about the author

D0981498

Chad Kultgen is the author of *The Average American Male* and *The Lie*. He is a graduate of the USC School of Film and Television and lives in California.

men, women & children

also by chad kultgen

the average american male

the lie

men, women & children

a novel

chad kultgen

HARPER PERENNIAL

NEW YORK • LONDON • TORONTO • SYDNEY • NEW DELHI • AUCKLAND

HARPER ⬤ PERENNIAL

MEN, WOMEN & CHILDREN. Copyright © 2011 by Chad Kultgen. All rights reserved. Printed in the United States of America. No part of this book may be used or reproduced in any manner whatsoever without written permission except in the case of brief quotations embodied in critical articles and reviews. For information address HarperCollins Publishers, 10 East 53rd Street, New York, NY 10022.

HarperCollins books may be purchased for educational, business, or sales promotional use. For information please write: Special Markets Department, HarperCollins Publishers, 10 East 53rd Street, New York, NY 10022.

FIRST EDITION

Library of Congress Cataloging-in-Publication Data is available upon request.

ISBN 978-0-06-165731-3

11 12 13 14 15   OV/RRD   10 9 8 7 6 5 4 3 2 1

Our planet is a lonely speck in the great enveloping cosmic dark. In our obscurity, in all this vastness, there is no hint that help will come from elsewhere to save us from ourselves.

carl **sagan**

men, women & children

Don Truby thought about Kelly Ripa's anus. He thought about what it would look like as he slid his penis into it. This image was all he could focus on in the forty-five minutes he had left of his dwindling lunch break. He took the largest bites he could from a Big Mac as he drove home, averaging ten miles over the speed limit. He felt both anxiety and shame about the frantic level of effort he was willing to exert in order to create a fifteen- or twenty-minute window in which he could masturbate. He allayed these concerns by reminding himself what his doctor told him a few weeks earlier during his annual physical: that, for every year a man lives past fifty, his chance of having some kind of prostate trouble, cancerous or otherwise, increased by 5 percent. And to combat these odds, his doctor added, it was wise to maintain as healthy a prostate as could be managed, which meant employing it in the creation of ejaculate as often as possible. Don was only thirty-seven, but he rationalized that regular masturbation could be considered a form of preventative medicine. This rationalization sustained him through the rest of his drive home.

With roughly thirty-five minutes left in his lunch break, Don entered his house. By then, his mode of excuse had moved from medical prevention to blaming his wife for her lack of willingness to engage in sexual activity with him. They had been married since they were in their early twenties and they had a thirteen-year-old son, Chris. Both of these facts were things that he understood could take a toll on the libido of any average person, man or woman. Nonetheless he couldn't help feeling that, in the past year, something had changed. The frequency of their sexual encounters had dwindled to once every month and a half, and his wife, Rachel, seemed completely uninterested in and unwilling to offer him fellatio or manual release as alternatives to intercourse when she wasn't in the mood, which had become excessively frequent. Don felt that he had no choice but to engage in the only sexual outlet on which he could still rely: semi-regular masturbation.

He entered the bedroom that he and his wife shared, sat down at their computer, and tried to suppress the feeling of self-pity that always seemed to creep up on him at exactly this moment. He reminded himself that because of the schedules of everyone else in the house, these twenty to thirty minutes were the only ones he would have to himself all day, and hence the only ones he could use to satiate his biological need to ejaculate.

The computer, which had been idle on the Windows loading screen for several seconds too long by Don's estimation, reverted to its boot-up screen. Don had seen this before with their previous computer. He knew it meant one of two things: Either the computer was just getting old and overused and it was time for it to be replaced, or more likely, he had browsed one too many pornography websites and accidentally infected it with some kind of virus or adware or spyware that had rendered it inoperative. He decided to power the computer off and give it one more chance to make it out of the load screen into some form of operational status, but when he turned the machine back on, the same thing happened again. He wasn't looking forward to taking the computer to the Best Buy Geek Squad, as he had done once before, but that was the least of his concerns. With twenty minutes left in his lunch break, and no hard copies of pornography anywhere in the house as a result of Rachel having accidentally found his collection some years ago—at which point she forced him to destroy it in front of her—Don gave a brief thought to masturbating using only his imagination. He hated masturbating without pornography, always finding the orgasm to be less satisfying. But in order to get to the limitless fountain of pornography on the Internet to which he had become so accustomed, he would have to resort to something he had never done. What he was contemplating would far surpass any level of indignity he might have felt for masturbating during his lunch break, or at work (as he had done twice before), or in his car outside his own home, or in virtually any other scenario in which he might have found himself in the service of ejaculating.

He opened the door to his son Chris's room, purging all thoughts of guilt or shame. He knew he would have no time for either of those if he was going to make it back to work before his lunch break was over. He had purchased Chris a laptop the previous Christmas, primarily for schoolwork and video editing. Chris had expressed interest in possibly pursuing a career in television or film postproduction, so when he asked for a video camera and a computer to edit on, Don and Rachel agreed to foster his curiosity. Don thought about these things for a fleeting moment before he opened the laptop and powered it up.

The procedure Don used to reset the Internet browser history on the computer in his and Rachel's bedroom had become second nature to him. It was not complex: He simply reset the entire history after each use of the computer for masturbatory purposes.

Don knew that Rachel wasn't savvy enough to understand why the browser history had been cleared. Very infrequently he would have to field one of her questions about the mysterious disappearance of a website she saw on *Oprah* from "that little drop down thingy," but a nonchalant "I don't know" or a "sometimes the whole thing just resets so it doesn't get viruses" always seemed to satisfy her questioning. He was well aware that this would not be the case with Chris, who knew far more about computers and the Internet than Don himself did.

Before he logged onto BangBus.com, the website he had gotten a separate and secret credit card specifically to pay for six months prior, he planned to look through the browser history of his son's computer and write down each website. He then planned to erase the browser history after using his son's computer for the five to ten minutes he assumed it would take him to reach the point of ejaculation. And, finally, Don Truby planned to type back in all of the websites that were originally in his son's browser history, in the order in which he had written them down. He knew of no technique that would have been more efficient, although there were several.

His son's browser history contained multiple social networking sites, a few music sites, some movie news websites, the Goodrich Junior High School website, and a few others that Don wrote down without giving them much thought. One site, however, was unfamiliar to him and gave no indication of its nature through its name alone: KeezMovies.com. With only a few minutes left to masturbate, Don's curiosity overrode his carnal urges for the brief second that found him navigating to KeezMovies.com instead of just writing it down and opening a browser window to BangBus.com. What he saw filled his mind with thoughts and reactions that were difficult to reconcile.

KeezMovies.com, Don learned, was a website that contained page after page of thumbnail images that represented streaming videos one could access by merely clicking on the thumbnail.

The videos ranged in length from a few minutes to well over thirty minutes, and they were all pornographic. The website was free and seemed to offer a much wider variety of pornographic content than BangBus.com. Don was immediately reminded of the time he found his father's secret stash of pornography. He was roughly the same age his own son was currently: thirteen. He had been in the garage on an innocent errand, recovering a wrench from his father's toolbox in order to tighten the chain on his bicycle. After several minutes of looking for the wrench in various places that seemed likely, Don found a cardboard box labeled "Junk from Old House" and opened it. Inside he found a dozen or so *Penthouse* and *Playboy* magazines as well as a Super-8 film reel. The film reel was the obsession of his adolescent existence. He had no idea if his parents even owned a Super-8 projector, and beyond that he would have had no idea how to operate such a device even if they did. He would, from time to time, when he became tired of using the same images in the dozen or so magazines, hold the film strip up to the garage light and use the tiny still images as fodder for his early masturbation sessions. He remembered most of them vividly, and certainly the discovery of his son's stash of pornography brought him back to the moment he discovered his own father's. It was strange.

At first, Don lamented the fact that technology had progressed to a point that a teenage boy's first experience with pornography would never again include the discovery of his father's stash. He realized that children reaching adolescence would never again need their parents to supply them with their first glimpses at human sexuality, intentionally or otherwise. Don felt a brief moment of sadness about not being a part of that moment for his son, about not being involved in what he considered an intrinsic part of growing up. Still, he was relieved that his son's pornographic tastes contained nothing homosexual or overtly abnormal. Then he saw the clock on his son's computer and he was reminded that he had only a precious few minutes left to masturbate before he had to get back in his car and drive back to his office, where he would spend four more hours trying to convince people to invest their money with, or to purchase a life insurance policy from, his employer, Northwestern Mutual. He had stopped, years ago, questioning how his life had become what it had become, but every so often, when he unbuttoned his pants, untucked his shirt, and threw his tie over his shoulder in order to masturbate with as little disrobing as possible on a lunch break from a job he despised, his mind would fire off some almost imperceptible objection. This isn't what he thought he'd be doing at thirty-seven.

The first thumbnail he clicked on opened a streaming movie starring a girl he had never seen, named Stoya. She was extremely attractive and extremely pale. Don had never found pale girls particularly appealing, but he knew that if he got caught in the trap of clicking on multiple videos until he found one he liked, he would most likely be late for work and he would have to deal with his manager. He pulled the elastic band of his underwear down so it fit just behind his testicles and applied a small amount of pressure.

Don had first implemented this technique many years ago after stumbling upon it purely by chance. He had been lying awake the whole night as a result of his wife pressing her buttocks against his genitals as she slept. He had tried gently grinding his erection against her, as this sometimes brought him to full ejaculation, but that night Don was wearing a pair of boxers that were made of a thicker material than normal, and this just made him more incensed. He knew that the jarring motion of all-out masturbation would surely wake his wife and bring a barrage of questioning that he was unwilling to endure. At some point his wife, Rachel, got out of bed and went to the bathroom. Don took the opportunity to pull his underwear down under his testicles for the first time and quickly masturbate, cupping his hand to catch the ejaculated semen and wiping it on the side of the bed before Rachel came back. He didn't know if the elastic band of his underwear being placed behind his testicles made his orgasm come any quicker or stronger, but he enjoyed it and from that moment on occasionally employed the technique, especially in scenarios that required him to complete his masturbatory session in a short amount of time.

And so it was as Don ejaculated into a McDonald's napkin, which he crumpled up and tossed back into the bag with his empty Big Mac container and french-fry sleeve. He shut his son's computer down and put it back where he had found it. He was momentarily reminded, once again, of putting his father's pornography back in its secret location in the garage, hoping his transgression would remain undetected. As he left his house, he knew it was excessively unlikely that the series of events necessary for his wife to discover his semen-covered McDonald's napkin in their own trash can would ever transpire. But he saw no sense in taking unnecessary risk, so he threw the McDonald's bag away in the neighbors' trash can.

On his drive back to work, he thought about his son and was again relieved that Chris's pornographic tastes seemed normal. As he walked back into his office, Don wondered what his son was doing at school, and as much as he didn't want to, he couldn't help wondering about his son's masturbatory habits— when he did it, where he did it, where or into what object he expelled his semen.

He gave only a brief thought to what his wife might think of their son's indulgence in pornography. He would not tell her about his discovery.

"Jesus Christ!" Danny Vance said. Chris Truby had just shown him a video on his phone depicting a transsexual with double-D breasts inserting her penis into the anus of a man who was wearing a hockey mask. Danny and Chris had been friends their entire lives, so Danny wasn't surprised that Chris would have pornography on his phone, but the nature of this specific video was more than slightly off-putting to him. Danny was even more disturbed by the fact that Chris chose to show him this material during lunch, giving any of the five or six teachers who monitored this thirty-minute period each day an opportunity to catch a glimpse, assume Danny was just as complicit as Chris, and suspend them both, forcing Danny to miss at least one, possibly two games and effectively ruining his eighth-grade season as starting quarterback for the Goodrich Junior High Olympians before it even started.

"What is that?"

"It's a tranny fucking some dude in the ass while he's wearing a hockey mask. Hilarious, right?"

"Hilarious? I'd go with *horrible, gay, repulsive*, a bunch of other shit before I'd go with *hilarious*. And what are you doing whipping that shit out at lunch? You're going to get us both in trouble."

"Relax. No one saw it."

Just as Chris put the phone back in his pocket, Brooke Benton sat down at their table and kissed Danny on the cheek. Brooke had blond hair, blue eyes, an athletic yet feminine build, and a bone structure that made her almost unanimously considered the most attractive girl at Goodrich Junior High. She was the squad leader of the Olympiannes, a junior high precursor to high school cheerleaders. She was also Danny's girlfriend of over a year.

She said, "Hey, babe, what were you guys looking at?"

Danny said, "You do not want to see it. Trust me."

Chris said, "You wanna see it?"

Brooke said, "What is it?"

Danny said, "Just leave it, babe. You seriously don't want to see it."

Chris said, "I can't really describe it. You'll have to see it for yourself."

Danny said, "Don't get caught."

Chris handed her his phone under the table. Brooke turned the phone on and winced at what she saw. She handed the phone back and said, "Gross. Those are guys having sex with each other? Are you gay or something now?"

Chris said, "It's not guys. It's a tranny and a guy. And yeah, I'm gay. I love to suck dick and take dicks up my ass and drink cups of jizz."

Brooke said, "You really have problems, Chris. You know that, right? You're not normal."

Chris said, "Whatever. I think it's funny as shit. Just because you guys are pussies. Fuck off. I have to go do a make-up quiz for Mr. Donnelly. I'm out." Chris left, walking behind Brooke's back and giving Danny a silent fellatio pantomime show as he did. Danny was used to Chris's overly sexual antics and offered no response.

Brooke said, "So are you getting excited for the first game?"

Danny said, "Yeah, are you?"

Brooke said, "Of course. I can't wait to see you out there and get to cheer for you and everything. This year is going to be awesome. I really think we're going to win district."

Danny said, "I hope so."

Brooke said, "Can you walk me home today?"

Danny said, "I don't think so, babe. Coach Quinn is doing his start-of-the-season thing after school."

Brooke said, "How long will it be? I can wait."

Danny said, "I don't know. Like half an hour maybe."

Brooke said, "Cool. I'll just hang out with Allison until you guys are finished. I can help her make banners for the game and stuff, anyway."

Danny said, "Okay, cool. Oh, wait, I actually forgot. My mom wanted to know if you wanted to come over for dinner tonight."

Brooke said, "Yeah, as long as my mom says it's okay. I'll text her after lunch."

Danny said, "Cool. And I think my dad can pick us up after Coach Quinn's thing, so we won't have to walk."

The rest of their conversation covered topics that ranged from schoolwork to movies and television shows. As Brooke entered into a detailed description of an episode of *The Soup* she had watched the previous night, Danny looked across the room at Tim Mooney, who rose from his seat, threw his trash away, and then wandered out of the lunchroom. Danny and Tim had been friends through grade school and even through the entirety of seventh grade. Danny knew that Tim would be one of the main reasons that the Goodrich Olympians stood a good chance to win district.

Tim left lunch ten minutes early, checked his e-mail on his phone very quickly to make sure his guild in *World of Warcraft* was still planning to raid Icecrown Citadel that night at the predetermined time, 7 P.M., and then headed to Coach Quinn's office with a specific purpose. He didn't want to be late for his American history class, but knew that a few minutes of tardiness would have no effect on his understanding of the day's lesson. He had already read ahead the night before and done the workbook assignment he knew would be given as homework that night so he could join his guild in their raid without having to worry about getting school work done after the raid ended at 11 P.M.

School was easy for Tim. He found most of it trivial, but knew it was necessary to do well so that he could maintain a grade-point average that would place him in AP classes once he got to high school, which would, in turn, assure him admittance to a good college. Although, lately, Tim Mooney was finding it more and more difficult to maintain this attitude.

His parents had been separated for a little more than a year. Tim had always suspected infidelity on his mother's part as the reason for their split, but neither of his parents ever discussed this with him. They each maintained that they just needed some time apart. When his mother, Lydia, first announced that she would be moving into her own apartment across town, Tim was surprised at how little impact it all seemed to have on his life. He stayed with his father so he could continue going to the same school, but he saw his mother frequently. Not that much had changed. Then, at the start of the summer before his eighth grade year, Tim's mother and father were officially divorced. Tim understood that this time would be difficult. His family no longer existed. His parents had no hope of working things out or living in the same house again.

A week or so after the divorce, Tim's mother made another

announcement. She was moving to California to live with a man named Greg Cherry who was in marketing. Tim was again forced to choose which parent he would live with, but this time the decision carried more weight. In all likelihood, he would see little to none of the parent he wasn't living with. Since he had already been living with his father, Kent, and had little interest in moving to a new school, he stayed where he was. His mother offered no objection. As a result of this decision, he hadn't seen his mother since she'd left, nearly four months ago. Her contact with him became more and more infrequent with each passing week, reduced to a phone call every Saturday that she usually chose to end short due to how busy she claimed to be.

Over the summer, Tim found himself staying awake until three or four in the morning every night. He played video games, *World of Warcraft* more than any other, and watched television, interacting with his father less and less, growing increasingly uncomfortable around him as Kent became more passive-aggressive and cold in the absence of his wife. One night, Tim stumbled across a documentary called *Manufacturing Consent*. After viewing it, he found some writing online by its subject, Noam Chomsky, and as a result began to feel that there wasn't really a point to anything, that free will was an illusion, and that the things most people invested time and energy in were systems of control designed by those who sought to manipulate the general population. He thought about this as he knocked on the door to Coach Quinn's office, interrupting him as he ate a sandwich and watched *SportsCenter*.

Tim was the best middle linebacker Coach Quinn had seen in years. He was bigger than most kids his age, much quicker, and generally more athletic, just like his father had been. He was essentially a one-man defense, holding most teams to under ten points per game almost single-handedly.

With the season opener against the Park Panthers less than a week away, Coach Quinn was more than confident that he would have a winning season and potentially even win district, which would afford him opportunities to pursue a head-coaching job at one of the area high schools.

Coach Quinn said, "Tim, come in."

Tim entered Coach Quinn's office and sat down.

Coach Quinn said, "You're looking outstanding in practice, Tim. You must be excited about the Park game coming up."

Tim said, "Actually, Coach, that's what I wanted to talk to you about."

Coach Quinn could feel a cold sweat forming on the back of his neck. Tim Mooney was a key component in what he felt was the best chance he'd had in years to ascend beyond the junior high coaching ranks. He said, "What are you talking about, Tim?"

Tim said, "Coach, I don't think I can play this year."

Coach Quinn said, "Excuse me?"

Tim said, "I just wanted to tell you that I'm quitting the team, Coach. I feel like it's what I have to do."

Coach Quinn said, "Where is this coming from, Tim? This is something you should really think about. Is anything going wrong? Maybe something at home?"

Tim said, "Yeah, everything's fine at home. I've thought about it a lot, actually. Sports just seem pointless."

Coach Quinn said, "Well, they're not pointless, Tim. They're the best times of your life when you're young—hell, your dad can tell you that. Are you really okay with throwing that away?"

Tim said, "I think so, yeah."

Coach Quinn said, "Well, I obviously can't make you play football, Tim, but I think you should seriously reconsider this decision. God gave you a gift, son. You don't just throw God's gifts away like that."

Tim said, "I'll think about it, Coach. But for now, I'm done for the season."

Tim stood up and turned to leave. Coach Quinn watched

him leave knowing that his best chance at the addition his wife wanted to their house was walking out of his office.

Tim left Coach Quinn's office and continued to his American history class. He sat next to a girl named Brandy Beltmeyer. Tim had never had a girlfriend, but he thought that Brandy would make a good one. She was very plain-looking, not the kind of girl most guys would probably consider interesting. Tim liked the fact that she was understated. She didn't get caught up in the same unimportant minutiae of being a teenage girl that all her peers seemed preoccupied with, and this made Tim curious about her. To Tim she seemed like the kind of girl who was probably extremely interesting to the people who took the time to get to know her.

Tim had been partnered with Brandy for a final English project at the end of their seventh-grade year, a book report presentation on *Huckleberry Finn*. They got along well and he liked the way her voice sounded when she said certain phrases that seemed unique to her and that she repeated often. "That is not even possibly real" was among his favorites.

Over the summer, Tim had sent Brandy a text message to see if she wanted to go to a movie with him, but she never responded. Unbeknownst to Tim, she would have been more than happy to see a movie with him but she never received the text message. In fact, she was disappointed that Tim never contacted her after their partnership, because she had developed a mild crush on him during the time they spent together and had fantasized that he would be the first boy to kiss her.

Tim's text message, which read, "Want 2 go 2 a movie maybe?" was intercepted by Brandy's mother, Patricia, who ran a local watch-group called PATI, which stood for Parents Against The Internet and was also an abbreviation for her own name, a combination she found to be clever. She formed the watch-group after seeing an episode of *Tyra* about a phenomenon called "sexting." In addition to forcing her daughter to divulge every password to every one of her e-mail accounts, her Myspace account, and any other online membership, when Patricia gave Brandy her most recent phone, she installed software on it that allowed her to access that phone from her own. And when Patricia saw the text from Tim asking her daughter to go to a movie, she immediately decided that it was too soon for her daughter to start dating and deleted it. Tim interpreted Brandy's lack of response as lack of interest and never made another attempt to gain her favor or attention. He still thought about her, however, and wondered if he had been too forward with his text message, or, more likely, whether Brandy simply found him unattractive.

Tanner Hodge, the Olympians' tailback, walked past Tim on his way to his own seat. "Let's kick some Panther ass," he said, and offered Tim a fist bump, which Tim returned. Tanner had no idea that Tim had just quit the football team.

Tim opened his book to the section he had already read the night before and wondered what his mother was doing at that moment in California as Mrs. Rector began her lesson about the Boston Tea Party.

chapter
three

Coach Quinn began every eighth-grade season by delivering a speech, on the week of their first regular season game, that was designed to motivate and excite his team. He had given this speech so many times that it was almost identical to each previous year's speech, with some small variation in inflection or tone and possibly one or two words changed.

Coach Quinn had tried several times in the past few years to secure employment as a high school football coach in various school districts. He used to be comforted by the complacence he felt in his position as an eighth-grade coach, but that had given way to frustration in recent years, primarily fueled by his wife's desire to live in a nicer house, drive a nicer car, and eventually even move to another city. He hoped this year would be his last at Goodrich Junior High School. But if he wanted to maximize his odds of employment elsewhere, he knew, a successful season was a must.

Some of the thirty-two eighth-grade football players had already begun to notice that Tim Mooney was not among them. Coach Quinn could hear their whispers asking about their star linebacker's absence. If he wanted to have any hope of salvaging the season, he knew he would need to address any questions and concerns his players had immediately, rather than ignoring them and hoping that Tim would come back to the team. With that in mind, Coach Quinn decided to improvise his season opening speech for the first time in his career.

He said, "Guys, sometimes Jesus throws you a curve ball. This afternoon, he threw us one that broke about four feet. But Jesus isn't trying to strike us out. Jesus would never do that. The reason he threw us a curve ball is because he wants us to swing at it. He wants us to hit a home run. That curve ball's name is Tim Mooney.

"For some reasons that are beyond all of my faculties to understand, Tim Mooney isn't playing this year. He came into my office this afternoon and told me he didn't see a reason to play, that football wasn't important. And I know you all probably think that's a bad thing, but I've come to a conclusion this afternoon. It's not a bad thing at all. A team is only as strong as its weakest link, and Tim was psychologically weak. He didn't have what it takes mentally to stick it out and help this team win a district championship this year.

"So I don't want to hear anything about Tim for the rest of the season. I've decided that Bill Francis is going to be our starting middle linebacker, and he's gonna make us all forget about Tim Mooney. Isn't that right, Bill?"

No player in the field house was more stunned than Bill Francis by the unfolding developments of that afternoon. He stammered slightly before responding, "Yes, sir."

Coach Quinn said, "As I look around this room, I see the talent. I know you know how to win district this year. And, let me just say this: For some of you guys, this is it, your eighth-grade season. Some of you guys will go on to play high school ball and some of you won't. So, for the ones who won't, this is going to be your last shot to do something special, to play that season of football that you'll remember for the rest of your life. Think about that in every game, in every play this year. Just do me that favor, just take a swing at that curve ball and we're gonna have a real shot, gentlemen—with or without Tim Mooney."

Coach Quinn paused for effect, took off his baseball cap, and said, "Now, our first game is coming up this Friday—the Park Panthers. We know they play hard, and we know they like to run the ball all over the field. We're going to have to be ready for that. So let's have a good practice today and focus on the Panthers."

As everyone stood and prepared for practice, Danny Vance sat in the back of the room near Chris Truby. He thought about Tim not being part of the team. He felt angry that Tim had found something more important in his life than football, and he felt even angrier at the fact that Tim had very likely taken away the Olympians' chance to win district. Despite everything Coach Quinn said, Danny had seen Bill Francis in practice. While he was unquestionably the best possible candidate to replace Tim as middle linebacker, he was nowhere near as good. Danny knew that, to have a real shot at winning district, he was going to have to lead the charge on offense, never really being able to count on the defense to hold a close game or make a timely stop. The entire season rested on his shoulders and it was all because of Tim.

At thirteen years old, Danny had only one dream in life, and that was to be the starting quarterback for the Nebraska Cornhuskers. His father had played for them. His older sister currently played volleyball for them. And his mother had been a cheerleader when his father played. That's how they'd met. He had been groomed to play football for Nebraska. He knew that, based on his passing ability, he would likely be the starting junior varsity quarterback when he went to ninth grade the following year, but it wasn't a guarantee, especially if they didn't win district. If another junior high or middle school won, he knew that team's quarterback would come into ninth grade with a little extra attention. If the Olympians could win district decisively, allowing him a chance to showcase his quarterbacking skills, he might even have a shot at making varsity as a freshman and being second-string behind Mike Trainor, who would be a senior, giving him a probable chance of starting on varsity as a sophomore: a feat only three other players had accomplished in the history of the school. And if he could put up impressive numbers and capture a state championship or two during his time in high school, he would garner attention from Nebraska. This was his plan. He vowed to maintain his plan even though Tim was making it more difficult.

He hoped that the defenses of the other junior high schools wouldn't be ready for a strong passing game. He knew no other eighth-grade quarterbacks had his arm or accuracy, and the other schools' defenses would assume the Olympians would run a heavy ground game. They would practice against run plays and get their corners and free safeties used to blitzing and stopping ground plays that got away from the linebackers. He had to have hope, and this strategy gave him that hope.

Danny looked over at Chris, who would be his go-to wide receiver this season. Chris would have to play to his full potential. He knew Chris was faster than most kids their age, and he had decent hands. Those things, combined with the fact that Danny was able to regularly throw a pass thirty-five or forty-five yards deep with accuracy, led Danny to believe they would have a shot at more than one deep pass play. He wondered if he could count on Chris, if he would be able to get the job done. As he wondered these things about his friend he noticed that, instead of paying attention to Coach Quinn, Chris was flipping through a series of pornographic images on his phone. From what he could see, they appeared to feature immensely obese women and abnormally skinny men engaged in various sexual acts.

Across the room, Tanner Hodge, the Olympians' starting tailback, was having a much less strategic reaction to the discovery of Tim's rejection of football. Like Danny, Tanner had dreams of pursuing the sport of football as a career, which meant being successful through high school and college, which he knew would be easier with a district championship in junior high.

But beyond the practical disappointment Tanner Hodge felt as a result of Tim quitting the team, he was offended on a deeper level; he felt a sense of personal insult. Tanner and Tim had been teammates on youth football and baseball teams since they were children. Tanner thought of Tim as his athletic equal, which, for Tanner, commanded more respect than friendship. Tanner felt a masculine connection, a camaraderie with all of his teammates. In Tanner's mind, Tim was flippantly dismissing this bond that they had all built over the course of several years playing various sports with one another. He was dismissing the very identity that they all, in some part, shared. That dismissal was unforgivable.

Tanner thought about the fist bump he shared with Tim a few hours prior and became incensed. Tim Mooney immediately became the focus of a rage and hatred that Tanner Hodge had never experienced. He wanted to punch Tim. He wanted to kill Tim.

In the gymnasium, Brooke Benton and Allison Doss made banners for the season opener. The girls had known each other since early childhood and had always been a part of some sort of cheerleading group together. They prided themselves on their craftsmanship in the area of banners and posters. They were working on a poster that depicted an Olympian cutting the head off a panther when Brooke said, "Your hair looks so hot. And you are seriously skinny this year. You look really good."

Allison, who had recently dyed her hair black, said, "Thanks. I went on a super diet over the summer and then I was like, 'I should do my hair different, too.'"

Brooke said, "Well, it worked."

Allison said, "Thanks."

Allison had lost twenty pounds over the summer as a result of simply not eating when she was hungry. She was five foot two and weighed eighty-two pounds. Despite the fact that she often felt lightheaded and occasionally suffered from nosebleeds, she felt disgustingly fat and was determined to lose a few more pounds to ensure that she wouldn't end up like her mother, father, or younger brother, who were all overweight if not obese.

She said, "So are you and Danny going to like do it this year or what?"

Brooke said, "My opinion is I don't think so. I don't know if we're ready, you know? And it's not really like either of us feels like we have to or anything. You know?"

Allison said, "Yeah. I guess so. I'm not rushing to do it or anything either. It's just like, you guys have been together for so long, it wouldn't be like you were doing it with some random guy just to do it or anything."

Brooke said, "I guess."

Hannah Clint, the first and only member of the Olympiannes to have C-cup breasts, joined the conversation, having overheard the last few comments as she worked on her own banner a few feet away.

Hannah said, "Um . . . I'm pretty sure you know next year we're going to be in the ninth grade—high school—and you know Mike Trainor is going to be a senior. He'll be the starting quarterback for North East and, Brooke, you'll probably have a pretty good shot at him. You're seriously way hotter than pretty much any of the cheerleaders who'll be there next year. And you're definitely not going to want to have it be your first time with him. He'll be able to tell that you don't know what you're doing."

Brooke had never liked Hannah. She tolerated her because she was a fellow Olympianne, but she felt that Hannah wasn't worth her friendship. Although she had no direct evidence, she felt that Hannah had been jealous of her since they were children. Brooke felt that Hannah was jealous of her beauty. Brooke felt that Hannah wanted to be everything that Brooke was, but that she always came up slightly short. Hannah had gotten her breasts before any other girl, and Brooke felt that had just made Hannah that much more pathetic in her quest to be the prettiest girl in school, because she clearly flaunted them more than necessary. Every so often, Brooke would lay awake at night thinking about Hannah's wardrobe and makeup and wonder if any male students had found Hannah more attractive than her that day. Hannah was unaware of any of this.

Brooke said, "He won't be able to tell anything."

Hannah said, "Are you kidding? You should just do it with Danny now, so you're not completely terrible for Mike."

Brooke said, "How would you know? You haven't done it with anyone," as she sent Allison a text message that read "Hannah is such a bitch."

Hannah said, "I gave a blowjob over the summer."

Allison said, "To who?" as she replied to Brooke's text message with "I know. She thinks her tits make her god's gift or something."

Hannah said, "This guy I met when my mom and I were in Florida. Here, look." Hannah took out her phone and began searching through her photos until she came to a photo of her with an unknown boy's penis in her mouth, clearly taken by herself during the act, the boy's head cropped out of the image. She showed the photo to Allison and Brooke.

Allison said, "Oh my god, was it gross?" as she sent a text message to Brooke that read "What a skank."

Hannah said, "No, it wasn't that bad. It was kind of salty, I guess."

Brooke said, "Did you let him, you know, finish in your mouth?" as she replied to Allison's text message with "I know, right?"

Hannah said, "Uh . . . yeah. How else would I know it was salty?"

Brooke and Allison simultaneously sent each other a text message that read "Gross!!!"

Hannah said, "Anyway, after this summer, I'm pretty sure that I'm seriously ready to actually do it, and I'm going to before I get to high school so I'm not completely retarded when I do it with a high school boy for the first time."

Brooke said, "My opinion is that you should probably know who you're going to do it with before you make that kind of decision."

Hannah said, "I was thinking Chris."

Brooke said, "Oh my god. That's gross. He's seriously repulsive. He showed me the grossest porn I have ever seen in my life today at lunch."

Hannah said, "So he showed you porn? Who cares? I just don't want to get to high school without having done it. And he's cute enough and I think he likes me so . . . whatever."

Hannah looked at her phone as it beeped to indicate a new text message and said, "My mom's here. See you guys tomorrow." Hannah picked up her purse and left the gymnasium.

Brooke and Allison had a short discussion about the likelihood of Hannah and Chris having sex before their eighth-grade year came to a close. They both seemed to think it was unlikely that this event would come to pass, but neither was willing to rule it out completely. And if they did have sex, Hannah and Chris would be the first among their peers to have done so, which was significant to both Allison and Brooke. Despite not being ready to have sex, Brooke confided in Allison that she had always thought she and Danny would be the first couple to have sex among their peers. They had been together longer than any other couple at Goodrich. To allow Chris and Hannah to have the distinction of being the first of their peers to have sex seemed wrong somehow to Brooke. Allison agreed and added that all of her dedication to a strict diet over the summer was done to attract a boy this year and she hoped that it would pay off.

Brooke did not discuss the fact that the competitive nature her father had instilled in both her and her little brother since birth made her incensed at the thought of Hannah beating her in anything, including being the first girl to be sexually active. It wasn't that Brooke had any desire to become sexually active. The opposite was true. She knew she wasn't ready to enter that phase of her life and even thought that doing it in the eighth grade was somewhat clichéd. She had seen enough episodes of *Tyra, Dr. Phil, Oprah*, and other talk shows dealing with teen pregnancy and prostitution to have developed an idea that sexual activity before the age of sixteen or seventeen was nothing she was interested in. But she could not ignore the desire to at least perform oral sex just to have done it at least once so that Hannah Clint would have nothing over her. Brooke had never received a grade below A-minus on any report card, test, or assignment. She was the captain of the Olympiannes and was determined to be the varsity cheerleading captain at North East High School by her junior year. That right was most normally reserved for a senior, but Brooke had resolved to achieve this rank as junior and was fairly certain that she would be able to attain her goal if she worked hard enough at it.

This ultracompetitive mode of thinking led Brooke to believe that, as the captain of the Olympiannes and the best-looking girl in the school, she should be the best at anything that any of the Olympiannes did, including being sexually experienced.

• • •

In the south parking lot of Goodrich Junior High School, Hannah Clint emerged from the building and got into her mother's fourteen-year-old Mercedes. Her mother, Dawn, said, "I bought you some underwear. We got a request from a subscriber so we have to do a quick shoot tonight."

As Dawn drove back to her mother's house, where she and Hannah had been living since Hannah was born, she looked at the leather armrest where her initials were monogrammed. This car was the last piece of her old life, the last real reminder of what she had left behind.

Dawn had once lived in Los Angeles. She had aspirations of becoming an actress, just like her mother, Nicole, had been. Nicole had a moderately successful career as a character actress in the 1950s. She appeared in only a handful of films, but her career gave her the chance to socialize with various people who were prominent in the entertainment industry and even become romantically involved with some of them. When she was in her early thirties, she was involved with three different men, any one of whom could have been Dawn's father. Upon becoming pregnant, she made the decision to move back home with her parents and have the baby. Once Dawn was born, Nicole had difficulty imagining herself moving back to Los Angeles in an attempt to pick up where she had left off. So she stayed in her hometown and raised her daughter by herself.

When Dawn graduated from North East High School, she moved to Los Angeles to pursue her own dream of becoming an actress. She was not met with the same early success as her mother, having been cast in a play or student film once or twice a year, but nothing substantial. As an attractive young woman, she had engaged in relationships with several men who subsequently expressed their intent to marry her and raise a family, but she wouldn't allow a relationship to stand in the way of her career goals.

On her twenty-eighth birthday, she was celebrating by

drinking with some friends at Bar Marmont. She began to think about the fact that she was getting older, about the fact that even the inconsequential auditions she forced herself to go on were generally filled with girls ten years younger than her, about the fact that maybe her lifelong dream was over. That night a television producer of moderate success bought her a drink, convinced her to give him her telephone number, and took her out to dinner the following week.

After a little more than a year of dating, they moved in together. A few months later he sold a show to CBS and in celebration he bought her a Mercedes with monogrammed seats. The show required an actress for the small role of an attractive, but slightly older, next-door neighbor. He promised Dawn that if CBS were to order the pilot to be produced he would give her the role. CBS did order the pilot to be produced, and he was true to his word, but the pilot didn't test well and the show was never ordered to series. Dawn was unimpressive in her minor role and, as a result, drew no new attention from agents, managers, or network or studio executives.

Two weeks after the pilot was officially rejected by CBS she became aware of the fact that she was pregnant. Her boyfriend reminded her that he had always maintained he never wanted children and said that he would have nothing to do with the child if Dawn elected to give birth to it rather than abort. He told her he would pay whatever amount of child support was required of him by law, but would in no way be a father.

The combined emotional trauma of the failed pilot, and the subsequent disintegration of the longest relationship she had ever had, led her to move back in with her mother in her hometown, just as her own mother had done. Hannah was born nine months later, and although the living arrangement was initially supposed to be temporary, the three generations of Clint women had lived under the same roof ever since that day.

At an early age Hannah told her mother and grandmother that

she, too, was very interested in acting. Nicole, having more years of insight into what the pursuit of such a statistically improbable goal can do to a person psychologically and emotionally, warned Dawn to encourage Hannah's interest in other areas. But Dawn, having been so close to some success of her own in this area without really getting what she felt was a fair shake, saw in her daughter the opportunity for another chance.

Because her child support checks were moderately substantial, Dawn never needed to have a job. She devoted every waking hour to making sure her daughter would find the success as an actress she had never had—that even her mother, who had acted in legitimate studio films, had never had. She enrolled her in acting classes, singing classes, dancing classes. She stayed up nights with Hannah, coaching her with techniques from countless books about acting, dancing, singing, and auditioning for jobs in all three of these fields. She was so willing to do anything to give her daughter the experiences in life that she was unable to achieve that she found herself locked in a relationship based on casual sex with the local community theater director, whom she found repulsive, just to ensure that Hannah would be cast in every production.

It was this fervent desire to help her daughter that gave Dawn the idea to create a website for Hannah. In the beginning it was no different from any other aspiring actor's website. It listed contact information, displayed headshots, a résumé, and a few video clips from various productions Hannah had appeared in. It wasn't until the summer before eighth grade, when Hannah began developing breasts, that Dawn had the idea to put a few images of Hannah in her bathing suit on the website, hoping that she might be able to get work in print ads for summer fashion.

A few weeks after uploading the first two images of Hannah in a one-piece red bathing suit, the site received its first e-mail—a request asking if a few more images of Hannah, this time in a two-piece bathing suit, could be posted. The e-mail went on to request that the photos of Hannah be taken lying down or bending over.

Curious, and also excited that the site had generated interest in Hannah, Dawn replied to the e-mail asking its sender if he was an agent or manager interested in representing Hannah or a photographer looking for models. The sender replied that he was neither an agent nor a manager nor a photographer, just a self-proclaimed fan of Hannah's.

Dawn then realized that the person e-mailing her might very likely have a sexual interest in her daughter. But the person hadn't yet asked for anything illegal. Dawn told herself that posting more photos of Hannah in various bathing suits wasn't a bad thing if it generated further interest, no matter where the interest came from. She also recognized that there might be an opportunity to turn the website into a business, to make some money. She e-mailed the sender asking if he would be willing to pay a monthly fee for access to a private section of the website that would feature the photos requested. The sender replied by explaining that he would gladly pay a monthly fee of twelve to fifteen dollars to have access to such photos and also to be able to request certain outfits or poses once or twice a month.

Despite being fully aware of the fact that what she was about to do was, at the very least, exploitive and possibly bordering on criminal with regard to the treatment of her own child, Dawn quickly set up a PayPal account and hired a web designer to build a members-only section on her daughter's website. She had a talk with Hannah to make sure she had no reservations about wearing some more revealing outfits on this section of the site. Hannah explained that she was proud of her body and understood that if she was to be discovered by a director like Darren Aronofsky or Paul Thomas Anderson and they wanted her to participate in a nude scene, she wouldn't hesitate to oblige them. This, she reasoned, was just practice for any such feature-film roles that might come her way in the future.

After four months of the member's-only section going live, Dawn had eighty-seven subscribers each paying $12.95 a month to see her daughter in bikinis and underwear in various poses. Dawn split the money with Hannah and told her not to tell anyone about it, including her grandmother. Hannah felt there was a salacious element associated with what they were doing and decided it was better to keep it a secret than to tell her friends at school. She liked doing it too much to risk being discovered and shut down. Hannah felt like she was famous every time her mother got an e-mail asking for a new pose or new outfit or just asking how she was doing or what her favorite color was. Even though her mother would never let her answer any of the e-mails or interact with any of her subscribers, she considered herself to have fans, and she viewed the experience as a type of training for what her life would be like when she had real fame, which was an inevitability in her mind.

As they got out of the Mercedes, Hannah said, "Do you think we could put up a video blog for the subscribers? Just like a little one-minute thing I could do every week? Like talk about my life and stuff? I think they'd like that."

Dawn said, "We'll see. Let's just stick with the pictures for now. Here." She handed her daughter a matching set of Hello Kitty bra and underwear along with a pair of Hello Kitty knee-high socks.

Hannah said, "Socks? What for?"

Dawn said, "To wear with the underwear," and shrugged at her daughter, offering no further explanation.

chapter four

After school, Chris Truby did his homework; ate dinner with his mother, Rachel, and his father, Don; watched an episode of *Two and a Half Men* with them; and then told them that he had a difficult science test the following day that would require him to put in multiple hours of studying if he was to make a decent grade. And certainly he would need a good night's rest as well, so Chris retired to his bedroom earlier than usual, leaving his parents in the living room.

Don looked at his wife. She had started a new job as an accountant for a nationwide collections agency six months before. The job offered no opportunity for exercise or movement beyond picking up the phone, typing on a keyboard, and making occasional trips to the bathroom or her car. Don could easily notice that Rachel had put on weight, maybe as much as eight or ten pounds, as a result of the job's sedentary nature.

Don's physical attraction to his wife had waned over the years of their marriage due to the combination of her aging features and his overfamiliarity with her body. But no matter how unattractive she had become to him, the basic need to engage in sexual intercourse spurred him to try to initiate some form of physical intimacy on a regular basis. Despite his frequent attempts, the last time Rachel had been willing to have sex with him was more than a month and a half ago.

With Chris headed off to his room for the night, Don leaned over to his wife and said, "Hey, what do you think?"

Rachel said, "About what?"

"About, you know . . ."

"Tonight?"

"Yeah—it's been almost two months, Rachel."

"No, it hasn't."

"The last time was after that barbecue at your sister's house. Chris was at a friend's house."

"Really? How do you remember that?"

"How do you not?"

"I don't know, I guess my new job is just making me tired."

"It's still early tonight. We can do it and you can be asleep by nine."

Rachel looked at Don. She knew she wasn't satisfying him and she didn't know exactly why, but the idea of sex with her husband was almost completely unappealing to her. She didn't know if it was because they had been together for so long, or because she knew she had gained some weight and felt less attractive, or because, like Don, she found his aging body and face less appealing than they once had been, but she certainly knew it was not for any reason having to do with her job, which was the excuse she used most often. Despite the fact that it was the last thing she wanted to do that night, Rachel said, "Okay, but it has to be quick."

Don said, "It will be."

"I mean really quick."

"Okay."

As Don inserted his penis into his wife's vagina, all he could think about were the images of the porn star Stoya. Since discovering her on his son's computer he had become mildly obsessed and had purchased memberships to several websites that featured her movies. It wasn't just that she was incredibly beautiful that aroused Don, it was that she genuinely seemed to enjoy having sex—something Rachel hadn't seemed to do in a very long time.

Don looked down at his wife's uninterested face and felt his erection softening inside her. Not wanting to waste what he assumed would be his only chance to have sex for at least the next month or two, he said, "Roll over."

Rachel said, "Why?"

"You know, for doggy style."

"Why? Just finish like this."

Don felt his erection dissipating a little more with each passing second that the negotiation continued. He said, "Please."

Rachel said, "Fine," and rolled over onto her stomach, propping herself up on all fours. Don stroked his penis a few times with his eyes closed, thinking of Stoya and what her face looked like when she was being entered from behind. To Don, she looked happy—and, more than her perfect body, her willingness to engage in any sexual position or to accept a penis in any orifice, Don found her happiness to be her most appealing trait. It was that image of Stoya, smiling and then biting her bottom lip as she was penetrated from behind, that Don kept in his mind as he gripped his wife's hips and slid his penis into her, imagining the same expression on her face that Stoya had in the countless videos he had seen.

Rachel closed her eyes and tried to imagine anything that would help her enjoy this. She wanted to feel attracted to her husband again. She wanted to feel desire for him. But it seemed that time in their relationship might have passed for her. As he thrust into her and grunted, she thought of their wedding night. She tried to remember how happy she was then, but couldn't conjure the emotion she used to associate with the memory of that day. Then she felt Don ejaculate in her vagina and slide his quickly shrinking penis out of her.

She said, "I'm going to the bathroom."

Don said, "Okay," and lay back in their bed, wondering if he would ever again have sex with a woman who enjoyed it.

A few feet down the hall, Chris wasn't studying for his science test. The test never existed. Instead he was downloading from a variety of torrent websites various collections of pornography depicting women over the age of fifty. While he waited for these videos to download he masturbated to a three minute and forty-two second video of a transsexual receiving a prostate massage from a man, which resulted in a massive ejaculation. This was the first time he had masturbated to transsexual pornography.

A few miles away, Allison Doss walked through her front door, dropped her book bag, and entered her family's kitchen, where her mother, Liz, her father, Neal, and her younger brother, Myron, were all eating. She had always considered her family to be overweight, and they were. She, too, had been overweight, until halfway through her seventh-grade year. On the first day of school that year, an eighth-grade boy named Gordon Hinks had given Allison the nickname "Muffin Top." She was surprised at how quickly she became accustomed to the emotional pain and torment she suffered. Her daily ritual involved crying in the girls' locker room for a few minutes before the start of school every day. She made no attempt to remedy the situation until a boy she was mildly obsessed with, another eighth grader and friend of Gordon named Brandon Lender, said exactly this to her: "I'd fuck you if I could find the hole."

The statement itself, combined with the importance it carried for Allison, coming as it did from her first romantic interest—a boy she drew pictures of in her notebook, whose last name she fantasized about having as her own, with whom she countless times imagined sharing her first kiss—led her to go home that night and skip eating dinner. Instead she retreated to her room and sought dieting advice on the Internet. She came across a posting on the website Everything2.com called "How to Become a Better Anorexic." The article outlined various dieting strategies to curb hunger pains, such as eating as much celery as possible because it contains no calories but causes your body to burn them as it is digested, or making sure the water you drink is as cold as possible so your body has to expend a few extra calories heating it. As well, this posting listed several links to pro-anorexia websites like Ana's Underground Grotto, which encouraged girls to become anorexic by allowing other girls to post photos of themselves that highlighted their hipbones, ribcages, and, in some cases, spines. These photos were commonly referred to within the pro-anorexia community as "thinspiration."

Allison found that the physical pain caused by hunger was just as easy to accept as a constant in her life as the emotional pain that came with being overweight was before. Over the next six months she created her own account on the Angels of Ana website and frequented sites like the Art of Reduction, Thin2be's Diary, and Hungry for Perfection. Although she had never met any of the people she communicated with on these sites, she felt they were her friends and she valued their advice and interaction far more than she did the guidance of her own family, who knew nothing about her treatment of food and eating.

Allison's mother, Liz, worked at Marie Callender's and always brought home pies. As Allison walked through the kitchen, Liz said, "Honey, I got a peach cobbler," which was Allison's favorite. The smell of the cobbler was almost more than she could deal with as she walked through the kitchen. She could feel herself begin to salivate and a slight tingling sensation in the back of her mouth became apparent.

Allison said, "Thanks, Mom, just leave it in the fridge and I'll get some later. I have to go get started on some homework."

Allison's father and brother said nothing as she went upstairs and logged on to Angels of Ana to look at pictures of girls who were thinner than she was and read postings about how to ignore cravings of favorite foods.

A few blocks away, Brandy Beltmeyer stood behind her mother, Patricia, who sat in her room at her computer doing what she called her "weekly check." This check consisted of Brandy being forced to give her mother the passwords to every website on which she had an account. Patricia would then log in to each of these sites, including her daughter's Gmail account, Myspace page, Facebook page, and her user account on Syfy.com. Patricia would read through every interaction her daughter was engaged in on each of these sites and question her if she found anything that seemed out of the ordinary. This was all done to protect her daughter from Internet predators.

As Patricia scrolled through the comments on her daughter's Myspace page, she came to one, posted by a male user named DILF whose age was listed as twenty-eight, that read, "U R HAWT."

Patricia said, "Who is this DILF guy?"

Brandy said, "I don't know, just some guy. I can't help it if some random guy finds my picture and thinks I'm cute."

Patricia said, "Well, I can," as she deleted DILF's comment. This garnered an eye-roll and sigh from her daughter. Patricia stood from her daughter's computer chair and said, "You know this is to make sure you're safe."

Brandy said, "I know."

Patricia said, "I love you."

Brandy said, "I love you, too."

Patricia left her daughter's room and went downstairs, where her husband, Ray, said, "You clean up her Internet or whatever?" Since he was in high school, Ray had worked in a local sporting goods store that was originally owned by his grandfather. His older brother now owned the shop, and Ray was next in line in the event that his brother wanted to retire. They used the same bookkeeping methods that were popular with their grandfather. There had never been a computer in the store. Ray still felt computers were unnecessary on many levels and refused to even create an e-mail account for himself.

Patricia laughed and said, "Yes, honey, I cleaned up her Internet." Then they settled in to watch a syndicated episode of *According to Jim*, which was their favorite show.

Upstairs, Brandy logged on to a Myspace account that she kept secret from her mother. Her username and identity on this account was Freyja. She decided on the name after doing a search on the Internet for "sexy goddess." She was directed to a page devoted to Freyja, the Norse goddess of love and sex. Freyja was believed to have been pulled in a golden chariot by a pack of wild cats. Brandy liked cats. Brandy donned gothic makeup and took pictures of herself in her bra and underwear with her phone and then uploaded them to this account, erasing the photos from her phone immediately after uploading. She gave incorrect information about her age and location and, despite the fact that she had yet to experience her first kiss, filled the blog section of her Freyja account with fictitious descriptions of sexual encounters and sexual preferences that she assumed men would want her to have, including bisexuality, a predilection for anal sex, and the need to be choked or spit on.

She communicated daily with her 5,689 friends and regularly made new ones. There were a few whom she communicated with more frequently than others. Dungeonmax, GothGod1337, and LovelyPallor were among them. They talked about a wide variety of subjects, mainly sexual, most of which Brandy knew nothing about, but could quickly research with a rudimentary Google search and then regurgitate, in some cases copying and pasting various bits and pieces of other blogs she would come across directly into instant messaging conversations. She was not overly interested in losing her virginity or performing any kind of sexual act at her age, but she found it an easy way to get the interest of moderate to large numbers of people who would engage in instant message conversations with her about a wide variety of subjects.

Brandy had invented her Freyja identity in the seventh grade, when her mother and father moved to a school district that forced her to go to Goodrich instead of the junior high school her grade school friends attended. As an alternative to making new friends at Goodrich, Brandy found it easier to find meaningful and entertaining interactions with people online. She still maintained a friendship with her best friend, Lauren Martin, and saw her on most weekends.

She worked very hard at keeping this secret from her mother, resetting her browser's history, cookies, and caches every fifteen minutes or so just in case her mother should come in and demand a surprise check of her computer, which she had done in the past. She also kept this Myspace page a secret from her classmates, assuming that knowledge of its existence would find its way back to her mother if any of her peers found out about it.

Freyja had eighteen new messages, many innocuous, two requesting nude pictures, and one from an obese married woman in gothic makeup from Tucson, Arizona, calling herself Lady Fenris and offering a ménage à trois with herself and her husband, who were both disease and drug-free.

A few blocks away, Tim Mooney finished eating a twelve-pack of nuggets from Chick-fil-A that his father, Kent, brought him home for dinner, along with one for himself. As Tim stood from the table taking his trash with him to the kitchen, Kent said, "Want to toss the ball for a while?"

Kent and Tim would frequently play catch with a football after dinner. It was something they did even before Tim's mother and Kent's wife, Lydia, left to live with this man named Greg Cherry in California who was in marketing. But since she left, Kent felt that tossing the ball brought them closer together as a father and son. It was something that solidified their bond as two men who were abandoned. Tim recognized this as well. He thought about agreeing to play catch with his father, and not telling him that he'd quit the football team a few hours earlier, but was unable to. He didn't want to lie to his father or to participate in any form of charade with his father. He had respect for his father and that respect, he thought, deserved the truth. He said, "Dad, I, uh . . . I quit the football team today."

The words were difficult for Kent to hear coming from his son's mouth, but he wasn't surprised. Since Lydia left, Kent had sensed his son pulling away, becoming more introverted, losing interest in the things that had always held his attention. Kent's normal reaction to his son's news would have been anger. Kent would have screamed at his son and threatened punishment unless his son rejoined the football team. But, like his son, since his wife had left, he found it more and more difficult to feel anything other than a certain hollow sadness. Kent said, "Oh. I see. Are you sure?"

Tim said, "Yeah. I just . . . Yeah. I'm sure, Dad."

Kent said, "Well, I'm obviously not going to force you to play. I mean, I can't force you to, but I think you should think about it. And I don't want this to be because of— Just think about it."

Tim said, "I already quit."

Kent said, "I know, but, just think about it. You can go back, I'm sure."

Tim said, "Okay."

Tim passed his father on his way to the kitchen, where he threw his empty nugget box in the trash and went to his room without saying another word. Kent threw away his own trash, opened the first of what would be seven Bud Lights that night, and sat in for a night of watching the World Series of Poker and, at several specific moments, wondering what his wife was doing in California, which resulted in him imagining her having sex with Greg Cherry, a man Kent had never met or even seen. He pictured him as being small and intellectual, physically weak, probably wearing glasses and appearing slightly effeminate—the opposite of Kent. Kent had difficulty imagining that his wife would leave him for a man who was similar to him in any way. He could only reconcile her decision to abandon her family by assuming she had realized that she wanted something completely different, at least for the time being.

Kent turned his thoughts to his son. He recognized that Tim had become more introverted and moody and rationalized that all kids his age must go through similar periods and that his mother's absence probably wasn't helping the situation. He held on to some hope that, after Tim emerged from whatever he was going through, he would return to football. Beyond directly illustrating the benefits of playing football, Kent assumed he could say nothing else to his son to speed this process up, so he decided to leave him alone to work things out on his own. Kent found that dwelling on how badly he wanted his son to rejoin the team left him with less time to think about his soon-to-be ex-wife, Lydia, living in California with Greg Cherry who was in marketing.

Tim sat down at his computer and logged on to *World of Warcraft*, the Shattered Hand server, five minutes before his guild was scheduled to raid Ulduar, the highest-level end-game dungeon in the game at the time. Tim's main character was a frostfire specced mage named Firehands who regularly had the highest damage-per-second in guild raids. He was a valuable member to his guild, which required his damage output to defeat all of the bosses in Ulduar.

As soon as he logged on, he was greeted in guild chat by other members who would be joining in the raid. At the bottom left of Tim's screen in the green guild-chat text a series of phrases appeared: "I thought your mom sucked my dick last night but when I reached down and felt stubble, I realized it was your dad. My mistake." "What's up, nigger?" "You fuck any junior high pussy yet?" "I wish I was in junior high again, I'd fuck every piece of 7th grade ass I could, even the niggers."

Tim had become used to the tone and content of his guild's chat. He believed that none of these people were actual pedophiles, homophobes, or racists, and he found humor in their explicit chat messages, understanding that most massively multiplayer online games had evolved a similar style and tone of communication within their player bases due to the fact that a large number of the players had spent so much time digesting the Internet's most base content that they were now desensitized to nearly everything most people would consider offensive. Even though Tim had never known the real names of his guildmates, he considered them his friends based on the frequency of their interaction, which was daily. He had no conversations of substance with these people and their exchanges involved little beyond *World of Warcraft*, racial humor, and explicitly sexual anecdotes that were rarely true. He had told none of them about his mother moving or about his decision to quit playing football, which were the two most important events of his life thus far. Tim enjoyed the surface-level communication he had with his guildmates. He didn't want anything more.

He knew Chucker only as the protection-specced paladin who was the greatest purveyor of fake racial hatred in the guild. He would never know that the person on the other end of the computer was a twenty-eight-year-old loan officer in Annapolis, Maryland, who had to beg his fiancée to let him play *World of*

Warcraft virtually every night and more often than not waited until she fell asleep so he could sneak off to the computer in their office and play the game.

He knew Baratheon only as the dwarven shadow priest who would respec to holy before every raid and then fail to properly heal the tank on at least one boss per instance, causing a wipe. He would never know that the person playing Baratheon was a six-foot-five, three-hundred-twenty-pound half-Korean, half-French Canadian college student studying engineering and accounting in order to make his parents happy even though he really wanted to play football.

He knew Selkis only as the night elf rogue who could outdamage most of the mages in their guild. He would never know that the person playing Selkis was a twenty-six-year-old perpetual college student who had no intention of ever graduating, ate a Wendy's Baconator at least once a day, and lived with his parents and their five cats.

At a chat command from the guild leader to "Get on Vent," Tim logged on to the guild's Ventrillo server, a third-party program that allowed the members of the guild to actually talk to one another using microphones; he put on his headphones; and they all entered the instance. Tim was happy not to think about his mother in California with Greg Cherry or his father sitting silently in the living room wishing he would play football again or the pointlessness of any of it for the next four hours.

A few blocks away, Carl Benton was uneasy about his daughter spending so much time with her boyfriend, Danny Vance. Carl was aware that his daughter had inherited much of her physical appearance from her mother, which meant that she would likely be the first sexual fantasy of many of the boys she went to school with. And more than a fantasy, she would likely be Danny Vance's first sexual experience. Carl did not like this. As he ate dinner with his wife, Sarah, and his seven-year-old son, Andrew, he said, "She spends a lot of time over there. Should we be as okay with this as we're acting like we are?"

Sarah didn't mind Brooke spending time at the Vances' house. She and Carl had known the Vances for several years, and their son, Danny, was among the less threatening boys of his age. Brooke had never cried as a result of anything he had done, which, as a junior high school teacher for many years before she retired, Sarah knew to be rare. She said, "I think we should be more than okay with it. She's having fun—let her be."

Andrew said, "Can I go eat dinner with the Vances?"

Carl said, "Very funny, turd."

After they finished dinner, Carl helped Andrew with his homework and then put him to bed. Then he went into his own bedroom to find Sarah reading a book he had never heard of. He said, "Honey, you're really not worried about Brooke and Danny?"

Sarah continued reading as she spoke. She said, "No. I'm really not."

Carl said, "She's getting older, you know what I mean?"

Sarah said, "Yes, I know exactly what you mean. If you're afraid she's going to start having sex, then talk to her about it."

Carl said, "That's not a father-daughter conversation. That's a mother-daughter conversation."

Sarah said, "We've already talked to both of them about sex. She knows better than to do something stupid."

Carl said, "Yeah, but we talked to them when she was still a kid. She's not anymore. Have you looked at her lately? Boys are going to be beating down our door pretty soon."

Sarah said, "Then we should be happy that she has a nice boy like Danny Vance to keep them away. She'll be fine."

Sarah put her book down on the nightstand and turned off her reading lamp. Carl went into the bathroom and brushed his teeth. When he came back, Sarah was asleep.

• • •

A few blocks away, and a few hours earlier, Jim Vance opened the door and came in with Danny and Brooke. Danny's mother, Tracey, had already set the table. She said, "Hello, Brooke. It's so nice to have you joining us for dinner tonight."

Brooke said, "Thanks, Mrs. Vance. It's nice of you to have me over."

Tracey said, "How many times do I have to tell you? It's Tracey."

Brooke said, "Sorry."

Tracey said, "It's all right. Dinner'll be ready in about ten minutes. You kids can go watch TV if you want."

Danny led Brooke into the living room. Tracey turned to Jim and said, "She is such a cutie."

Jim said, "Just like you used to be."

Tracey said, "Used to be?" and then spanked Jim, who laughed and kissed his wife before going into the kitchen for a Beck's.

Once dinner was ready, all four of them took their seats around the table and Jim said, "So, how's the team looking this year?"

Danny said, "Well, Tim Mooney quit today, so it's going to be a lot tougher to win without him, but I think we'll be okay. Coach Quinn is going to let me pass a lot this season and Chris should be able to get down the field, so I think we'll have a shot at district."

Jim said, "Tim Mooney quit?"

Danny said, "Yeah."

Jim said, "Why?"

Danny said, "Coach didn't say."

Tracey said, "That's so sad. I bet he's going through a tough time with his mom being gone and everything."

Danny said, "Whatever."

Tracey said, "Well, Brooke, how are you doing this year?"

Brooke said, "Pretty good. We're just getting ready for the season to start, too. It's pretty exciting. I can't wait to see Danny play. I know they're going to be awesome."

The rest of the dinner conversation was about the various junior high schools Danny would face in the regular season and about *American Idol*, with Tracey adding some anecdotes about the neighbor's cat, who seemed to be defecating on the Vance's front steps with almost daily regularity. After dinner, Brooke helped Tracey clear the table. Tracey said, "Brooke, would you like a ride home? Jim can take you."

Danny said, "Oh, we were going to play some *Rock Band* and then I was just going to walk her home, if that's cool."

Tracey said, "As long as your mom is fine with you kids walking out after dark, Brooke."

Brooke said, "Yeah, she's cool with it. I mean, we're only like five minutes away."

Danny and Brooke went up the stairs to his room.

Jim said, "You don't think they're . . . having sex, do you?"

Tracey said, "I doubt it. But maybe you should have 'the talk' with him."

Jim said, "Jesus Christ, really? How old were we when we started getting it on?"

Tracey said, "We were in college, but that doesn't mean they're going to wait that long. Better safe than sorry. Maybe you should buy him some condoms."

Jim said, "Oh my god, are you serious? Don't they just learn everything about sex from TV and the Internet? Do I really have to do this?"

Tracey said, "Don't be stupid." She kissed him and added, "Just have the talk with him."

Jim took a swig from the Beck's he was currently drinking and said, "I don't see why I have to do it."

Tracey said, "I did it with our daughter and you have to do it with our son. That was the deal."

Jim said, "I know, I know. I'll do it this weekend. I don't want to get in his head before their first game."

Upstairs, Danny turned on his Xbox 360 and raised the volume on his television so his parents could hear nothing but the sounds of the *Rock Band* introductory video coming from his room. Then he sat down on his bed next to Brooke and kissed her. They had been in the habit of pretending to play *Rock Band* or do homework with loud music playing for almost a month while they engaged in various forms of foreplay, never removing clothing, but getting slightly more aggressive with the placement of their hands in each successive encounter. Danny had felt Brooke's small and still-forming breasts through her shirt; Brooke had felt Danny's erection through his pants as it pressed against her legs and genitals. Danny had ejaculated in his pants as a result of these encounters once before. Embarrassed, he said nothing about it and pretended that the event never occurred. Although it was strangely arousing to Brooke, she remained silent about the incident as well, assuming that Danny's silence indicated his unwillingness to address the matter.

As Danny retraced every step he had taken in their most recent groping session, kissing Brooke's neck, moving his hand from her hip toward her breast, tonguing her ear, and eventually moving his hand to her left breast, he knew that the only possible next step, the only way to keep the evolution of their physical relationship steady, was to put his hand under her shirt. He moved his hand off Brooke's breast, back down toward the bottom of her shirt, and slid his fingertips just under it, barely grazing her stomach. She moaned.

Danny hoped that Brooke would be unable to detect his nervousness as he slid his hand slightly higher, placing his full palm on her stomach, his fingertips brushing the bottom of her bra. He stopped his hand here for a moment and rubbed her stomach, not sure if this brazen action would constitute enough progress for one night in Brooke's mind.

Although Brooke was enjoying herself, it was difficult for her not to think about the image on Hannah's phone of her performing fellatio on a random and unnamed boy. She had no choice but to compare herself to Hannah, and when she did, she felt inferior. As Danny rubbed his hand against her stomach, she made the decision that Hannah wasn't going to be the only one to have had a boy's penis in her mouth in the eighth grade. And, beyond that, she rationalized that Hannah didn't love the boy she shared her first sexual encounter with, so Brooke could still be the first girl in eighth grade to perform fellatio in a loving relationship and that was more important than just being the first to do it.

She moved Danny's hand out from under her shirt. Danny said, "I'm sorry. I didn't mean to go too fast or anything."

Brooke said, "You didn't," and then rolled over on top of him and kissed him. She kissed him down the neck and lifted up his shirt, at the same time moving down and kissing his chest and stomach while rubbing his erection through his pants.

Danny could feel himself on the verge of ejaculating again. He said, "What are you doing?"

Brooke said, "Something."

Danny said, "We don't have to do this. Are you sure we're, you know, like ready for this and everything?" He was nervous and unsure about how to behave in such a situation. Although he and Brooke had been engaging in increasingly more sexual behavior over the past few months, he had come to the conclusion that he wasn't ready for anything beyond what they had been doing. He hoped that Brooke felt the same way.

She said, "I know we don't have to, but in my opinion it's fine if we do. We've been together for a long time. We should." Brooke perceived Danny's hesitation to be some kind of obligatory and unnecessary chivalry on his part. She certainly didn't want to have sex, but she had convinced herself that performing oral sex on her boyfriend of over a year wasn't, in actuality, as significant as it might seem. Furthermore, she reasoned that she'd rather have her first attempt be on a person she loved than on a stranger, as Hannah had done. She said, "Just relax."

She noticed the smell immediately. She found it vaguely unpleasant and wondered if Danny had taken a shower after football practice. She knew that he sometimes didn't if the practice was light. She took his penis into her mouth, careful not to graze it with her teeth. The instructions for performing oral sex she had read in various magazines and on websites all mentioned a man's distaste for having teeth be involved in any way.

Danny had run through every nonsexual thought his mind could conjure during the experience in an effort to avoid immediate ejaculation—algebra equations, football plays, *Grand Theft Auto* cheat codes, the image of his grandmother urinating in her pants at the last family Christmas—but he reached a point at which he could no longer hold back. He had no idea what the proper etiquette was to let Brooke know what was about to happen. All he could do was tap her shoulder three times in rapid succession, which only served to confuse her enough to remove his penis from her mouth slightly just as he ejaculated. She first felt his semen hit her on the upper lip and go slightly up one nostril; the second contraction of Danny's prostate expelled semen onto Brooke's cheek, which caused her to recoil. The final contractions of Danny's prostate resulted in semen being deposited all over his Old Navy boxer shorts and Goodrich Olympians T-shirt.

They were silent for a few seconds, Danny looking directly at his ceiling, not wanting to make eye contact with Brooke, feeling slightly embarrassed. Brooke, too, felt some embarrassment at not being able to contain the semen better. She had heard that guys prefer a girl who swallows the ejaculate. The smell of it was slightly disgusting to her, though, and the taste, she imagined, was even worse. She wasn't sure that she'd ever be able to swallow semen. She tried wiping the semen off her face with her hand, but its texture made it difficult to manage. She said, "Um, I think I need a towel or something."

Danny said, "Okay, hang on," and got up off his bed, still without making eye contact with her. He went into the upstairs bathroom and found a hand towel. He used it on himself first, cleaning up as much of the semen as he could, hoping that his mother wouldn't find it on his clothes when she washed them the next day. Then he went back into his room and handed the towel to Brooke, who eventually managed to clean herself up satisfactorily, despite getting some of the semen Danny put on the towel on her face and hands a few times.

Brooke said, "Did you like that? I mean, did I do it okay?"

Danny said, "Um, yeah."

Brooke said, "Was there anything I could have, like, done better?"

Danny said, "Um, I don't think so."

Brooke said, "Okay, cool."

Danny said, "Yeah."

Brooke said, "Well, in my opinion, I'm glad we did it, aren't you?"

Danny said, "Yeah."

The truth was that neither of them was glad. Danny felt strange upon the act's completion, as did Brooke. They had crossed some line, performed some act that signified their emergence into an adult world. Whatever innocence they once had was, although not completely gone, tarnished in some way, and they both recognized this.

Danny knew immediately that he didn't want to do this again anytime soon. And, more than repeating this act, he feared that the escalation of their physical relationship would now culminate in sexual intercourse, something he felt unsure about and unready for. He wondered if he could do anything to stave off this eventuality until he felt more ready. His thoughts drifted to ideas of breaking up with Brooke. It might be his only option.

Brooke, too, regretted doing what she'd done. Her sense of competition had driven her to perform the act, and she took some solace in feeling that she was on equal ground with Hannah Clint, but she assumed that Danny would now expect at least that level of physical intimacy at every subsequent encounter. Brooke knew she wouldn't be able to meet his expectation, let alone exceed it with sexual intercourse, which is what she logically assumed he would require in the near future. She, too, began contemplating a breakup.

Danny and Brooke walked downstairs past Danny's parents, who were watching *Dancing with the Stars* at Tracey's behest, and out the front door, any evidence of their sexual activity unnoticed. When they came to Brooke's house, she leaned in to kiss Danny on the lips, their standard parting display of affection, but Danny said, "Is it cool if we just hug? You just had my, you know, like in your mouth."

Brooke said, "Yeah, it's cool."

They hugged. Brooke went inside to find that everyone else was already asleep. She was relieved to be able to avoid the strange conversation with her mother or father that she had assumed would happen—the conversation in which she would have to lie about the details of the night and hope that her mother or father wouldn't notice any evidence of the night's actual activities. She made her way upstairs where she washed her face properly, finding a few tiny bits of Danny's semen in the hair above her right ear, then got into bed and stared at the ceiling for a few minutes, trying to overcome the strange nausea she had felt since performing fellatio on Danny. She reached for her cell phone and sent Danny a text message that read, "luv u."

Though content that night as he went back home and lay in his bed, Danny was also trying to overcome a certain nausea, one that came from an all-consuming uncertainty he felt about his future with Brooke and what impact a breakup might have on his eighth-grade year. He briefly thought about having to perform oral sex on Brooke in order to placate her at their next physical encounter. He realized he would have absolutely no idea how to perform even the most rudimentary version of the act. He decided he wouldn't make the attempt unless she asked. He replied to her text with one that read, "u 2."

Brooke Benton and Allison Doss each held one side of a twenty-by-six-foot butcher-paper banner that read, "Olympian Strength, Win! Win! Win!" stretching it tight as they stood near the end zone closest to the Goodrich Olympians' field house. Hannah Clint, along with the other Olympiannes, stood nearby facing the home crowd doing various cheers, kicks, and claps. Hannah's mother, Dawn, was on the field taking photographs of the girls. She had convinced Principal Ligorski and Mrs. Langston, the Olympiannes' coach, to let her serve as the photographer and organizer of the Olympianne scrapbook that year, agreeing to perform these services at no cost, thereby saving the school the seven hundred dollars that was normally charged by the local photographer. Dawn saw it as an opportunity to get some impressive action shots for her daughter's website that would be impossible to get otherwise.

In the stands, Don Truby, Jim Vance, and Kent Mooney stood next to each other. Don passed a flask of bourbon to Jim, who declined the offer, prompting Don to pass it to Kent, who drank generously and said, "Thanks. Needed that more than you know."

Don said, "Work getting shitty?"

Kent said, "Nah, no more shitty than usual. Just Lydia being gone and Tim not playing tonight, you know?"

Don said, "Yeah, Chris mentioned Tim quitting. Sorry about that, man. But on the bright side—and I know this probably isn't what you want to hear right now—but with the wife thing, you're better off, man. Seriously. You're a free man. You can bang any chick you want."

Kent said, "I haven't really been in a bangin' mood lately, Don."

Don said, "I'm just saying, Rachel lets me bang her maybe once a month. I'm stuck with her, man. That's what married guys have to deal with until we fucking die."

Jim Vance said, "Speak for yourself."

Don said, "Oh, Mister 'My kid's the fucking quarterback and I fuck my wife three times a day' over here. Fucking bullshit."

Jim said, "It's not bullshit. Tracey and I still have sex at least a few times a week. So not all married guys are in your situation, Don."

Don said, "Fuck. Twice a week?"

Jim said, "Yeah."

Don said, "Really?"

Jim said, "Yeah."

Don said, "Jesus fucking Christ. Lucky piece of shit. I actually—I don't know why I'm fucking telling you guys this—I actually got so desperate a few days ago I used Chris's computer to look at porn." He took a long pull from his flask.

Jim said, "Oh my god. You're a disgusting individual. You know that, right? You need help."

Don said, "Don't we all?"

Jim said, "Kent, you think Tim might come back out this season?"

Kent said, "I don't know. I don't know what his deal is. He just seems like his heart's not in it, but I think it's just a phase, you know? I'm hoping he will."

Jim said, "I think we all are."

In the announcer's booth, Principal Ligorski switched on his microphone and said through the PA system, "Ladies and gentlemen, welcome to the first game of the season here at Goodrich Junior High. Thanks for coming out tonight to support your team. And now, here they are—your Goodrich Olympians!"

On the field, Brooke and Allison pulled their banner as tight as they could. The field house doors opened and the Goodrich Olympians eighth-grade football team ran toward the field, each player screaming. The visiting team, the Park Panthers, were not granted such an entrance. They stood silently at the opposite end of the field, watching as Danny Vance led his team at full speed, tearing through the banner held by Brooke and Allison. Brooke tried to make eye contact with Danny as he ran by. She had come to the conclusion, in a day's time, that she did not want to break up with Danny. In fact, she wanted desperately to stay together, but still was uneasy about the new nature of their physical relationship. She planned to put off any future sexual encounters as long as she could and then, if she was pushed to do so, she would talk to Danny about how she felt, at which point she assumed he would break up with her.

She wanted to blow him a kiss as he ran on the field, but he never looked anywhere other than straight ahead as he tore through the banner. He, too, was consumed with thinking about the nature of their physical relationship. The game and his role in it should have been his primary focus, he knew, but he found that the only thing in his mind was a slow replay of Brooke putting his penis in her mouth and eventually of semen spraying her face. It disturbed him. He had seen pornography, but the sight of his own penis in the mouth of a girl he actually knew was somehow far more disturbing to him. He came to the conclusion that he would avoid any kind of situation that led to a physical encounter with Brooke until she forced the issue. Then he would tell her how he felt and endure whatever her reaction might be, presumably a breakup.

The parents of the players clapped and cheered at their appearance on the field. Kent took out his telephone and thought about sending a text message to his son, Tim, to tell him that the game was starting. He put his telephone back in his pocket without sending the text message, assuming there was no point.

The two Olympian co-captains, Danny Vance and Chris Truby, walked out to the fifty-yard line along with two players from the Park Panthers and the referees. Danny called heads to win the coin toss and elected for the Olympians to receive the ball first, and a few moments later the game was underway.

Chris Truby, as the fastest player the Olympians fielded, served as their kickoff and punt returner. The opening kickoff of the game was a line drive that bounced several times before finally making it to Chris, who returned it for twelve yards before being brought down in a dog pile near his own thirty-five-yard line.

As Danny Vance and the rest of the Goodrich Junior High School offense took the field for their first drive of the season, Coach Quinn pulled him aside. Despite the fact that it had already been predetermined that the first play of the game would be the X fade, a passing play designed to deceive the defense—making them think all of the receivers were running short routes while Chris Truby stalled on the line and then sprinted down the sideline as the primary receiver—Coach Quinn said, "Danny, let's switch it up. Run the seven-three-nine flip." Danny had no time to protest Coach Quinn's decision to go with a running play as the first play of the season. He ran out onto the field, into the huddle, and said, "Okay, seven-three-nine flip on one. Ready—break!"

The abrupt change of play caused some minor confusion. Danny quelled it by saying, "I know we were supposed to run the X fade, but Coach Quinn changed it. So let's do it. Hit your blocks." They ran the play for a loss of one yard, as a result of Randy Trotter missing his block assignment and letting one of the Park Panthers' defensive ends straight into the backfield.

From the sidelines, Coach Quinn sent in Tanner Hodge with the next play. It was the four-two-six pitch wide right, another running play. Danny ran the play as Coach Quinn requested, for another loss, this time for three yards, as a result of Tanner attempting to run through the incorrect hole. The third play was another running play, this time executed for a gain of four yards leaving the Olympians with fourth and ten. In spite of the fact that little more than forty-five seconds had passed in the first quarter of the game, Danny called a time-out and went to the sidelines. He approached Coach Quinn, who immediately said, "What are you doing?" Danny said, "Coach Quinn, don't punt. Let me throw. We can get a first here with the Xfade or a deep cross. Just let me hit Chris. We can get this."

In the stands, several parents of the other players made comments in Jim's general direction like, "What's your kid doing calling a time-out, Vance?" and "Does he think he's in the NFL?" and "It's the first goddamn quarter."

On the sidelines, Coach Quinn thought about the likelihood of Danny completing a pass to Chris Truby for enough yards to get a first down. He knew the Park Panthers wouldn't be ready for a pass play. They already had a player lining up deep in anticipation of the punt. It seemed like it might work, but more important to Coach Quinn was making Danny understand that he couldn't undermine a decision that came from the coach and certainly couldn't undermine a decision that cost his team a time-out.

Coach Quinn believed he was more than just a football coach to the players on his team. He believed he was teaching them skills that they would carry with them into whatever endeavors they may encounter in their later lives. Discipline and the ability to follow instructions from a superior were skills he thought every one of his players should have by the time they made their way into high school. He took personal offense at Danny's defiant attitude, but also saw it as an opportunity to teach Danny the value of subservience.

And beyond all this, Coach Quinn had recently been through two significant events in his life that left him feeling somewhat powerless. After attempting unsuccessfully to conceive a child with his wife for three years, Coach Quinn had been told by a fertility doctor that his sperm count was insufficient to father a child. There were methods by which he and his wife could conceive a child using his sperm, all of which were surgical—leaving the decision on which method would be employed entirely up to his wife. Then, within a week of learning about his low sperm count, Coach Quinn was passed over for the head-coaching position at a high school in a neighboring district. The position would have meant more money and would have signified a move toward his true goal, coaching at the college level.

Coach Quinn used his hours on the field as the leader of the Goodrich Junior High Olympians as his time to take control back in his life. And, as much as he believed that his players needed to learn discipline and respect, he also needed to administer these things in order to feel like he had control over something in his life. He looked at Danny and said, "We're kicking it, Danny. Take a seat." And, in that moment, some switch was thrown in his mind that made him decide that this game, and every subsequent game, would be dominated by the running game, if only because he needed to have absolute control over something and that something was the eighth-grade football team he was coaching.

Danny took his helmet off and sat down on the bench next to Chris and watched Jeremy Kelms kick a twenty-five-yard punt. Brooke saw Danny sitting on the bench and took a momentary break from cheering to approach him and say, "You look seriously awesome out there. I love you." Danny said, "Thanks. I gotta stay focused, babe," and then put his helmet back on. Brooke understood. She turned back to the crowd and began cheering again.

The Goodrich defense took the field and in the stands Jim said, "I guess we'll see how bad we need Tim out there. Here we go."

Kent nudged Don, prompting him to offer his flask again and took a deep drink from it. He had never watched a youth football game in which his son wasn't playing. He obviously wanted his son's school to win, but he found himself wishing not only for his son's replacement to fail but to be significantly injured in that failure. He wanted it to be more than obvious to everyone watching that his son, the way he had been before his mother left, was sorely missed.

The Park Panthers ran a quarterback sneak as their first play and gained eight yards, their quarterback running straight past a diving Bill Francis and finally being stopped by the free safety, who moved up to cover the middle linebacker's mistake. Jim said, "Shit. That's not a good sign." Kent was happy. He thought again about sending a text message to his son and again thought better of it. He was content to know that Tim was missed.

Tim was at home checking his Myspace account, thinking only briefly about the fact that he was missing the season opener. He tried to find some small part of himself that cared or missed playing football, but he couldn't; it seemed meaningless to him. His nightly raid had been canceled due to the raid leader, at the age of twenty-six, taking the next few days to move out of his parents' house and into his first apartment. Tim had no new messages from his one hundred and two friends, most of whom were other Goodrich students, but some of whom were people he'd met through Myspace based on various common interests, people who belonged to fan pages for Noam Chomsky or *World of Warcraft*.

Near the bottom of his home page, six profiles were suggested to Tim as people he might be interested in based on other common friends. One of them was a profile for a gothic-looking girl named Freyja who claimed to be twenty-five years old. Freyja's resemblance to Brandy Beltmeyer, the girl Tim had unsuccessfully attempted to ask out on a date via text message the year before, was uncanny. The makeup Freyja had on was transformative enough to stir significant doubt in Tim's mind that this person actually was Brandy Beltmeyer in some type of alter-ego disguise, but the small scar over her left eyebrow, which he knew Brandy also had, erased whatever doubt the makeup had conjured.

He saw that Freyja was online and had the impulse to send her an instant message asking if she knew Brandy Beltmeyer or was related to her in some way, or perhaps even overtly proclaiming that he knew her true identity. Instead, he clicked on Freyja's picture section and viewed twenty-three albums containing pictures of Brandy dressed in various gothic outfits and makeup schemes. He found it a strange coincidence that her profile was randomly suggested to him by whatever means Myspace defined these suggestions. Tim reasoned it must have had something to do with he and Freyja both having a large number of friends who had links to other friends who were involved with fantasy and gothic games and lifestyles. He read some of her blog entries: "My First 3some," "Anal Only Hurts A Little At First," "My First 3some With 2 Grls," and "Swallowing." He wondered how many of these blog posts were based on actual experience, or if they were all fabricated. If they were based in reality, he wondered if his sexual inexperience had played a part in her ignoring his text-message movie invitation the year before. He had a vague notion that Brandy's mother ran some kind of parental watch-group for Internet abuse, based on the fliers his father had received advertising monthly meetings at Brandy's house and giving helpful tips for parents to keep their children safe from Internet predators. He wondered if her mother knew her daughter was Freyja.

Tim wrote a brief e-mail to Freyja. It read, "The Myspace references thing popped you up when I logged on. Just thought I'd say hi." He didn't want to let Brandy know that he knew who she was. He decided to see what her reaction would be to his e-mail before doing anything else.

Brandy had just sent a response to an e-mail from Dungeon-max, part of an extended conversation about *True Blood* regarding which of the vampires they found to be the most sexually attractive, when she saw a new message from Tim appear in her in-box. The subject line read, "Hello." She was instantly nervous and slightly afraid. She frantically wondered if she had been discovered by one of her classmates—and not just any classmate, but one whom she had had romantic interest in the year before. She opened his e-mail and read the message, which seemed innocuous enough not to warrant any alarm. Nothing in the message led her to believe he knew it was her, and even if he did, it didn't seem like he was the type to divulge this information to her mother or anyone else for that matter. Despite her understanding of the situation, Brandy decided to ignore his message and delete it.

In his room, Tim waited fifteen more minutes for Brandy to respond. In those fifteen minutes she never went offline and she never sent a response. He assumed her reasoning was identical to the time he sent her the first text message: that she was uninterested.

Danny was allowed to pass twice in the first half, each time resulting in a gain of over fifteen yards, once resulting in a touchdown throw to Chris Truby, who was alone in the end zone.

Despite the success of both passing plays, Coach Quinn forced Danny to execute a battery of running plays. The final play of the first half found Danny Vance handing the ball off to Tanner Hodge for a gain of three yards. As the Goodrich Olympians ran off the field into the field house for a halftime pep talk, the score was thirteen to seven in favor of the Park Panthers. In the wake of the football team, the Olympiannes took the field to put on a halftime show they had been practicing all week.

In the stands, parents freely issued conjecture on the state of the team, the outcome of the season, and the mistakes that would surely be made in the second half. Jim, Don, and Kent were among these parents.

Don, who was inebriated, said, "Well, it's not looking good, huh, guys?"

Jim said, "Nah, we're fine. Danny and Chris will hook up a few more times before the game's over. You'll see."

Kent said, "It's not going to matter much if our defense can't stop them from scoring."

Jim said, "I know. And Park probably has the weakest running game of any school this year. I hate to sound like a broken record but you have to find a way to get Tim back out here."

Kent just nodded.

On the field, the Olympiannes formed a pyramid with Allison Doss at the apex. Dawn Clint knelt by the pyramid, snapping photos of her daughter, who was in the second tier of the pyramid. She found that from a certain angle she was able to take some in which Hannah's buttocks were slightly exposed, shots she knew would be favorites of her subscribers. Upon review of a series of ten photographs she took, she found that one actually allowed the viewer to see a small part of Hannah's vagina on the side of the underwear she wore beneath her cheerleading skirt. She deleted this image immediately.

The pyramid was to be held for ten seconds, at the end of which Allison Doss was to stand up on the shoulders of the two girls supporting her, scream "Go Olympians," and then fall back, to be caught by Mrs. Langston and Rory Pearson, the only male member of the Olympiannes. Allison stood at the correct moment but found herself unable to scream "Go Olympians," due to becoming abruptly and extremely light-headed. She fell backward from the top of the pyramid, unconscious and bleeding from the nose. As Mrs. Langston caught her limp body and became aware of the blood trickling out of her nose, she yelled, "Doc!" Mr. Kemp, the school's athletic trainer, made his way to her as quickly as possible from the sidelines. Mrs. Langston told the rest of the Olympiannes to continue the show with basic cheers and individual gymnastics while she and Mr. Kemp took Allison to the field house.

In the field house, Coach Quinn was explaining to the football team that the offensive line needed to pick up the slack in order to make sure the running game was as effective as it was designed to be. Danny became aware of the fact that Coach Quinn had no intention of letting him pass and was unsure of how to change the situation. He was on the verge of voicing his opinion when Mr. Kemp and Mrs. Langston carried Allison Doss through the front door, prompting Coach Quinn to stop his speech and say, "She okay?"

Mr. Kemp said, "I think so, just got a little light-headed, nose bleed. Nothing serious. Just needs to lay down for a few minutes."

Coach Quinn said, "Okay, you can use my office if you need or anything in the training room." Then Coach Quinn turned his attention back to his team and began his speech about the importance of a solid ground game again.

In the training room, Mr. Kemp and Mrs. Langston laid Allison down on a table that was generally used to tape athletes' joints before games. Mr. Kemp retrieved some smelling salts from the first-aid cabinet and brought Allison back to consciousness. He gave her a washcloth to wipe the blood from her nose.

She said, "What happened?"

Mrs. Langston said, "You passed out on top of the pyramid."

Mr. Kemp gave her a grape Gatorade and said, "Just sit here as long as you need and drink this and you'll be okay. I have to get back out on the field. Mrs. Langston, you okay in here?"

Mrs. Langston said, "Yeah."

Once Mr. Kemp was gone, Mrs. Langston said, "Should we call your parents or anything?"

Allison didn't want her family to have reason to suspect that anything might be abnormal with her. She said, "No, they're both working and wouldn't be able to come anyway. I'm fine, really."

Mrs. Langston said, "Allison, you don't have to talk about this if you don't want to, but I want you to know that I'm here for you if you do. Have you been eating okay?"

This was the first time Allison had been directly confronted about her eating habits, the first time anyone had recognized that something might possibly be out of the norm. She said, "Yeah, I had a big lunch today. I mean, I know I've lost a little weight, but I think it's just because I'm going through puberty or something, you know? Same thing with the nose bleeds. I read online that you just get them sometimes as you grow."

Mrs. Langston said, "That can be true. I just want you to know that if you want to, I'm always here to talk." Mrs. Langston had coached Allison in the seventh grade as well. She had always liked Allison and felt sorry for her, knowing that once she got to high school, she would be too overweight to make the cheerleading squad. So when she returned to eighth grade, not only thinner than she had been in seventh grade but thinner than virtually every girl in her class, it seemed likely, at least in Mrs. Langston's mind, that Allison might have developed an eating disorder, although she reassured herself that she had no conclusive evidence to support her suspicion. Mrs. Langston had never dealt with something of this magnitude, and wasn't exactly sure how she should handle it or if she should alert a third party, so she decided in that moment to let Allison come to her if she felt it necessary; otherwise, she would remain silent.

Allison said, "Thanks." Then she looked at the Gatorade and said, "Could I actually just get some water?"

Back in the main room of the field house, Coach Quinn delivered the final words of his halftime speech; then the team stood and began to file back out onto the field. Danny Vance thought for a moment about approaching Coach Quinn privately before they left the building, to air his complaint about not being allowed to use his passing capability as frequently as he thought he should be. Instead, years of discipline and forced respect for authority, instilled in him by his father through various organized youth athletic endeavors, motivated him to remain silent and hope that Coach Quinn would realize the Olympians should utilize the pass play far more in the second half than they did in the first.

The first play Coach Quinn called in the second half was the four-three-six option, another running play. The next two plays of their first series of the second half were also running plays, resulting in a net gain of three yards and forcing a punt. As Jeremy Kelms delivered a thirty-two-yard punt, Danny watched from the sidelines, wondering what he should do about the obvious lack of coaching ability that was hindering his team. Brooke came up behind Danny and said, "You look really good out there, babe." Danny found her voice to be annoying and shrill at that moment, a sound that broke his concentration on the game. He said, "Not now, we're losing." This was the same response and attitude that Danny's father would display toward his mother when she would ask a simple question while he was watching a professional or college football game in which his preferred team was behind, although Danny would never have recognized the similarity. Brooke said, "Sorry," with sincerity, and returned to her place among the Olympiannes as they began a cheer with "Go! Fight! Win!"

For the next quarter and a half, Coach Quinn called only running plays that resulted in no additional scoring. The Park Panthers were able to exploit the Olympians' weak middle defense to score an additional touchdown, bringing the score to twenty to seven with slightly more than five minutes left in play as Danny Vance and the Olympians' offense took the field again.

Chris Truby ran into the huddle from the sidelines and whispered the play to Danny as was protocol. He said, "Five-three-two flip" and took his place in the huddle, waiting for Danny to repeat the play to the rest of the offense. Danny looked at the clock and knew that another run play was a mistake. He decided at that moment to take matters into his own hands and said, "X fade on two, X fade on two. Ready—break!" Chris was the only player on the team who knew that Danny had changed the play, and he offered no complaint, because the play Danny called was a pass play with him as the primary receiver.

As the offense lined up, Coach Quinn immediately knew that something was wrong, based on the formation. He was on the verge of calling a time-out, but before he could, the ball was snapped and the play was in motion. Chris Truby hitched on the front line for a few seconds as Danny dropped back in the pocket, and then Chris took off down the sideline with as much speed as he could generate. He overtook the right side cornerback and was alone within a matter of seconds. Danny threw the ball to Chris, who caught it and ran to the end zone for a touchdown. Coach Quinn was confused by what he saw. He didn't know which of the players had decided to change the play he called, but the outcome was beneficial to his team, so he decided he would allow this one transgression against his authority to go without acknowledging it. There would be no reprimand, no inquiry into the matter.

After the extra point, the score was twenty to fourteen with slightly under five minutes left in play, and the Olympian defense took the field. By this point in the game, the Park Panthers had recognized that the weakest point in their opponents' defense was right in the middle. If they could get a run play through the defensive line, it was almost guaranteed to get past the middle linebacker and would only be stopped by the free safety, which would usually result in enough yardage for a first down or close to it. With a seven-point lead and little time left in the game, the Park Panthers' coach decided that the best strategy was to call run plays up the middle for the remainder of the game.

The first such play resulted in a gain of seven yards. The second, a gain of five for a first down. The third, a gain of fifteen for a first down. The fourth, a gain of four. The fifth, a gain of nine for a first down. The sixth, a gain of eighteen for a first down and a field position on the Olympians' twenty-yard line with slightly under two minutes left in play. Even if they didn't score a touchdown, they could easily kick a field goal, making it virtually impossible for the Olympians to win.

The next play was another run up the middle. Every member of the Olympian defense expected it, and one member, a lineman named Eric Rakey, decided that instead of going for the tackle, he would attempt to strip the ball, knowing that a turnover might be the only thing that would allow the Olympians a chance to win their season opener.

As the Park Panthers' tailback came through the hole immediately to Eric's right, Eric raised his hand and swatted at the ball in the tailback's hands as hard as he could, causing a fumble that was recovered by Bill Francis.

The Olympians' offense took the field on their own eighteen-yard line with one minute and forty-two seconds left on the clock. The first play called was the seven-six-two smash, a running play. Danny knew that Coach Quinn had made no attempt to reprimand him for calling his own play earlier in the half, but he felt that doing it again might incur some form of punishment. He ran the play as called for a gain of one yard. The next play was also a running play. He ran it as called for a gain of two yards. On third down, Coach Quinn called another running play. This time, Danny decided to override his coach in an attempt to win the game. Danny called the wide-right fly, a play designed to get Chris Truby as deep as possible while making it seem as though the intended receiver was much closer to the line of scrimmage in the flat on the right side.

Danny connected with Chris for a gain of thirty yards, putting the Olympians just over the fifty-yard line. In the stands, the parents credited Coach Quinn with finally deciding to pass. On the sidelines, Coach Quinn called his last time-out. As the offense made their way to the sidelines, Danny correctly assumed that calling his own play a second time might have been a mistake.

Coach Quinn said, "I don't know what in the hell is going on, but that's the second play this game that I've called that got changed in the huddle. Now who's doing it?"

None of the players said anything. Coach Quinn said, "Well, it can only be one of two people. It's either the guy I sent the play in with or Danny. So who is it?"

Again, no one said anything. Danny was surprised that Tanner Hodge, the tailback who had brought the original play into the huddle, said nothing. Tanner wanted to win the game as much as anyone else and also recognized that Coach Quinn clearly had some personal reasons for calling running plays that were not working.

As the referee blew the whistle to resume play, Coach Quinn said, "Fine. We'll be running extra laps tomorrow. Right now, you run the five-three-four flip. Got it?"

The entire team responded in unison, "Yes, sir!"

As they took the field, Danny called a huddle and said, "Guys, I was the one changing the plays, and I'm going to do it again right now. If we're going to win this game, it's going to be with a pass to Chris. Are we all cool with that?"

The other members of the Olympian offense nodded or answered in the affirmative. Danny had their support. He said, "Okay, then, we have thirty-four seconds left and about fifty yards to cover. Coach Quinn has no more time-outs, so let's do it in two plays. First one, Y left hook, on two. Ready—break!" Danny passed the ball for a gain of twenty-four yards, leaving the Olympians with twenty-eight seconds and twenty-three yards to the end zone. Coach Quinn sent in Randy Trotter with a new play—a running play. Danny looked over to the sidelines. The coach was looking directly at Danny. He knew that Danny was the one calling his own plays. Danny understood that he was already going to endure some punishment for what he had done, so he had no reason to run Coach Quinn's play at this point. He called the Z cross, another pass play to Chris Truby, and executed it for a touchdown. After the extra point, the Olympians were ahead twenty-one to twenty with less than ten seconds left on the clock. The Park Panthers were unable to score again in that time, resulting in the Olympians claiming a victory in their first game of the season.

As the players ran off the field toward the field house, Hannah Clint found Chris Truby and said, "Hey, you were seriously awesome out there."

Chris said, "Thanks," as he stared at her breasts.

She said, "You're cute," quickly kissed him on the lips, and then giggled and ran off with the other Olympiannes. Chris continued on into the field house thinking about how underwhelming his first kiss had just been.

In the parking lot after the game Jim, Don, and Kent stood near their cars waiting for their sons to be released by Coach Quinn. Jim said to Don, "Well, it looks like our kids are going to be carrying the team this year."

Don was drunk. He said, "Guess so."

Jim said to Kent, "If Tim was out here, it wouldn't have even been a close game."

Kent said, "Yeah, I know. That kid they got playing his spot is pretty terrible."

Jim said, "You should really talk to him."

Kent said, "Yeah."

The Olympiannes came off the field and out into the parking lot. Dawn found Hannah and said, "Hey, I got some good shots." Hannah said, "Cool. I tried to really pop my boobs out. Did you get that?"

Dawn said, "Yeah, I think so. You looked great."

Brooke and Allison left together. Brooke's mother, Sarah, was waiting in the parking lot. She said, "How was the game, girls?"

Brooke said, "We won and Danny threw the winning pass. It was awesome."

Sarah said, "That's great. Allison, your mom called me and asked if I could give you a ride home, so you're with us tonight."

Allison said, "Thanks, Mrs. Benton."

In the field house, the team celebrated and congratulated Danny and Chris on their successful plays, the plays everyone correctly recognized as being the sole reasons for their victory. Coach Quinn was livid. He said, "Everyone sit down and shut up!" He knew it would go against school district policy to curse at a student, even in the current context of a sporting event outside of school. He found it difficult to control his temper, but managed to say, "I know we won, and that's a good thing, of course, but the way we won is not a good thing. You all know I don't like singling people out, but tonight one person on this team undermined my authority, and I can't have that if we're going to have a team that works together as a unit. Danny Vance, you played a hell of a game, there's no question about that, but you played that game for yourself, not for your team."

Danny tried to protest, "Coach, we wouldn't have won without—"

Coach Quinn said, "That's enough! You don't know what we would or wouldn't have done if you would have run the plays I called. Now, like I said, we won, that's a good thing. But next week, Danny—since you proved tonight that you're not a team player—you're benched. Kramer, you're starting. And that's the last we're talking about it. Go home tonight. Be happy we won and come back Monday morning ready to put in some hard work at practice. We have Irving next week. They may not seem like much, but we can't take them for granted. So let's get it done. Everybody in."

On Coach Quinn's command, the entire team gathered in the center of the room and put their hands together. Coach Quinn said, "One, two, three," and everyone in unison screamed, "Olympians!" Then Coach Quinn headed to his office in the field house, leaving the team to gather their equipment and file out into the parking lot, where their parents were waiting.

On the ride home, Jim told Danny how immensely proud he was of the way he played. He went on to explain that he thought the team couldn't have won without him, and that Coach Quinn should be calling far more passing plays than he did. A few minutes into the ride home, Danny received a text message from Brooke that read, "Great game, babe. Ur super hawt. Movies 2moro?" He replied, "Sure. Cu 2moro." Danny made no mention of his reprimand, or of the fact that he wouldn't be starting the following week.

It rained on Saturday. This made parking at the Westfield Gateway Mall more tedious than it usually was for Dawn Clint. As she drove through the rows of cars looking for a parking space that was close enough to the main entrance for her liking, she envied her daughter, who sat in the passenger's seat sending and receiving text messages at a rapid pace. Dawn said, "Who're you texting?"

Hannah said, "Just a friend from school."

Dawn said, "Uh-oh. Just a friend from school whose name you won't tell me. I think my daughter's texting with a boy. What's his name?"

Hannah said, "Chris."

Dawn said, "And is Chris cute?"

Hannah said, "Yes."

Dawn said, "Am I going to get to meet this Chris?"

Hannah said, "Um . . . I'm pretty sure you can let me text without the inquisition."

Dawn said, "Sorry. Sorry. Just curious."

Hannah and Chris had been texting that morning about nothing in particular. The conversation was initiated by Hannah, who sent a text message that read, "How u feelin after the big catch last night?" to which Chris replied with a text message that read, "Pretty good I guess. What r u up 2?" Hannah described a day at the mall with her mother, which was a usual occurrence for her on the weekends. Chris described a day at home with his parents, watching college football with his father, which was a usual occurrence for him on the weekends.

At one point Chris sent a text message that read, "What wuz up with the kiss last night?" to which Hannah replied with a text message that read, "I like you, dummy." This shift in the conversation, from the mundane outlining of their day's plans to their attraction to each other, led down a path that prompted Hannah to send Chris a text message that read, "Have U ever had sex?" to which Chris replied with a text message that read, "No. Have U?" to which Hannah replied with a text message that read, "Only oral." This text is what made Chris leave the living room, where he was watching football with his mother and father, and go to his room, where he masturbated in his bed throughout the rest of the conversation.

Through these text messages, Hannah admitted that she had performed oral sex only once before and she might need some practice. Chris offered to be her practice partner as he continued to masturbate. Hannah said she'd think about it. Chris asked her to tell him exactly what she'd do to him if they were to be alone together. Hannah took a few seconds before responding. She wondered if someone other than Chris could possibly see these text messages. Up to that point, they had written nothing pornographic, but she was approaching the line. She ultimately decided that, even if Chris were to show these text messages to any of his friends, like Danny Vance, they would only make her more desirable to the rest of the male population at Goodrich Junior High School.

As Dawn pulled into the closest parking space she could find, Hannah sent a text message to Chris Truby that read, "I wud totally suk ur cok until ur cum dripped down my throat. GTGFN. At the mall." Despite the arousal he was experiencing as a result of the text message conversation with Hannah, he found himself unable to achieve orgasm. He turned his laptop on, went to a site called Tnaflix.com, and searched specifically for a streaming video of a man receiving oral sex from a woman while another woman slid a phallic-shaped glass rod into his anus. Chris had recently discovered a type of pornography that dealt with prostate stimulation and submissive male sexual behavior, and it seemed to be the only type of pornography that would arouse him enough to achieve orgasm. He tried to think of Hannah performing oral sex on him while she inserted a dildo in his anus. That thought, along with the image of the man in the video being fellated and simultaneously penetrated, was enough for Chris to ejaculate as his parents watched the second quarter of the Nebraska-Colorado game come to a close.

Danny Vance and his father, Jim, were also at the Westfield Gateway Mall that morning. Jim had promised Danny that if he threw a touchdown pass in their season opener, he would buy him a new Xbox 360 game. Jim also thought this would give him a chance to engage in the conversation about sex with his son that his wife demanded occur.

As they walked from the main entrance of the mall toward GameStop, Jim said, "So, what'd Brooke think of how you played last night?"

Danny said, "She was into it."

Jim said, "I bet." Not knowing how to ease into the conversation, Jim said, "You get a little action after the game or what?"

Danny said, "What?"

Jim said, "I don't know. I just . . . I was joking, I guess."

Jim was relieved to arrive at GameStop, which brought an end to the conversation. As Danny browsed various games, Jim took the time to attempt to formulate another plan of attack. It involved lunch at Danny's favorite place to eat in the mall: Chick-fil-A.

After purchasing the latest edition of *Madden* for Danny, Jim and his son walked toward the food court in silence. As they approached the expanse of tables and fast food restaurants, they became aware of a large crowd of parents and children in the middle of the food court, forming a large line that ended at a table where people seemed to be turning in applications of some sort and then having their photos taken. Danny had no interest in whatever it was. Neither did his father. They ignored the line of people and proceeded on to Chick-fil-A, where Danny ordered a Number 5 twelve-piece meal with large fries. Jim got a chicken sandwich and they sat down to eat.

Jim said, "So, you and Brooke, are you guys, you know . . ."

Danny said, "Are we what?"

Jim said, "You know it seems like you're getting kind of serious. You see each other a lot, you know . . ."

Danny said, "Yeah, I guess we're serious."

Jim thought about when his father had this exact conversation with him. His father was far blunter about it than Jim found himself capable of being. One morning, when Jim was fifteen years old, his father had walked into his bedroom and said, "If you feel the need to have sex with some girl at your school, make sure you use a rubber. I don't care if you do it in our house, but make sure you use a rubber, that's the most important thing. Having sex with a girl is fun, and I know you're going to do it at some point, if you haven't already, but having a kid is not fun. I mean, you're an okay kid and everything, and so is your sister, but you should use a rubber every time. We good?"

Jim took a bite of his chicken sandwich and sat across from his son in silence wondering why he found it so difficult to engage in what should be a normal conversation that all fathers have with their sons at some point.

Across the food court, Hannah and her mother entered the mall and saw the line of people leading up to the table and photographer. They were both immediately curious. As they approached the table, they found out that a new reality show called *Undiscovered* was in the process of a nationwide talent search in malls across America. The show was going to focus on twelve kids aged six to sixteen who were in various parts of the country but who all wanted to eventually get to Hollywood to pursue careers in the performing arts. Hannah and Dawn were both more than excited. Dawn took an application and sat down with her daughter to fill it out.

The two-page application included standard profile information like height and weight as well as a résumé section that Dawn filled with Hannah's numerous local theater roles. A line on the application indicated that a website could be included if the applicant had one. Dawn thought about including Hannah's website, but ultimately chose to omit it.

The application also contained an essay section in which the applicant was asked to write about where he or she saw him or herself ten years in the future. Hannah enjoyed filling out this section of the application. She thought very often about what her life would be like in the future. She knew it would include living in a large house with a swimming pool in Los Angeles, and she knew she would have an attractive boyfriend who would probably also be famous, but maybe not quite as famous as she was. She knew, also, that she would have a nice car and get to go to parties with famous people every night if she chose. She rarely thought about what she would do, specifically, to get these things, but she was sure she would have them. She mentioned all of this in her essay.

After turning in the application, Hannah posed for a photographer who took a few pictures of her, which were filed along with her application. They were told by one of the people collecting applications that they would hear something within a few weeks if Hannah was selected to move to the next step of the casting process.

As Dawn and Hannah made their way back out into the mall, Hannah said, "How cool would that be, to, like, actually be on a show?"

Dawn said, "Pretty cool." She thought about how difficult things had been for her in her attempts to be an actress in Los Angeles. For her, the path to getting on television included years of acting classes, bad auditions, and drinks and dinners with various denizens of the town who claimed to be able to offer her help on her path but in reality only wanted to have sex with her. And, worse than all these things, her path included endless rejection from producers, agents, managers, and so on. Now, it seemed, things had changed. Her daughter might never have to endure any of the things she did in her attempts to become an actress. For her daughter it might all be as simple as filling out a two-page application. She envied her daughter and wondered how different things would have been in her own life if she had been born twenty-eight years after she actually was.

On the ride home from the mall, Jim felt some anxiety. His wife had specifically told him to have the conversation about sex with their son before they returned. In preparation for this conversation, Jim had stopped at Walgreen's on the way home from work two days before. He was more than familiar with aisle 12 of the

Walgreen's near his office. He had been purchasing condoms from the family planning section in that exact aisle ever since Danny was born and his wife, Tracey, decided not to return to her regiment of using oral birth control. But he found that walking into the family planning section of aisle 12 in Walgreen's was difficult for him when his intent was to buy condoms for anyone other than himself, especially for his son. Far more difficult, however, was bringing a box of twelve Trojan latex condoms with spermicidal lubricant to the front register and thinking the entire time about the possibility of his son actually using them. He had such a high level of anxiety about the entire incident that he offered certain unsolicited information to the seventy-four-year old woman who checked him out. He said, "These aren't for me." When she said nothing in return, Jim said, "They're for my son." He knew the memory of the event would probably stay with him until he died.

In the car with Danny, Jim said, "Why don't you open the glove box?"

Danny said, "What? Why?"

Jim said, "Just open it."

Danny did as he was instructed. Inside the glove box, amid the clutter of receipts for oil changes, pens, napkins, Taco Bell mild sauce packets, and the owner's manual for the car they were riding in, was a Walgreen's bag.

Danny said, "Okay?"

Jim said, "Well, open the bag."

Danny opened the Walgreen's bag to find a box of twelve Trojan latex condoms with spermicidal lubricant. He said, "Uh . . ."

Jim said, "I'm sure you already know all about sex and how to do it and how to use condoms, so I'm just telling you to use those if, you know, if you and Brooke, you know . . ."

He looked at his son, who stared at him with what Jim interpreted to be a half-horrified, half-insulted expression.

Jim said, "I know this is weird and I'm probably the last person on the planet you want to have talking to you about this shit, but that's the way it has to be. Would you rather be talking to your mom about this right now?"

Danny said, "No."

Jim said, "Exactly, so just know that your mom and I don't care if you and Brooke start, you know . . . I mean, we care. You should definitely not be doing it anytime soon or anything, and you should wait until you're ready and all of the other crap I'm supposed to say here, but I know how it goes. I was young once. I had urges, too."

Danny said, "Dad. C'mon. Do we really have to do this?"

Jim said, "Just let me finish, then it's over. Now, like I said, your mom and I aren't trying to convince you start having sex or anything. We're not doing that at all. But if you do get to a point where you think you're going to do it, we'd rather have you doing it in our house, where it's safe, than in some parking lot or something. And please just use those every time if you start doing it, okay?"

Danny said, "Okay." Then he took out his phone and sent Brooke a text message that read, "My dad just gave me condoms," to which she sent a text message that read, "Gross," to which Danny sent a text message that read, "I know." Despite their text messages, both Danny and Brooke began to think about actually having sex with one another in a more concrete way than they had previously. Brooke had certainly thought about it more than she would have admitted to anyone, but the act of performing fellatio on Danny had made her more than apprehensive about attempting anything sexual again. She felt like she had taken an important first step and had attained what she felt was the highest echelon of sexual experience of any of her peers, and she was comfortable with remaining at that level of progression for the immediate future. But with Danny's father essentially giving them his blessing, she began to think about the exact scenario in which she might lose her virginity to Danny—about the fact that, if she were to have sexual intercourse, she would be on an even higher echelon of sexual experience, one that she alone occupied, sharing nothing with Hannah Clint, being above Hannah Clint, better than Hannah Clint.

Danny, too, was comfortable with their level of sexual activity—even slightly uncomfortable with it—after having received oral sex from Brooke. He was almost certain that he didn't actually want to have sex at this point in his life. He enjoyed the oral sex that Brooke had performed on him, but he was made uncomfortable by it at the same time. He wasn't fully ready for it when she did it, and he wasn't certain that he would be ready for it a second time. But now, with his father essentially giving him a free pass to have sex in his own home with a free supply of condoms, he began to imagine having sex with Brooke in his bed or in his shower.

Danny sent another text to Brooke that read, "What shud I do w/them?" to which she sent a text message that read, "Idk keep them I guess, in case."

chapter
seven

After dropping her son, Chris, off at school, Rachel Truby continued on to work. She found Monday mornings to be soothing. Her weekends at home with her family had become increasingly uncomfortable for her. The excuse she used most in order to avoid having any kind of sexual contact with her husband, Don, was that her activities during a standard day of work left her too exhausted to entertain the idea of anything outside of a warm bath and sleep when she got home. But this excuse never carried her through the course of an entire weekend.

As the curiosity about why she had come to feel this way began to drift away, her mind began to focus on the various tasks she knew would be awaiting her at the collections agency, and the Howard Stern radio show, which her husband had installed a Sirius satellite radio in the car specifically to listen to, went to commercial.

The commercial was for AshleyMadison.com, a website designed to help people who were in monogamous relationships, including marriage, find partners with whom they could engage in affairs. Despite Rachel's waning desire to engage in any kind of sexual activity with her husband, she had never entertained the idea of seeking a sexual relationship outside of her marriage. Somehow, knowing that it could potentially be as simple as filling out a profile on a website changed that. She began to think of the logistics involved in engaging in an extramarital affair.

She thought there would be some complication with getting a night away from her husband and son. She wondered if she could do it on a lunch break, or if she could possibly take an afternoon off work by telling her employers that she had a doctor's appointment. Maybe she could even use a visit with her sister, who lived a few hours away, as an excuse. It seemed to her that it wouldn't be prohibitively difficult to find the time. But actually meeting the man she would have an affair with seemed strange to her. Even though she knew she was being paranoid, she had some reservation that such a man might turn out to be a serial killer or a rapist. Obviously no one would know what she was really doing, or where she was really going, when she met the person. She would be helpless if indeed this theoretical person arrived at their chosen meeting spot with nefarious intent.

When she got to work, she powered up her computer, sent a few work-related e-mails, got a cup of coffee and bagel, printed out a memo detailing the delinquent accounts she was responsible for overseeing, put that memo on her manager's desk. Then she pulled out her personal laptop, so as to avoid being caught using her work computer for non-work-related activities, and logged on to AshleyMadison.com.

She was able to create a free profile within a few minutes. She wrote a brief paragraph describing what she was hoping to find on the site: a man to make her remember what it was like to enjoy sex. She opted to omit her picture from the profile, thinking that perhaps someone she knew might also be a member of the site. But then it occurred to her that, even if that were the case, this person would also want to keep their involvement with the site discreet, so they would have no reason ever to reveal their discovery of her account. To quell whatever anxiety she had about the issue, she took a picture of herself with the digital camera mounted in the top of her MacBook's screen, cropped it so that her head was not visible, and posted it.

Seeing herself without a face, Rachel became painfully aware of the fact that she had gained weight. She knew that this was the case, but seeing herself like this made her question why her husband still wanted to have sex with her as frequently as he did. She thought about retaking the picture, but didn't. She felt it was better for her potential affair partner to know exactly what to expect, were they actually to meet, and in some way she also hoped it would deter anyone from actually soliciting her. Cheating on her husband was not something she took lightly. She convinced herself that she was signing up on AshleyMadison.com more out of curiosity than anything. Even if she was to get an interested party, she would more than likely ignore him.

With that in mind, she published her profile, logged out, and told herself that she would check her account after lunch to see if anyone had sent her any indication of interest.

Don Truby sat at his desk on that same Monday morning wondering if he would have enough time to go home and masturbate at lunch. He doubted he would, but after a weekend in which his wife verbally agreed to a sexual encounter when she was half-asleep, but never delivered, Don needed to masturbate.

He knew his supervisor wasn't going to be in for at least another forty-five minutes to an hour, as was the case on Monday mornings, and his supervisor was the only person who might be looking for him. Don closed his office door with the intent of looking at enough vaguely erotic Internet images—images that would not be blocked by his company's firewall or filters—to arouse him to the point that he could go into the men's bathroom on the first floor, where there were no Northwestern Mutual employees, and masturbate quickly into the toilet.

He started at ModelMayhem.com, a website where amateur and aspiring models would post their pictures, allowing aspiring or established photographers, commercial directors, and so on, to be able to search for specific types of models for various projects. Don searched for brunettes with pale skin, something to mimic the adult film actress Stoya with whom he developed a mild obsession. He found several models fitting the description; a few had pinup-style images in their portfolios. Don found these images to be satisfying and arousing. He refined his search to display only models that had pinup-style images in their portfolios. After looking at these images for ten minutes or so, and attempting to give himself an erection by rubbing his penis through his pants, Don realized that in order to become aroused enough to be able to masturbate to completion at work, he was going to need to view legitimate hardcore pornography, which, despite his almost mind-numbing level of libidinous urge, he was unwilling to do, fearing the loss of his job.

He noticed an ad in the sidebar of ModelMayhem.com for a website called TheEroticReview.com. It was a database of reviews, compiled by the website's users, of their encounters with prostitutes. The idea of having sex with a prostitute had been one he revisited with more and more frequency over the past six months or so, ever since his wife had begun flatly denying his requests for sexual activity. He had concerns about having sex with a prostitute, though. His first was how to even go about finding one that wasn't an undercover police officer. TheEroticReview. com seemed to take care of this first concern.

Finding the time to get away from his wife and child for long enough to have a sexual encounter with a prostitute also seemed problematic to him, but he reasoned that he could potentially do it on a lunch break instead of going home to masturbate. He was also apprehensive about being able to find a prostitute he considered attractive enough to warrant paying for sex. If he could see pictures of the prostitutes on the website, then this problem seemed solved to him as well. He clicked on the ad and was redirected to TheEroticReview.com.

Don was surprised to find how intricate the site was. Not only was he able to read a seemingly limitless number of reviews by men who had already procured the services of the prostitutes on the site, and given honest accounts of their interactions, he was also able to search for virtually any physical type of prostitute imaginable. There were fifteen categories, each with a drop-down menu that Don was able to use to find specifically what he was looking for. For build, Don chose thin. For height, Don chose five-foot-four to five-foot-six. For age, Don chose eighteen to twenty-four. For hair color, Don chose black. For hair type, Don chose straight. For hair length, Don chose chin length. For breast size, Don chose thirty to thirty-one. For breast cup, Don chose B. For breast implants, Don chose no. For breast appearance, Don chose perky. For piercings, Don chose nipple. For tattoos, Don chose none. For pussy, Don chose shaved. For ethnicity, Don chose white. For transsexual, Don chose no. This was as close to the physical description of Stoya as Don was able to come.

His search criteria returned four results that were within twenty miles of his zip code. He began to read the reviews of each of their services and he came to understand that an entire subculture existed of men who engaged in regular sex with prostitutes and then posted reviews of their experiences. Some men, it seemed, had even become aficionados in this world of prostitution and their reviews held more weight within the community than other reviews.

Don's mild fascination with the culture surrounding regular

customers of prostitutes subsided as he came to the reviews for
and images of a prostitute named Angelique Ice. Every review
she had was an eight or above, many claiming that she would
"go the extra mile" or that it "didn't feel like you were paying for
it" or that she was "the real deal." Along with her flawless collection of reviews, Angelique Ice remarkably resembled Stoya. She
was slightly taller and maybe a little less petite, but Don found it
uncanny. He assumed that he would never have a chance in his
lifetime to have sex with the real Stoya, but for what most reviews
claimed was around eight hundred dollars, he could certainly
have sex with a girl who looked enough like Stoya to satisfy him.
Don sent himself a text message with her name, Angelique Ice,
so he wouldn't forget her.

When Rachel came back from lunch, she checked her account
on AshleyMadison.com and found that she had received an indication of interest from a man whose screen name was Secretluvur. In order for her to view the message he sent, Rachel had
to purchase credits on the website, which gave her greater access
to the site's features, including the ability to communicate with
other members. She used a separate credit card that she always
paid the bill for, just in case Don was observant enough to notice
the charge on the family card.

Once she was granted access, she read Secretluvur's message.
It read, "I saw your profile and it seems like we're in need of the
same thing. I've never done this, always been a little too scared, I
guess, but I'd love to keep talking if you're up for it and see where
this goes. Sorry I didn't post a picture. I just thought it was best
if I didn't take any chances as far as somebody I know finding
out about this. I can send one to an e-mail address if you'd like,
though."

Rachel didn't mind that Secretluvur didn't send a picture. It
actually augmented the feeling of excitement she was experienc-

ing surrounding the interaction. It made Secretluvur seem far more mysterious than she assumed he actually was. She replied with a message that read, "Hi, I've never really done anything like this either. Maybe we are looking for the same thing. I'm open to talking a little more to see where this goes, too. And you don't need to send me a picture or anything. It's probably safer to keep our correspondence limited to this website anyway. I look forward to your next message." She didn't know whether she should sign the message with her real name or her username, which was Boredwife12345. She opted not to sign the message at all.

chapter
eight

Principal Ligorski began the Monday morning announcements by congratulating the Olympian football team on its victory in the season opener and specifically praising Chris Truby and Danny Vance for their last-second touchdown pass that enabled the win.

Hannah Clint sat a few seats away from Chris Truby in their first-period American history class. They had not communicated with each other since the flurry of sexually explicit text messages they had engaged in two days before. At the mention of his name in the announcements, Hannah smiled at him. She felt slightly uncomfortable and wondered if Chris felt the same way. He did. He smiled back. After the announcements ended, Mrs. Rector went to the dry-erase board and wrote "9/11." She said, "What do these numbers mean to you?" A few students raised their hands. Mrs. Rector acknowledged a student named Regina Sotts.

Regina said, "It's September eleventh. The day that terrorists attacked the World Trade Center."

Mrs. Rector said, "That's correct, Regina. Other than the attack on Pearl Harbor, it was the only time a foreign force has attacked anything on U.S. soil. In each of these cases, the attitude and political policy of our country were changed. You guys are all probably a little too young to actually remember 9/11, so today I'm going to put you in groups of two, and you're all going to have a week to interview someone who was old enough to remember it and then give a presentation on Friday. You can talk to your parents, a teacher here, anyone you want about what it was like and how it changed our country."

Mrs. Rector spoke for a few more minutes about the assignment, and then she began pairing students off into groups. Chris and Hannah were paired together. After the pairings were made, Mrs. Rector allotted the rest of the class time for the groups of two to discuss whom they were going to interview as well as the manner and details of their presentation.

Chris pulled his desk next to Hannah's and said, "So, I guess we should probably interview, like, one of our parents or something."

For the entirety of the class period, Chris was unable to stop himself from taking quick glances at Hannah's breasts, and though she was fully aware of this, she offered no protest. She found it flattering and in some way it made her feel valued and important.

Hannah said, "Yeah, I'm pretty sure that seems like it would be the easiest way to go."

Chris said, "We can just talk to my dad or my mom or something if you want."

Hannah said, "Yeah, that sounds cool."

Chris said, "Okay, cool."

Hannah said, "What should our presentation be like?"

Chris said, "I don't know, what do you think?"

Hannah said, "Uh . . . I'm pretty sure we need like some kind of poster board or something."

Chris said, "Okay."

Hannah said, "But not, like, with the Twin Towers blowing up or whatever or anything, you know?"

Chris said, "Yeah."

Hannah said, "Maybe with, like, pictures of firemen and police officers and everything, you know? Like, kind of patriotic."

Chris said, "Cool."

They continued discussing their project and what their presentation would entail. At no point did they ever discuss the kiss Hannah gave Chris after the football game, the explicit text messages they had sent to each other, or the likelihood of any sexual activity between them.

As class came to an end, Chris told Hannah that he thought they could interview his parents that night if it offered no conflict with her schedule, which it didn't. They agreed to meet at his house that evening after his football practice concluded and then they each proceeded in opposite directions down the main hallway of Goodrich Junior High School.

Walking to her next class, Hannah took out her phone and sent Chris a text message that read, "C U 2nite." She was tempted to include something sexually explicit but didn't, convincing herself that she should wait for Chris to make the next advance, which she hoped would be included in his reply. Chris read her text and was disappointed that she failed to include any indication of her sexual interest in him. He took this omission as a sign that she had lost interest over the past two days. He felt that he might have lost an opportunity to have his first sexual encounter. He wondered if he should include something in his reply to test her level of interest in explicit sexual conversation at the very least, and possibly in actual sexual activity. Instead, Chris replied to her text message with one that read, "C U 2nite 2."

• • •

When the lunch bell rang, Tim Mooney went to his locker to retrieve the lunch he had packed the night before. His father, Kent, had shirked the responsibility of buying groceries over the weekend, so Tim's options were reduced to a peanut-butter-and-jelly sandwich with one piece of bread or cold turkey cutlets, which had been in the refrigerator for at least a month if Tim's memory served him correctly. He opted for the peanut-butter-and-jelly sandwich.

Tim walked into the cafeteria and took a seat near the back of the room toward one of the corners, away from most of the other kids. As he sat down, a few of his classmates, members of the football team, began raising their speaking voices loud enough for Tim to hear.

One of them said, "Well, I guess we didn't need that pussy-ass bitch as middle linebacker anyway."

The other one said, "We're better off without that faggot."

The other one said, "Totally."

The other one threw an empty milk carton in Tim's direction, which drew attention from Mr. Donnelly, who was one of the faculty monitors during that lunch period. When questioned about his motives, the student who threw the milk carton said, "I was just trying to hit a three, Mr. Donnelly," to which Mr. Donnelly replied, "Well, why don't we keep the basketball-playing in the gym?"

Tim had already dismissed the incident as meaningless. His gaze had wandered to Brandy Beltmeyer, who also sat alone a few tables away from him, eating her own lunch and reading *Breaking Dawn*. Tim found it slightly off-putting that she would be reading a book from the *Twilight* series, but he was still tempted to pick up his lunch and sit down at her table. He wondered what her reaction would be. Over the past week, due to his quitting the football team, Tim had taken his place as a sort of pariah at

Goodrich Junior High. Given Brandy's own lack of friends at the school, though, he assumed she wouldn't perceive association with him as negative.

Tim thought for several minutes about what he considered to be a brazen action in the Goodrich Junior High cafeteria and eventually his thoughts began to drift to the various YouTube videos he had recently become interested in—lectures and clips from television programs hosted by or featuring Carl Sagan and Neil deGrasse Tyson.

Recognize that the very molecules that make up your body, the atoms that construct the molecules are traceable to the crucibles that were once the centers of high mass stars and exploded their chemically enriched guts into the galaxy enriching pristine gas clouds with the chemistry of life. So that we're all connected—to each other biologically, to the earth chemically, and to the rest of the universe atomically.

Tyson's explanation of the interconnected nature of the universe made Tim feel insignificant, and in that insignificance he was able to allow himself to let go of any anxiety he might have had about approaching Brandy.

Tim thought about these predictions, that the universe would end in either a big crunch or an eventual sundering of itself from its own unstoppable and constantly increasing rate of expansion. He found comfort in this as well. In the end, he knew that nothing any human being had ever done or would ever do would mean anything, because it would all be washed away in time. He applied this inescapable truth to how he felt about Brandy Beltmeyer. If the actions of Hitler, Gandhi, Jesus Christ, anyone who had ever existed or would ever exist, were all meaningless, then surely sitting down next to Brandy Beltmeyer was equally meaningless.

As several of his classmates watched with curiosity, Tim

picked up his lunch and walked fifteen feet to where Brandy was sitting. She looked up from her book and said, "Uh . . . what up?"

Tim said, "Nothing, just thought I'd sit with you if it's cool."

Brandy said, "Uh . . . whatevs."

Tim sat down and said, "You're into *Twilight*?"

Brandy said, "I guess. I started reading the first book and then I pretty much figured I should finish the whole series. It's okay."

Tim wanted to ask Brandy about the message he sent her on Myspace about her alter-ego, Freyja. He considered that an outright conversation about it might be too much. He knew that nothing mattered, and yet he also realized that, even in the face of that universal truth, at least to him, something about talking to Brandy did matter, and despite the philosophy that had motivated him to sit next to her, he felt he shouldn't push the issue further. This did matter, at least to him.

They continued to talk for the rest of the lunch period about nothing in particular. Tim wanted to bring up the text message he sent over the summer but thought better of it as well. He was content to keep this first interaction of the eighth-grade year with Brandy at arm's length. He was content to have someone to talk to about anything, someone who seemed not to mind his company.

As Brandy talked to Tim, she felt some of the old affection she had developed for him in seventh grade coming back to her. She remembered fantasizing about Tim kissing her, and she found herself returning to that fantasy as they talked. The act of sitting next to her without invitation was something she found attractive.

Brandy wondered if Tim would ask her about Freyja's Myspace profile. It was a secret she had kept for the entirety of its existence. She was aware that Tim already knew it was her, and some part of her wanted to discuss it with him, just to have someone to talk to about it. But she didn't mention it. Just like Tim, she was content to have someone at school to talk to.

When the electronic tone sounded, signifying the end of the lunch period, Tim said, "Thanks for letting me sit with you," to which Brandy replied, "No prob." They each wanted to say more but were hesitant. They each presumed this burgeoning relationship to be far more fragile than it actually was. Nonetheless, they said nothing else to each other as they left the cafeteria from separate doors, each making their way to classrooms in different parts of the building. For the rest of the day, they each thought about the other and wondered if they would be sitting together the following day at lunch. The prospect of this made them both happy.

chapter nine

Allison Doss and Brooke Benton arrived at Rory Pearson's
house an hour after school ended to do their geometry homework. Despite exhibiting several highly effeminate traits—as
well as being the only male member of the Goodrich Junior
High Olympiannes and being sexually attracted to men—Rory
maintained that he was straight because his parents were fer-
vently religious and made a point of telling him daily that no
homosexuals would be allowed into heaven and, in fact, that all
homosexuals would burn in Lucifer's hell. Rory's mother regularly attended meetings of a militant antihomosexual Christian
group that touted the slogan "God Hates Fags" along with several other "God Hates . . ." slogans referring to other groups.
Rory planned to remain untruthful about his sexual orientation
until he could leave for college. He found Allison and Brooke to
be good friends. He assumed they knew he was homosexual but

simply never questioned him about his desire to remain secretive about it.

As the girls came in, they were surprised to see Rory's older brother, Cal, who was a freshman at North East, and his friend Brandon Lender playing *Band Hero*. Allison hadn't had any interaction with Brandon Lender since the end of her seventh grade year, when he said to her, "I'd fuck you if I could find the hole." Allison still felt some part of the crush she'd developed for Brandon as she saw him sitting on the Pearsons' couch holding a pair of drumsticks.

Hearing the girls enter, Brandon and Cal turned around. Cal said, "'Sup ladies?"

Brooke said, "Not much. Just homework."

Allison said, "That's about it."

Brandon said, "Sweet."

After the brief interaction, the girls headed to Rory's room at the back of the house. They got out their geometry textbooks and began the night's homework assignment.

Allison said, "I didn't know your brother was friends with Brandon Lender."

Rory said, "Yeah. I guess they're both starters on the JV football team or something. I don't know. He's a bitch, if you ask me."

Brooke said, "Your brother or Brandon?"

Rory said, "They're both kind of bitches, if you really boil it down. Who cares? Let's get this done—then we can watch the Mike Tyson *Oprah*."

Brooke said, "In my opinion, you watch that thing way too much. We watch it literally every time we come over. How are you not tired of it?"

Rory said, "Are you fucking kidding me? Please. I've watched it pretty much every day for like a year. I'll keep watching it until my DVR wears out and then I'll watch it online. It's the best thing that has ever happened on TV."

They finished their homework and then all got in Rory's bed

to watch the episode of *The Oprah Winfrey Show* in which she interviewed Mike Tyson. Allison wondered what Brandon thought
of her now that she was thin. After a few minutes of watching,
Allison said, "I'm gonna go to the bathroom."

Rory said, "You want us to pause it?"

Allison said, "No, it's cool. BRB."

Allison left Rory's room and went toward the bathroom nearest to the living room, where she last saw Brandon Lender. She
found Brandon playing *Band Hero* by himself. She said, "Hey."

Brandon paused the game and said, "Hey."

She said, "Where's Cal?"

Brandon said, "He went to the store. We needed some *mas*
beverages and his parents wanted him to pick up something for
dinner before they get home from work in like an hour or whatever."

She said, "He walked to the store?"

Brandon said, "Nah, nah, he snatched up his learner's permit
this week. He's completely mobile as of, like, two days ago."

She said, "Oh."

Brandon said, "You can sit down if you want."

She walked over and sat down next to him. He said, "So you
must have went on like a *Biggest Loser* diet boot camp or some
shit over the summer, right?"

She said, "Yeah, I just kind of started watching what I ate
more."

He said, "Well, it shows. You're, like, a serious piece."

Allison found nothing demeaning in what Brandon said. She
found his approval of her appearance to be a just reward for the
hard work she had done over the summer and continued to do by
forcing herself to omit meals regularly.

Brandon said, "You ever kiss anybody?"

She said, "Not exactly."

He took her hand and said, "Come here."

Brandon led her into Cal's room and shut the door, locking it as he did. Allison saw Cal's shoulder pads and helmet sitting on the floor next to his bed. She could smell the sweat that saturated the cloth in both of them. Brandon walked over and sat on Cal's bed, patting the area next to him. Allison sat down beside him. Brandon reached up, put one hand behind her head, and forced her mouth to his. Allison had imagined her first kiss being different from the one she experienced now. This kiss was more forceful and sloppy than she had foreseen in her imagination— nothing sweet about it, too urgent. She pulled back a little and Brandon said, "What's the deal?" as he took off his North East Football T-shirt.

This was the first boy Allison had a crush on, the first boy she had thought of in a romantic manner, the first boy she imagined being in this exact scenario with. That meant something to her, and now he was sitting next to her in a bed with his shirt off. When Brandon reached back up and pulled her toward him again, she gave in. He kissed her roughly and put his hand under her shirt, pawing at her ribcage and breasts. Allison liked everything about her body except her breasts. She knew boys liked big breasts and hers were among the smallest of any girl in the eighth grade. She opened her mouth and let Brandon insert his tongue into it, deep enough that their teeth knocked together repeatedly. It was unpleasant, but she was too concerned with attempting to detect any dissatisfaction Brandon may have had with her breasts to protest.

Allison knew she wasn't ready for anything that she assumed was about to happen, but she didn't want to disappoint Brandon. She didn't want to feel the same rejection she had felt that last time they'd spoken, in the seventh grade.

She had had her first menstruation over the summer, but it had been somewhat erratic and irregular in the months that followed, so Allison had only had cause to insert two tampons into her vagina. These were the only experiences she knew that involved anything being inserted into her. This was much different.

She wished Brandon's technique were gentler. The texture of his hands was rough and his motion was jerky and too deep, at times painful. He eventually removed Allison's shirt, skirt, and underwear so she lay completely nude in Cal Pearson's bed. He then stood up and removed his own jeans and underwear, leaving his knee-high football socks on, pushed down around his ankles. She noted this and added it to the list of details that she would always remember and would always wish had been different.

Brandon lowered himself back down on top of her and said, "Have you ever done this before?"

Allison said, "No."

He said, "Cool."

Allison said, "Have you?"

He said, "Yeah, I'm in high school. I've fucked like three times. It's awesome. You don't really have to do anything. It's mainly on me. Just lay there. You're actually pretty lucky that I've done it enough to know what I'm doing. You'll totally love it."

Allison said, "Do you have a girlfriend or anything?"

He said, "Fuck no."

She waited for Brandon to do whatever he was about to do. She felt remarkably like she was waiting for an injection to be administered by a doctor. She hoped that she was making the event worse in her mind with anticipation than it would turn out to be in reality. She looked up at Brandon. He was looking away from her, concentrating, propping himself up on one arm, and then he entered her.

It was unlike anything Allison had ever felt. It didn't seem like something that big should ever be inserted into her vagina. As he thrust into her with more and more intensity, she felt his penis pushing against her hymen and said, "Ow, ow—slow down." Brandon said, "Oh, yeah. The first time for you is gonna hurt a little, but it's like something you kind of have to do to just get it over with. I have to pop your cherry. You know what I'm saying? We can stop if you want, I'm down. But eventually you're gonna have to let some dude do it. My dick's already in and everything, but I'm not, like, a rapist or some shit. Your call."

Allison thought about this for a brief second. It seemed rational enough, what Brandon was saying. She had heard that a girl's first time could hurt, but that it got better each successive time thereafter. She reasoned that she was already there, already having sex, and it was with a boy that she had a crush on for a long time—the first boy she ever really liked. She said, "It's cool."

Brandon said, "Cool," and thrust his hips forward with more intensity than he had before. On the fourth such thrust, he ruptured Allison's hymen and said, "Boom—popped that cherry," and put his tongue in her ear as he continued to thrust in and out of her.

The pain was intense, but she had become used to experiencing physical pain from hunger. She had developed countless techniques that she employed to ignore pain. In this case she chose to think about a time when she was younger and her parents took her and her little brother on a vacation to SeaWorld in Orlando, Florida. She had a specific memory of that day—something inconsequential, but a memory to which she had always attached great happiness.

Her father had stopped at an ice cream stand and, without her even having to make the request, bought her a waffle cone with chocolate ice cream and sprinkles—her favorite kind of ice cream cone. There was something about the look on her father's face as he gave it to her that would always remind her of happiness, of a time when an ice-cream cone could mean the world to her. She missed her father in that moment, as she lay in Cal Pearson's bed with Brandon Lender on top of her, inside of her. She wondered what her father was doing at that moment.

Brandon said, "Oh yeah, I'm almost there," and then he shuddered and bit down hard on her nipple as he thrust into her one last time with all of his force. He said, "Oh shit. That was like fucking an Olsen twin or some shit. You cool?"

Allison nodded, on the verge of tears. Brandon said, "Cool," as he pulled out of her and looked down at his penis. He said, "Snap—murder scene on my dick. I'm gonna hit the bathroom down here. You cool with the one upstairs to clean up and everything?"

Allison nodded again. Brandon said, "Cool," then put on his shirt and pants and headed out of Cal's room saying, "You should probably hurry up. Cal could be back here soon, and he probably wouldn't be that cool with me and you fucking in here."

Allison lay on Cal's bed for a few seconds, just feeling the pain between her legs. She wasn't a virgin anymore, which relieved her on some level, but she wished it had been different. She pulled her skirt back up and put on her shirt but held her underwear in her hand, not wanting to get blood on them. As she stood from Cal's bed, she felt a combination of blood and semen run down her leg and wondered if sex would be like this every time. She hoped not.

After she washed what she could off her legs and vagina in the upstairs bathroom, she put her underwear back on and came back downstairs, where Brandon sat on the couch playing *Guitar Hero* by himself. She thought about sitting down next to him but got no indication from him that it was something he wanted so she didn't. Instead, she said, "Do you want my number to text me or anything?"

Brandon said, "Just get me on Facebook if you want to fuck again or something. But don't put any shit on my wall or anything. Seriously. This shit is probably best on the d-low. Ya heard?"

Allison said, "Okay." She took out her cell phone, found Brandon's Facebook page, and sent him a friend request along with a message that read, "I had a good time hanging out 2nite." She thought about how Brandon had compared her to an Olsen twin as she walked back into Rory's room. He said, "Okay, that was, like, fifteen minutes—you were either taking the world's biggest shit or you were totally flirting with my brother or Brandon. Talk."

Allison thought briefly about telling Rory and Brooke every-thing that had just happened, but found that she felt the same way about having just had sex for the first time as she did about not eating. It was a secret that carried some shame for her, but also some power. It was hers and hers alone. She said, "A lady never talks about what she does in the bathroom."

Rory said, "You little slut," as Allison climbed into his bed, hoping not to bleed through her underwear, and they all contin-ued watching Oprah and Mike Tyson. After half an hour or so went by without her friend request being accepted by Brandon, she began to wonder if he was ignoring it. She chose to convince herself that he had just left his phone at home or hadn't checked it since she sent the friend request.

To take her mind off wondering when or if Brandon would add her as a friend, Allison began to compose, in her head, the post she would write on the Ana's Underground Grotto mes-sage board when she got home. She would omit any feelings of shame, guilt, or doubt that she might actually have had during the act as she wrote the post. She decided the focus of her post would be the idea that if a girl were to maintain her diet and get thin enough she could get any boy she wanted—even one who, less than a year before, had thought she was fat enough to insult. She wondered how many complimentary comments she would get on her post.

Chris Truby sat in his room masturbating and watching a video clip of a girl urinating while a man had anal sex with her. Han-nah Clint was on her way to his house in order for them to begin work on their 9/11 project by interviewing his parents, who were in the living room watching a rerun of *Deal or No Deal*. He was about to ejaculate at the moment in the video clip when another man entered the frame and urinated into the girl's open mouth as the man who was having anal sex with her said, "Drink that piss, you slut." Chris found a dirty sock on the floor a few feet away, inserted his still-erect penis, and continued masturbating for a few seconds, still watching the girl drink urine while being penetrated anally, until he himself ejaculated into the sock. He found this method of masturbation to be the most economic when his parents were still awake. It required no trip to the bathroom for cleanup. He merely had to remove the sock, which contained all of his semen, hide it under his bed for twenty-four hours, and then deposit it in the family dirty clothes hamper with the rest of his laundry. He would hide his socks in order to give the semen a chance to dry so there would be no chance that his mother might accidentally come across a wet spot in the cloth, smell it to determine what it might be, and then discover that he had been masturbating into his socks.

After buttoning his pants, Chris lay on his bed feeling calm, as he usually did immediately after masturbation. He wondered if Hannah had ever masturbated or watched pornography. He wondered if she would object to him showing her some on his computer after they finished interviewing his parents. He wondered if she still harbored any sexually explicit thoughts or feelings for him, or if they had evaporated. He assumed none of these questions would be answered that night.

The doorbell rang some minutes later and Chris's father, Don, answered the door to find Hannah, whom he was not expecting. He said, "Hello?"

Hannah said, "Hi, um, is Chris home . . . or?"

Don said, "One second," and as he turned around, Chris was already making his way toward the front door.

Chris said, "Hey, Dad, uh, I spaced. Forgot to mention—this is Hannah. We're working on a project for school. Need to interview you and Mom tonight."

Don looked at Hannah. She was holding a notebook and wearing a tight, low-cut shirt, and he could see that, even at thirteen or fourteen years old, her breasts were larger than his own wife's; they had the perfect shape of newly formed breasts, before any sagging had set in with age. Don felt some guilt about the envy he felt for his son, but it passed almost immediately. Don said, "Well, Hannah, it's nice to meet you. Come on in and let's see what we can do about this interview."

Don led Hannah and Chris into the living room, where Rachel Truby sat on the couch watching television. Don said, "Honey, this is Hannah. She and our son are working on a project for school and they need to interview us. You up for it?"

Rachel was tired, and her thoughts had been concentrated on Secretluvur, and the possibility of excitement that he represented, and the fact that to experience that excitement she would have to cheat on her husband. She was glad to have something to take her mind off it, at least for a few minutes. She said, "Sure. What are we being interviewed about?"

Chris said, "9/11."

Don said, "Jesus. They're having you do a project on 9/11? That's some pretty serious stuff."

Rachel said, "I think it's good. You guys probably don't even remember it, do you?"

Chris said, "Not really."

Hannah said, "I'm pretty sure we were too young."

Rachel said, "Well, let's go in the kitchen. I'll make us some drinks and you guys can ask us whatever you want."

Once in the kitchen, Hannah took out her notebook and opened it to a blank page. Chris said, "Are you going to write this down? We can just voice-memo it."

Hannah said, "I guess we should do both, maybe."

Chris said, "Cool," took out his phone, opened a voice-memo application, hit the record button, and set it down on the table in front of his mother and father. Don looked at his wife and wondered if it was possible that this act of family bonding, which had been rare in recent months, would curry him any favor with her later that night, and invite some sort of sexual interaction. He hoped it would.

Chris began, "So I guess, um, what was it like on 9/11?"

Don said, "Go ahead, honey," and put his hand on her arm, using the opportunity to initiate some form of physical intimacy that he hoped he could escalate to a sexual advance later in the night.

Rachel said, "Well, I guess it was scary for everyone. I think we all felt pretty safe, I mean as a country, up until that point, and then none of us did. It was just really, really scary. I don't know how else to put it."

Hannah said, "Um, how did you, like, find out that it was happening and everything? Did you get a text or . . ."

Don said, "A text? No. Text messages weren't really a thing back then. We didn't even have cell phones yet, did we, honey?"

Rachel shook her head and said, "No. We didn't get them until that year for Christmas, actually. And we got them because we thought if anything like 9/11 ever happened again we should be able to get ahold of each other as fast as possible."

Don said, "Yeah, we actually found out about it from a regular phone call—like a landline phone call. My brother, who lived in New York at the time, called us up and just said, 'Turn on the TV. We're under attack.' And then he hung up. He's a weird guy and plays jokes and things from time to time, but I could tell from his voice that something was seriously going on, so I turned on the TV about one minute before the second plane hit and we, Chris's mom and I, both sat there watching it."

Chris said, "Where was I during all of this?"

Rachel said, "You were asleep in your room. We didn't know if we should wake you up or what we should do. I mean, you were so young, you wouldn't have understood what was going on or anything."

Chris said, "What were you guys doing when your brother called—like, actually doing?"

Don knew exactly what they were doing: They were having sex. It was at a time in their relationship when morning sex before work was common and they both enjoyed it. It was difficult to have sex at night because Chris was young and didn't sleep well through the night, but he slept in the mornings and this gave them a daily sexual opportunity. Don remembered the entire encounter. Rachel woke him up by slowly stroking his penis into an erection and then began to fellate him. He reached down and pulled on one of her legs, which had become his standard means of indicating that he wanted his wife to position her vagina over his face to engage in mutual oral sex. They did this for the next few minutes and then Rachel moved down and slid Don's penis into her vagina while she sat facing away on top of him. It was one of Don's favorite positions, because he enjoyed the way Rachel's buttocks looked as he spread them apart with his hands to get a better view of his penis sliding into her. He remembered how her body used to look, how she used to enjoy sex. It seemed to him that she had become a different person and his desire to have sex with her now had nothing to do with her, it was just a base desire that all men had to put their penis into things, and his wife was just that—a thing. A person he used to know and used to be attracted to, but now just a thing, the closest thing to him in physical proximity that had places for him to put his penis. Don felt pathetic, but was made to feel even more pathetic as he thought about the fact that this thing in which he wanted to put his penis wouldn't even allow it with any acceptable frequency. He thought briefly about telling his son and this girl he'd just met the truth, that he was having sex with his wife when the world was ending— just how it should have been—but he knew that that would end any chance of having sex with her that night. So he let Rachel field the question.

Don said, "Honey, you want to take this one?"

Some small part of Don thought that maybe his wife would

tell the truth, but she said, "We were getting ready for work, you know, mind on a million other things. Definitely not thinking that our country was going to be attacked. And then we got that call and turned on the TV and just sat there all day. We didn't even go to work, just watched the news all day and tried to make sense of it."

Chris said, "Did you guys know anyone who was in it—like, actually in the buildings or anything?"

Don said, "No, like we said, your uncle Cliff was in New York at the time but he wasn't anywhere near the Twin Towers. That's probably the closest we were to having someone we actually knew in it. Didn't make it any less scary, though."

Hannah said, "I read online that there were a lot of candlelight vigils and group prayer gatherings and stuff. Did you guys do any of that?"

Rachel said, "No. We just stayed home and watched TV, mostly. I honestly just felt like somebody knocked the wind out of me. I didn't want to do anything except sit and watch TV."

Hannah said, "Um . . . what was the biggest news story that was happening right before 9/11?"

Rachel said, "I don't know. I can remember there was this interview that Anne Heche did where she said she talked to aliens in an alien language and everyone was saying her career was over because she was crazy and then 9/11 happened."

Chris said, "Who's Anne Heche?"

Don said, "She's an actress. Was dating Ellen DeGeneres for a while."

Hannah said, "What else? Um . . . did you guys support the war in Iraq and everything?"

Don said, "Well, yeah. I think everybody pretty much did. I mean, we didn't know at the time that there weren't going to be any weapons of mass destruction and that the whole thing was a big ploy to get more money for Bush and his oil buddies. We were just pissed off that we got attacked and the Bush administration did a real good job of making us all think that Iraq was behind it when in reality they had nothing to do with it."

Chris said, "How about, do you think there will be another attack in our lifetimes?"

Rachel said, "I have no idea. I hope not, but it seems pretty impossible to stop people who are willing to kill themselves in the process of killing you, you know? I mean, if another terrorist really wants to walk into Westfield Mall with dynamite strapped to his chest and blow himself up, how can we stop him? We can't, really. I guess we just have to hope that maybe the one good thing Obama might be able to do is make the world see us a little differently, and then maybe the terrorists won't want to do those things anymore."

Chris said, "You got anything else, Hannah?"

Hannah said, "No, I'm pretty sure we got enough. Thank you so much, Mr. and Mrs. Truby."

Don said, "No problem. I hope we helped you guys enough to get an A."

Chris said, "I think it's one of those deals where everybody is going to get an A as long as they turn something in."

Don said, "Oh, well, then I hope you learned something," and then he laughed.

Chris said, "Do you want to go type some of this stuff out and start putting together our presentation?"

Hannah said, "Sure."

Chris said, "Peace out."

Hannah said, "Thank you guys again so much for helping us out. And it was really nice meeting you." Then she and Chris went back to his room, leaving Don and Rachel alone. Don stood up from his chair, moved behind Rachel, and started rubbing her shoulders. He said, "It's weird how long ago all of that seems, isn't it?"

Rachel didn't want him to touch her, but she felt guilty some- how about letting this fact be known, so she continued to allow him to rub her shoulders, her guilt tied in some way to the fact that they'd just recalled a moment of mutual trauma in their lives. She wished she could ignore the fact that it was her husband long enough to enjoy it. She said, "Yeah. It's weird that enough time has passed that they have our kids doing school projects about it."

Don said, "I know," and he leaned down to kiss his wife. Her guilt held her in place. She accepted his kiss and even kissed him back. Don's surprise was too extreme to be hidden. He backed away from her, looked at her, and said, "I love you." Rachel wasn't sure whether she still loved her husband or not. She knew she wasn't attracted to him in any way, but they had built a life together. He wasn't a bad husband or a bad father. They were still friends on some level. She said, "I love you, too."

He took her by the hand and said, "Let's go." She allowed him to take her into their bedroom, still thinking about that morning of 9/11 when they were having sex, when there was no question in her mind that she loved her husband. She wondered if she would ever feel that way again. She thought about the years that had passed since then and about Don. She knew he hadn't done anything to deserve the treatment he was getting from her. With that thought in her mind, she turned off the light in their bedroom, took off her clothes, and had sex with Don.

In an effort to give him what she knew he wanted that night, she didn't just lie still and allow him to grind his penis into her without reaction. She got on top of him, turned around so she was facing away from him, and rode him in the position she knew he enjoyed the most. She tried not to, but couldn't stop herself from imagining Secretluvur's penis in her vagina instead of Don's. She found this to be beyond absurd, based on the fact that she didn't even know what Secretluvur looked like—which made it clear to her, in that moment, that she at least had to meet him.

Don watched his wife's buttocks move as she had sex with

him. He hadn't seen them from this position in almost a year, and he was saddened by what he saw. His wife's body was never perfect, but it had been, at one time, beautiful to him. Her buttocks were his favorite part. They weren't muscular or amazingly shaped, but they were exactly what he liked in that part of a woman's body, slightly flabby without being dimpled with cellulite, and easy to grab hold of while in certain sexual positions. All of that was gone. All Don could see was cellulite and an absence of form. He was almost too repulsed by the sight to conclude the act, but he was uncertain about when his next sexual encounter might occur, so he forced himself to continue. He fantasized about Stoya and tried to ejaculate as soon as possible, in order to end what he felt was a perversion of the sexual memories he had of his wife. While he was thinking about his penis entering Stoya's anus, and the look of excitement and happiness on her face as he did this, Don was able to ejaculate after only a minute and forty seven seconds of being inside his wife. Both he and Rachel were relieved upon the conclusion of their sexual act.

Chris sat at his computer desk while Hannah sat on his bed. He offered to transcribe the interview with his parents, based on the fact that he perceived himself to be the faster typist. The transcription took around forty-five minutes. After finishing, Chris turned to Hannah and said, "So should we work on how we're going to present this, or . . . ?" Tired of wondering if Chris was ever going to make an advance, Hannah said, "Or . . . we could do something else."

Chris, still believing that Hannah had lost interest after their initial kiss and flurry of sexually explicit text messages, said, "Like what?"

Hannah rolled her eyes and said, "Come here."

Chris left his computer chair and sat beside her on the bed. She kissed him, this time for much longer than their first kiss after the football game. Chris was more than happy that the second kiss of his life seemed to be better than the first. He could feel an erection developing as he grabbed the back of Hannah's hair and pulled her head back hard. He had seen this maneuver employed in virtually limitless numbers of pornographic videos and the women always seemed to respond well to it. Hannah's reaction was to say, "Ow, what are you doing?"

Chris said, "I don't know. Sorry."

Hannah said, "It's cool. Just like you don't have to be so . . . you know?"

Chris said, "Yeah, sorry."

She took the hand that Chris had used to pull her hair and put it on one of her breasts, then said, "Here."

It was the first breast Chris had ever felt. He had seen countless breasts in the various videos he watched, of all shapes, sizes, and colors. He was surprised at how soft Hannah's were. He was under the impression that breasts would be harder, like a flexed muscle. Hannah said, "You want to feel them under my shirt?"

Chris said, "Yeah," and put his hand under her shirt and then wedged his fingers under her bra until he flipped the cup up over her breast, exposing her nipple to his fingertips. His erection was full now as he felt Hannah's naked breast in his hand. She said, "Do you like it?"

Chris said, "Yeah."

Hannah said, "Have you ever had a blowjob?"

Chris said, "Uh . . ."

Hannah said, "It's cool if you haven't. I'm not expecting you to be, like, all experienced or anything."

Chris said, "Then no."

Hannah said, "Lay back."

Chris lay back on his bed as Hannah unbuttoned his jeans and pulled them down around his knees, followed by his underwear. She remembered the only other time she had performed oral sex as being a rather quick process that ended with an un-

expected ejaculation in her face. Wanting to avoid a similar scenario, she said, "When you're about to come, just tell me."

Chris said, "Okay."

Hannah licked the underside of Chris's penis and noticed
that it wasn't quite as hard as it had been when she felt it prod-
ding her through his pants. With each passing second, Chris's
penis became more and more flaccid. Hannah said, "Am I doing
something wrong?"

Chris said, "No. Just keep going." Chris was embarrassed and
unsure of why he was unable to maintain an erection. His mind
could only conjure images of a pornographic video he had seen
called *Cockgobblers 4: Facefuck Mountain*. The women in this
video allowed the men to thrust their penises so far into their
mouths that they frequently caused gagging, tears, and, on occasion, vomiting. This is what Chris wanted. This is what he
thought of when he thought of oral sex.

Hannah said, "This isn't working. Do you want to try like
squeezing my boob or something?"

Chris said, "No, sit up against my wall," as he positioned her
on his bed, sitting with her back flush against his bedroom wall.
He took off his pants and then said, "Now open your mouth."
Hannah did as she was instructed, and then Chris put his limp
penis between her lips and began thrusting in and out of her
mouth. After several seconds he began to achieve another erection.

As Chris continued to thrust in and out of her mouth, he
closed his eyes and conjured images from *Cockgobblers 4: Facefuck Mountain*, specifically the image of a girl with red ponytails
crying as two men, each holding one of her ponytails, using them
as handles for her head, forced their penises into her mouth at
the same time.

Hannah didn't know how to react to the situation. She had
been the initiator and the one to control the situation the first
time she had performed oral sex. In this instance she felt as

though she wasn't even there. She felt as though Chris could have been inserting his penis into any inanimate object and there would have been little difference. This feeling wasn't pleasant for Hannah, but she endured it because her end goal was to have sex with Chris—not specifically with Chris, but he was the best candidate for it, especially at this point. Hannah was determined to lose her virginity as soon as possible and to potentially have intercourse a few more times before the end of eighth grade. She thought there might still be a chance to lose her virginity that night.

She reached up, pushed Chris's hips back far enough to force him to stop what he was doing, and said, "Do you want to fuck me?" Chris did want to have sex with Hannah, but he was unsure if he could maintain an erection at that moment without reenacting something at least vaguely similar to a scene from *Cockgobblers 4: Facefuck Mountain* that contained nothing but aggressive and, in some cases, abusive oral sex. Chris said, "No, I just want to do this." Hannah acquiesced and allowed him to insert his penis back into her mouth and continue to thrust.

She looked up at him and saw that his eyes were closed. She looked around his room, noticing small details she hadn't seen before as Chris used her mouth, adding a bit more force as their encounter continued. He had a small stack of CDs on his desk. She wondered why he had CDs, where he bought them. She assumed they were gifts from someone. She wondered who. She saw that he had an Einstein mouse pad and wondered if that too was a gift, or if Chris idolized Einstein in some way. She didn't figure him to be the type who would.

Chris thrust into her mouth as hard as he could three more times, bringing Hannah to the verge of gagging, until he began to ejaculate. He then pulled his penis out of Hannah's mouth, giving her the opportunity to cough and choke as he ejaculated on her face and in her hair.

Chris put his underwear and jeans back on and then offered

Hannah a box of Kleenex. She said, "Thanks." Chris said, "No prob. Do you want me to like, you know, go down on you or something? I mean, I could probably do it. I think I know how, kind of." Hannah had never had a boy perform oral sex on her, but was slightly too traumatized by the sexual encounter she'd just experienced to consider anything further. She said, "You can next time. I should probably be getting home," as she wiped the semen and tears from her face.

Chris said, "Oh. Okay. I'm just saying, I mean, I've never done it before, but I'm not opposed to it or anything. I really wouldn't mind."

Hannah said, "Yeah, it's cool. Next time. Can I use your bathroom, maybe?"

Chris said, "Sure, it's just right around the corner. I'm pretty sure my parents are in their room, so you should be good."

Hannah went to the bathroom. As she cleaned his semen out of her hair, she thought about what sex would be like with Chris, what it would be like to lose her virginity to him, if this first encounter was any indication. Even if it was, she didn't really care. She needed to lose her virginity this year, and she felt like she was close to being able to do it with Chris. She finished her clean up and went back into Chris's room.

Chris said, "Do you need my dad to give you a ride home or anything? I can get him."

Hannah said, "No, I just have to call my mom. She'll pick me up."

Chris said, "Okay, cool."

Hannah called her mother and then sat on Chris's bed with him for another fifteen minutes before her mother arrived. They talked about their school project for the entirety of the fifteen minutes, choosing to evade any possible conversation about what had just happened between them.

Once in her mother's car, Hannah received a text message from Chris that read, "I luvd ramming my cock down ur throat."

Hannah replied to Chris's text message with one that read, "It made my pussy so wet—next time I want u 2 fuck me." Chris replied with a text message that read, "Send me a pic of ur pussy." Hannah replied with a text message that read, "Not til u fuck it."

Chris turned on his computer and attempted to masturbate while watching pornography depicting regular vaginal entry sex between one man and one woman. He was unable to maintain an erection through the process and ultimately was only able to ejaculate while watching a video of a bound woman having live eels inserted into her vagina and anus.

When Hannah got home, her mother said, "So how was the project with Chris?" putting an emphasis on Chris's name that denoted romantic interest on her daughter's part. Hannah said, "It was fine."

Dawn said, "Just fine? Did you guys, like, totally make out?"

Hannah thought about telling her mother everything that happened but instead said, "No, we didn't, like, totally make out. We just worked on the project."

Before she went to sleep, Hannah turned on her computer to see if there were any new subscribers to the members-only section of her website. There were none.

Patricia Beltmeyer had only hosted three meetings of her Internet watch-group, Parents Against The Internet. Each of these meetings generated what Patricia considered moderate interest, attracting anywhere from three to six parents of her daughter's classmates. After increasing her group's visibility by introducing an e-mail list as well as through fliers she left in Principal Ligorski's office each week before her meetings, Patricia hoped that the fourth meeting of PATI would yield a higher number of attendees. In anticipation of a more robust turnout, Patricia ordered two large cheese pizzas from Papa John's and asked Allison Doss's mother, Liz, if she could bring over a few pies from Marie Callender's, where she worked. Liz had attended two of the last three meetings. She had only a general interest in policing her children's use of the Internet, but found the group to be a welcome opportunity for social interaction outside of her family and coworkers.

Liz was the first attendee to arrive. She brought with her two pies, a lemon meringue and a blueberry. As she handed the pies to Patricia she said, "So does it look like there might be a few more people tonight?"

Patricia said, "I can't be sure, but I think so. Did you get a chance to do any of that stuff we talked about last week—adult passwords for your family computer or anything?"

Patricia had a list of computer and cell-phone protocols that she recommended all parents follow in their own homes, and with their own children, in order to ensure what she called an Internet-safe environment. Liz had implemented exactly none of these protocols. She had little knowledge of computers or technology in general, and despite Patricia's tutoring in these meetings, Liz retained too little of it to be able to apply it when she returned home. Beyond that, she had almost no concern that her daughter, Allison, or her son, Myron, were being exposed to any of the risks Patricia seemed to be concerned about when they used the Internet. Liz viewed these meetings as nothing more than a chance to get out of the house and talk to people who were not a part of her immediate family.

Liz said, "It's going pretty good. Seems like my kids are safe."

Patricia said, "And what about your husband?"

Liz said, "What about him?"

Patricia said, "It's not just your kids who are at risk when they use the Internet or cell phones or video games. Your husband is at risk, and so are you, Liz."

Liz couldn't imagine how she would ever be at risk as far as her use of any of the things Patricia mentioned was concerned. She said, "Oh, well, I'll keep that in mind next time I check my e-mail. How do you keep your family safe?"

Patricia said, "Well, my husband doesn't use the Internet, really. He's kind of old-fashioned that way, I guess, and, you know, I make my daughter give me all of her passwords, and I monitor every text message and e-mail she gets."

Liz said, "Are they here tonight?"

Patricia said, "Ray's playing poker with some friends, and Brandy's up in her room. I tried to get her to help me tonight, you know, to show everyone that you can still be a cool parent to your kids and keep them safe from the Internet at the same time, but she has a lot of homework to do, so she'll probably be in her room all night."

Patricia's excitement to hear a knock at her door was quelled when she opened it to find the Papa John's delivery man. Patricia paid for the pizzas and Liz helped her set them out on the kitchen table along with the pies and two two-liter bottles of Diet Coke. As they finished preparing the refreshments, the next actual guest arrived.

Kent Mooney had no idea what to expect when he'd decided to attend this meeting, but he thought it might give him some insight into why his son, Tim, wanted to play online video games instead of football. With his wife gone for more than four months at that point, he had also begun to think about dating again. He knew he wasn't fully ready to do it. When he and his wife, Lydia, had been separated, but still lived in the same town, he never saw a need to consider other women. Now that she'd been living in another state for four months, he began to realize that at some point he would need to put himself back out in the world and interact with women again. He thought that this PATI meeting might be a decent place for him to practice, to at least talk to a woman in a social setting.

After Kent introduced himself, Patricia said, "Well, it's very nice to meet you. Thank you for coming, and we'll make you feel just as welcome as we can for your first meeting. There's some pizza and pie in the kitchen. Help yourself, and we'll start just as soon as a few more people get here. Should be in the next ten minutes or so."

Kent went to the kitchen and immediately questioned his decision to attend his first PATI meeting. He wondered if he would actually gain any knowledge about his son, anything that could help him get Tim to play football again. He felt certain, after meeting Patricia and Liz, that this meeting would not yield any valuable interactions with the opposite sex. He began to convince himself that he should leave, faking an urgent phone call or something similar. He concocted a plan to walk back into the living room, start a conversation with Patricia about online video games, pretend that his phone was vibrating, answer it, act surprised and concerned, and then say, "Okay, I'm leaving right now. I'll be there as soon as I can," flipping his phone shut and apologizing profusely for having to leave while explaining that an emergency at home was forcing him to go before the meeting started.

As Kent came into the living room, Patricia was answering the door, and as she opened it, Kent saw Dawn Clint for the first time and decided that maybe he should stay at the meeting after all.

Although Dawn considered herself Internet-savvy, especially since she'd started running her daughter's website, she had become increasingly concerned about one of the members on that website who had begun to request photos of her daughter that were of an increasingly pornographic nature. She was worried that, by even reading the e-mails, she might be creating some grounds to implicate herself in some kind of Internet or child-endangerment crime, even though she made very sure that the images of her daughter on the website were not even remotely pornographic and were only slightly lewd, which, she rationalized, was subjective anyway. Dawn realized that she could just have looked up the specific laws she was concerned about on the Internet, but she felt, no matter how irrational she knew her feelings to be, that a Google search of these laws might alert the authorities to her activities. She wanted no record on her computer that might indicate she knew she was doing anything wrong, just in case it could ever be used against her. Instead, she thought she might be able to bring up certain issues in the meeting that might illuminate her on the specific laws that she felt she was coming increasingly close to breaking. She hoped that Patricia would know something about all of this, and although she thought the watch-group itself, and the meetings it held, were ridiculous, she hoped they might help her this one time.

Dawn came in and introduced herself to Liz and Kent. Kent immediately noticed that she wasn't wearing a wedding ring and thought about slipping away to the bathroom to remove his, but it was too late. He saw Dawn look down at his hand at the same time he looked at hers. He made a mental note to take the ring off after the meeting.

Although Kent held on to a small sliver of hope that somehow he and his wife would work things out, he knew that she was in California with Greg Cherry, having sex with Greg Cherry. At the beginning of their separation, he was too emotionally distraught to think about having sex with anyone other than his wife, and he remained so for many months after she had moved out of their home. But since she moved to California, his libido had picked up. In the past month or so, he had promised himself that, even if he and his wife were to work out their differences and end up together, he would not squander this opportunity to have sex with someone who was not his wife—perhaps even more than one woman if he could. He had begun to see his wife's decision to leave him for another man as an insult, and where he once felt only emotional pain, he was now beginning to feel anger, and with that anger he was beginning to subscribe more and more to an eye-for-an-eye philosophy. He wasn't sure yet how he would let his wife know that he was having sex with another woman—how he would get the information to his wife that he was no longer a broken man without her, but instead a man who was desirable to other women and capable of having sex with them—but he knew that once she was aware of the fact, she would more than likely regret giving up what they had together for the company of Greg Cherry.

Dawn Clint was the first woman Kent had seen since his separation who made him think about sex again in a carnal and pornographic way. As their hands touched in a brief handshake, Kent imagined what her breasts looked like, what her nipples were like, if she liked to have them sucked during the sexual act, if she had ever engaged in anal sex or had any kind of sexual interaction with a woman. These thoughts seemed almost foreign to him, because he hadn't had them in so long, but they were welcome.

Dawn found Kent attractive and wondered who his wife was, if she had met her through her dealings with the Goodrich booster club or other various school functions. She said, "So, does your kid play football or. . . . Just trying to figure out if I've met your wife or anything. My daughter's an Olympianne."

Kent said, "No. You haven't met her, I'd guess. The short version of the story is, my kid doesn't play football this year. He did last year, but he decided not to this year. Plays a lot of video games instead now. That's why I'm here, I guess. And my wife is in California."

Dawn said, "Oh, business trip or something?"

Kent said, "No, more like she's living with another guy."

Dawn said, "Oh, oh, I'm sorry. I didn't mean to . . . I saw the ring and just . . . I'm sorry."

Kent said, "It's okay. I probably should have said ex-wife. The divorce is still a little fresh, I guess." Not wanting to give the impression that he still had any feelings for his ex-wife, Kent added, "But we've been separated for a long time, so . . ."

They continued to talk for a few more minutes, Kent shifting the conversation to more innocuous topics like movies and television shows. When he asked what she did for a living, Dawn just said that she worked for an Internet startup company as a webmaster. Kent found himself more interested in the specifics of her job than he would have thought, but his lack of skill in talking to women stopped him from probing the matter further.

His lack of interest in his own job, accompanied by that same lack of skill in talking to women, led him to answer the same question, when it was posed to him, with, "I work in sales for a shipping company. Nothing exciting." Despite Kent's missteps in the conversation, they got along well; they shared an easily recognizable attraction, made stronger by the fact that they were each aware of the other's mutual availability.

Dawn had been involved with only a small number of men in the thirteen years since moving in with her mother after her life in California. She had considered only one of them a boyfriend, and she knew from the beginning of that relationship that it would never result in marriage, based on her inability to ignore certain of the man's habits that she found unbearably disgusting, including his habitual use of chewing tobacco. Something about Kent made her irrationally hopeful. She was hesitant to let herself think that anything would come of their meeting, especially given the fact that Kent's marriage was only recently legally concluded. Nonetheless, she found herself flirting with Kent uncontrollably and hoping that he would ask for her phone number before the end of the meeting.

Eventually, five more parents of Goodrich Junior High School students arrived, and Patricia decided to start the meeting after each of them had had a chance to eat some pizza or pie. She gathered everyone in her living room and said, "I want to thank everyone for coming tonight. And I'd like to start by letting you all know that you should be proud, because this is the biggest turnout Parents Against The Internet has ever had. So when you go home tonight, feel free to send out e-mails or pass on fliers letting even more people know about our meetings.

"Now, I usually like to start every meeting by opening it up to anyone who might have specific questions, but since we have a few new faces tonight, I thought I'd kick it off by telling you guys a little bit about us, about PATI, and then you can all introduce yourselves.

"I started PATI, which stands for Parents Against The Internet, a while back, after I just read and heard too much about how dangerous the Internet and cell phones and video games and all that stuff can be if you're not careful—especially for kids who are reaching the age ours are reaching. I basically just want to help as many parents as I can to be informed about what they can do to protect their kids and their families and even themselves from the dangers of the online world, which get worse and worse every day as new technology comes out. I guess that's about it. So, now, Kent and Dawn, why don't I turn the floor over to you, so you can tell us a little bit about yourselves and also how you heard about PATI?"

Kent and Dawn exchanged a knowing glance, slightly horrified and slightly amused by what they realized they had stumbled into. Kent said to Dawn with mock chivalry, "Ladies first," to which she replied with mock flattery, "How gentlemanly of you." They were clearly bonding to some degree in their mutual assessment of their inaugural PATI meeting as being slightly absurd.

Dawn said, "I'm Dawn Clint. I have a daughter, Hannah, who goes to school at Goodrich. I'm doing the Olympiannes' scrapbook this year, if any of you have a daughter who's on the squad." Dawn paused to see if this bit of information got any reaction. It didn't. She continued, "Um. . . . Well, I heard about your group through a flier that I found in the principal's office, and I just thought I'd check it out, because I guess you can't be too safe, right? And that's about it."

Patricia said, "Well, welcome to the group. Kent?"

Kent said, "My name's Kent Mooney. My son, Tim, goes to Goodrich. He used to play football, but he's been playing a lot of video games lately, kind of retreating from the world, it seems like, so I thought I'd come and find out all I could about how I can get him back to normal life."

Patricia said, "And how did you find out about PATI?"

Kent said, "Oh, uh, one of your fliers was actually sent home with Tim's last report card."

Patricia said, "Oh, really? Well, that's just wonderful. I had spoken to a few teachers about the idea, but I had no idea they were going to implement it. That's really just . . . so wonderful. Okay. Well, I suppose we can get the open-questions portion of the meeting started with you, then, Kent, since you've already brought up your son's problem. Video games are bad. It doesn't matter what you read, or how many studies claim they're harmless. I can show much better studies that claim the contrary. Video games are terrible on almost every level for a child's development. They teach children to be antisocial and to engage in violent attitudes and behavior. Video games called 'first-person shooters' are very widely believed to be the cause of the Columbine tragedy, and flight-simulator programs, which are a version of video games, were instrumental in training the terrorists who flew the planes into the Twin Towers on 9/11. Nothing good has ever come from video games."

Kent said, "But how do you really feel about video games?" Dawn couldn't stifle a laugh.

Patricia said, "I know I come off strong sometimes in my reaction to video games and their impact on our youth culture, but it's a serious matter. Does your son play many different games, or is there one that he plays more than the others? Some are far worse than others."

Kent said, "He plays *World of Warcraft* almost exclusively, as far as I know. He has an Xbox but he doesn't really ever play it anymore. He's always on the computer."

Patricia said, "Well, *World of Warcraft* is one of the worst games out there. A couple in China played it so much, and for so long, that they neglected their baby for three days and it died from dehydration. Another man in Korea played it for so long that he forgot to eat or drink, and he died in the seat he was playing it in. Kent, and anyone else who is aware of their child playing this game, I urge you to get them stop. Uninstall the game from his computer immediately and never let him reinstall it. If you need help with that, I can print you out an FAQ about it."

Kent, feeling that Patricia's reaction to the game was slightly unwarranted, said, "I'm not sure it's that bad. He still does well in school; it's not like the game is destroying his life or anything. It just seems like he's been a little more introverted lately, and I thought maybe the game had something to do with it. I was really just looking for more of an explanation of what the game is like, if you might know that kind of thing."

Patricia said, "I know exactly what it's like. I've seen the television commercials. It's a virtual world, Kent, where your son has made an avatar. An avatar is a visual representation of the person playing the game, which very often has demonic or evil-looking features. And, when he's plugged into that avatar, he thinks that that world, the *World of Warcraft*, is the real world. This world doesn't matter anymore. His friends don't matter, school doesn't matter, you don't matter, he doesn't even matter. The only things that matters are his avatar and the other *World of Warcraft* avatars, which he thinks are his real friends."

On some level, as Kent listened to Patricia's anti-video-game rhetoric, he felt like defending his son, like telling the whole room that he wasn't a deviant, like the picture Patricia was painting—the boy who sat in his room all day playing a game and not taking the time to bathe or eat or drink or relieve himself. In a strange way, Patricia's tirade left Kent feeling closer to his son than he had in a long time.

Patricia said, "Does that answer your question, Kent?"

Kent said, "Yeah, I think so. Thanks."

Patricia turned to Dawn and said, "Dawn, as the other brand-new PATI member, I'd like to open the floor to you if you have a specific question."

Dawn said, "Yeah, thanks. Um . . . I guess, you know, my daughter is getting to that age where she's starting to, um . . .

develop, and you know, you worry about what can happen, especially when she's on the Internet all the time and Facebook and always texting and all of that. I was just wondering if you knew what the laws were about, like, I guess, what people can and can't say in e-mail or can and can't post on the Internet, I guess as it relates to Internet predator type stuff and child pornography. Things like that."

Patricia said, "This is a very good question and one that I've actually researched quite a bit. This is something that we should all be paying much more attention to than we do, because in our state the laws are far more lenient than they should be. Essentially, anyone can say anything they want to your children online if they don't know they're minors. So my best advice is to go home after tonight's meeting and set up a practice role-play session with your kids. It might seem weird at first, but you should be playing the role of potential Internet predators, and your kids, of course, would play themselves. Start off by asking them something very normal, like what their favorite movie is or something like that, and see how they respond. The first thing they should ever tell anyone online that they don't know—and I know it's scary to think that your kids might be talking to people they don't know online, but they are. You just have to accept that and hope you've drilled them and coached them enough to be able to handle themselves.

"So, anyway, the first thing your kids should do is ask who the person is and tell the person that they're under eighteen. Once that's done, it then becomes illegal for that person to bring up any kind of sexual topic. If they do, it's all right there in your computer, and I can show you how to go into your kids' computers and call back up whatever chat sessions they have logged in their history, so you can see who they've been talking to and what they've been talking about. Anyway, I hope that kind of answered your question, Dawn."

Dawn said, "Kind of. I was also wondering what kind of images are legal and illegal to put up on the web. I mean, say my daughter sent a picture of herself in a bikini or something like that to someone in an e-mail or something—is that against the law?"

Patricia said, "I don't think that is, no. I'm pretty sure that, as long as your daughter isn't nude in the pictures, she's not doing anything illegal. But I would have to say that if your daughter is sending people images of herself in a bikini, you should probably have a talk with her as soon as possible about online etiquette and decorum. I know none of our kids are thinking about jobs and their adult lives yet, but I guarantee you that none of them will want some compromising photo of themselves floating around the Internet when they start raising families and looking for jobs and all of that. We're already starting to see people lose their jobs because of pictures they post on Facebook or Myspace. Our kids are really going to be the first generation that has lived their entire lives on the Internet. So any image they've posted of themselves, from childhood on, is going to be out there for anyone to see. So it's our job to make sure that those photos are tasteful."

Dawn said, "Thanks. That pretty much answered what I think I was asking."

Patricia said, "And as long as we're on the subject of Internet predators, and what is safe and unsafe for our children to be doing online, I think I would also add that, statistically speaking, the reason I even started this group in the first place, really— the number-one threat our children face when they're online—is adults posing as children their age. I know it's a terrible thing to think about, but we should all be extremely aware that there are adults out there in chat rooms, on AOL Instant Messenger— playing *World of Warcraft*, Kent—who are acting like children in order to gain the trust of our kids. It's very disturbing and it's what we all have to fight against. Our kids have grown up using the Internet and cell phones; they're not stupid. They know that, if an adult is interacting with them through this technology, that adult is probably not to be trusted. But if they think they're interacting with one of their peers, they're statistically far more likely to divulge personal information because they see no harm in it. Again, and I can't stress it enough, the number-one threat to a child's online safety is an adult posing as one of their peers. This can come in the form of a fake Facebook account, an online avatar in a video game, or even an adult hacking into a child's social-networking site and then using that child's online identity to interact with that child's peers. It's a difficult thing to monitor, but you should have a conversation with your kids and tell them that, if any of their friends start behaving abnormally online, there might be cause for concern that their account has been hacked. And they should immediately call that friend to see if they're online and actually the person on the other side of the computer."

The other members of the PATI meeting asked questions, ranging from what action should be taken if a parent accidentally discovers their child masturbating while viewing pornography on the Internet to how many hours a day a child should be allowed to use the Internet. Neither Kent nor Dawn found any of Patricia's answers regarding anything that was brought up to be that informative or enlightening.

After the initial round of questions came to a close, Patricia spent twenty to thirty minutes reviewing various cell phones that had either just been released or were about to be released in time for Christmas. She went over details such as price, functionality, preloaded applications and software, and which phones she felt were the safest for their children to use based on ease of monitoring and controlling use.

At the meeting's conclusion, Patricia handed out a four-page document, which she'd created the night before, containing much of the information about new phones that she'd just covered. The document also included various websites where parents could download software for their children's computers and cell phones that would grant the parents remote access to the children's devices, as well as the ability to log keystrokes in order to obtain passwords and transcripts of chat conversations that might have been deleted by their children. This part interested Kent more than anything else in the meeting.

Kent was still thinking about what he might find out about Tim's lack of interest in football using such software as he walked out of Patricia's house just behind Dawn. Patricia said, "Kent, Dawn, it was a pleasure to have you guys out tonight. I hope you got some good info and it helped a little. And, of course, I hope to see you back next week."

Kent and Dawn both engaged in the expected pleasantries and noncommittal banter, which Patricia knew meant she would not be seeing them again. She wondered what she could do to make the meetings seem more important. As she closed the door behind them, Patricia thought about renting out a meeting room at the Ramada Inn in order to give the meetings a more formal feeling.

Dawn and Kent, both wanting a chance to talk without the other PATI attendees around, made small talk until they were the only two left meandering around in front of Patricia's house.

Kent said, "Which way are you parked?"

Dawn said, "Over here," and pointed down the street.

Kent said, "Oh, I'm the other way, but I'll walk you to your car if you want."

Dawn said, "Sure." She hadn't been walked to her car since she was in high school. She found a certain charm in the offer. She assumed that Kent had been so out of practice with dating that he held on to things like walking a woman to her car or maybe opening the door for her.

Once at her car she said, "This is me."

Kent said, "Nice car."

Dawn said, "It's old."

Kent said, "So, uh . . ." He laughed, "I really haven't done this in a while, so I guess I'll just do it—would you want to get dinner or something, or drinks or coffee or . . ."

Dawn said, "Or what?"

Kent said, "Or . . . I don't know, I guess I covered everything we could do on a first date, didn't I? I just wasn't really sure how to end that sentence, I guess."

Dawn said, "Oh, first date? Well . . ."

Kent said, "I'm sorry, was that too forward? I don't really . . ."

Dawn said, "I'm just joking with you. Yes, I would love to get dinner with you. How's this weekend?"

Kent said, "Oh! Fine with me. Saturday night?"

Dawn said, "Saturday night it is. Here, what's your number?" She pulled out her cell phone. Kent gave her his number and she added him to her contacts, sending him a text message that read, "Looking forward to Saturday night." He added her to his contacts as Dawn and then said, "What's your last name again?"

Dawn said, "Clint," which he added to her contact page, and then said, "Mine's Mooney," which she added to her contact page.

As he drove home, Kent felt strange about having set up a date. He knew logically that it was all part of moving on, and he was somewhat surprised at how little difficulty he encountered in his first endeavor to reenter the dating pool. It gave him hope, and he found his thoughts drifting to what Dawn's breasts looked like naked. Kent began to experience the excitement that comes with the promise of a new sexual partner—something he hadn't felt in a very long time.

Kent's son, Tim, had just finished a twenty-five-man Trial of Champions raid in which no gear dropped that was useful to the character he had run the instance with. He told his guildmates good night, waited for each of them to tell him how much they wanted to "fuck his mother in every hole," "hang him from a tree like a filthy nigger," or "fuck him in the ass and then wipe their dicks across his lips to give him a cum-flavored shit mustache," and then signed up for the following night's raid in the guild calendar and logged out of *World of Warcraft*.

He logged on to his Myspace account and searched through his friends to find Freyja. Tim took the next fifteen minutes to compose a three-paragraph-long e-mail in which he detailed his romantic interest in Brandy Beltmeyer and his curiosity about her alter ego and all of the activities she had described being a party to in her blog entries, specifically the anal sex, threesomes, and bisexual encounters. He admitted that he'd never had any kind of sexual interaction, beyond a few awkward attempts at masturbation that had yet to yield an orgasm. He then highlighted the entire e-mail, pressed the backspace key, and wrote, *I had a good time at lunch today.* He knew she hadn't responded to the first e-mail he'd sent to Freyja, but he felt now that some ice had been broken, that their individual outcast statuses at Goodrich Junior High had somehow merged into something mutual, something that would compel her to respond this time. He clicked the send button. She wasn't online, but he assumed that she got text message updates on her phone alerting her to any incoming messages or friend requests associated with her various Myspace and Facebook accounts. He left himself logged into his account in the hopes that she might respond more quickly if she saw he was online, perhaps even beginning an instant-message conversation.

While he waited, Tim minimized his Myspace page, opened a new window, and logged into his Facebook account. He had several new wall posts, most of which were his classmates deriding him for not playing football. Tanner Hodge was the most prolific of the posters in this vein. Tim thought about changing his account's privacy settings to disallow the public posting of comments on his wall, but he had come to enjoy some element of it. A part of him found pleasure in knowing he was responsible for any anguish felt by his peers. Their posts on his wall confirmed their continued unease due to a decision he made.

He then noticed a new post by his mother. Tim had shown her how to make a Facebook account a few months before she and his father had separated. Both he and his mother had tried to convince his father to make a page as well, but he refused. Tim hadn't heard from his mother in almost two weeks. He had e-mailed her in response to the last one she sent him, but she had not yet responded.

He clicked on her post, which was titled Napa. He saw a series of forty-three photos chronicling a weekend trip his mother and Greg Cherry had taken to various Napa Valley wineries. The last time Tim's mother had posted photos was the week after she left for California, when she posted a series of shots chronicling her breast augmentation surgery. The photos, featuring images of his mother out with her girlfriends drinking a few nights before the surgery, images of her on the way to the surgery, and finally images of her new breasts in a bikini, were difficult for Tim to view, but somehow the absence of Greg Cherry in all but one of the seventeen made them easier to witness than the Napa series.

Greg Cherry was in all forty-six of the Napa photos. Seeing his mother with a man who wasn't his father disturbed him and made her absence in his own life that much more concrete. Her new breasts, almost twice their original size, along with a new, much shorter haircut and a tan that was much too orange, made her seem like a different person to Tim. He wondered if this was the person she'd always wanted to be but was held back, held to some identity she had come to despise, because of himself and his father. There were photos of his mother drinking wine, laughing, dancing, kissing Greg Cherry, living a life that involved neither Tim nor his father—and it was a good life, a life she enjoyed.

Tim's stomach churned a little bit and his neck warmed. He could feel his forehead beginning to sweat. As he clicked through each photo, forcing himself to look, he told himself that this was the way things were. His mother would never again be a significant part of his life. His thoughts drifted to Carl Sagan and "The Pale Blue Dot," a video he had found on YouTube. This doesn't matter, he told himself. He could be looking at photos of his mother having sex with the entire Cornhusker football team—it didn't matter. Eventually, she would die, his father would die, Greg Cherry would die, even he would die, and beyond all of their deaths, beyond anything they had ever done in their lives—the football games played or not played, the saline breasts implanted or not implanted, the conversations spoken or not spoken—all of those things done or not done by everyone he knew, or would ever know, would be forgotten in time if they were even remembered to begin with. And, far beyond that collective discarding of anything they had managed to leave behind, humanity itself would burn out, leaving no impression on a universe that would itself be torn apart under its own forces, leaving no trace of anything. This undeniable truth of reality propelled him through the series of Napa photos, through the images of Greg Cherry with arms around his mother, through the images of his mother lowering her shirt's neckline to feature her manufactured cleavage while drunk, through the images of his mother captured candidly through a camera held by Greg Cherry, who was only feet away from her, through all the rest of the images of Tim's mother, to the final three photos—which somehow trumped all of the rational philosophies he had mustered and made him so nauseated that he nearly vomited.

The first of these three photos depicted Greg Cherry and Tim's mother, Lydia, kissing in a gazebo as the sun was setting. It reminded Tim of a postcard, the image seeming too perfect to be real. Up until this photo, the captions accompanying all of the others had been innocuous, relaying the time or date of the trip and the location, occasionally including an attempt at humor. The caption attached to this first photo of the final three, however, read, "He chose a perfect moment for it." Tim wondered what this "it" was, but he had a feeling he already knew. He clicked the next button to get his answer.

The next photo was an image of Greg Cherry on one knee in the same gazebo, with the same sunset as a backdrop, as he extended an open ring box to Tim's mother. The caption read "The ring was beautiful, especially as the sun was setting. What do you think I said?" Tim wondered what his mother must have said, even though he again had the feeling he already knew. He clicked the next button to get his answer.

The final photo was an image of his mother, with the ring on her finger extended toward the camera, as Greg Cherry kissed her on the cheek. The caption read, "YES!!!" Tim stared at the screen for several minutes. His mother was marrying another man. He didn't understand where the emotions he was feeling stemmed from. He knew logically that this was to be the eventual outcome of his parents' separation, certainly of his mother's move to California to live with Greg Cherry. Despite his rational understanding of the events as they were unfolding, he found he didn't want them to be real. But they were.

He noted that the pictures had been posted just fifteen minutes before he had logged on. That meant that he was among the first to see these images, to witness this moment of his mother's happiness. He stared at Greg Cherry's eyes in the final image. He seemed equally happy. Tim didn't hate Greg Cherry the way he thought he should. He didn't even know him. He represented a happiness that Tim and his father were unable to supply Lydia with, and that made Tim feel resentment toward the man, but not hatred.

Unable to look for more than a moment at the photographic evidence of his mother's wholesale rejection of him and his father, Tim checked his Myspace account and found no response from

Brandy Beltmeyer. He logged out and started up *World of Warcraft*, hoping to spend an hour or so running daily quests in an attempt to take his mind off his mother and Greg Cherry. When he logged on with his main character, Firehands, he saw that the cooldown on his alchemy transmute had reset, so he went to the Ironforge auction house in order to buy the necessary materials to perform the transmutation. As he clicked on the buyout price of eighty-four gold for a stack of Frost Lotus, he saw a message in guild chat from Selkis that read, "Why you logging back on nigger? Forget to jerk off to your toon?" Tim thought about not responding, just finishing his transmute and then logging off, but he felt an overwhelming need to let someone else know about his mother. He typed a message in guild chat that read, "I just found out via Facebook that my mom is getting remarried."

Instantaneously, multiple members of Tim's guild sent their reactions to the news. The messages read, "Is she marrying a nigger?" "Does she fuck niggers?" "Is your dad a nigger?" "Can I fuck her be4 she gets hitched?" "I thought ur mom died after I raped her last night, but I still raped her again." "Where's the bachelorette party?" "You're gonna have a mulatto half-bro."

This continued for several minutes. Tim offered no response. He just read the scrolling green text. Tim understood that the responses were absurd, too detached from the actual event to have any real perspective, but they put him at ease nonetheless. They made him realize that none of the people in his guild, none of the people he talked to on a daily basis and considered friends, had any stake in anything that happened in his real life. And this led him to realize that he had no stake in theirs. They could be going through similar turmoil, or going through situations that were even worse, and he would never know—or, if he knew, if one of his guildmates should divulge any personal information as he just had, he knew he wouldn't care either, and that he might very well be the one responding in guild chat with equally insensitive comments. It reminded him that nothing mattered.

After running his final daily quest at the Tournament of Champions, Tim quit the *World of Warcraft* program, revealing the Facebook window he left open. He knew that looking at his mother's pictures again was a mistake, but he couldn't help himself. He needed to see them. He wanted to force himself to look at them, to scour them for every detail that might relay how happy his mother was without him and his father in her life. He wanted to be done with missing her. He wanted to recognize her as a person he no longer knew. He wanted to hate her.

As he clicked the general link to the Napa photo album, he was met with a message from Facebook that read, "This user has made his or her photos private." Tim understood that she had posted the photos without realizing that all of her Facebook friends would be able to view them. He assumed that, in the few hours he spent on various websites and playing *World of Warcraft*, she made the Napa album private specifically to block him from seeing the photos it contained. This, he reasoned, meant that she was thinking about him and, he believed, trying to spare him whatever emotional pain the knowledge of her engagement to Greg Cherry might have caused. He thought briefly about sending his mother a Facebook message congratulating her on her engagement, but thought better of it, not wanting to seem petty. Instead, he logged out and decided not to tell his father. He would pretend he never knew, that he'd never logged on and saw his mother's Napa photos before she made the album private.

chapter eleven

Allison Doss had become something of a celebrity on the message board at Ana's Underground Grotto after posting her account of her first sexual experience with Brandon Lender. She had almost one hundred replies to her initial post, and a dozen or so personal e-mails, all commending her on sticking to her diet and seeing the tangible results. She also had far more traffic to her profile on another pro-anorexia website, which resulted in a glut of comments on her photos, all praising her beauty. She was checking this profile on her cell phone at lunch to see if any new comments had been added when Danny Vance and Brooke Benton sat down next to her.

Brooke noticed that she was snacking on a Hostess Cupcake and said, "You off your diet?" After spending more time than usual in the past few days on the various websites that supported an anorexic lifestyle, Allison had been swayed, by various posts she found more than convincing, to experiment with bulimia. She said, "I figured one wouldn't hurt. What are you guys up to?"

Danny said, "Just trying to focus for the game tonight."

Brooke said, "In my opinion, you should relax a little. The game should be no problem, babe. Irving is a terrible team, right?"

Danny said, "Yeah, but that doesn't mean we don't have to be focused and play hard." Danny had not told anyone about Coach Quinn's decision to start Josh Kramer in his place. He hoped that Coach Quinn would change his mind, but Danny hadn't noticed any indication that he had in any of the practices that week. Danny took a bite of the chicken-fried steak that had been served for lunch and said, "God, this is gross."

Allison said, "I'll eat it if you don't want it."

Danny said, "All yours," and pushed his tray to her, adding, "I'm going to hit the vending machines or something." Danny left the table, leaving Brooke to watch as Allison ate Danny's chicken-fried steak. Brooke said, "I don't want to tell you what to do or anything, but in my opinion, I just know you worked really hard to, like, stop being chubby. Maybe you should take it easy or something." Allison said, "I know. One day off the diet won't hurt, though."

It had been so long since Allison had allowed herself to eat anything other than celery, apples, and an occasional can of tuna that her taste buds experienced a slight amount of pain as the salt in the gravy passed over her tongue. The amount of food in the three or four bites Allison swallowed was more than she was used to allowing herself to eat at lunch. It filled her, but she continued to eat, knowing that it wouldn't stay in her stomach long enough to be digested. After half of the chicken-fried steak, Allison moved on to the mashed potatoes and then on to the slice of frozen cheesecake that was served with the meal as desert.

She kept up her conversation with Brooke, but wasn't paying

enough attention to what she was saying to remember anything they had talked about; by the time the tone sounded signaling the end of the lunch period, she was too focused on tasting everything she put into her mouth.

On the way to her next class, Allison stopped in the girls' bathroom, her stomach in pain from being overfull. She entered the nearest available stall happy that no one else was in the bathroom. Then, as she was putting down a paper toilet-seat cover, she heard the door open and Sherri Johnston walked in talking loudly on her cell phone. Allison became paranoid that she might not have enough time to vomit and still make it to geometry class without being tardy. If she had to leave the bathroom without forcing herself to vomit, all of the food she ate would be digested. It would become a part of her. This disgusted Allison.

She heard Sherri Johnston say, "No, I'm in the bathroom, retard. Fine, meet you in front of Mrs. Ground's room in like five seconds." Then Sherri Johnston left the bathroom, leaving Allison alone once again.

She had never forced herself to vomit, and although she was nervous, she also found that she was excited to some degree. She was adding a new technique to her regimen for remaining thin. Eating was something she enjoyed far more than starving herself. Even if she found the forced vomiting too disgusting, she knew she would implement the technique from time to time, if for no other reason than to allow herself the pleasure of eating with some regularity. But if she found the vomiting to be tolerable, or perhaps even enjoyable, then it might replace disallowing food altogether.

She read a dozen or so blogs on various websites that gave instructions on the best methods to induce vomiting, and although several methods were suggested that involved drinking things like ipecac, salt water, mustard-seed water, or hydrogen peroxide, Allison assumed that gagging herself with three fingers was the most practical for speed and convenience while at school. It also seemed a waste of effort to Allison to purchase or prepare a drink that would induce vomiting if this was something that she might do only once in her life. If she responded favorably to it, then she would consider alternative methods.

She put a finger into the back of her throat as far as she could, just to test what putting fingers in the back of her throat and holding them there would be like. Her gag reflex initiated immediately, causing her to salivate and choke. She shook her head and her eyes started to water as she spit into the toilet bowl. Her resolve weakened as second thoughts overpowered her original intent. She forced herself to think of the food in her stomach, the gravy turning to fat deposits on her legs, the chicken-fried steak being broken down into green soupy liquid by her stomach acid, the cheesecake congealing into cellulite on her buttocks. She imagined that she could feel these processes occurring in her body as she thought about them. This brought about a mild wave of nausea and helped to nullify any doubt she might have had about going through with it.

She wiped her eyes, bunched her middle three fingers together, took a deep breath, and forced them to the back of her throat. She held the fingers at the back of her throat, despite a gag reflex that seemed to come with more strength this time. After heaving twice with no results, she forced her fingers to the back of her throat a third time, further back than she had the prior attempt, and was met with a stream of vomit that contained all of the undigested food she had eaten for lunch. She had vomited before with different illnesses, but never in this manner. It felt good, clean, made her body feel immediately lighter. It was similar to the feeling she experienced in the morning after a night of eating nothing.

All of the pain she felt from overeating was relieved immediately. It was a strange feeling. Where Allison had become used to the constant and slowly increasing physical pain that accompanied purposeful starvation, this was almost the direct opposite—a quick buildup of pain that was relieved just as quickly. And there was no hunger. She felt just as satisfied as she had after the meal.

Much of the vomit coated her hand, as she'd been unable to remove it from her mouth in time. She would get better at this, she thought, as she stared down into the toilet bowl, amazed by the fact that its contents had been in her body only moments before. She flushed and went to the sink, washing her hands, wiping her eyes, and swishing some water in her mouth. She chewed a piece of gum on her way to geometry. On every blog she read, this was an almost mandatory rule, necessary to mask the scent of vomit.

She took her seat with a few minutes to spare and wondered if anyone could tell what she had just done. She smiled to herself and took out her cell phone in the minutes that were left before class began. She logged in to her Facebook account and, even though he still hadn't accepted her friend request, she sent Brandon Lender a message that read, "Hey, just wanted to c wut u were up 2 =)."

Don Truby, Jim Vance, and Kent Mooney stood next to one another in the bleachers at Goodrich Junior High School, just as they had at the season opener. They watched the opposing team, the Irving Aardvarks, leave their bus and jog to the visiting team's sideline. One Aardvark stood out to them—Kevin Banks. Kevin had grown six inches and gained almost twenty pounds of muscle since his seventh-grade football season, making him easily the biggest football player on the field. Jim said, "Look at the size of that kid."

Don said, "Did he play for them last year?"

Kent said, "I don't know. If he did, he grew."

Don said, "Fuck, that is a big fucking kid," then took a drink from his flask and said, "Have you guys ever heard of the Erotic Review?"

Jim said, "No."

Kent said, "Jesus, Don, we know you're hard up and every-thing, but all you talk about is sex and porno websites. Doesn't it ever get old to you?"

Don said, "Hmm. Not really. Have I been any different since high school?"

Kent said, "I guess not. But I just don't get why we have to talk about your sex life every time we get together."

Don said, "I don't want to talk about my fucking sex life, Kent, I want to tell you about this fucking website. Is that okay with you?"

Kent said, "Doesn't really matter if it is, does it?"

Don said, "No. So, the Erotic Review is this fucking website, right, where you can go and basically read reviews of whores, and then it has the whores' contact info and everything. It's like an online whorehouse or something."

Jim said, "I'm surprised you didn't invent this site."

Don said, "I know. I just kind of stumbled across it and it blew my fucking mind. You guys should check it out."

Jim said, "Why would I need to check out a website that has prostitutes on it?"

Don said, "Right, I forgot, you and your wife have sex all the time. Well, Kent, *you* should check it out. You've probably been hard up for a while, right?"

Kent said, "I have been, but I don't think I'll be needing your whore website. Because I actually have a date tomorrow night."

Don said, "What? That's great. Congrats, man. With who?"

Kent pointed down to the field, where Dawn Clint was taking photos of her daughter and the other cheerleaders holding the banner that the Goodrich Junior High School Olympians were preparing to run through, signifying their arrival to the field. He said, "Dawn Clint."

Don said, "Holy fuck. Her daughter came over to my house this week, doing some project on 9/11 with my son. She has some fucking huge tits already. How'd you swing that, you lucky fucker?"

Kent said, "I went to this Parents Against The Internet thing and she was there. We kind of hit it off, and I just asked her out."

Jim said, "How was that thing? I've gotten a few fliers about it. Seems kind of stupid."

Kent said, "Yeah, the woman who runs it is a little too into it, if you know what I mean."

Jim said, "Yeah."

Don said, "Fuck, man, Dawn Clint is a serious piece of ass. I mean, for being a certain age and everything. Congrats, man. You better hit that shit."

Kent said, "I'll do my best," as the Olympians ran through their banner and onto the field.

Running toward the Olympian sideline, Chris Truby watched Hannah Clint. As she bent over, he focused on trying to see her vagina. He couldn't. He wondered if he could convince her to engage in some kind of sexual act while she was wearing her Olympiannes outfit. He wondered if this would allow him to maintain an erection and came to the conclusion that it might, but only if she also allowed him to penetrate her anus while he spit on her face, which was a specific type of pornography he had recently been watching while he masturbated. Something beyond the obvious demeaning nature of the act of spitting on someone was appealing to Chris, something in the saliva itself that was sexual to him in a way that not much else was.

Although Coach Quinn was not starting Danny, he still allowed him to take center field for the coin flip, which the Olympians won, electing to receive. After a twenty-three-yard kickoff return, the Olympians' offense took the field led by Josh Kramer. In the stands, Jim Vance was beyond confused. He said, "What in the hell is going on? Who is that kid? Is that Josh Kramer? Where's Danny?"

Don said, "He's over there. Sidelines."

Jim said, "What the hell is going on?"

Kent said, "Maybe it's some kind of trick strategy or something."

Don said, "Or maybe they just want to see what that big son of a bitch is going to do to our quarterback before they put Danny in."

Josh Kramer had been instructed by Coach Quinn to run a seven-three-nine rush, a running play to the right side, as the first play of the game. He called the play in the huddle and made his way to the line of scrimmage. The play required him only to take the snap, then turn around and hand the ball to Tanner Hodge, who would run it through a hole that was to be made on the right side of the line. Overcome with nervousness at the thought of making any kind of error in his first play as a starting quarterback, Josh Kramer turned left instead of right after the snap to find that Tanner Hodge was not there. He was, instead, running in the other direction, the proper direction of the play. Having no real choice, Josh gave in to instinct, tucked the ball, and tried to run it himself, making the most out of a broken play. After three steps he was met by the defensive end, Kevin Banks, who tackled him in an excessively violent manner.

Don said, "Jesus Christ. Is this pro wrestling? He fucking body-slammed that kid." The crowd gathered in the Goodrich Junior High School bleachers collectively gasped as Josh Kramer lay motionless on the ground. Mr. Kemp and Coach Quinn ran onto the field to find Josh still conscious but having trouble breathing. Mr. Kemp said, "Can you talk?"

Josh let out what seemed to be a constant exhale and shook his head. Mr. Kemp said, "I think you just got the wind knocked out of you. Give it a few seconds, you'll be fine." Josh shook his head again and pointed to his ribs on the left side. Mr. Kemp applied pressure to the area he indicated, and Josh Kramer screamed in pain. Mr. Kemp said, "Okay, okay. Lay still, try to breath. You might have a fractured rib. I'll get the cart. Sit tight."

Mr. Kemp ran to the field house, got the golf cart, and drove Josh Kramer off the field for further examination as the crowd cheered his exit. Coach Quinn, having no choice, looked to Danny Vance and said, "You're in. Five-two-six power left. Don't run anything else." As the game resumed, Danny entered the huddle and called the five-two-six power left just as Coach Quinn had demanded. It was clear to Danny that any running play, but specifically any running play to the right, would be nullified by Kevin Banks. He knew that their only hope to remain competitive in this game was to implement a strong passing game, but he had disobeyed Coach Quinn once before and didn't want to be benched for game three or maybe even for the rest of this game. Danny resolved to follow every instruction Coach Quinn gave and to run every play he called, win or lose. He hoped he wouldn't suffer the same fate as Josh Kramer at the hands of Kevin Banks.

As Danny took his place behind the center, Brooke looked on from the sidelines. She was worried for Danny and wasn't sure how she would react if he should sustain an injury.

Danny ran the five-two-six power left as instructed, resulting in a loss of three yards as Kevin Banks effortlessly pushed two Olympian linemen aside and met and tackled Tanner Hodge in the backfield just as he was catching the flip from Danny. On third down, Coach Quinn called another running play that resulted in another loss of yardage bringing Jeremy Kelms out to punt. On the sideline, Chris Truby approached Danny and said, "If we don't pass, we're not going to score. That big fucker is going to pound us all night." Danny said, "I know, but I'm doing what Coach Quinn wants. I got lucky that Josh got hurt. I never told my dad about being benched; now maybe I won't have to. I'm not about to go through that again."

Chris said, "Then this fucking game's over, man."

For the remainder of the first half, Danny followed all of Coach Quinn's instructions and ran every play he called. This included only one pass play, which resulted in the Olympians' largest gain of the game, a twenty-two-yard reception by Chris Truby that also resulted in their only first down of the half. Danny felt lucky that the Aardvarks seemed to have almost no offensive capabilities. Kevin Banks was their whole team. When the Olympians went into their field house at halftime, they trailed the Irving Aardvarks by seven points.

Tim Mooney and Brandy Beltmeyer had been friendly at school in the days after the first lunch they spent together. They shared another lunch, and if they happened to see one another between classes they would talk. While Tim's father was at the football game, Tim was at home, playing *World of Warcraft* and watching for Brandy's alternate personality, Freyja, to log on to Myspace. As soon as she was online, Tim decided to take matters into his own hands and initiate an instant-message conversation.

She had some pause about communicating with Tim through her Freyja account, but after spending some time with him at school, and becoming romantically interested in him again, she found she couldn't help herself.

The conversation began innocuously with Tim asking her why she wasn't at the football game. Having already discussed their mutual disdain for school sports, Brandy took this a joke, and responded by telling Tim that she *was* at the football game, and that she never missed one. She went on to tell him that she just loved hanging out with all of the jocks and cheerleaders. With the ice broken, Tim couldn't help himself. He wrote, "So why didn't you ever respond to my e-mail?"

Brandy responded with, "No one knows about this account. I wasn't sure I should be talking to someone I actually know on it."

Tim wrote, "But now you're okay with it?"

Brandy wrote, "Yeah."

Tim wrote, "I've read your blogs. Some pretty crazy stuff."

Brandy wrote, "Oh shit, none of that is real. Don't think I'm some sex fiend or something."

Tim wrote, "I figured. Why write it at all, though?"

Brandy wrote, "I kind of want to be a writer like when I grow up."

Tim wrote, "Cool. But you want to write porn?"

Brandy wrote, "I don't know. Romance novels or something. Maybe porn. What's wrong with porn?"

Tim wrote, "Nothing."

Brandy wrote, "You have to have seen porn before, right?"

Tim wrote, "Yeah, but not that much."

Brandy wrote, "I'm not like a porn addict or anything. I've just seen some here and there, you know? I mean, if you're on the Internet at all you pretty much have to see some sometime."

Tim wrote, "Yeah."

Brandy wrote, "Anyway, I should probably log off this account. My mom is going to do a random check any second. I can feel it."

She had told Tim about how her mother forced her to divulge all of her passwords and how her mother monitored everything she did online, except her Freyja Myspace account. Steeling his resolve by thinking about the insignificance of any single human life or even of humanity as a whole, Tim wrote, "Okay. You want to go out sometime, like see a movie or something?"

Brandy wrote, "Uh . . . yeah. When?"

Tim wrote, "Tomorrow?"

Brandy wrote, "Okay. I'll have to tell my mom I'm going to the library or something."

Tim wrote, "Who goes to the library?"

Brandy wrote, "I'll think of something better. Logging."

Tim wrote, "Night."

Brandy didn't respond, having logged out of the Freyja account. She didn't know what she could tell her mother in order to escape the house without being questioned, but she knew she'd think of something. She was excited and kind of nervous to be going on her first date. She wondered if Tim would try to hold her hand or try to kiss her. She wondered where they would go, if Tim's dad would be picking them up and dropping them off. She thought about texting Tim, but didn't want to seem too eager.

Patricia came in to Brandy's room a few minutes later and did a surprise check of her computer, just as Brandy had assumed she would. Brandy had become adept at removing any trace of Freyja from her computer. Patricia went through all her usual steps, her usual protocols and came up with nothing abnormal. She told her daughter that she loved her and went back downstairs to watch television with her husband.

Tim remained logged in to his Myspace account and looked at Brandy's pictures as Freyja. Her body was far more attractive than he would have thought based on the clothes she wore to school. Her face, too, was prettier than he had noticed when he gave it more scrutiny than usual. Tim found Brandy's instant-messaging technique refreshing and even attractive. Abbreviated words, acronyms, and emoticons were acceptable when texting but not when given access to a full keyboard—this was Tim's philosophy on the matter, and he was happy to see that Brandy seemed to share it. He assumed that she probably wasn't conscious of her instant-messaging etiquette, that it was just something she did naturally. He wondered what movie they should see, and he wondered what his father's reaction would be to the news that he would have to be the chauffeur on his son's first date. Tim hoped that the news of a first date might alleviate some of the tension between them. He thought about what he should do on the date, if he should try to hold Brandy's hand and maybe even try to kiss her.

Don was slightly jealous of Kent's upcoming date with Dawn Clint. He looked down on the field at Dawn. She was wearing tight track pants and a zip-up hoodie with the zipper down just low enough to make out the top of her cleavage. Knowing that Dawn was willing to date the father of another student at Goodrich immediately sent Don's mind into a brief fantasy about having sex with her in the parking lot at the football game.

Don said, "So, what are you guys going to do on your date?"

Kent said, "We're just getting dinner."

Don said, "And then you're going to fuck her, right?"

Kent said, "Jesus. I doubt it. I don't know. How would I know if she even wants to?"

Don said, "How is it that I'm married and you've been single for a year and you don't know this shit and I do? If she agreed to go on a date with you, she's willing to fuck you, retard."

Kent said, "I'm sure that's not entirely right, but we'll see what happens."

Don said, "You have to make whatever happens happen, dipshit."

Kent said, "Is this what you learned on that prostitute website you were talking about?"

Don said, "No, it's fucking common knowledge."

Jim said, "Would you two shut up? The second half is starting."

Almost the entire second half of the football game was uneventful. The Goodrich Olympians scored a touchdown on a fluke running play in which Kevin Banks tripped over one of his own players and was unable to tackle Tanner Hodge as he had done in virtually every previous play. The other running plays the Olympians attempted were met with failure at the hands of Kevin Banks, but still Coach Quinn demanded that no passes be thrown, and Danny abided.

The Aardvarks' offense failed to score again until the game was nearing an end. With two minutes and fourteen seconds left in the game, the Aardvarks were able to drive the ball down field far enough to attempt a field goal. The kicker, Tony Shane, had successfully kicked only two field goals in his life among the twenty-two he had attempted. Nonetheless, he was the only player on his team who was able to successfully kick a field goal at all. So, with the ball on the nineteen-yard line, no one, including Tony, thought he would be able to give his team the lead, but that's exactly what he did.

The score, after Tony Shane's successful field goal, was ten to seven with the Aardvarks leading and two minutes, nine seconds left in the game. Danny quelled his urge to explain to Coach Quinn that their only chance to pull out a victory was to let him pass, hoping that maybe he would see it on his own, maybe he would call a passing play and give them a chance to win. Coach Quinn, however, did no such thing. He called a series of running plays that resulted in a fourth down with twelve yards to gain for a first down. As Danny ran to the sidelines, expecting the punting team to come out with only one minute and twelve seconds left, Coach Quinn said, "What are you doing?"

Danny said, "I thought we'd be punting."

Coach Quinn said, "Nope. You wanted your chance to pass? This is it. X cross wide. Run it."

Danny ran back to the field and called the play in the huddle. Of all the passing plays they could have run in that situation, Danny knew the X cross wide to be the worst possible. It put only one receiver in first-down range and that receiver would likely be in double coverage with the corner and free safety. The play was designed to draw the secondary out of position so the quarterback could throw a short pass to a receiver just beyond the line of scrimmage, who might have enough room to run for a few extra yards.

Danny knew it was hopeless, but he found some pleasure in obeying Coach Quinn's demand, assuming it would fail. The fact that it was a passing play was even better because, on the off chance that Danny was able to complete the pass, he would be lauded as a hero. Danny ran the play as instructed for an incompletion. The Aardvarks regained possession and were successful in running the clock out. The Olympians lost, and although they still had a chance to make it to the district playoffs, they could likely only lose one more game—and their two most difficult opponents were still ahead of them.

chapter twelve

Rachel Truby tried not to seem overanxious as she ate breakfast
Saturday morning and listened to her son and husband recount
the events of the football game from the night before. Once
Don finished the story, she said, "I'm going to head to my sister's this afternoon and I'll probably end up staying the night."
Rachel did this from time to time. Her sister lived almost two
hours away in Grand Island, and she ended up staying overnight
on most visits. Don found nothing about this strange. He said,
"Okay," and began to think about what he would do with a night
to himself.

Rachel had no intention of visiting her sister. She had been
communicating with Secretluvur daily, and their online interaction had reached a point of familiarity that led to him asking to
meet her. She agreed and made the necessary arrangements.

Chris finished his scrambled eggs and hoped that his father

wouldn't want to spend the night doing something with him. Seeing a movie or getting pizza were his father's usual bonding activities. Chris had been looking forward to spending the night sending sexually explicit text messages to Hannah Clint in the hope that he might convince her to take and send pornographic images of herself in various poses and perhaps even with her fingers and potentially other various objects inserted into her vagina and anus.

Don said, "Maybe I'll call up Kent or something, get some beers. We haven't done that in a while." Beers were the furthest thing from his mind, however. Don had already begun to plan out exactly how he might be able to meet Angelique Ice. With his son home, bringing her there was out of the question. This, he reasoned, was also a bad idea on the off chance that Angelique Ice would leave something behind, a stray hair or a bobby pin that would alert his wife to the presence of another woman in her absence. A hotel would be Don's only option. It would have to be somewhere slightly secluded. There was no sense in potentially encountering an acquaintance or even a friend of Rachel's during his attempt at infidelity. Don decided to wait until his wife left to get on the computer and find the best location for his first encounter with a prostitute.

Every day, Tim Mooney checked a Facebook group started by Tanner Hodge called Tim Mooney Is Gay. Tim enjoyed reading the posts his classmates made about him. It was while he was checking this Facebook group that he saw a post from Eric Rakey that read, "First loss of the season = gay." He wondered if he would be blamed in any way by his classmates, or by his father, for the loss. Subsequent posts gave no indication that the loss was to be blamed on poor defensive play, so he assumed the offense was at fault. Nonetheless, he was not looking forward to talking to his father, but had no choice, emerging from his bedroom to find his father drinking a Starbucks coffee and reading a newspaper, which he'd thought they stopped subscribing to over a year ago. Tim assumed that his father picked the newspaper up while he was out getting coffee. It was unusual.

Tim said, "Dad, I need a favor tonight," expecting an immediate reprimand for not playing football and possibly even a chiding that would place full blame for the Olympians' loss on his shoulders.

Instead, Kent said, "I have plans tonight." His demeanor wasn't angry or cold. He actually seemed happy.

Tim said, "Oh, I just—it's kind of important."

Kent said, "What is it?"

Tim said, "I kind of have a date."

Kent said, "So do I."

Tim was beyond surprised. He immediately wondered if somehow his father had become aware of the fact that his mother was getting remarried. The fact that his father's date and his mother's remarriage were happening so close together seemed far more than coincidental. Nonetheless, Tim didn't bring up the subject of his mother's pending nuptials. It was strange for Tim to see both of his parents moving on from each other, but somehow in the case of his father he didn't feel as bad, didn't feel as abandoned. He actually felt some happiness for his father. He imagined his father posting pictures of his date on Facebook, and his mother seeing these images and feeling some regret for having left him. He knew this would never happen, in part because his father didn't actually have a Facebook account.

Tim said, "So who is it?"

Kent had reservations about telling his son about Dawn Clint. He was unsure about how he might react, about what he might think of his father going on a date with the mother of one of his classmates. Kent said, "Just a woman I met a few days ago. Who's the girl you're going out with?"

Tim said, "Just a girl from school."

Kent said, "I assumed that much. Is she a cheerleader? Does she play sports? Tell me about her."

Tim was slightly surprised by his father's interest. He said, "She doesn't really do anything. She wants to be a writer, and we get along pretty well, I guess. I don't know. We're seeing a movie."

Kent said, "Well, like I said, I wish I could help you out, but I kind of have my own thing going on. Is there any way you could get her mom or dad to take you guys?"

Brandy's mother and father didn't know she was going on a date, and it had to remain that way. Tim knew this. Another plan—inviting Brandy over to his house to watch a movie—began to materialize in Tim's mind. He said, "Yeah, I'm sure we can work it out. What are you doing on your date?"

Kent said, "Just going to dinner."

Tim said, "Well, good luck," as he got a glass of water and sat down at the table across from his father.

Kent said, "Thanks. You too."

In an effort to extend this moment, which for Tim was the closest he and his father had come to recapturing a piece of their relationship that existed before his mother left, Tim said, "Can I get the sports page?"

Kent gave it to him and had to hold back a smile. This felt good. It was a feeling he hadn't had with his son in more than a year. It felt familiar, like it used to feel between them. He wondered what his wife was doing, if she missed him at all, if she missed Tim. Then he found himself not caring about the answers to these questions. It felt good not to care about her.

Danny Vance woke up to the sound of his phone vibrating against his nightstand. It was a text message from Brooke Benton that read, "Sorry bout the game :(call me if you want 2 hang 2day." He didn't respond. All he could think about was the fact that, in all likelihood, his chances at going to district were done, and so too were his chances to have any advantage as an entering freshman the following year at North East.

Danny brushed his teeth and went into the living room, where his mother and father were sitting on the couch. Jim said, "Tough one last night. What is Coach Quinn doing with all of those run plays, anyway? He should let you pass more."

Danny said, "I know."

Jim said, "Can anyone talk to him about it? There have to be more angry parents than just me, right?"

Danny said, "Probably."

Jim said, "You want me to call him, see what the hell he's thinking, get him to let you use that arm?"

Danny said, "No. He already ruined the season."

Tracey, sensing that her son was distraught, said, "Honey, it'll be okay. It was just one game."

Danny said, "Yeah, but now we have the toughest two teams in the district still in our schedule, and we can really only lose, like, one more game and still have a shot at district. It's pretty much over."

Jim said, "You can't think like that. You think Peyton Manning thinks like that? Or Drew Brees?"

Danny said, "Probably not."

Jim said, "That's right. Just put it in the past and move on. Think about your next game. Who are you guys playing next week?"

Danny said, "Scott."

Jim, "Well, concentrate on kicking Scott's ass. And remember, they're probably not going to have a kid as big as the one Irving did."

Tracey said, "You should go do something with Brooke. Take your mind off the game—clear your head, honey. I'll take you to the mall or to see a movie or something if you want. I have to get out and get some things anyway this afternoon, or if you guys would rather go see a movie tonight, I can drop you off and pick you up."

Danny said, "Yeah, I guess so." He sent Brooke a text message that read, "Want 2 c a movie or something 2nite?" She replied almost immediately with a text message that read, "Y :)." Danny said, "Okay, Brooke wants to. I guess just let me know when you want to go, Mom, and I'll tell her to be ready." Then he went to his room to see if the write-up of the game had been posted on the school's website yet. He wanted to find out how his performance was perceived, if the blame for the loss would fall on his shoulders, or if it was obvious that Coach Quinn was at fault.

Jim turned to his wife and said, "What do you have to get at the store?"

Tracey said, "Just some groceries and stuff for the house."

Jim said, "We need rubbers, too. Don't forget."

Tracey said, "Will you just get snipped so we can stop with the condoms already?"

Jim's vasectomy had been a point of argument for a few years in the relationship. He knew it made sense. They had two children and neither of them wanted a third. But the thought of his scrotum being opened by a scalpel or laser, and of the subsequent internal incisions that would be made in the inner workings of his genitals, were so off-putting to Jim that he could find no enthusiasm for it. He didn't like using condoms every time he and his wife had intercourse, but he had grown used to them over the years and had difficulty remembering how sex felt without one. He reasoned that he could endure the decreased level of pleasure derived from the act of protected sex for the rest of his life if it meant that his genitals would remain intact, unaltered. And despite what he assumed to be the low risk of error involved with the procedure, Jim had heard stories at his office of botched vasectomies leaving men numb in the scrotum, or requiring a second visit to correct whatever error the doctor might have made during the initial visit. He had even heard of abnormal reactions to properly performed vasectomies that left men with lumps of congealed blood in their scrotum the size of a third testicle. Even though he'd heard that these men's lumps eventually went away, the thought of a lump of congealed blood sitting his scrotum for any amount of time made Jim uneasy. He had come to the conclusion that if he ever underwent the procedure, it be would something he did entirely for his wife.

After searching for a suitable hotel online for a few minutes, Don began to think about the logistics of his encounter with Angelique Ice. They would never be seen in public together. He would arrive at the hotel before she did, secure the room, and wait there for her to meet him. Once he realized there was no need to drive out of his way, he settled on the Cornhusker Hotel and reserved a room with the same credit card he used to purchase memberships to pornography websites.

With the location of his first act of infidelity solidified, Don went to TheEroticReview.com and found Angelique Ice's page, which listed her phone number along with directions on how exactly to contact her. A text message was to be sent to the phone number provided with the phrase "date today," "date tonight," "date tomorrow," or "date soon" as the only text in the body of the message. Don took out his phone and thought one last time about what it was exactly that he was on the verge of doing— cheating on his wife. If he was ever found out, it would no doubt ruin his marriage. And yet he felt his marriage was already ruined. This was something he had to do to remain sane. He texted the phrase "date tonight" to the number provided, and then closed the web browser and deleted the browser history.

He sat in the chair staring at the desktop wallpaper his wife had insisted remain on the computer—an image of Hillary Clinton. He remembered having a minor argument with her about it. Don was not a fan of Hillary Clinton and didn't want to be forced to look at her every time he turned on his own computer. Rachel explained that she would just keep putting the image back up as the computer's wallpaper every time Don removed it. Eventually, Don acquiesced. Now, Don found he was glad his wife insisted on this image being used as their wallpaper. As he stared at it, all guilt and nervousness he was feeling about his decision to have an extramarital affair, let alone with a prostitute, subsided. He was making the right decision. This was his final thought before his phone rang. He answered it and had his first conversation with Angelique Ice.

Angelique Ice said, "Hello, this is Angelique. Are you looking for a date tonight?"

Don said, "Uh, yes. I've never done this before, so you'll have to kind of help me through this. Like, when do I give you the money and . . ."

Angelique said, "What's your name?"

Don tried to think of a fake name but failed. He said, "Don."

Angelique said, "Well, Don, I never talk about that on the phone. So if you'd like to go on a date with me tonight, here's how it works. I do in calls and out calls, so we can meet at my place or your place—"

Don cut her off, "Is a hotel okay?"

Angelique said, "Yes. That's fine."

Don said, "Good. I already booked one."

Angelique said, "Okay, that's fine. We can meet there, and once I get there we can talk about the other thing, but if you're calling me that means you probably saw my site, so you know what I'm looking for in our date."

Don said, "Your price, you mean?"

Angelique said, "Well, again, I don't have a price. We're going on a date. I don't date cops, though. Are you a cop?"

Don said, "No."

Angelique said, "Okay. Well, like I said, once we meet, we can talk about what you want to do on our date and what I want to do on our date and I'm sure we can work something out. So, how's ten o'clock tonight for you?"

Don said, "That's fine."

Angelique said, "And where would you like to meet?"

Don said, "I got a room at the Cornhusker."

Angelique said, "Okay. Do you want to meet in the bar at ten, then?"

Don said, "Actually, could I just meet you in the room? I don't really want to risk having someone I know see me with you. No offense."

Angelique said, "None taken. I'm very discreet, but I do usually like to meet my dates in a public setting before the date starts for safety reasons."

Don said, "Oh. Well, how long would that meeting take?"

Angelique said, "Just a few minutes. And I reserve the right to cancel or end the date at any time. You should know that."

Don said, "Okay, so meet up in the bar at the Cornhusker at ten."

Angelique said, "It's a date."

Don said, "Okay," and hung up. His hands were sweating. The gravity of the fact that he had just successfully solicited his first prostitute began to sink in. Where he had thought there might be guilt or second thoughts, there was only a giddy joy, something akin to what he'd felt in high school when he would sneak out of his bedroom window, ride his bicycle across his sleeping neighborhood, climb into his girlfriend's window, have sex with her, sneak back out, ride his bicycle back across his neighborhood, sneak back into his own home, back into his own bed, and fall asleep without his parents ever knowing he was gone. It was happiness.

After leaving her home in the early afternoon, Rachel Truby went to the airport Ramada Inn and checked herself into a room.

Having no idea about Secretluvur's appearance or demeanor, and having some doubts about her ability to have an affair at all, she had yet to make up her mind about how far she was willing to allow things to progress with this stranger. No matter what the night's outcome would be, Rachel was happy to have a night sleeping in a bed without her husband next to her, no matter if she was alone or sleeping with another man. She took a shower and stretched her legs out in the hotel sheets. She set the alarm on the nightstand to go off at six-thirty, giving her an hour and a half to get ready before meeting Secretluvur in the hotel lounge. She hadn't taken a nap in the middle of the day in a long time. Sleep came easy for her as she closed her eyes, looking forward to waking up without her husband in the room.

Tim Mooney logged on to his Myspace account, saw that Brandy was logged into her Freyja account, and sent her an instant message that read, "My dad has plans tonight. He won't be able to take us to a movie. I can meet you somewhere, though. I have a bike." Brandy responded with an instant message that read, "If your dad's going to be gone, I could just come to your house and we could watch a movie there. I'll just have to tell my mom that I'm riding my bike to a friend's house or something." Tim thought of the prospect of Brandy in his house without his father there. He wrote an instant message that read, "Sounds good. I think my dad is leaving at about 7 o'clock. Want to come over at 7:30?" Brandy replied with an instant message that read, "See you then."

Tim emerged from his room to find his father sitting on the couch watching a rerun of *Everybody Loves Raymond*. He thought for a moment about telling his father that he was going to have Brandy over. He assumed his father wouldn't mind, but on the off chance that he would, Tim decided to keep the information to himself. He said, "So, you ready for your big date?"

Kent said, "Yeah, I think so. Did you work yours out?"

Tim said, "Yeah. Her mom's going to take us to see a movie."

Kent said, "What are you seeing?"

Tim was thrown momentarily. He said, "Uh . . . don't know yet. We're just going to see what's showing when we get there."

Kent said, "Well, have fun. And I don't know what time I'm coming back, so if I'm not here when you get back, don't worry. I got that new college football package—feel free to watch it when you get home. Huskers are on tonight."

Tim said, "Thanks. I'll probably just play WoW when I get home."

Kent had hoped that Tim's interest in the sports page the day before had signified some new interest on his son's part in becoming that athlete he used to be, moving back toward the person he used to be. His response diminished those hopes. Kent said, "Well, maybe when you take a break you can check out some football."

Tim said, "Maybe."

Danny Vance and Brooke Benton decided they didn't want to see a movie after all. Instead, Danny had his mother drop them off at the mall for a few hours. They were content to meander through the place talking. Brooke had mentioned that spending time together, just being in each other's company, was all she wanted. She actually preferred it to seeing a movie. She felt as though the forced silence required at a movie was a waste of time she'd rather spend talking to Danny.

Brooke made a few attempts to hold Danny's hand as they walked, but he would not clutch her hand in return. Ever since the night she had performed fellatio on Danny, Brooke had noticed that something was strange between them. She assumed that Danny's abnormal reaction to her affection was due to the fact that they hadn't so much as kissed each other on the cheek since their last encounter. She further assumed that he was disappointed in her for not having repeated her performance in the week or so that had passed. The opposite was true.

Although Danny was beginning to experience normal sexual urges, they were still new to him, and he certainly didn't feel that he was ready for what he and Brooke had done. He had tried to put the event out of his mind, feeling anxiety every time he thought about it. It marked a progression in their physical relationship that seemed likely to be marching toward a conclusion involving sex relatively soon. This was far beyond what Danny was comfortable with, but—feeling a certain amount of pressure to appear normal—he had already decided that if Brooke were to initiate sexual intercourse with him, he would not stop her.

They passed Dippin' Dots and bought a cup to share. They sat down on a bench and ate. Brooke said, "We never really talked about what we did. You know?"

Danny said, "Yeah."

Brooke said, "Should we?"

Danny said, "I don't know."

Brooke said, "Well, in my opinion, we probably should because I don't know if, like, I'm ready to do it again, you know?"

Danny said, "Really? That's cool."

Brooke said, "You're not mad?"

He said, "Babe, it's totally cool."

Brooke said, "Really? You're not just saying that?"

Danny said, "No. It's cool."

Brooke said, "I mean, we can still make out and everything. I just don't know if I'm ready for, like, you know, what we did and everything. I think I just kind of wanted to do it to say that I had done it or something. I'm glad you were the first guy I ever did it with, though."

Danny said, "Me, too."

They ate their Dippin' Dots, and when they finished, Brooke

said, "Can we go to Verizon? My phone is shitting the bed again."
Danny kissed her on the cheek and said, "Sure, babe," and then
held her hand as they made their way to the Verizon store.

Don Truby told his son, Chris, that he was going to get a few
beers with Jim Vance, and if he ended up having too many he
might end up staying the night on the Vances' couch—something he had done from time to time, though not often. Chris
found this early notification of an unlikely scenario suspicious,
but he didn't care enough about his father's actual intentions to
question him as he walked out the front door.

Chris had become interested in videos produced by and
featured on a website called TheEnglishMansion.com. The
English Mansion was a collective of dominatrices, sexual
slaves, submissives, and various purveyors of specialized sexual
fetishes in the arena of men being dominated by women who
produced pornography in the areas of humiliation; forced bisexuality; male genital torture—known as cock-and-ball torture,
or CBT—which most often included the testicles and penis
being bound with twine or string until they turned black and
blue while being forcefully slapped or kicked, and sometimes
included the penis and testicles being probed with needles or
electrocuted; latex play; and cuckolding, with a slight leaning
toward interracial cuckolding. Chris found all of this arousing.
He had replaced what he had found sexually exciting in the
Cockgobblers series of movies—the all-controlling nature of
the men who were forcibly ramming their erections into the
throats of various women, sometimes even against their will, it
seemed—with its exact opposite. He found something highly
erotic in the full surrender of dominance. Having no control
over the situation, not even enough to move—in some cases
men were bound so completely in combinations of full-latex
bodysuits, chains, shackles, stocks, and so on that they even re-

quired aid to breathe properly—aroused Chris in a way that no other form of pornography had.

He especially enjoyed videos of men being examined by dominatrix doctors. After his father had gone, leaving him with the whole house to himself, he masturbated with his bedroom door open while watching one such video, which featured a nude man in a leather hood with the mouth zipped shut strapped to a doctor's table, with a milking device attached to his penis, as his doctor, dressed in a white latex bodysuit, violently inserted a dildo into his anus. And, while all of this was happening, a black man with an abnormally large penis was having anal sex with the man's wife a few feet from the doctor's table he was strapped to. His wife was excessively vocal about how good the black man's penis felt, and about how much larger it was than her husband's, and about how her husband would never be able to satisfy her sexually like this man.

Chris found the interracial cuckolding aspect of this specific video to be as arousing as any other part of it. He imagined being tied to his chair with a vibrator in his anus while Hannah was having vocal sex with Jordan Shoemaker, a black student at Goodrich Junior High. He was near the point of orgasm when he stopped, quit out of his media player, and moved from his desk chair to his bed. He continued to stroke his penis, maintaining his erection, still thinking about the video he'd been watching, when he sent Hannah a text message that read, "Wut wud u do w/my hard dick right now?" He didn't know if she would respond in any kind of a timely fashion, but decided to prolong his masturbation session for a few minutes, giving her time to answer. She replied to his text message in under a minute with one that read, "I'd put it in my wet pussy." Chris wished she'd said something about gagging on it, or about squeezing his testicles as hard as she could. He sent her a text message that read, "And what wud u do w/ur hands?"

Hannah replied with a text message that read, "Rub them on

u." The lack of specificity or inventiveness in her answer was not arousing to Chris. He prompted her by sending a text message that read, "What wud u do 2 me if I was tied up?"

Hannah didn't know what to make of this text message. She wasn't experienced enough with anything sexual to know what to do with a boy who was tied up, and thought it slightly strange that Chris would ask something of that nature. But she still considered him the best and quickest opportunity to lose her virginity. She sent a text message that read, "I'd slide ur dick n my pussy & ride u till u came."

Although Chris would have preferred a response that included a description of how Hannah would insert something into his anus, or twist his testicles to the point of pain, or sit on his face to the point of smothering him, he was able to derive enough excitement to ejaculate from the thought of lying motionless, bound completely, as Hannah used his erection for her own pleasure.

He thought about sending Hannah a message that read "I just came," but thought better of it. Instead, he sent one that read, "When r we hanging out?" Hannah replied with one that read, "Whenever u want to fuck me." Having ejaculated a large amount of semen into a dirty sock, Chris's sexual arousal was gone. He had almost no interest in having sexual intercourse with Hannah, or with any girl for that matter. He was more interested in emulating something from one of the videos he had seen at the English Mansion. He assumed it would be more than difficult to get a girl to comply with any of these acts, being as far from the norm as they were. Still, he thought, he might be able to get Hannah to comply. She had been willingly accepted his almost abusive sexual treatment of her during their last encounter. He replied with a text message that read, "Up 2 u," accidentally getting some of his semen on his phone.

•　　•　　•

Brandy Beltmeyer came into the kitchen, where her mother was typing up a new document to present in the following week's PATI meeting. It was an overview of websites that parents commonly mistake as predator-free, even though, according to Patricia, they were breeding grounds for danger. The list included sites like eBay, Twitter, TMZ, and ESPN. Brandy said, "Mom, I'm going to go Lauren's to watch a movie." Although Lauren attended Dawes Middle School, she still lived close enough to Brandy that a bicycle ride was not uncommon.

Patricia looked at her watch and said, "Well, it's getting kind of late. Are you spending the night there? Has her mother okayed this?"

Brandy had used Lauren as an excuse a few times before. Lauren had been her best friend since early childhood, and although they didn't attend the same junior high school, they maintained a close friendship.

Lauren's parents were less strict than Brandy's. Although they didn't condone their daughter, or any of their daughter's friends, engaging in questionable behavior under their watch, they had no interest in completely policing their daughter's activity, online or otherwise. From time to time Lauren's parents recreationally smoked marijuana and saw nothing wrong with it.

Lauren herself was similar to Brandy in her social standing at Dawes Middle School. She had a few friends whom she had known since grade school, but she seemed to have been left out of the popular crowd once the seventh grade started the year before. She didn't mind her position in the social structure of Dawes Middle School, though. As long as she could maintain a few close friends like Brandy, she was content.

Brandy sent Lauren an e-mail detailing what her actual plans were and requesting that Lauren be an accomplice in whatever cover story might be necessary. Lauren had used Brandy as a cover story twice before, and the two of them clandestinely met with two boys from Lauren's school in the basement of one of the boys' houses. Nothing happened with the boys, but Brandy enjoyed being able to live her life out from under the eye of her mother. In this case, Lauren agreed to cover for Brandy if her mother should call the house looking for her.

Brandy said, "Yeah, her mom said it was okay if I spent the night."

Patricia said, "Do you want your dad to take you?"

Brandy said, "He's asleep in his chair. You don't have to wake him up."

Patricia said, "I can take you."

Brandy said, "You really don't have to. It looks like you're pretty hard at work on whatever that is."

Patricia, in an effort to be more trusting of her daughter and to allow her to spread her wings as a young adult, said, "Okay, but take your cell phone so I can track you and call me when you get there."

Brandy said, "Okay."

When purchasing a cell phone package for her family, Patricia made sure to get one that included GPS tracking capabilities from one master phone to all other phones. Her husband, not one to use cell phones, left his sitting on the kitchen table, eternally plugged into the wall. His GPS icon on Patricia's tracking screen was always at home. Her daughter's locations were more varied: school, Lauren's house, the mall, the movie theater, and so on. Patricia knew the exact routes to each of these locations on her phone's GPS map, and any deviation from the known path would surely be cause for concern. Brandy knew this as she rode to her bicycle to her friend Lauren's house. Once there, she called Lauren, who came out and met her on the front porch. Brandy gave her the cell phone and said, "I just called my mom and told her I'm here. Just keep the phone in your room, and if she calls, just tell her I'm in the bathroom or something and I'll call her when I get out. Then send me a message on Facebook and I'll call her from Tim's house."

Lauren said, "You're just going to be like, 'Hi, let's hang out, and by the way, can I use your computer and be logged into Facebook the whole time?' That's a little weird."

Brandy said, "My laptop's in my backpack. He won't care."

Lauren said, "You can't call from his house. Your mom won't recognize the number."

Brandy said, "I'll just tell her you got a new phone and I had to use yours because my battery died."

Lauren said, "But why would I change my number?"

Brandy said, "I don't know, you got a cheaper plan or something."

Lauren said, "Your mom will see right through that. What time are you coming here?"

Brandy said, "Whenever I leave, I guess."

Lauren said, "Which is?"

Brandy said, "I don't know, midnight or something."

Lauren said, "Okay, I'll leave my window open, just crawl in. I won't be able to open the door without waking up my parents."

Brandy said, "Okay. Thanks for helping out."

Lauren said, "Whatever."

Brandy got on her bicycle and rode to Tim's house, hoping that her mother wouldn't call her cell phone but knowing that, in all likelihood, she would at some point.

Dawn Clint had no interest in Kent Mooney meeting her mother on a first date, so she instructed him to send her a text message when he was at her house and she would come out. She received the text at 7:33 P.M. and said good-bye to her mother, Nicole, who said, "This one sounds nice. Don't do anything stupid." Dawn offered no response. She knew that Hannah was in her room doing something, so she didn't bother to say good-bye. Dawn told her mother that she didn't know how late she would be out and that she'd left money for pizza on the kitchen table.

She checked her makeup one final time in the hallway mirror and left.

Kent was standing near his car. She wondered why he wasn't in the driver's seat. As she approached, she said, "Why aren't you in the car?" Kent said, "I was just getting the door for you," as he opened the passenger's side door. Dawn wondered if Kent might actually be a genuinely nice guy. When she left Los Angeles, she'd thought a move back to Middle America might yield a larger field of nice guys. To date, it hadn't. She had almost given up hope of finding one, assuming she would have sexual relationships with whichever men were the most attractive to her until she was no longer desirable, and that by then, with luck, her daughter would have some kind of lucrative career in entertainment that she could manage, nullifying the need for a man in her life. Kent was the first nice guy she had met.

Once in the car, she said, "So how have you been since our PATI meeting?"

Kent said, "Pretty good, I guess. Just working and doing the usual stuff. You?"

Dawn said, "Yeah, I guess pretty much the same thing."

Kent didn't know how to continue the conversation, and after a few seconds of silence he began to fear the date was already going badly. Dawn assumed Kent was nervous and took it upon herself to forward the conversation. She said, "So where are we off to tonight?"

Kent, realizing that his choice of restaurant might not be appealing to Dawn, said, "You know, I didn't even think to ask if you like Indian food."

Dawn said, "I love it."

Kent said, "Okay, good. The Oven okay, then?"

Dawn said, "Yeah, I love that place. Not that I go that often, but I've been, you know. It's really good."

Kent said, "Yeah, I used to go all the time—" and stopped himself from finishing the sentence with what would have been *with my wife.* When selecting a location for their dinner, Kent had decided to make it a place that he and his wife used to frequent, in an effort to force himself to forget her, to make the things they held sacred become more meaningless to him, to rid his world of places that she held some sway over. It wasn't fair to Kent that she got to move to a place where neither of them had ever lived or even visited. For her there were no taboo restaurants, no stores that conjured memories of them buying groceries together, no street corners that held phantoms of conversations they had in the rain because the keys were locked in the car. Kent needed to start taking the places in his town back, and the Oven was one of his favorite restaurants. He hadn't been since Lydia left him.

Once at the restaurant, they ordered a bottle of wine and several dishes to share. In the beginning, their conversation was light and innocuous. By the third bottle of wine, they were discussing things that carried slightly more weight. Dawn had recounted the entire story of her time in Los Angeles as an actress and how Hannah came to be conceived. Kent had divulged to Dawn that, until recently, he had fostered hopes of some reconciliation with his wife. It was this topic that prompted Dawn to say, "What made you start thinking differently about your ex-wife?"

Kent said, "Honestly, I know this will probably sounds like a pickup line or something, or maybe it's showing my hand a little too early, but . . . meeting you was kind of part of it. The night we met, I realized I was wasting my time on my ex-wife. Pretty much every night, up until that night, I'd sit in my living room watching TV and wondering what she was doing. That night, I wondered what you were doing."

Dawn wasn't quite sure how to react. She felt it was sweet and trusting of Kent to tell her something that personal, but it also seemed to her that Kent might be placing too much importance on her and whatever relationship they might be about to begin. Then again, she thought, wasn't she placing a similar amount of importance on him and the possibilities he held for her future?

Kent took her lack of an immediate response as a bad sign and said, "I'm sorry. I shouldn't have, I mean, that was way too much wasn't it?"

Dawn said, "Uh, no, no," and in that moment decided she was going to see where this relationship with Kent—with a nice guy—could go. She was going to choose to align herself with the possibility that what he was saying was genuine and heartfelt and not be scared by his willingness to be open with her. She continued, "It was actually about the most flattering thing a guy has ever said to me, believe it or not. I think it's really sweet."

They shared a smile and the conversation turned to their children. Kent told Dawn about Tim's decision to quit playing football and how disappointed he was in his son. Dawn told Kent about Hannah's passion for acting and her plans to help her daughter in any way she could. She omitted any details about her daughter's website, assuming that Kent, or any normal person, would find it strange or possibly morally negligent. Dawn went on to explain her living situation, how she and Hannah lived with her mother. She was embarrassed by it, to some degree, but she admitted that she didn't see the scenario changing anytime soon. She had thought about moving back to Los Angeles at some point, but it seemed pointless unless she was moving there to help Hannah navigate the entertainment business when she was a little older.

As they left the Oven, Kent considered it to have been a successful first date. He enjoyed Dawn's company, and she seemed to have enjoyed his as well. Approaching Kent's car, Dawn said, "You want to go get a drink somewhere? It's still kind of early." So they went to a bar a few minutes away, and at Dawn's behest played a touch-screen game called *Erotic Photo Hunt* that was featured in a small monitor near the bar. It was fun. Kent realized, while touching a woman's fake third nipple in the game, that he hadn't had fun in a long time. He decided that he wouldn't try to kiss Dawn at the end of the night, that he wouldn't do anything to jeopardize the possibility of a second date with her.

After the bar, Kent drove Dawn back to her house and walked her to the door. He said, "Well, thanks for coming out with me. I had a really good time tonight and if you're up for it, I'd love to do it again sometime."

Dawn said, "There better be a date number two," and then kissed him. They were both slightly inebriated, and they tasted alcohol on each other's mouths as they kissed. Kent found Dawn to be a good kisser and Dawn found the same to be true of Kent. She was the first woman Kent had kissed since his wife. It was foreign but enjoyable. Even though he hadn't kissed his wife in more than a year, he still vividly remembered every aspect of her technique and could easily compare it to Dawn's. He found Dawn to be superior, more sexual somehow.

The kiss concluded and Dawn said, "Call me tomorrow." Kent said, "I will. Have a good night," and then turned and walked back to his car. Dawn went inside and answered the standard questions from her mother and her daughter about how the date was and then went to her bedroom. She took out her cell phone and composed a text message thanking Kent for the date. She debated whether or not to press the send button. Her initial impulse was to delete the message, not wanting to seem overly enthusiastic and risk scaring him off. This is what she would have done with any other man with whom she'd gone on a first date. But, reminding herself that she was going to let herself get involved this time, that she was going to give in to her impulse to be open and allow herself to feel something for Kent, she overcame her inhibitions and sent the text message.

Kent received it on his drive home. He liked Dawn. While driving, he replied to her text message with one that read, "Had fun, too. Sweet dreams tonight," which made Dawn smile.

• • •

Brandy Beltmeyer and Tim Mooney sat on his bed watching episodes of *Tim and Eric Awesome Show, Great Job!* that Tim had saved on his digital video recorder. Brandy's laptop was powered up on the floor next to them, and she was logged into her Face-book page awaiting any message from Lauren about her mother having called.

Tim and Brandy had yet to touch each other. Tim was unsure about how to escalate what he assumed Brandy assumed was a friendship to a level that would warrant any kind of touching. He didn't necessarily have any intention of doing anything sexual with her. He had fantasized about Brandy laying her head on his chest as they watched television and stroking her hair or maybe kissing. Once again he conjured thoughts of "The Pale Blue Dot" and various other scientific essays, theories, and opinions about the nature of our universe that explained our insignificance and said, "You know, we could, uh, lay on my bed if you want."

Brandy said, "Okay," and they did, still not touching. Brandy, too, was unsure about how to make the transition to any kind of physical contact. She had always been under the impression that it was the duty of the male to initiate anything in that direction. For her to act outside of this unspoken rule would seem awkward. But, then again, she reasoned, it was already awkward as they lay there side by side in his bed, not touching, actively maneuvering their bodies so that not even the slightest contact was made.

Saying nothing, giving no warning, she reached out, took Tim's arm, and moved it so that she could lay her head on his chest, putting his arm around her as she did. Tim, too, said noth-ing as it was happening, unsure of what it meant, of what he was supposed to do next. He opted to do nothing, to just enjoy her lying on his chest, as Tim Heidecker performed his character Spaghett on television. He smelled her hair and listened to her laugh at the show. This, Tim thought, was what it must be like to have a girlfriend. He wondered if she thought the same thing about him, and he wondered when or if that subject should even be brought up. So he remained where he was and watched television, content with exactly what was happening.

Brandy, with her head on Tim's chest, listened to his breathing and to his heart. She, too, thought that this was what having a boyfriend must be like. She, too, wondered when, or if, that subject should be talked about. Obviously they would at least have to kiss before there was any talk of becoming a couple, and she knew she wouldn't be the initiator of their first kiss. So she remained where she was and watched television, content with exactly what was happening.

After a few hours, Brandy raised her head and said, "I should probably go. I can't even believe my mom hasn't called me yet."

Tim said, "Okay. I'll walk you to the door."

On Tim's porch, he hugged her but did not kiss her, despite wanting to more than anything in that moment. He said, "Thanks for coming over."

Brandy said, "Yeah, no prob."

They both wanted to know when their next meeting would be, when they would hold hands, when they would share their first kiss, but neither said anything or initiated any movement toward these things. They were both too nervous, too unsure about the other's response if they should ask or do something of that nature. Tim Mooney stood on his porch and watched Brandy Beltmeyer ride her bicycle off into the night, hoping that her mother hadn't called her and that he would see her again outside of school very soon.

Once Brandy was back at Lauren's house, she checked her phone, only to find that her mother had never called. Brandy found this strange; she wondered if something was wrong with her phone. She thought about calling her mother to make sure everything was all right, but opted not to. She decided not to press her luck, not to look a gift horse in the mouth.

•   •   •

Patricia sat in her daughter's room at her daughter's computer. She meticulously sifted through all of her e-mails, Facebook and Myspace messages, wall posts, and any other file on her daughter's computer that might reveal anything incriminating. She had been doing this for hours when her husband, Ray, came in. Ray said, "You still in here?"

Patricia said, "Yes, I am."

Ray said, "You've been at it for a few hours now."

Patricia said, "I know, and I haven't been able to find anything. We're lucky, Ray."

Ray said, "Then maybe you should take it easy on her a little bit."

Patricia said, "You're right. I'll just call her and check in to make sure everything's okay at Lauren's house and then I'll come to bed."

Ray said, "Don't call her."

Patricia said, "What?"

Ray said, "You just went through her entire computer, doing whatever you do, and you said yourself—she's clean as a whistle. Just let her be a teenager tonight. Show her you trust her. Let her grow up a little."

Ray sometimes initiated conversations with his wife about being less overbearing with their children. Patricia usually dismissed his arguments, but in this case he seemed to make sense. She looked at her phone as it sat on her daughter's desk. Her daughter was becoming a young adult, and her husband was right. She deserved the space that she needed to grow on her own. Patricia tried hard not to take for granted how well-behaved her daughter was, and she believed that giving her a night away from home, without a phone call to check up on her, would strengthen their relationship. She found that she trusted her daughter.

She said, "You're right, honey."

Ray said, "Let's go to bed."

• • •

Don parked his car further away from the front entrance of the Cornhusker Hotel than necessary, put a piece of gum in his mouth, and checked his hair in the rearview mirror. This was it—he was really doing this. He reached over into the passenger's seat, took the envelope containing eight hundred dollars that he had gotten from the bank that afternoon, and tucked it inside his jacket pocket, questioning the decision to wear a jacket to this encounter as he did. The jacket had seemed like a good idea earlier in the day; it seemed like it might lend some importance to what he was doing, make it classier than it actually was. Now it just seemed like a failed and pathetic attempt to do those things.

Don entered the Cornhusker, checked in at the front desk, got his room key, and then went to the bar. He was five minutes later than the time he and Angelique Ice had agreed upon. This was done on purpose. Don had no interest in waiting at the bar for her. He wanted to spend as little time in public as possible, on the off chance that someone he knew might spot him. There were no other patrons in the Cornhusker's lounge, just Angelique Ice, who sat at the bar drinking a martini. Don recognized her immediately. She was slightly heavier in person than in her photos, but Don found her attractive nonetheless. She certainly wasn't as soft and out of shape as his wife.

He approached her and said, "Angelique?"

She said, "You must be Don. You're cute."

Don saw this as part of her act. He knew she couldn't actually find him attractive, or that, if she did, the circumstance of their meeting would render any genuine attraction she had for him null. Still, it was nice to be complimented, nice to have someone tell him she was attracted to him. His wife, Rachel, hadn't called him anything remotely close to cute in longer than he could remember.

Don said, "You're not so bad yourself. So how does this work?"

Angelique said, "Well, we have a drink and then we go on our date."

Don looked around and saw that no one else was in the place. His fear of being discovered hadn't completely subsided, but he agreed to one drink, having some desire to get the full experience of a meeting with a prostitute. He also reasoned that a drink might not be a bad idea. He was more nervous than he wanted to be. He wanted to enjoy this. He ordered a shot of whiskey and drank it instantly, and then ordered another and did the same.

Angelique said, "Is this really your first time? I know you said it was on the phone, but a lot of guys say that."

Don said, "You can't tell?" as he ordered a final shot of whiskey.

Angelique said, "Well, you seem like a nice guy and you're pretty clearly nervous. Let's continue our date in your room."

Don said, "Sounds good," left some cash on the bar, and led Angelique Ice up to the room he had booked.

They said nothing on the elevator up to the room. Once they were inside, Don said, "So how exactly does this work?"

Angelique said, "Well, for a donation of eight hundred you get to have a standard date with me, which is full-service and lasts for an hour. For sixteen hundred you get the full GFE."

Don said, "GFE?"

Angelique said, "Girlfriend Experience. I stay the night with you and wake up with you tomorrow and we get to be with each other all night."

Don wanted the GFE. His primary desire was to have sex with Angelique Ice, to do things to her that his wife hadn't allowed him to do in a year or so, to feel a body that was still young and semi-tight, to hear a woman moan as though she were enjoying herself as a result of something he was doing. But, beyond that, Don wanted to fall asleep with a woman who wasn't his wife and to wake up with her. Don said, "Well, I only brought eight hundred with me. I have another hundred and twenty, but I can't cover sixteen hundred."

Angelique said, "Then we can just do the hour date. Or for the extra hundred and twenty I guess I could let you do anal, even though it's usually an extra three hundred."

Don said, "There's no negotiating for the GFE, then, I guess."

Angelique sat on the chair across from the bed and took off her shoes. She said, "There's always negotiation, but I can't do GFE for that low."

Don took that to mean that she would be going on other "dates" as soon as she was done with Don. He wondered if he was the first of the night for Angelique Ice, or if she had just come from another "date." He thought about asking her but assumed it was against protocol, and more than that, it was something he didn't really want to know.

Don thought about having anal sex with Angelique, about whether it would be worth all the money he had on him. He had seen videos of Stoya engaging in anal sex and seeming to enjoy it. He hadn't had anal sex with his wife in what he calculated was around five years. He said, "Okay, let's do nine-twenty then."

Angelique said, "So you want anal?"

Don said, "Yeah."

Don could already tell he was going to have to do this at least one more time. He was going to have to get the GFE. Angelique said, "So you place your donation on the table now, and then we start our date."

Don took out the envelope, laid it on the table, and then took out the one hundred and twenty dollars he had in his wallet and put that next to it. Angelique opened it and counted the money. Don said, "So, do we make small talk now, or do we just get right to it? I mean, do you want to hear about what I do for a living or something?"

Angelique said, "If you want to tell me, you can," as she took off her blouse, revealing her black lingerie. Don looked at her pale skin and medium-sized breasts. He became excited at the thought of having anal sex with her, an act that would be happening within an hour's time. Don tried to calm himself, not wanting to seem overanxious or to ejaculate prematurely. He wanted to get the full hour if he could. He said, "Well, I'm an account services manager at Stanley."

Angelique removed her skirt, revealing panties that matched her bra. She turned around and bent over, giving Don a view of her buttocks. To Don they were almost perfect. He could see the hint of cellulite forming, but she was young enough that it didn't take away from their shape. Still bent over, she reached between her own legs, pulled her panties to the side, and slid a finger over her own anus as she said, "So what does an account services manager do?"

Don could feel an erection forming. He was sure this would not last the entire hour as he said, "I coordinate daily sales activities regarding distributors. I also manage relationships with various accounts and ensure that all internal applicable projects are complete, and I occasionally assist with marketing programs relating to distributors."

Angelique said, "That sounds really complicated," as she turned around and approached the bed where Don was sitting.

Don said, "It's not," as she straddled him, took off his jacket, and unbuttoned his shirt. Don reached up and tried to pull her head toward his to kiss her, but she said, "That's only with the GFE."

Don said, "Oh, sorry, I don't really know the protocol or anything."

Angelique said, "It's okay," then slid off his lap and unbuckled his belt. She unzipped his pants and took them off along with his shoes and socks. She turned around again and sat on Don's lap facing away from him. They were both still wearing underwear, but Don was on the verge of ejaculating already. *This is what it's like to actually be attracted to the person you're having sex with—*

this ran through Don's mind as Angelique removed her bra and panties and turned to face him.

Don found her body attractive. She had smallish breasts and a little extra weight in certain places, but nothing that made her look fat, just curvy. She was by no means perfect, but Don was aware of the fact that he didn't live in New York or Los Angeles. For a girl who made a living as a prostitute in his town, she was very attractive. He said, "Can I touch your boobs, or . . . ?"

Angelique said, "You can do anything you want to me, but you can't kiss me. I mean, you can't hit me or anything, either, but you can touch them, lick them, whatever."

Don put his mouth on her right nipple. It became hard immediately, and she moaned. He knew the moaning was most likely an act, but it was an act she did well, and Don found himself giving in to the illusion she was trying to create for him. It was what he was paying nine hundred and twenty dollars for, after all.

Angelique Ice licked her palm and reached down to Don's penis. She stroked it for a few seconds, until Don had to stop her before he ejaculated. She said, "You don't want me to touch your cock?" Don didn't want her to see that, after only the most rudimentary sexual interaction, he was already so aroused that he was on the verge of orgasm. Something in his male psyche wanted to show Angelique Ice that he was sexually adept, that if he were to become a repeat customer, her next interaction with him would be pleasurable for her—that, among all her clients, he was one of the best, one she looked forward to seeing. He said, "We should get a condom."

Angelique got off his lap and went to her purse. Don had brought his own, being skeptical of the integrity of any condom used by a prostitute. But now that he had been put slightly at ease by meeting Angelique Ice, he almost felt embarrassed when he said, "Would you mind if we used mine?"

She said, "If they're still in a sealed box, then I don't mind."

Don went to his jacket and removed a box of three Trojan

latex condoms with spermicidal lubricant. He handed it to Angelique to inspect. She approved, opened the box, and took out
one of the condoms. She said, "Lay down." Don got into the bed
and did as instructed, his erection throbbing. He felt as though
he hadn't had an erection like this one since he was in high
school. He hoped the condom would take away enough sensitiv-
ity in his penis to allow him to prolong the experience.

He stared at the ceiling and felt Angelique Ice take his erection in her hands and roll the condom down the length of it,
saying, "Such a big dick," as she did. Don knew he had an average-sized penis. He knew that Angelique Ice told every one of
her clients that he had a "big dick" or a "huge cock." It was all
part of the experience; it was bought and paid for. He tried to rid
his mind of these thoughts, to make himself believe she wanted
to be there, wanted to have sex with him. That was the chief
thing he was seeking in this endeavor: to have sex with someone
he believed wanted to have sex with him in return.

Once the condom was on, Angelique Ice stroked Don's penis
a few more times; then she climbed on top of him and slid his
erection into her vagina. Don looked up at her as she sat on top
of him. She was smiling. It was a sweet and sexy smile, one he
had never seen on his wife's face. He gripped her hips, which
were shapely and soft in the way Don liked, and thrust into
her. She closed her eyes and opened her mouth, taking a deep
breath, moaning, and then biting her bottom lip as Don continued to move his hips under her. She was giving all the signs Don
needed to believe she was enjoying herself.

She reached down and moved one of Don's hands from her
left hip to her breast, giving Don an even stronger illusion that
this was a normal sexual encounter, that Angelique Ice was engaging in sexual intercourse with him for no other reason than
because she found it pleasurable. She said, "Your dick is so hard.
I love feeling it in my pussy." Don gave no verbal response.
Instead he pulled his hips back, removing his penis from her,

barely avoiding climax. He rolled her over onto her back, licked her nipples for a few seconds, listening to her moans, feeling her hands running through his hair, enjoying giving pleasure to a woman through sexual interaction, the thoughts of it all being an act on Angelique Ice's part slowly fading.

He inserted his penis back into her and she grabbed his buttocks, pulling him deeper in. Don pressed himself to her, wanting to feel every inch of her skin against his. He wanted to kiss her, to feel like this was real, but he knew he couldn't. It was at that moment that he knew he would be making another appointment with Angelique Ice, there was no question. Whatever guilt he might feel after the act had concluded would be incidental, and he assumed he would feel none anyway. He wondered when the soonest available time he could see her again was as she said, "Fuck me."

The missionary position was Don's least favorite. As a result, he was able to maintain a medium-paced rhythm as he penetrated Angelique Ice for several minutes without nearing climax. He began to sweat and feel self-conscious about it. Before he could apologize or wipe his face with his hand, though, Angelique Ice reached up and wiped the sweat from his forehead with her own hand, then wiped it across her breasts and said, "So fucking hot."

Don looked at the clock. They had been engaged in sexual intercourse for almost thirteen minutes. Don knew he couldn't last much longer. He was reaching the point at which the physical effort he was exerting was producing diminishing returns for the amount of sexual pleasure he was receiving. He rolled off of Angelique Ice and said, "Get back on top of me but face the other way."

She said, "Oh, a fan of reverse cowgirl, are we?"

Don said, "Yeah."

She said, "You want to fuck me in the ass like this so you can watch that big cock go in and out of my little pink asshole, don't you?"

Don said, "Yeah."

Angelique Ice climbed on top of Don, with her back facing him, and inserted his penis into her vagina. She rocked back and forth on his penis as he groped her buttocks. Don was enjoying himself and was on the verge of an orgasm but wanted to make sure he was getting everything he paid for, so he said, "I thought we were doing anal."

Angelique said, "Patience, patience," and then looked back at Don, smiled, and began sucking on her index finger. Her smile made Don think of Stoya. Don wondered if Stoya enjoyed herself while she was having sex in her movies or if it was just a job to her, just an act. He couldn't tell. It seemed real to him in her movies. And Angelique Ice was approaching Stoya's level of performance as she reached back and inserted her index finger, now glistening with her own saliva, into her anus. She moaned, actually seeming to enjoy it. Don stopped all his thrusting motion and tried to stave off orgasm. He could feel her finger pressing against the shaft of his penis through the wall of her rectum. It was easily the most pornographic sex he had ever been party to; just the thought of what he was doing was almost enough to make him reach orgasm.

Angelique removed her finger and said, "Do you want to put it in or do you want me to?"

Fearing that any further contact of Angelique Ice's hands on his penis might produce a quick end to the encounter, Don said, "I will."

She said, "Hurry. I want that big dick in my tight little asshole now."

Don removed his penis from her vagina, moved his hips back a few inches, angled them for proper entry, and forced his erection into Angelique Ice's anus. She looked back over her shoulder, smiled at him, and said, "You like fucking my little asshole?"

Don said, "Yeah," and then bent over entirely, so that all Don could see was her buttocks moving up and down slowly with

Don's erect penis in her anus. He could feel his prostate starting to contract. This was it. He clutched her buttocks and let out a loud grunt as Angelique Ice sat down hard on his erection, taking the entire length of it in her rectum. She said, "Yeah, come for me, baby. Come right in that asshole." Don's leg twitched a little as the last amount of semen produced by his orgasm was pumped into the condom. Angelique rode Don for a few more seconds, smiling at him from over her shoulder again, and then dismounted him and said, "Did you like that?" as she rubbed his chest.

Don liked it more than anything he had done in his adult life. He had convinced himself in his youth that having sex with a prostitute was somehow demeaning for the woman and pathetic for the man. It was strange how easily the convictions of youth fade away with the apathy of age, he thought. He said, "That was incredible."

Angelique said, "Well, I'm glad you liked it. You paid for an entire hour and I can stay for it if you want."

Don said, "Yeah, that would be good, actually. I'm gonna go to the bathroom and get rid of this."

Don went to the bathroom and removed the condom, checking his penis for any evidence of it having just been in someone's anus. There was none. He gave his penis a cursory wash with the bathroom washcloth and returned to the bed, where Angelique was still naked and waiting. He said, "I don't know if this is against the rules or anything, but could we just lie in the bed together, and maybe you put your head on my chest or something?"

Angelique said, "No, that's fine. We have a little over half an hour left. We can do whatever you want."

So they lay there in the hotel bed where they just had anal sex, with Angelique Ice's head on Don Truby's chest. Don tried to think of the last time he and his wife had done anything intimate like that—not engaging in any kind of sexual act but just lying together, feeling each other's breathing, just being together. He couldn't remember. Don fell asleep with the rhythm of Angelique's breathing, and she woke him up when she had to leave. She said, "So, I'm glad you had a good time."

Don said, "Yeah, thanks. I mean, I'd like to do it again if you want to."

Angelique said, "Like a second date?"

Don said, "Yeah. I guess so."

Angelique said, "Well, you know how to get in touch with me, and you know what I need if you want a longer date. So just send me a text whenever you want."

Don said, "Okay."

After she got dressed Don got out of bed and walked her to the door of his hotel room. The interaction hadn't been strange to Don until that final moment. He wanted to kiss her good-bye. He had never had sex with a girl and not given her a kiss good-bye when they parted ways. He said, "I know I can't kiss you. Can I give you a hug or something? I don't know what to do really at this point."

Angelique said, "A hug is fine."

They hugged and Angelique Ice left his hotel room. Don went back to the bed and went back over every second of the encounter in his mind. He decided he would stay the night in the hotel. A night alone was something he hadn't had in years. He tried to conjure some amount of guilt for what he had just done and wasn't able to. He had never thought of himself as the type of man who was capable of having sex with a prostitute, but now he realized that not only was he that exact type of man, but he was the type would do it repeatedly until the day he died.

The alarm in Rachel Truby's hotel room went off. She got out of bed and put on her makeup and a black dress that she had smuggled out of her house without her son or husband noticing. She looked in the mirror and thought to herself that she used to look much better, less tired, in better shape. She assumed this type of thing happened to all women at some point in their lives, and she further assumed that she was at that point in hers.

By the time she had brushed her teeth, put on deodorant, and decided she looked the best she possibly could, she still had twenty-four minutes until she was scheduled to meet Secretluvur. She decided that a drink before he showed up might not be such a bad idea, so she headed downstairs to the bar. Once there, she saw only one other person sitting in the bar, a slightly overweight black man. He looked at her as though he was waiting on someone, and she became aware of the possibility that this was Secretluvur. The initial moment of meeting a complete stranger would always be awkward, she thought, but the circumstances surrounding this specific meeting made it more so. She decided to sit at the bar and get a drink without asking him his identity, to wait until the agreed upon time and see if anyone else showed up. But before she could order a drink he said, "Are you . . . boredwife?"

Rachel said, "Uh, yeah. Hi—Secretluvur?"

Secretluvur said, "Yeah."

The only other person in the room was the bartender, who heard the entire conversation. It was slightly embarrassing to Rachel to have this meeting played out in front of a complete stranger, whom she assumed was passing judgment on them both, but the meeting could be conducted in no other way. Rachel had never had any kind of physical interaction with a black man. She had wondered what it might be like, whether all of the stereotypes about large penises were true. Secretluvur had a nice-enough looking face, and although he was slightly overweight, he seemed to have broad shoulders and she assessed him to be muscular under the sport coat and slacks he chose to wear for their first meeting.

He said, "So, I don't really know how this is supposed to go down."

Rachel said, "It's new to me, too. I guess we have a few drinks, talk a little, and then see what happens."

He said, "Sounds good. What'll you have?"

Rachel said, "Cosmo."

He motioned to the bartender and said, "She'll have a—"

The bartender cut him off, "I heard her."

He said, "Okay," then turned to Rachel, who had moved over to sit next to him, and said, "So what kind of work do you do?"

She said, "It's boring. Bookkeeping-type things. It's kind of a terrible job, actually, but I just got it this year, and so I've been trying to tell myself to stick it out. It pays pretty well, I guess. What about you?"

He said, "Exact same thing. I guess I've had the job a lot longer than just this year, though. I been at the same place now for, let's see, ten years. Wow, you never think you're gonna be at some place, doing something you don't like, for that long. And then one day you meet up with a potential Internet affair and you kinda get your whole life in perspective, you know?" Rachel laughed. Her husband hadn't made her laugh in a long time. Her husband was funny, and she laughed at some of the things he did or said, but he hadn't made her laugh in a long time.

Something in Secretluvur's attempt at humor, something beyond the way it was amusing, made Rachel appreciate him. It was as though his attempt to make her smile, to make her laugh, to make her enjoy the time she was spending with him, was a display of his value, and, in turn, an admission that through that display he saw value in her. He wasn't trying to amuse himself or the bartender, the way her husband would have. Secretluvur didn't care if anyone else in the world found his joke funny, as long as Rachel did. It was this attempt to make her laugh that made her decide to have sex with him that night, and it was that decision to have sex with him that made her further decide to let him do anything he wanted to her, and to do things to him that she had never done with her husband. She wanted to be a different person that night.

The bartender brought her the cosmopolitan, and she reached for her purse. Secretluvur said, "I got this," and paid for the drink.

They talked long enough for Rachel to have one more drink, which he also paid for. The conversation was about nothing specific to their lives. Neither of them spoke about their spouses, their children, where they lived; neither of them divulged their actual names. They spoke about movies, television shows, music, sports, celebrities—the generalities of life that everyone experiences in a way specific to them. She learned that his favorite television show was *The Wire*, and he learned that hers was *Six Feet Under*. They shared a mutual disdain for reggae, which she found strange for a black man and then immediately felt ashamed for having felt that way.

As she took the last sip of her second drink and put the glass back down on the bar, she said, "So . . ."

He said, "So . . ."

She said, "I guess we should . . ."

He said, "I don't want you to think that this has to happen tonight or anything like that. We can just talk tonight if you want. This ain't like a real pressing thing or anything. I mean, you seem like a real nice woman, and you look fine as hell, but—"

She stopped him there. She had never been called "fine as hell" by anyone, and it turned her on. She could feel something in her that had been buried for a long time starting to come back to the surface. She said, "I have a room here if you want to join me."

He said, "Okay. Okay. We can do that," and she took Secretluvur by the hand and led him up to her room.

Once inside the room, Rachel had no intention of giving herself any time to think too much about what she was doing, or to convince herself that she shouldn't have sex with Secretluvur. She pushed him toward the bed and kissed him. He was the first black man she had ever kissed. It was something she had resigned herself to believing would never happen in her life. He was a good kisser, and along with the exhilaration that came from the circumstance itself, Rachel was excited by the way he grabbed the back of her hair and pulled it gently as they kissed.

She pushed him back down onto the bed and straddled him, never taking her lips off his. This level of sexual aggressiveness was something she hadn't been able to conjure for her husband in several years. Even when they used to have sex more frequently than they had in the past year, she never found herself capable of feeling such animal lust for her husband, certainly nothing on the level that she felt for Secretluvur as she unzipped and unbuckled his pants.

She put her hand under his shirt and felt his stomach. It was big, fat, but she could feel the muscle underneath. She wondered if Secretluvur had been an athlete in high school or maybe even college. She wondered whether her husband had ever played football against Secretluvur in high school, and thought that if he had—if the world was that small—then she was merely living out one of her possible futures there in that hotel room.

She slid her hand down into his pants and under the elastic waistband of his underwear—which was the same style her husband wore—and found his penis. It was large. It wasn't gigantic, but it was noticeably larger than her husband's in both length and girth. This discovery only served to enhance the carnal desire Rachel had conjured for Secretluvur. She hoped that, along with being well-endowed, Secretluvur would also fit the stereotype of being a skilled and insatiable lover.

She pulled his underwear down a little bit so that his penis and testicles were exposed. Then she moved down and began to fellate him. Rachel hadn't performed an act of oral sex in some time. She tried to think back to the last time she had put her husband's penis in her mouth, but she was unable to produce the memory. A small part of her was concerned that she wouldn't be able to perform to the standards Secretluvur might be used to. She tried to imagine what his wife was like. She wondered if she was black.

As she took Secretluvur's penis in and out of her mouth, fondling his testicles with one of her free hands, it became erect. It didn't gain much size beyond what she already knew it to be. She found this to be far different from her husband, whose erect penis was almost triple its flaccid size. Secretluvur said, "Yeah, baby, suck that thing."

Rachel and her husband had passed through a phase early in their relationship in which they would employ pornographic commands and requests to one another during foreplay and during the act of intercourse itself. In the past several years, however, neither she nor her husband had uttered a word during these acts. She had almost forgotten that such a technique had once been a part of her repertoire. She remembered how much she enjoyed feeling a little dirty while she performed oral sex and found that this was a perfect opportunity to relive some of her sexual youth. She said, "You like it when I suck your big dick?"

Secretluvur said, "Yeah."

Rachel said, "You want to fuck me with that big dick?"

Secretluvur said, "Yeah."

She reached down and pulled off her panties under the dress she was wearing. Then she moved up and straddled him, both of them still fully clothed save for their now-exposed genitals. Rachel would have liked to have been nude, but she maintained her urgency to ensure there was no turning back. She reached over to the nightstand, where she had placed a CVS bag containing condoms she had purchased before arriving at the hotel. She handed the box to Secretluvur and went back to performing fellatio on him as he removed one of the condoms, unwrapped it, and then handed it to her.

In her entire life, she had never put a condom on a man's

penis. It had always been the man's job. Although Rachel did remember a point in her life when she thoroughly enjoyed sex with
her husband, she recalled some unshakable feeling that sex was
a favor to him. And, as she was kind enough to perform this favor,
so should he be kind enough to handle all of the perfunctory
activities and protocols that were necessary before it could be
carried out. This was different. This was not a favor.

Rachel took the condom in one of her hands and continued
to lick the underside of Secretluvur's penis. As she pulled her
head back, she got her first really good view of his penis. It was
not only large, but slightly misshapen. It curved to the right a little bit, and the head seemed to be a little bit too small for the rest
of it. This only made Rachel want it inside her more. It was so foreign, so different from the penis she was used to, from the penis
she felt a continual obligation to touch and to allow to penetrate
her, that she had to know what it was like. She quickly rolled the
condom down the length of his penis and slid it into her vagina.
She could feel it stretch her a little more than her husband. The
sensation wasn't necessarily more pleasurable, but it was different in a way that Rachel found appealing. She slowly rocked back
and forth, getting used to the feel of Secretluvur inside of her. He
reached down and grabbed her hips, squeezing them.

She was aware of the fact that she wasn't in the best shape
anymore and she was slightly self-conscious, but she didn't ask
him to move his hands. He seemed to be enjoying himself, to
like the way his fingers felt as they massaged the soft, doughy
area above her buttocks. And it was at that moment that she realized why it was that she was there with Secretluvur, why she'd
sought out another man to have sex with, and why she couldn't
bear having any kind of intimate contact with the man she had
sworn to love for the rest of her life. It had little to do with her.
Over the past year, she had come to the conclusion that her husband found no joy in having sex with her. She had become aware
of the fact that he no longer found her attractive or sexy, and this,

in turn, made her hate any sexual act with him. It was as if they were both just doing it to maintain their routine.

She moved her hips more quickly, then lifted herself up slightly and sat back down on Secretluvur's penis, forcing it in and out of her vagina with increased friction. He reached up and fondled her breasts through her dress and then said, "Turn around. I want to see that ass."

The low, almost growling quality in Secretluvur's voice made Rachel believe that he did, in fact, want to see her ass, no matter how unappealing it might have been to most men. So she obliged his request and turned around, keeping his penis in her. He said, "Oh, yeah, now lay down." Again she obliged, bending her torso down so that her face was against the bed as she rode his erection. Secretluvur groped her buttocks with hands that were strong and rough. Rachel could feel the calluses on his hands and she wondered what they were from. His job seemed white-collar enough. Maybe he was lying about his job, or maybe he just worked out a lot or played softball or something. Whatever the reason for them, she enjoyed the way they felt on her skin.

Secretluvur said, "Oh, baby, my God, that ass," and he began to move his hips with more force, slamming them against her as he thrust his erection into her. She felt his fingers slowly moving from the outside of her buttocks toward her anus. Her husband had attempted to have anal sex with her from time to time, and early in their relationship, she had indulged him on occasion. So she offered no protest when Secretluvur licked his index finger and put it into her anus up to the first knuckle, saying, "That is some hot shit, baby."

He made no move to go deeper with his finger or replace it with his penis. He was content to have sex with her in this manner for several minutes until he ejaculated. The force of his thrusts, the shape of his penis inside her, and the knowledge that he was so aroused by the site of her buttocks that he climaxed caused Rachel to have an orgasm at the same instant. It was one of the most intense she could remember, causing her legs to tremble slightly.

Secretluvur said, "Damn, baby, that was something."

Rachel said, "Yeah," as she climbed off of him, turned around, and moved up to lie on the pillow next to him. They were silent for several minutes, neither really knowing what to say to the other. If this was truly Secretluvur's first encounter with infidelity, then Rachel assumed it was reasonable that he wouldn't have anything to say, just as she didn't. She tried to conjure some amount of guilt for what she had done and found herself unable to. She had never seen herself as the type of person who could cheat on her husband, and as she lay there next to the man who just had his index finger in her anus and his penis in her vagina simultaneously, she realized that she was that type of person now.

Secretluvur eventually said, "So, I don't know how you want the night to go, but I can't really stay. I hope that's okay."

Rachel said, "Yeah. Not a problem," realizing only in that moment that she might have preferred to spend the night with Secretluvur.

He said, "Okay, I just want to make sure we cool, you know. Without getting into all of the stuff we probably shouldn't be talking about, I kind of have to get back to you-know-who."

She said, "Oh, oh, yeah, I guess that makes sense." Rachel hadn't given any thought to the possibility that Secretluvur might not have arranged to spend the entire night away from his wife and family, if he had one. He said, "But I would love to do this again if you want to. I mean, I don't know how you're feeling about everything right now, and you might need some time to think on it, but . . ." he leaned over, kissed her, and then said, "Damn, that was some hot shit right there."

Rachel said, "Yeah. We can meet up again. I guess we should just keep talking through the site."

He said, "Okay. So this is like an official . . . secret thing then?"

Rachel smiled and said, "Yeah. I guess so."

He kissed her one more time and then went to the bathroom, where he removed the condom, washed his penis, and zipped his pants back up. Before he left, he said, "Can I just feel that ass one more time?" Rachel allowed this. They shared one last kiss before he left.

Rachel stayed in the bed they just had sex in. She could smell Secretluvur in the sheets, on her hands, on her lips. She smiled. As she closed her eyes, drifting into a relaxed sleep, she was happy that she had had an orgasm with a black man; she was happy that she would have at least one more with him; she was happy that she didn't have to wake up next to her husband. She closed her eyes and breathed slowly, drifting into a contented sleep.

Allison Doss completed her latest post on Ana's Underground Grotto at 2:13 A.M. It was a detailed description of her first encounter with forced vomiting, including the clean and empty feeling she had immediately afterward. She explained that she understood mia would now be a friend of hers, just as ana already was. She uploaded the post and then went into the kitchen. Her parents and little brother were all asleep. She opened the refrigerator and saw that her mother had brought home a new peach cobbler. She left the lights off, took the peach cobbler, got a fork, and sat down at the kitchen table.

After eating half the cobbler, she found that her stomach ached. She forced herself to eat more until the entire thing was gone. She licked the spoon clean, rinsed it off in the sink, put it back in the silverware drawer, and then took the empty container the cobbler had come in to her bedroom and hid it under her bed, intending to throw it away in the dumpster behind her house tomorrow when no one was around.

She went to her purse and retrieved a bottle of ipecac syrup that she'd bought at CVS earlier in the day. In the bathroom, she drank a glass of water, following the instructions outlined on the back of the ipecac bottle, and then drank two tablespoonfuls of the syrup. She vomited within four minutes and she was happy.

chapter thirteen

Principal Ligorski began his Monday morning announcements by congratulating the Goodrich Odyssey of the Mind team on its second-place showing at a competition that weekend. And he ended them by encouraging the Goodrich football team to remain enthusiastic about the rest of the season and to prepare for their game against the Scott Shining Stars the following Friday, adding that the entire school should come out to show support for their team at the next game.

Most members of the team had used the weekend to reconcile themselves to their loss. Tanner Hodge had not. Instead, he obsessively thought about why they hadn't been able to overcome the Irving Aardvarks in a game he felt they should easily have won. Tanner convinced himself that all blame for the loss was to be placed with Tim Mooney and his decision not to play in the eighth-grade season. Having to deal with an entire morning of his classmates consoling him and telling him they were sure the following Friday would produce a win that would get the Olympians back on track only made Tanner angrier with Tim Mooney. By the time he found himself sitting across the cafeteria from Tim during his lunch period, Tanner could no longer suppress his rage.

He waited until Mrs. Rector, who was the only faculty member lunch monitor that day, was on the other side of the room, and then he took the orange he had sitting on his lunch tray and threw it toward Tim Mooney as he said, "Faggot." Instead of hitting the intended target, the orange struck Brandy Beltmeyer, who was sitting next to Tim, in the shoulder. Tim followed the orange's trajectory back to Tanner Hodge, who was walking away from his own table toward Tim, saying, "We lost because of you, homo."

Tim looked back to Brandy and said, "You okay?" She said, "Yeah. Don't get into it with him." Although up to that point Tim had found the anger of some of his classmates amusing, he no longer found any levity in it once it manifested itself in violence toward Brandy. Tim stood from his own table, bringing himself face-to-face with Tanner Hodge as he said, "You realize it couldn't have been my fault because I wasn't there, you idiot."

Tanner said, "Yeah, that's why it *was* your fault, fuckface. And if we don't make it to district it'll be because of this game."

Tim said, "Who cares?"

Tanner said, "I do, faggot," and then pushed Tim backward, causing him to fall over the bench part of his table onto the ground. Tanner took the opportunity to jump on top of Tim, swinging wildly. A crowd of students, Brandy included, immediately surrounded them. Some were screaming, some clapping, some silent in shock, having seen nothing like this in their lifetimes. The ruckus eventually gained the attention of Mrs. Rector. She had been a teacher in some capacity for almost fifteen years, and although she had seen her fair share of disagreements, arguing matches, and on occasion even a shove, she had never seen an altercation of this magnitude. Each of the boys involved was easily stronger than she was, and she knew it. In a minor panic, she reflexively did the only thing that came to mind, which is what she had been trained to do.

The year Eric Harris and Dylan Klebold killed twelve students and one teacher at Columbine High School, the school district that governed Goodrich Junior High School made mandatory the installation of panic buttons in locations throughout each of the schools in the district. The buttons were to be pressed in any situations of violence. Faculty members were made to undergo training each semester in order to ensure that they were knowledgeable about the locations of each of these buttons in their individual schools as well as properly refreshed on the protocol necessary to operate the buttons if a scenario should arise in which they might be needed. In addition to these panic buttons, each school was to employ a full-time armed security guard.

Mrs. Rector ran to the nearest of these panic buttons, entered her faculty code, which armed the button, and then pressed the button itself. The Goodrich PA system emitted an alarm, causing most of the students surrounding the fight to disperse, but the fight itself continued. Mrs. Rector did as she'd been trained to do and remained by the button she pressed. She recalled the exact phrase from her Emergency Violence Scenario course: "Remain near the emergency indicator and wait for armed security to arrive. Never attempt to approach the situation of violence."

In the parking lot, Officer Blidd, Goodrich Junior High School's armed security guard, was enjoying a Newport cigarette when he heard the alarm sound and received the accompanying signal on his two-way radio. This was the first time he had ever been called into action in his ten years as an armed security guard. Not knowing what to expect as he entered the building, but assuming it would be something akin to a Columbine massacre if a member of the faculty saw fit to press a panic button, he drew his gun and, being a religious man, said a quick prayer asking his god to aid him and to keep him safe.

By the time Officer Blidd arrived in the cafeteria, Tim had used his advantage in both size and general athletic ability to turn the momentum of the fight in his favor. He was kneeling on Tanner Hodge's chest, striking him in the face repeatedly.

Not sure if either of the students was armed, Officer Blidd approached them cautiously, allowing Tim to land several more punches than he would have otherwise, knocking Tanner Hodge into unconsciousness. Once he was close enough to assess the situation as a standard fight between two male students, Officer Blidd holstered his gun, said, "Break it up," and pulled Tim off Tanner Hodge, who remained unconscious on the ground.

Brandy Beltmeyer watched the event unfold. Although she had no taste for violence, being protected by Tim, and watching his brutal victory over Tanner Hodge, made him seem much more attractive than he already was to her. She hoped that he wouldn't get into any serious trouble over this, because she found herself wanting to see him again as soon as possible.

Officer Blidd found it slightly absurd that he had to handcuff both of the boys involved before taking them to the principal's office, but that was the protocol his training dictated for any kind of violent altercation. He valued his job and didn't want to be held responsible for any wrongdoing that could result in his losing it. So he removed two pairs of handcuffs from his belt and said, "Can you put your hands behind your back, please?" The students watched as Tim complied, none of them having seen anything like this before. With Tim handcuffed, Officer Blidd moved to Tanner Hodge to find that he was regaining consciousness. Officer Blidd said, "Sorry, kid, I have to cuff you."

Tanner said, "What?"

Officer Blidd could tell he was more than shaken from the beating he'd sustained. He said, "You were in a fight. I have to cuff you and take you to Principal Ligorski."

Tanner said, "Are you serious?"

Officer Blidd said, "Yeah, sorry. I have to."

Tanner Hodge offered no resistance as Officer Blidd hand-cuffed him, stood him up, and then walked both him and Tim down the hallway to Mr. Ligorski's office, with Mrs. Rector fol-lowing them to give her account of the event for the official re-cord—which was that she hadn't seen the initial moments of the episode, but it was her opinion, judging from the aftermath, that Tim was clearly the aggressor. She added that she knew nothing about the nature of the brawl, or the reason for its occurrence, before going back to her classroom, slightly shaken and hoping that she wouldn't be further involved.

Mr. Ligorski brought each student in individually to hear his account of the interaction. Tim's recounting of the incident was the more accurate of the two, allowing for some embellish-ment only in the description of the damage caused to Brandy Beltmeyer from the orange thrown by Tanner. Tanner's account was much less truthful, taking any opportunity he could to paint Tim as the initial assailant and provoker of the entire event. After hearing both of their renditions, Principal Ligorski came to the conclusion that they were both to receive punishment in the form of three-day suspensions, which, for Tanner, also carried with it the added punishment of ineligibility for the upcoming game against the Scott Shining Stars. Both Tanner and Tim were then made to undergo individual, hour-long counseling sessions with Ms. Perinot, the school counselor.

Tim's father was in his office, reading reviews of restaurants in neighboring cities that might serve as possible romantic set-tings for his second date with Dawn Clint, when he received a phone call from Laurie Fenner, Principal Ligorski's receptionist, informing him that his son, Tim, had been involved in behavior that required disciplinary action. That action, Kent was further informed, involved Tim being held in the principal's office until a parent or guardian could pick him up from school. Kent told his supervisor that he had a family emergency that required immediate attention and took the rest of the day off. He used his drive to Goodrich Junior High School to calm himself, to defuse the anger that ignited almost instantaneously in him. He thought that he and his son had been doing well the past week or so, certainly better than they had been since Lydia Mooney moved to California. He couldn't help thinking that, if Tim had still been playing football, everything would be fine, none of this would have happened.

When Kent Mooney arrived at Goodrich Junior High School, he was told that Ms. Perinot, the school counselor, wanted to speak with him. She told him that after talking with his son, Tim, for an hour or so about various things in his life that she felt led to his violent outburst, she came to the conclusion that he might be suffering from some form of clinical depression. She recommended that Kent take Tim to see a psychiatrist, due to the fact that she was not qualified to give a valid medical diagnosis.

Kent, deriving some hope from Ms. Perinot's suggestion, asked her if she thought his depression might be the cause behind his decision to quit football. Ms. Perinot couldn't be sure, but she told Kent Mooney that depression in teens, as well as in adults, can be the cause of erratic behavior or behavior that is highly abnormal for the person afflicted. She told Kent that he was, of course, free to take Tim to anyone he wished if he sought further help for his son, based on her suggestion, but she recommended Dr. Ray Fong specifically. She had known Ray for several years, since high school. They had engaged in a brief romantic relationship during their college years that ended amicably and, although Ray Fong was married and had children and Ms. Perinot had a boyfriend of four years, they still met once every few months for drinks or dinner that led to sexual intercourse. Ms. Perinot handed Kent Mooney Dr. Ray Fong's business card and thought about the last time they had sex. She had asked him to ejaculate on her breasts, and he had obliged her.

Sex with her boyfriend was never pornographic, and she used her encounters with Ray Fong to explore her more carnal desires. She thought that Ray probably used her for the same purpose.

Kent found his son waiting in Principal Ligorski's office. He said, "Come on, let's go home." Nothing was said by either Kent or his father on the drive back to their house until Kent said, "Your counselor thinks you're depressed. Do you?"

Tim said, "I don't know. She told me the same thing."

Kent said, "Do you want to see a shrink?"

Tim didn't know if he was depressed or not. He felt that, if he had been, it had been fleeting. He had experienced a strange feeling of detachment from his own life after finding out that his mother was getting remarried, but he felt that detachment slipping away the more time he spent with Brandy Beltmeyer. Nonetheless, the prospect of having someone he could talk with about anything that might be happening in his life was interesting to him. Brandy was beginning to fill that role, but he still felt uncomfortable about bringing up anything regarding his mother with anyone. He said, "I don't know. I guess."

Kent said, "Okay, I'll set it up."

Tim went to his bedroom and logged on to *World of Warcraft*, looking forward to using his suspension as a time to do some valuable midday raiding and rep grinding. Kent called Dr. Ray Fong and set up an appointment for his son the following day. He hung up hoping that whatever psychological mending Tim needed to get back to his former self would happen soon enough for him to return to playing football before the end of the season.

Dr. Fong's office was exactly what Tim expected: dark wood bookshelves, various diplomas on the wall, and a couch. As Tim came into his office, Dr. Fong said, "Hello, Tim. How are you doing today?"

Tim said, "Fine."

Dr. Fong said, "Good. That's good to hear. So why don't you have a seat wherever you feel comfortable, and if you don't mind,

I'd like to use our first session to just get to know you a little bit and to give you a chance to tell me anything that you want to about you, or your father or your mother, or anything that might be going on at school. Just anything, really, that you feel you want to talk about. That okay?"

Tim said, "Yeah," and sat down on Dr. Fong's couch.

Dr. Fong took out a small notepad and a ballpoint pen, crossed one leg over the other in his chair, and said, "Okay, then, let's begin."

Tim was surprised by how clichéd the entire situation was, how much it seemed like a scene from any movie he had ever seen that involved a psychiatrist and a patient. He said, "Well, what do you want to know?"

Dr. Fong said, "I want to know what you think you should tell me, Tim. Whatever's important in your life right now."

Tim said, "Well, I guess, my dad thinks I should be playing football. That's probably the most important thing to him right now."

Dr. Fong said, "And how do you feel about football? Is it important to you?"

Tim said, "It was last year, but this year I guess it's not as important. It actually kind of seems less than important, really. Pointless, in fact. I guess most things are pointless, though."

Dr. Fong said, "And what are some of the things that aren't pointless to you?"

Tim said, "I don't know. I play *World of Warcraft*."

Dr. Fong said, "And this is a game of some kind, a Nintendo game maybe?"

Tim said, "No, it's a video game, but not Nintendo. It's a computer game. You play it online with millions of other people."

Dr. Fong said, "And you're probably very good at this game?"

Tim said, "I guess. It's not really about skill, though. It's more just about how much time you put in and how familiar you can get with the different enemies and stuff in the game."

Dr. Fong said, "And these other people you play the game with, are they your friends from school?"

Tim said, "No. They're just my friends in the game. I mean, they're my friends, but I've never met any of them in RL."

Dr. Fong said, "RL?"

Tim said, "Real life."

Dr. Fong said, "I see. And do you have any friends in . . . RL, at school perhaps, that you interact with as often as you interact with your friends in the game?"

Tim said, "I used to, but since I stopped playing football, I've kind of lost most of those friends. There's a girl, though, that I've kind of been hanging out with. She's cool."

Dr. Fong said, "Very good. And do your mother and father approve of her?"

Tim said, "We just started hanging out. My dad's cool with it. My mom isn't really in the house anymore. She moved to California with another guy."

Dr. Fong said, "I see. I didn't see that in the file I got from Counselor Perinot."

Tim said, "I haven't really told anyone about it."

Dr. Fong said, "Well, I'm glad you're comfortable enough here to tell me. It's important that you feel free to discuss anything you feel is relevant to your current emotional landscape."

Tim had held the secret of his mother's remarriage for some time. He felt that this was as good a time as any, and as good an environment as any, to divulge it. He said, "I also found out, through my mom's Facebook page, that she's getting remarried to the guy she moved to California with."

Dr. Fong said, "I see. And what is your reaction to that?"

Tim said, "At first I was pretty sad, I guess—or just confused, really. Then I started not to care that much about her or about anything. Have you ever seen 'The Pale Blue Dot'?"

Dr. Fong said, "No. I haven't. Is this a movie? Or a video game?"

Tim said, "No, it's this thing—it's a thing that Carl Sagan wrote and then some people made videos to go with it and put them on YouTube."

Dr. Fong said, "I see. And is this something you used to watch with your mother?"

Tim said, "No, it's something I just started getting into not too long ago. It basically lays out the fact that we're all insignificant and nothing we really do matters in the grand scheme of existence. It was what kind of made me get over the fact that my mom is with some other guy now. Wait, do you tell my dad anything we talk about in here?"

Dr. Fong said, "No, I don't. Anything said in this room stays in this room, between you and me."

Tim said, "Okay, cool, because my dad doesn't know about my mom getting remarried."

For the remainder of the hour, Tim and Dr. Fong discussed Brandy Beltmeyer, the Olympian football team, Greg Cherry, California, *World of Warcraft*, the altercation between Tim and Tanner Hodge, and the awkward silences that he and his father seemed to have become adept at in the past months.

As the session came to a close, Dr. Fong told Tim that in just the hour they'd spent together he was able to come to a diagnosis of clinical depression. Dr. Fong told Tim that he hoped he felt comfortable enough with the environment they had created to continue seeing him. Dr. Fong recommended a treatment that included a continuation of their sessions, in conjunction with the use of an antidepressant called Anafranil. Dr. Fong explained that the drug was used to treat patients diagnosed with depression, as well as obsessive-compulsive disorder, and he also found it to be especially effective with depression in teens.

In actuality, Dr. Fong knew the drug was no more effective than Zoloft, Prozac, or Luvox in teens. But his wife worked as a pharmaceutical sales representative for Mallinckrodt Pharmaceuticals, the company that manufactured the drug Anafranil.

When given a choice among antidepressants, Dr. Fong always prescribed Anafranil in order to boost his wife's sales numbers, even if it was only by a small increment. Dr. Fong wrote Tim a prescription and told him to schedule an appointment for the following week, which Tim did.

When Tim's father picked him up from Dr. Fong's office, Tim handed him the prescription. Kent said, "What's this?"

Tim said, "Some kind of antidepressant."

Kent liked the fact that Dr. Fong had wasted no time in administering concrete treatment to his son. If all that was needed to get him back on the field was a pill, then this process would be easier than Kent had first imagined. Kent said, "Okay," and drove to the CVS pharmacy nearest to their house.

Before going to sleep that night, Tim looked at bottle of pills. He was curious about their effect. Dr. Fong had told him that the pills must be taken regularly for a few weeks before any effects would be felt, but the swallowing of the first pill was symbolic to Tim. It was an admission that something was wrong, that he could not handle whatever he was feeling without the aid of drugs. Tim swallowed his first Anafranil, and as he was lying in bed he took out his phone and sent Brandy a message on her Freyja account that read, "I missed eating lunch with you today." She sent a reply that read, "Me, too."

chapter
fourteen

Five weeks passed.

Tim Mooney was starting to feel less disconnected from his life and also less concerned with the things that had made him feel this way. From time to time, he even imagined what it would be like to meet Greg Cherry, and he came to the conclusion that Greg Cherry was probably a very nice person if he possessed qualities that lured Lydia Mooney all the way to California to live with him and even marry him.

Kent saw the change happening in his son. He was less brooding—not necessarily happier, but certainly things between them seemed to be more civil, more amicable. Kent continued to date

Dawn Clint. Things were going well between them, so well that Kent knew the next time they saw each other would likely result in a sexual encounter. He felt that their last date could have ended in this manner had he wanted it to, but he was too nervous. He had convinced himself that, after such a long time without sex, he might not be able to perform. Since that last date, Kent had visited his doctor, told him about his concerns, and asked if he could get a prescription for Viagra. His doctor obliged him, writing a prescription that could be refilled five times for five 100-milligram tablets. Kent was excited to see Dawn again.

Dawn was excited to see Kent again as well. She found it slightly strange that at the end of their last date, after a long kiss at her front door accompanied by her giving his buttocks a playful squeeze, and an outright invitation to enter her house, Kent declined her offer. She decided that he was probably nervous about engaging in a sexual relationship with the first new woman after his wife. This served to further reinforce her estimation of Kent as a nice guy. She was happy to take their relationship as slow as Kent dictated. She kept herself busy by focusing on her daughter's career.

The producers of the reality show *Undiscovered* contacted Dawn to inform her that they found Hannah's application to be among a chosen few that exhibited certain qualities they were looking for. Hannah was being advanced to the next round of the casting process, which included the production of a short video showcasing some of her talents and her home life. After the video's review, the producers would then decide if she would move on to the next round of casting, which would consist of a personal interview with the executive producers of the show in Los Angeles. When Hannah was informed of all of this, she asked her mother if she could post something about it on her website to let her fans know that she was about to be famous. Her mother discouraged her from doing this, remembering her own experience with the television pilot she'd had a role in. She told Hannah that she hadn't made it on the TV show yet, and even if she did, it was a much more celebrity-esque thing to do to let her website fans find out about it for themselves. Dawn had a feeling that Hannah's website might hold her back in the future. She thought about shutting it down, erasing any evidence of its existence, but the money generated by the website was good, and Dawn had seen countless compromising photos and videos of beauty pageant contestants and other minor celebrities surface into the mainstream media that only served to augment their exposure. She chose to leave it up.

Hannah continued to exchange illicit text messages with Chris Truby. This exchange escalated to include images and videos of various forms of masturbation from both parties. Hannah did all of this in the hope that she would eventually have sexual intercourse with Chris. They attempted it twice, but both times the act turned into some version of oral sex or masturbation, the last one culminating in Chris asking her to insert her finger into his anus while he masturbated. Hannah found this request disgusting but obliged him, assuming she would be able to maneuver herself onto his erect penis. Instead he ejaculated within seconds of her finger being inserted. She was becoming discouraged with the situation, but still felt that Chris was the best candidate with whom to lose her virginity. Hannah kept her dealings with Chris a secret from any of her Olympianne squadmates. She would tell them about it once she had accomplished her goal, and she would omit any of the things that she found strange or disgusting, such as the insertion of her finger into Chris's anus at his behest.

•   •   •

Chris Truby found his interest waning in any form of pornography that didn't involve women humiliating or penetrating men. He began to find that the only way he could achieve an erection and eventual orgasm was to at least imagine being tied down, spit on, abused, or otherwise compromised at the hand of a dominant woman. He understood that this was making his encounters with Hannah difficult, and he tried various methods to reorganize the way he thought about standard intercourse. He extensively researched masturbation techniques on various websites designed to help men associate sexual pleasure with vaginal intercourse.

The most common of these methods seemed to involve a product called the Fleshlight, which was a latex cylinder with an opening at one end that was fashioned into the shape of a vagina. The opening was designed for a man to insert his erect penis so as to simulate vaginal sex. Not having the access to purchase such a device, Chris researched how to build his own and was directed to a website with intricate instructions. The easiest of these to build was only good for a single use, but this was acceptable to him. The makeshift device's two main components were a Nerf ball and a cardboard paper towel tube. Chris had both of these items, and he found it easier to make the device than he thought it would be. He shredded the Nerf ball as instructed into small pieces, discarding the outer pieces of the ball that were coated in paint. Chris used a layer of duct tape to seal one end of the paper towel tube, filled the tube with the shredded Nerf foam, and then pumped a generous amount of hand lotion into the tube. The instructions on the website he read also said that, to further simulate the feeling of an actual vagina, the entire device could be microwaved for forty-five seconds. Not wanting to alert his parents to what he was doing, he omitted this step. And, to further conceal his activities, he hid the used devices in his backpack until he left for school the next morning, at which time he would throw them into his neighbor's trash can, fearing that there might be some reason for his parents to look through their own trash and discover his makeshift vaginas.

Once he had the first device built, he achieved an erection by watching one of his favorite videos, which included a man sealed in a latex vacuum bag, with only one opening in the material for his mouth, drinking urine directly from a woman's urethra as she squatted over his face. With an erection achieved, Chris held his device on the bed in the estimated position that Hannah's vagina would occupy if they were to have vaginal intercourse in the missionary position. He opened an image of Hannah's face on his phone and set it down on his bed under his own face, in a rough estimation of where her head might be if they were actually having sex. Chris thrust his penis into the cardboard tube filled with Nerf foam and lotion, forcing himself to think about sex with Hannah. After the fourth such attempt with the fourth such device, Chris was able to achieve orgasm. He felt that he would eventually be able to have sex with Hannah.

Allison Doss continued to implement forced vomiting in her dieting strategy. She had gained a certain amount of expertise and felt that no one could possibly know what she was doing. Although she preferred using the ipecac syrup to induce vomiting, she mastered the skill of using her own finger to trigger the desired reaction. She found it necessary in certain situations, where she hadn't anticipated food being served but was clearly expected to eat.

Despite the pleasure she got from eating and then forcing herself to vomit, she found it more and more difficult to control her cravings for food. She attributed this to the fact that she was allowing herself to taste so many things. When she had limited her diet to celery, tuna, and water, she'd found it easy to forget what other things tasted like and therefore simple to have no cravings. Allison convinced herself that she would eventually wean herself from forced vomiting, but not yet. She was still enjoying it and she felt that she could still control her cravings.

She sent Brandon Lender ten more messages on Facebook. He responded to none of them.

Brandy Beltmeyer viewed Tim's suspension as a sacrifice he made in the service of protecting her honor. It made him immensely more attractive to her, and in the weeks that passed, she spent as much time as she could with him. But her mother, Patricia, made it virtually impossible for her to find more than a night a week and some extra hours after school. She told Tim about her mother's overbearing nature and made sure he understood that he should only ever communicate with her through her Freyja Myspace account. All of her other methods of communication were monitored by her mother. Tim agreed to keep their relationship a secret from her mother, if only because he wanted it to continue.

Brandy began to use her Freyja account almost exclusively to communicate with Tim, abandoning most of her other Myspace friends and neglecting her blogs and posts. She came to understand that she'd created the account at a time in her life when she felt very alone and it had served its purpose. It found friends for her and gave her interaction with people who valued what she had to say. Tim had replaced these people, and he had replaced them in a more meaningful way. He was real, and the things they discussed were not lies or based on a false identity. She didn't feel as alone as she had when her parents first moved. Eventually, she even removed some of the friends she had gained who were interested only in having sexually explicit conversations with her. She deleted all of her e-mail conversations with these friends and all of her own blog entries as well. She even removed all of her photo albums and replaced her profile picture with an image of a painting of Freyja she'd found online.

She and Tim shared their first kiss in the Goodrich Junior High School south parking lot one day after school, and after that they agreed to consider themselves an official couple. This designation included many behaviors they had already adopted, such as sitting together at lunch and leaving notes in each other's lockers. But it also included new behaviors, such as holding hands and publicly recognizing each other as boyfriend and girlfriend.

They were content to kiss from time to time and do nothing beyond this. They each found happiness in the other's company, and they felt no need to push what they had into a level of physical intimacy that neither of them felt comfortable with yet. And although Tim might have felt some sexual urges at one point, he found that they were waning. It was a side effect of the Anafranil. He was aware of it and not altogether disappointed. He assumed a sexual relationship would only complicate his life, and he was happy with the level of simplicity he had achieved.

Patricia had gained a few new members in her Parents Against The Internet watch-group. She used her relationship with her daughter as an example of how parents and their children should interact with regard to the Internet and its use. She remained unaware of her daughter's secret Myspace account.

Don Truby saved enough money to purchase a Girlfriend Experience with Angelique Ice and considered himself lucky that his wife was leaving for another Saturday night so soon after the trip that had allowed Don his first encounter with Angelique. Once again, however, Rachel did not visit her sister. Instead, she made a second rendezvous with Secretluvur, and this time she spent the entire night with him, just as her husband did with Angelique Ice. Don and Rachel both found their experiences with their respective partners fulfilling in ways that the same experience within their marriage never could be. When they returned home the following morning, after each of their acts of infidelity, they were surprised to find that their relationship seemed to have improved somehow. They were more cordial with each other and happier in general. They each realized that sexual encounters outside their relationship made their relationship itself far more tolerable. They resigned themselves to living lives of constant infidelity, perhaps with Secretluvur and Angelique Ice or perhaps with multiple partners. Rachel had been receiving responses to her profile on AshleyMadison.com from several potential partners. As well, Don had performed several more searches on TheEroticReview.com and found a moderate number of prostitutes that offered the Girlfriend Experience, each of them unique and interesting to him for reasons that included varied hair color, tattoos, piercings, breast implants, and so on. For both Rachel and Don, the exact natures of their new adulterous lives had yet to reveal themselves, but they had found some happiness that didn't exist before in their relationship.

After two weeks of his wife, Tracey, withholding sex, Jim Vance agreed to schedule a vasectomy. He made the appointment as far in the future as he could, giving himself ample time to prepare psychologically for what he assumed would be a terrible ordeal.

Danny Vance and Brooke Benton had been content to scale their physical relationship back to where it was at the beginning of the year. As a result, Danny found it much less difficult to concentrate on football. In addition, Coach Quinn realized that no matter how much he wanted to teach Danny and the rest of the team a lesson about obeying their superiors, he was in contention for another head-coaching job at a high school in a neighboring district. His record this season would mean more to the athletic director of that district than any lesson he could teach his players. So he allowed Danny to pass and pass often. This decision fueled the Goodrich Junior High School Olympians through a five-game winning streak, as they defeated the Scott Shining Stars, the Lefler Lions, the Lux Lightning Bolts, the Mickle Missiles, and a team Danny considered to be among the two best teams in their district, the Dawes Trojans. This winning streak left them with a six-and-one record going into the final two games of the season against the Pound Squires and the Culler Cougars. Danny knew they could lose one of these games and still make it to the district playoffs. Of the two teams they had left to play, he felt the Squires would give them the most trouble.

chapter
fifteen

The Monday after the Olympians' win over the Dawes Trojans, Allison Doss was standing at the dry-erase board in Mr. Donnelly's geometry class, attempting to find the locus of an equation that was part of that day's workbook assignment, when her back began to hurt. The pain was minor at first. Allison dismissed it as muscle soreness from the previous Friday, when she'd accidentally fallen from the top of a three-person pyramid while cheering at the football game. She wrote $x^2 + y^2 - 6x + 4y - 23 = 0$ on the dry-erase board, received a satisfactory nod and congratulation from Mr. Donnelly for providing the correct answer, and then took her seat, the pain intensifying slightly. She rubbed her lower back for the rest of the class period and dry-swallowed two Advil caplets from her purse, but by the end of Mr. Donnelly's geometry class she was in an abnormal amount of pain.

Thinking that the pain might be related to an impending

menstrual cycle, and having no tampons in her purse, Allison visited the restroom between classes with the intent of purchasing a tampon from the vending machine and inserting it just in case her period was beginning. Once inside the girl's restroom, she purchased the tampon and went into a stall to insert it. As she pulled her pants and underwear down, she thought briefly about the fact that the last thing inside her vagina was Brandon Lender's penis. She wished that he would respond to her Facebook messages.

Just as she was about to insert the tampon, the pain in her back intensified to such a degree that she doubled over in pain. It seemed to move through her back and into her lower abdomen, which made her positive that it was related to her menstrual cycle. But in the past, it had never caused pain to this degree. She wondered if it had anything to do with the forced vomiting that had become a habit for her. If it was related, she felt that enduring intense physical pain every so often was a small price to pay. This was the last thought she had before she felt a heavy flow of blood stream down her thigh. She quickly rolled off a handful of toilet paper and did her best to stop the blood from making its way to her pants and underwear, which were around her ankles. Looking at the blood on the toilet paper, she noted that it was an odd shade of brown, much darker than any blood she had seen before. Along with the blood there were some smaller pieces of semisolid material. Allison had no idea what this was. Her assumption was that it was some kind of mucus associated with menstruation that she hadn't expelled during any of her previous menstrual cycles. She became nervous and frightened, slightly frantic.

She threw the bloodied toilet paper into the toilet and flushed it, but still felt blood flowing out of her vagina and down her legs. The pain in her back and abdomen were now at a level of intensity that made it difficult for her to concentrate on what she was doing. As she tried again to roll off another handful of toilet paper, the pain reached a point of intensity that overwhelmed Allison, causing her to collapse in the stall unconscious. She remained there for almost five minutes until a fellow student, Regina Sotts, happened into the restroom to urinate quickly before her next class and noticed a pair of shoes sticking out from under one of the stalls. After knocking on the door and inquiring as to the condition of the stall's occupant—and receiving no answer—Regina kneeled down in a prone position that allowed her to see under the door. Seeing that Allison was unconscious and that she was lying in a slowly expanding pool of blood, Regina alerted the first member of the Goodrich faculty she saw in the hall outside, Mrs. Langston, who then notified both Principal Ligorski and Mrs. Heldinberg, the school nurse, who assessed the situation and quickly decided that an ambulance was needed.

Allison regained consciousness as two paramedics lifted her onto a gurney, strapped her down, and rushed her through the halls of Goodrich Junior High School to an ambulance waiting outside. Allison was frightened and uncertain about what exactly was occurring, but above all she was glad this was happening while virtually all other students were in class, so that only the faculty members involved and Regina Sotts would know what was happening. She wondered how long she could keep it a secret from the rest of the school. She was not looking forward to the embarrassment of explaining it to anyone.

The paramedics asked Allison a series of questions dealing primarily with what she had had to eat that day, if she had ever experienced a menstrual cycle before, and so on. It wasn't until they had her in the ambulance that one of them asked, "Are you sexually active?" Allison had to pause for a moment before answering. She said, "No. I mean, not really."

The paramedic said, "I know this is really personal, but we have to know the answers to these questions if we're going to be able to help you, okay?"

Allison said, "Okay."

The paramedic said, "So we need to know if you've had sexual intercourse with anyone. And there's nothing wrong with that if you have. You're not in any kind of trouble or anything. We just need to know."

Allison said, "I mean, yeah, I guess I have."

The paramedic said, "Okay,"

Allison felt another wave of intense pain in her back and abdomen and again passed out. When she regained consciousness this time she was in a hospital, nude except for a surgical gown. Her mother and father were present. Her mother was crying and holding her hand. Allison noticed a needle in the back of her hand. She followed the tube connected to the needle to find a bag filled with some kind of fluid that was flowing directly into her vein. She assumed it to be some kind of medication or nutrients. The thought of something going into her body that she couldn't expel at will made her nauseous. She thought about tearing the needle out, but she knew that would bring up questions from her parents and a reinsertion by a doctor at some point. She hated needles and was thankful that she had been unconscious when it had been inserted the first time. With some concentration on the thought of the needle in her hand, she was certain she could feel the contents of the bag flowing into her vein and then being circulated through her body, swimming through her blood. She was on the verge of vomiting but held it back. She felt better having control over the act, comforted that she wasn't completely powerless in the situation.

Allison said, "What happened?"

Her mother, Liz, said, "We don't know, baby. The doctor just said somebody found you at school bleeding in the bathroom. We're waiting for them to come in and tell us what's going on."

Allison said, "Am I okay?" It was then that she realized she'd stopped bleeding. She looked at the needle in the back of her hand and wished that the bleeding hadn't stopped. She could accept the thought of fluid coming into her body if some of it was also leaving in equal or greater measure.

Her father, Neal, said, "They think so. The doctor's supposed to be in here in a second. How do you feel?"

Her eyes never left the needle in the back of her hand. Allison perceived it to be throbbing with the tick of a clock that was hanging on the wall over the door in her room, pumping her body full of things she couldn't get rid of, bloating her, making her thick and watery. She wanted to tell her father that she felt fat and disgusting, but she said, "I guess I feel okay. I just want to know what's happening."

Her mother said, "So do we, baby, so do we."

Dr. Michael Stern came into the room holding Allison's chart, shutting the door behind him. He sat down and said, "Hi. I'm Dr. Stern. How are you feeling, Allison?"

Allison said, "Okay, I guess. Am I, like, okay, though?"

Dr. Stern said, "The short answer is yes. The longer answer is a little more complicated."

Liz said, "What does that mean?"

Dr. Stern said, "It means that I need to tell you a few things that might be a little shocking, but the main thing to keep in mind here is that your daughter is going to be fine."

Neal said, "Okay."

Dr. Stern said, "Allison, you had what's called an ectopic pregnancy that self-terminated."

Liz said, "Pregnancy? What? How? Allison, are you . . . ?"

Allison immediately began crying. She said, "I'm sorry, Mom."

Neal said, "I can't believe this. You were pregnant? How many . . . I don't even know what to say. This is just . . ."

Dr. Stern said, "Again, I know this is a difficult thing to hear, but you have to remember that the most important thing here is that your daughter is okay. An ectopic pregnancy means that the fertilized egg develops in a place other than the uterus. In

Allison's case, it was growing in one of her Fallopian tubes. It's actually very serious and if it's not caught in time it can be extremely bad. So the fact that your pregnancy self-terminated was actually a very good thing. It probably saved your life. We did notice that you're a little undernourished, which can sometimes happen with an ectopic pregnancy—the fetus, because it's growing in an environment that's less than optimal, can sometimes take more than it normally would from the mother's nutrient supply. Do you have any questions about anything?"

Allison, still crying, said, "Can I go home?"

Dr. Stern said, "The pregnancy was only in about the fifth week, and it doesn't look like it caused any excessive damage to your Fallopian tube, but we'd like to keep you here overnight for observation, just to be on the safe side."

Allison said, "I want to go home."

Liz said, "They have to keep you here."

Allison said, "Will you guys stay with me?"

Neal said, "I can't believe . . . I just can't." Neal began to cry. It was the first time Allison had seen her father cry. She began to sob harder at the sight of it.

Dr. Stern said, "If you need anything, just have a nurse page me. And obviously take as much time as you need." Dr. Stern left.

Neal said, "Alli, I'm glad you're going to be okay, but I can't stay here tonight. I just—I don't know what to think. You were my little girl."

Allison said, "I still am, Daddy."

Neal said, "I don't think so," and left the room.

Allison began to cry convulsively. She said, "Mom, will you stay with me?"

Liz said, "Yes, baby." She hugged her daughter.

Allison said, "Does Daddy hate me?"

Liz said, "No. He loves you. He's just a little confused. So am I. Alli, how could you do this?"

Allison said, "I'm so sorry."

Her mother stayed through the night with her, sleeping in a chair in the corner of the room. Allison didn't fall asleep for a long time into the night. She stared at the ceiling, trying not to think of the needle in her hand, of the fluids being pumped into her body. She thought about the fact that Dr. Stern had never mentioned the possibility of anorexia or bulimia being the cause of her miscarriage, and of the fact that these things hadn't even been detected by the doctors. Once she left the hospital she would still have those things; she would still have control.

Liz went home to pick up some supplies for the night, and then stopped by Goodrich Junior High School to collect Allison's things before coming back to the hospital. Among them was Allison's phone. While her mother slept, Allison logged into her Angels of Ana account and began composing a post about her experience with the miscarriage and about how proud she was that the doctors hadn't detected her eating disorder. She complained about being fed intravenously but claimed that she would get the weight back off as soon as she left the hospital the following morning. Within a few minutes of uploading her post, she had two responses, each one congratulating her on keeping her secret and on maintaining the proper attitude about losing the few pounds she might be gaining while in the hospital. This support from girls she felt were her peers was important to Allison. It was support she knew she would get nowhere else.

After reading the responses, she opened her Facebook application and found that she still had no response from Brandon Lender to any of the multiple messages she had sent him. She took the opportunity to send him another message, one that carried enough gravity to perhaps garner a response. This one read, "I just had your miscarriage." Two minutes later she received his response, which read, "Whoa, that is some seriously fucked up shit." She was happy that he responded and took it as a sign that he was still interested in her.

As she began to feel the exhaustion of the ordeal setting in, she closed her eyes and thought again of that day at SeaWorld when she was younger and her father had bought her an ice-cream cone without her having to ask. She wondered if her father would ever see her as that little girl again and knew that the answer was no. She would never be that little girl again.

chapter
sixteen

Dawn Clint shot almost thirty minutes of new footage of her daughter answering various questions about her goals in the entertainment industry, performing various activities in and around Goodrich Junior High School, and wearing different outfits, all at the request of the producers of the reality show *Undiscovered*.

The most important and rigid of these requests, however, was that the video submission be no longer than five minutes. Having only rudimentary video-editing skills, Dawn was in the process of looking for a professional video editor when her daughter, Hannah, informed her that her friend Chris Truby was very skilled at video editing and would probably be happy to do it. Dawn was skeptical of allowing a thirteen-year-old boy to edit what could be the most important piece of video that her daughter had yet appeared in, but there were still a few weeks before the video was to be turned in and she decided that if Chris did a bad job she would still have time to hire a professional editor. Dawn made a copy of the video file containing all of the footage and e-mailed it to Hannah, along with footage of her performance as Annie in the local production of *Annie* from the year before.

As she e-mailed the file, she thought about the last time she had sex with the theater director. It was at least five months ago. She hoped that she wouldn't have to do it again, for reasons that included her burgeoning feelings for Kent Mooney as well as her desire to see her daughter succeed on a level higher than the local community theater.

Hannah sent Chris a text message that read, "Want 2 edit my video for the reality show?" Chris replied with a text message that read, "Sure, want 2 come over and help 2night?" Chris assumed that at some point after editing the video, he and Hannah would engage in some kind of sexual interaction, and he was anxious to attempt intercourse, confident in his ability to perform after having practiced with his various makeshift vaginas. Hannah replied with a text message that read, "Y."

Dawn picked Hannah up from school and drove her to Chris Truby's house. She said, "It can only be five minutes, but make sure he gets all of your outfits in it and make sure he gets the answers to the questions that were in the producers' e-mails." Hannah said, "I will, Mom," then got out of the car and went into Chris Truby's house, where she was greeted by both Don and Rachel Truby. She had been to Chris's house three times before, and each time she had noticed something distant between Don and Rachel. This time they seemed much happier to her, closer. Don said, "Chris is in his room. He has his computer all ready to go."

Rachel said, "So this is pretty exciting. A reality show."

Hannah said, "Yeah, I guess so. I mean, I'm not on the show or anything yet, but it could be really cool, you know, like a start to my career and everything."

Rachel said, "Well, good luck. We're pulling for you."

Hannah said, "Thanks," and went into Chris's bedroom.

Chris was sitting at his computer when she walked in. He had already broken the large video file Hannah had e-mailed him into smaller clips and was in the process of making a rough assembly of them in an order he thought made more sense than the order in which they were originally presented. He had trimmed many of the clips down, as well, and added a selected portion of Hannah's performance as Annie. The total run time of the new clip was twelve minutes. He told all of this to Hannah and then said, "So you should watch it, then tell me what you think we should cut out." Before he played the clip for her, they talked briefly about Allison Doss and her episode in the girls' restroom. Neither of them knew exactly what happened, but had both heard that it was serious enough to have paramedics take her away. Allison had not updated her Facebook and had posted nothing on Twitter, so no one knew exactly what was happening with her.

After the conversation about Allison, Chris played his version of the video back for Hannah, who claimed to feel that all of it was integral. She found it too difficult to make any decisions about what should be omitted. Chris said, "Okay, let me take another pass at it and I'll see what I can do." Hannah sat on his bed and watched as he worked. She didn't understand the subtleties and nuances of what he was doing, but was able to follow most of the broader actions he was taking. She offered protests a few times when she perceived him to be cutting out a portion she found especially interesting. In these cases, Chris told her that she misunderstood what he was doing, that he wasn't cutting these portions out at all, just moving them into another bin so he could rearrange them and edit them as individual clips.

Eventually, Hannah just let Chris work. She lay down on his bed, smelling his pillow. It smelled like his shampoo, a smell that was now familiar to her. She didn't like the way it smelled, like a stereotypical male bath product—like deodorant, almost. She assumed he used Axe or some other product that was marketed for men and wondered if he was the person who decided what type of products he used or if his mother just assumed that Axe would be something her son would like, and Chris never offered any protest because he didn't care, and thus his body soap and shampoo would forever remain Axe. She wondered if he would ever buy a different kind of shampoo when he went away to college and had to buy his own bathroom products, or if he would just succumb to habit, to familiarity. She wondered if anyone had control over these types of things.

After almost forty-five minutes of editing, Chris said, "Okay, I have it down to around six minutes. See what you think." Hannah watched the clip and, although there were a lot of things she'd liked in the original video, she had to admit that it was much better the way Chris had arranged it. She wondered if one day she'd be sitting in a real editing room working with a real editor, maybe even on the reality TV show for which she was making this video. She had the impression that once a person was featured on a TV show, reality or scripted, or was given a part in a movie, they had complete control over the production and over how they were edited. Chris was a good editor from what she had seen. Maybe she would take him with her when she became famous and he could be her personal editor.

She said, "I think it looks good. I mean, I miss a bunch of the stuff, like with me talking about what I like to do with my friends and with me doing gymnastics and everything, but it's cool. I'm pretty sure we still have to cut out a minute, though, right?"

Chris said, "Forty-three seconds, to be exact, but that's not a problem. Just let me tighten some stuff. I just wanted to see if you thought it was okay with these major chunks. I won't take any of the basic parts out of it, I'll just trim the heads and tails and take out pauses and things like that."

Hannah said, "How long will that take?"

Chris said, "Not too long. I can do it after you leave and e-mail it to you tonight."

Hannah said, "Cool," then got up off Chris's bed and walked

over to where he was sitting. She swiveled his chair around and sat in his lap.

Chris said, "My mom and dad are still up."

Hannah said, "We can be quiet."

Chris said, "Hang on," then got out of his chair, cracked his bedroom door, and snuck out into the living room to find his father asleep in his chair and his mother nowhere to be seen. Chris assumed she was in her bedroom. He snuck back into his room, shut the door, and put a T-shirt by the crack under it. He went back to Hannah and said, "What time is your mom coming to get you?"

Hannah said, "Whenever I text her. But it can't be too late. We have time, though."

Chris said, "What do you want to do?"

Hannah said, "I want you to fuck me."

Chris would have preferred her to say, "I want to fuck you," but he had been preparing for this moment and felt that he was ready to assume the dominant role that Hannah required. Chris said, "Okay, let's fuck."

They moved to his bed. Hannah lay down, removing her clothes as she did so. Chris removed his clothes as well. Chris looked at her naked body and started masturbating. Hannah said, "Do you want me to suck your dick?"

Chris tried to recreate the exact circumstances in which he'd been able to successfully ejaculate into a cardboard paper towel tube filled with lotion-saturated Nerf foam. Then he said, "No, just spread your legs."

She did as she was told and watched Chris standing at the edge of his bed, his flaccid penis in his hand, his eyes closed. She wondered what he was thinking about. She wondered if she wasn't attractive enough to fully arouse Chris. She assumed that there could be no other reason for his inability to achieve an erection in her presence unless some abnormal sexual behavior was employed. She knew that men liked big breasts, which she had, but she wondered if she was missing some other quality that they also liked or liked in a more profound way. She wondered if her vagina smelled bad, if she was slightly too fat in any area of her body, if her face wasn't pretty enough, if her hair wasn't done well enough, if her makeup wasn't applied properly enough, if her voice was too shrill, if her feet were too big, if she should have painted her toenails, if her hands were too rough, if her teeth weren't straight or white enough, if she had some innate deficiency in dealing with men because she never had a father.

Eventually, Chris achieved erection. Hannah remembered reading a post on a website about what men liked during sex that recommended complimenting the size of their erect penises in pornographic terms. She said, "Your hard cock is huge." Chris said nothing in response. He knew that he had a small window of time to insert his erection into Hannah's vagina before it withered.

He had a difficult time entering her due to the fact that her vagina was dry. With no foreplay, not even kissing, Hannah wasn't aroused in the least. The combined complications of Hannah's dry vagina and Chris's lack of interest in traditional sex were taking their toll.

With each thrust, he could feel his penis losing rigidity. He forced it in with his fingers as it softened anyway. Once in, his penis was fully lifeless again. Hannah said, "Are you in?"

Chris said, "Yeah, I think so."

Hannah said, "Uh . . . I'm pretty sure you're not."

Chris said, "No, I am."

Hannah said, "Are you moving?"

Chris said, "No," knowing that the most minor movement of his hips backward would result in the full extraction of his penis, which was now far too limp to be put back in.

Hannah said, "Well, don't you have to, to, like, have sex?"

Chris said, "Yeah."

Hannah said, "I'll move, then," and moved her hips under him, causing his penis to slide out.

She said, "Put it back in."

He rolled over on his back, frustrated. Hannah stared at the ceiling, not knowing exactly what to say, convinced that something was wrong with her, that every encounter she ever had with a man would result in similar disappointment. She said, "Is there something I'm doing wrong, or . . ."

Chris said, "No, I don't know. I'm sorry." Chris wanted to tell her what he found to be sexually arousing, but based on her reaction when he asked her to put a finger in his anus, he knew it was a waste of time. He assumed his sexual preferences were aberrant, and wondered if he would ever meet a girl who would not only indulge him but also enjoy the same things he did. He didn't think he would. He convinced himself in that moment that his life would be filled with sexual frustration and secrecy.

Neither of them made any attempt to engage in further sexual activity. Hannah said, "I guess I should text my mom." Chris said, "Okay." They averted their eyes from each other as they both put their clothes back on. Chris liked Hannah and Hannah liked Chris. Part of Hannah wanted to just be held by Chris, wanted to wait to have any kind of sexual encounter with Chris or anyone, and there was a part of Chris that just wanted to hold Hannah and fall asleep with her, smell her hair, wake up with her, wanted to wait to have any kind of sexual encounter with Hannah or with anyone.

When Hannah's mother arrived, Chris walked her to his front door and said, "I'll send you the video tonight."

Hannah said, "Thanks," then left without giving Chris a hug, which had been a regular part of their parting protocol.

As Chris finished cutting the video for Hannah, he checked his phone constantly, waiting for a text message from Hannah. Hannah did the same with her phone, waiting for a text message from Chris, waiting for some indication that they would still talk to each other, that this night hadn't ruined the undefined but increasingly comfortable relationship they had manufactured over the past months. The text messages never came.

chapter
seventeen

"So, my V-card is gone," said Hannah Clint to a shocked hand-ful of Goodrich Junior High School Olympiannes. Among them was Brooke Benton, who said, "You had sex with Chris?"

Hannah said, "Yep. Last night in his room."

Up until that moment Brooke had felt fine, even good, about where she and Danny had decided to take their physical rela-tionship. She was happy that she had performed oral sex on him once, because it quelled some desire in her to match what her peers had done, to go as far as they had. And at that time, she knew only of Hannah Clint and the oral sex she had performed on an unnamed boy the summer before. But in that moment, as Hannah Clint divulged her news to the entire Olympianne squad—except for Allison Doss, who was still not back in school following her episode in the east wing girls' bathroom—Brooke felt insignificant. Until that moment, she had been as experienced as any other girl at Goodrich Junior High School. Hannah had taken a step that Brooke hadn't, and now stood in a place that Brooke didn't.

As the other girls asked Hannah what it was like to have sex for the first time—wanting to know details about the intricacies of the act itself, the feel of a penis, if pain was involved—Brooke said, "She only had sex with Chris Truby. He's gross anyway."

Before Hannah could offer a rebuttal, Mrs. Langston entered the girls' locker room and asked everyone to sit down. She said, "Before practice today, I thought I should mention that I got some news today about Allison. The first thing you should all know is that she's going to be okay." Mrs. Langston didn't know the details of what had happened to Allison. Allison's mother, Liz, had called Principal Ligorski and lied, explaining to him that Allison was having some complications with her first menstruation and would be out of school for the rest of the week. This information was disseminated to the rest of the faculty to relay to their students as they saw fit.

Mrs. Langston said, "Just like all of you, Allison is going through changes and having her period and her body doesn't seem to want to cooperate like it should. So she's going to be out for a few days and we're going to need someone to take her place at the top of our pyramid tomorrow night."

Mrs. Langston continued on, assigning another Olympianne to take Allison's spot at the top of the pyramid, but Brooke wasn't paying attention to anything going on around her. All she could think about was the fact that Hannah Clint had had sex before her, and that the sex she had was meaningless, with Chris Truby. It seemed to Brooke that, if anyone was supposed to be having sex, it should be her and Danny. The same feeling that had compelled her to perform oral sex on Danny before the first game of the season compelled her this time to start contemplating having sex with him. She didn't feel any readier to engage in the act than she had when she and Danny decided to scale their physical relationship back, but it didn't matter to her. It seemed to be a matter of principle more than anything. She considered Hannah a slut, like the caricatures of teen girls on any of the Tyra Banks shows she had seen. Her mind was made up: She would not be outdone by a slut.

Chris Truby was in the cafeteria eating lunch with Danny Vance when word reached him, through Tanner Hodge, that the news was out that he had had sexual intercourse with Hannah Clint. Tanner offered his congratulations by saying, "Lucky fucker. How are those titties? You get your dick between 'em?"

Chris said, "No."

Tanner said, "Faggot."

Chris was trying to understand what was happening. To his knowledge, he and Hannah had engaged in what he considered a failed attempt at intercourse. He certainly hadn't reached orgasm. He knew that Hannah had failed to achieve one of her own. He had engaged in no thrusting to speak of. His limp penis had been resting just inside the opening of her vagina for a few seconds. From the countless hours of pornography he watched, Chris knew that what he and Hannah had done was not sex. He wondered why she would have spread the rumor, and beyond that he wondered if this meant that she wanted to continue their attempts at a normal sexual relationship or if it meant that she was done with him. Perhaps she had realized that she wasn't going to get what she wanted from him, decided to create her own reality in which she had gotten it, and used that as the reality she presented to their peers. In either case, Chris was happy to be known as the first boy in the eighth grade to have sex, and the fact that it was with Hannah Clint, the proprietor of the largest breasts in their class, would only serve to raise his status with not only the boys, but the girls at Goodrich Junior High School as well.

Danny said, "Jesus, man. That's some big news. When were you going to tell me about it?"

Chris said, "Yeah, I don't know. I guess I just wanted to kind of keep it on the down-low, you know?"

Danny said, "Sure. You can show me pictures of trannies fucking each other in hockey masks, but you can't tell me you nailed Hannah Clint?"

Chris, easing into the lie a bit, said, "Look, man, I just didn't know if she wanted everybody knowing, and I definitely need to hit that shit again, so . . . I was just protecting my investment."

Danny said, "Oh, yeah, your investment."

Chris said, "So when the fuck are you and Brooke gonna get down to business?"

Danny was happy in his relationship with Brooke. He didn't feel the need to match Chris or any of his peers in terms of their sexual experience. He said, "I don't know. Whenever we get around to it, I guess."

Chris, now fully embracing the new identity Hannah's lie afforded him, said, "Pussy. Hannah and I just started hooking up, like, last month, and I already fucked her. You guys have been together for over a year."

Danny said, "Yeah, lay off, dickhead."

Chris said, "Touchy, touchy. My bad. Just keep jerking off every night. I don't give a shit."

Danny said, "Thanks."

Across the lunchroom, Tim Mooney sat with Brandy Beltmeyer. It was something they each looked forward to daily. They considered the time they spent with each other during their lunch period to be the best part of their day. Tim said, "I think my dad is going to the football game this Friday, so he won't be home if you think you can fake your mom out and want to come over and watch a movie or something."

Brandy said, "I don't know. I might be able to, but she hasn't done one of her surprise inspections of my computer in a while, which always makes me hella nervous. I just like being there when she does it, so I can know what's totally going on. If I'm not there, I'm always worried that she's digging around through my stuff."

Tim said, "Okay, cool, well, whatever."

Brandy, "Uh-oh, it looks like somebody's a little sad that he might not get to see me this Friday."

Tim smiled and said, "Whatever. I could care less about seeing you."

Brandy smiled and kissed him on the cheek. The kiss went unseen by Mr. Donnelly, the faculty lunch monitor. Displays of affection between students were officially limited to holding hands and hugging on campus. Anything beyond that could be grounds for suspension or, at the very least, after-school detention. Tim liked the fact that Brandy took pleasure in breaking this rule.

Brandy said, "Let me text my mom and see how she responds. If it seems like she's busy with other stuff Friday night, then I'll come over. If not, I probably can't."

Tim said, "Okay," and kissed her on the cheek, which also went unseen by Mr. Donnelly.

After the lunch period ended, Brandy sent her mother a text message that read, "Lauren wants 2 know if I can C a movie w/ her Friday." Brandy's mother, Patricia, replied with a text message that read, "Okay . . . as long as it's not too late." Brandy replied with a text message that read, "K, we'll get tix for an early 1." Patricia replied with a text message that read, "Okay, I love you." Brandy replied with a text message that read, "U2." She then logged into her Freyja Myspace account and sent Tim a message that read, "See you Friday." Tim received a notification on his phone that he had a new message from Freyja just before his earth sciences class. He read the message and responded with one of his own that read, "Can't wait," before swallowing an Anafranil tablet.

chapter eighteen

The Pound Squires maintained one of the worst football fields in the district. The grass, what little there was, was never mowed or managed. Most of the field had given way to large patches of dirt, which had turned to mud after a heavy rain the day before the Goodrich Olympians arrived as the visiting team in the eighth game of the eighth-grade season.

Some opposing players and coaches speculated that it was these substandard playing conditions that made the players on the Pound Squires football team more resilient and better than many other teams. It was accepted that they were not the most skilled team in the league, but they were easily the toughest, the most robust, and the players with the least adherence to the rules of football. Every opponent the Squires had faced that season left the game having suffered at least one season-ending injury among their players.

Danny Vance took all of these things into account as he took the field for the Olympians' first offensive drive. His plan of attack was similar to what he had done in many of the prior weeks: a strong passing game designed to spread the defense's secondary thin and allow for shorter pass completions for a series of first downs that would ultimately lead to a red-zone drive for a touchdown. This plan was set into motion and executed perfectly, yielding six first downs for the Olympians followed by an eight-yard touchdown pass to Chris Truby.

After a three-and-out offensive series from the Pound Squires, Danny took the field again, this time anticipating the shift in defense that usually came after he delivered a successful passing drive. Coach Quinn, anticipating the same thing, called a running play to Tanner Hodge to open the second Olympian offensive drive. The play was run for a loss of three yards as the Squires' defense seemed to be adhering to their original run-protection defensive plan, sending their free safety in to blitz on virtually every play. Danny saw this, and when the next play brought into the huddle from Coach Quinn was the six-three-eight flip right, another running play, he called time-out and made his way to the sidelines to discuss something with Coach Quinn.

Since Coach Quinn had loosened his philosophy, allowing Danny to pass more frequently in the hopes of winning more games, he and Danny had developed a more cordial relationship. They were almost friendly. Danny said, "Coach, I don't think they're shifting for the pass. I think we should keep passing until they drop the safety back or show any sign that they might be playing pass protect."

Coach Quinn had trusted Danny in the games leading up to this one, and as a result the Goodrich Olympians hadn't lost another game. He had no reason to doubt Danny in this situation. Coach Quinn said, "Sounds good. One-four-two fly left?"

Danny said, "Yeah, that should work," and ran back to the huddle, where he relayed the new play to the rest of the team.

Danny took the snap, dropped back four steps, turned his head to the left to check Chris Truby, his primary receiver, and was sacked by the Squires' defensive tackle. In the huddle, Danny asked Randy Trotter if he missed his block assignment and Randy explained that it had nothing to do with his block assignment. He claimed that one of the Squires' defensive linemen had tripped him, allowing the defensive tackle to make his way into the backfield unhindered. The trip went unnoticed by the two referees officiating the game. Danny assumed this type of illegal play was a major component of the strategy the Squires had employed in most of their victories.

He attempted another pass play, which resulted in an incompletion due to blatant pass interference that the referees failed to call. Danny knew that the referees who oversaw eighth-grade football games were far from NFL level, but he was surprised that they'd missed what he considered an obvious pass-interference call. He assumed that the Pound Squires would continue to play in this manner and hope that the referees would miss more calls than they would see. He decided to call a run play, which resulted in a gain of two yards and brought the punting team onto the field.

The Pound Squires were able to score a touchdown and an extra point on their next drive. The fact that every member of their offensive line was holding on almost every play was a large part of the reason for their successful drive. They were penalized for the act only twice in a drive that consisted of eleven plays.

As the game reached halftime and the Pound Squires headed to their field house, leaving the Olympians to occupy their own sideline, the score remained seven to seven, and Danny Vance was having a difficult time seeing how exactly he could secure a victory against a team who employed illegal tactics to such a degree and seemingly without penalty.

As the team came together and each player took a knee around Coach Quinn, who was delivering a speech about the necessity of ignoring the Squires' gross misconduct on the football field and continuing to play a clean game, Chris Truby was staring at Hannah Clint, who was cheering roughly twenty yards away on the same sideline. He hadn't talked to her since the entire school had fallen under the impression that he and she had engaged in sexual intercourse. It was clear to Chris that Hannah had spread the rumor, but it was unclear to him why she would have done it. He had thought about sending her a text message, but thought better of it, content to live the lie that he was more sexually experienced than he actually was. A text message probing into the purpose behind the exaggeration might bring it all tumbling down. Still, Chris liked Hannah and didn't want their relationship to end. As Coach Quinn shifted topics in his half-time pep talk and began outlining various techniques for the defensive line to overcome being held on every play, Chris decided to let Hannah make the first attempt at any further communication between them.

Brooke Benton watched her boyfriend, Danny Vance, as he knelt in front of Coach Quinn. She found him attractive and she even felt that her love for him was genuine. These things alone were not enough to compel her to overcome her certainty that she was not ready to have sex with him. But as she looked at Hannah Clint cheering next to her with a smile on her face, Brooke thought she looked older, more adult than the other Olympiannes. It was something Brooke wanted for herself. She began to convince herself that she needed to have intercourse with Danny as soon as possible.

Brandy Beltmeyer said good-bye to her mother and father, got on her bicycle, and rode away from her house toward her friend Lauren's house. She continued on this path for a few blocks, until she was out of what she considered her mother's range of surveillance. Then she changed her course and headed to Tim Mooney's house. She was excited to see him.

Brandy's mother, Patricia, had become increasingly suspicious of the amount of time her daughter was supposedly spending at her friend Lauren's house. She knew them to have been close friends since early childhood, but it seemed that Brandy was spending almost twice the amount of time with Lauren that she was used to.

After Brandy left, Patricia logged on to her computer and opened her Spector Pro keystroke logging program. Spector Pro was Patricia's last line of defense when it came to knowing everything her daughter did online. Up to that point, she hadn't felt the need to use it. She was under the impression that her daughter was open and honest about all her online activities, and their weekly Internet checks had seemed satisfactory. It was only the increased time Brandy was spending away from home that had made Patricia curious enough to access a Myspace, Facebook, and iChat summary report of her daughter's computer through Spector Pro. The summary report was long, and Patricia was tired of looking at a computer screen all day. She opted to print out the report and review it for any anomalies as she and her husband watched *American Idol*.

Patricia read through the first few pages of the summary report finding nothing out of the ordinary. There were several iChat conversations with Lauren, several Myspace and Facebook messages sent to Lauren and other friends, and several school-related e-mails to and from teachers. Intending to peruse the entire summary eventually, Patricia set the stack of papers down on the coffee table when she heard Ellen DeGeneres make a particularly humorous comment, deciding to devote her full attention to the show for a few minutes. After watching the show to completion and falling asleep in her chair next to her husband, who was asleep in his own chair, Patricia woke up and went to bed, leaving the unread summary report on the coffee table.

Brandy arrived at Tim Mooney's house unaware that her

mother had a printed copy of every website she had visited in the past two weeks, every username and password she used to access those websites, and every keystroke she had typed to compose messages or chat conversations on those websites. Tim was playing *World of Warcraft* when she came in. Since beginning his Anafranil regiment, he had found that *Warcraft* was a more enjoyable game than it had been without the effect of the drug. He had begun to feel he had almost no control over any of the occurrences in his life. His mother's remarriage, which was taking place in a state he had never even visited, to a man he had never met; his own relationship, which could exist only through deceiving the mother of the girl he was involved with; his father's growing impatience with his decision not to play football—these were all things Tim felt he had no control over. But when he logged on to *World of Warcraft*, he found some comfort in the fact that he knew every square inch of Azeroth, Outland, and Northrend. He knew every detail of every boss encounter in every instance. He knew the relationship he maintained with each of his guildmates, and he knew those relationships would never change. There would be no surprises when he played; there would be nothing beyond his control. He spent more time playing and interacting with his guildmates than he had in the past, using any stray ten minutes or more to log on and complete a daily quest or just check the auction house for anything that might be of interest, which is what he was doing when Brandy arrived.

Tim told his guildmates good-bye when his doorbell rang and logged off after the first two comments appeared in guild chat in response to his departure, reading, "Is your mom's pussy stretched out from that nigger she's marrying yet?" and "What about her butthole? Niggers love butthole."

Tim and Brandy spent the night watching an episode of *Locked Up Abroad*, which they both found enjoyable. During the course of the episode, Brandy said, "I don't know if this is totally off-limits or whatever, but why does your dad go to the football games if you're not playing anymore?"

It was in that moment that Tim realized that he had never asked himself this question. He knew the answer. His father wanted him to play football, wanted things to be like they used to be, so badly that he maintained his normal pattern of behavior, ignoring the obvious changes that were happening around him. Tim said, "I guess he likes football. He's friends with some of the other dads, I guess."

Brandy said, "Oh. It just seems weird, you know?"

Tim said, "Yeah. I guess it does."

After the episode of *Locked Up Abroad* came to an end, Tim turned off the television and kissed Brandy, who was happy to return the kiss. They continued to kiss and hug for the next thirty minutes without removing their clothes or elevating their physical interaction to a level that included anything beyond kissing and hugging. This made them both happy.

Don Truby was far less inebriated than he usually was at the beginning of the second half. He knew that he was generally a happier person as a result of having a sexual relationship outside of his marriage. He wanted to tell Kent and Jim about Angelique Ice, about the new life he was leading, but he knew it was potentially dangerous to let anyone know about his infidelity.

Jim Vance had scheduled his vasectomy to occur two weeks later, choosing to wait until his son's regular football season had concluded, not wanting to risk any complication with the surgery forcing him to miss a game. Looking for some support in the matter from his friends, he said, "So, I'm getting a vasectomy in a few weeks."

Kent Mooney said, "Ouch."

Don Truby said, "She finally broke you down, huh? Getting

the old nuts cut. I'd do it, too, if I had a wife forcing me to do it, I guess."

Jim said, "She's not forcing me. We've talked about it for a long time and it seems like the best thing to do."

Don said, "Yeah. I bet you've talked about it. Did the conversation go something like this—'If you don't get your balls chopped off, I'm never fucking you again'?"

Jim couldn't help but laugh. Don's recounting of the conversation wasn't too far from the truth. Kent said, "I don't know if that's something I could ever do, honestly. Just the idea of it is . . ."

Don said, "Well, you might want to get over that unless you want to have a kid with Dawn Clint."

Kent said, "Well, we'd have to have sex first."

Jim said, "How long have you guys been dating?"

Kent said, "I don't know, maybe a month or so."

Don said, "And you haven't fucked her? I had no idea what a pussy you'd become."

Kent said, "I'm working up to it. We're going out tomorrow night. It'll probably happen then. I just haven't been ready, exactly."

Don said, "Like, you can't get a hard-on?"

Kent said, "No, emotionally ready, you jackass."

Don said, "Wow. You'd be less of a pussy if you just had a limp dick."

Kent said, "Like I said, it'll probably happen soon. How're things with you and your wife going? You seem a little happier than usual."

Don suppressed the urge to tell them about his new status as a connoisseur of prostitution and said, "Yeah, things seem to be getting a little better, I guess."

Kent said, "That's good to hear," as the Olympians kicked off to the Pound Squires, who returned the kick for fifteen yards. The Squires' next play was a run up the middle. Their offensive line employed several illegal blocks that left only Bill Francis, the middle linebacker who replaced Tim Mooney, as the last possible defender who could stop the fullback from breaking into the open field. Bill saw the fullback running toward him, so he lowered his head and closed his eyes, hoping that there wouldn't be a significant amount of pain involved in their impending impact. He leaned into what he assumed would be the impending collision and fell down as his upper body's weight set him off balance without the tackle he was expecting ever occurring.

The Squires' running back had merely performed a rudimentary side step in order to avoid Bill Francis, who he could clearly see wasn't watching the play at all. As Bill lay on the ground, he rolled over just in time to see the Squires' fullback sprinting off into the distance, twenty-five yards down field, for a touchdown.

In the stands, Kent Mooney said nothing, but he knew that his son would have made the tackle. Don and Jim remained silent as well, knowing that Kent couldn't have been happy about what he'd just seen.

The Olympians' offense took the field with slightly less than two quarters of play left in the game, the score fourteen to seven in favor of the Squires. Getting any form of offensive momentum going proved too difficult for Danny Vance in the face of the Squires' incessant illegal tactics.

The remainder of the game saw no further scoring from either team, making the outcome a fourteen-seven loss for the Goodrich Junior High School Olympians. No one said anything specifically about Bill Francis's missed tackle on the bus ride back to Goodrich Junior High School, but it was obvious to all the players and coaches alike that his inept play was the clearest reason for the loss.

Before the players were allowed to leave the field house back at Goodrich Junior High, Coach Quinn delivered a speech in which he blamed the loss on the illegal methods employed by the Pound Squires. He told his players that they were still in contention for the playoffs, and that it was imperative that they win their last regular season game. Without that win, they would have no chance at making the playoffs. He assured them that the loss against the Squires was a fluke, and that no team in their league would have been able to beat a team who cheated that much and was penalized for it so little. Coach Quinn knew that blaming Bill Francis would only create discord. The team had to be unified heading into the final game if they were to win against the Culler Cougars, who were, in Coach Quinn's opinion, the best team in their league. Without a win against them, Coach Quinn knew that his consideration for the high school coaching job he desperately wanted would likely dissipate.

Kent Mooney came home and went directly to his son's room with the intent of making him feel guilty enough about the Olympians' loss to return to the team for their final game. When he opened the door, his son was sitting at his computer playing *World of Warcraft* with his headphones on. Kent stopped at the door and thought about the reality of the situation. Even if he could convince his son to return for the final game, Coach Quinn would surely not let him set foot on the field after missing the entire season. There was no point in talking to his son. Kent shut his son's door without Tim knowing he had ever been there and went to his own room.

He saw on his bedside table the pamphlet Patricia Beltmeyer had given him at his first and only meeting of Parents Against The Internet. Looking through it, he came to the section that outlined how to download and install various types of surveillance software on any child's computer. Kent thought about what Patricia had said regarding the nature of the game his son seemed to be spending more and more time playing in the past month. Though he knew that Patricia Beltmeyer was far too overbearing in these matters, Kent couldn't help wondering if he should be concerned about his son, wondering if the amount of time he spent playing *World of Warcraft* was directly influencing his decision not to play football. Kent decided to install a program on his son's computer the following Monday, when Tim was at school, that would allow him access to his son's *World of Warcraft* account. At the very least, maybe he could come to a greater understanding of the game, and therefore a greater understanding of his son, which, he reasoned, couldn't possibly be a bad thing.

Confident in his decision, Kent sat on his bed and reached over to the spot where his wife used to sleep. He felt her pillow. He had bought new sheets the week after they separated, but in that moment he realized that he'd never replaced the pillows. He thought about Dawn Clint and the date they had planned for the following night. He was almost certain that he would have sex with her for the first time after the date. She would be the first woman since his wife that he would have sex with. She deserved new pillows at the very least, he thought.

chapter
nineteen

Danny Vance woke up Saturday morning after a particularly vivid dream involving his participation as a soldier in a war that was being waged on an alien world against the indigenous and technologically superior creatures of that world. It took his mind a few seconds after waking up to recalibrate itself and recall the reality that the Goodrich Olympians were six-and-two with one game left in the season, a game that would be played against a team that was arguably the best in the district. Another loss meant they would be out of the playoffs and the eighth-grade football season would be over for every member of the Goodrich Junior High Olympian football team.

He checked his phone and saw that he had a new text message from Brooke Benton. It read, "Sorry bout last nite :(not ur fault :) want 2 hang 2day?" He replied with a text message that read, "Sure. Let me take a shower and I'll call u."

Danny Vance showered, brushed his teeth, and came into the kitchen, where he found his mother and father. His father said, "You okay?"

Danny said, "Yeah. I guess. We just have to win this last game, which seems tough, you know?"

Jim Vance said, "Yeah, but you can do it. Keep that chin up."

Danny said, "I will. I might need a ride to hang out with Brooke today."

Tracey Vance said, "Okay. I can take you. Just let me know when."

Danny Vance ate breakfast and knew that the final game of the regular season would be the toughest he would have to play. The Culler Cougars didn't cheat, like the Pound Squires. They didn't have a freakishly tall player, like the Irving Aardvarks. They were just extremely good. They ran plays with precision. Their defense was difficult to fool. Their special teams were the best in the district. A win against them would be possible only if every member of the Olympian football team played the best game of their season. It was possible.

A few hours later, Danny had his mother take him to Brooke's house, where they planned to watch a movie with her little brother, Andrew, whom she was babysitting while her parents were shopping for a new bed. Once Danny arrived, Andrew informed them that he had a test on Monday that he felt he hadn't properly prepared for. Andrew was identical to his older sister in that he, too, was instilled with a deep need to outperform his peers in any manner that presented itself, be it athletic, academic, or anything else.

Andrew went to his room to study, leaving Brooke and Danny to occupy the living room alone. Brooke scrolled through the movies that were available on demand and found nothing that either of them wanted to see. Brooke had *Wall-E* saved on her DVR, which Danny agreed to watch for what he estimated to be the one-hundredth time. It was Brooke's favorite movie, and, as such, Danny had sat through it more times than he could remember.

Brooke had no real plan when she started kissing Danny a few minutes into the movie; she just knew she needed to lose her virginity as soon as she could in order to make herself feel that she was still the alpha member of the Olympians. Danny didn't object to kissing Brooke, but when she reached down and started unbuttoning his pants, he said, "What are you doing?"

Brooke said, "I don't know. My brother will be in his room until my parents get back, probably, and they won't be back for like a few hours at least."

Danny said, "But I thought we talked about this."

Brooke said, "I know we did, but in my opinion we might want to, you know, give it another try or something."

Danny said, "Why?"

Brooke said, "Because we've been together for a long time, and it's something we should be doing. We love each other, right?"

Danny said, "Yeah, we do, but . . . we have the biggest game of the season coming up. I want to be focused on it. I mean, if we lose, we're out of the playoffs."

Brooke said, "I know. I just thought maybe this would help you relax a little."

Danny said, "I don't know. I don't think we should."

Brooke said, "Well, in my opinion we should. And I think we should like . . . have sex, too."

Danny said, "I don't get why you're wanting to do this now. I thought we were cool with not doing anything but kissing and stuff for a while."

Brooke said, "I was cool with it, and once we have sex we can totally go back to just kissing and stuff if you want to, but we should do it at least once, just to, like, get it out of the way and everything."

Danny thought about this. He had put the possibility of

having sex out of his mind since his conversation with Brooke weeks before in which they agreed to scale back their physical relationship. He was comfortable with the level of physical intimacy they had agreed on. It made him more able to concentrate on football, which was important to him. He assumed that having sex with Brooke would make concentrating on the final game difficult. He wondered why she had changed her mind so quickly and he couldn't help thinking about the time she'd performed oral sex on him. It was pleasurable and it was something that he thought about with moderate frequency, especially when he masturbated. Sex with Brooke, he presumed, would be even more pleasurable.

He said, "Can we just agree to not do anything until after the game this week and then we'll talk about it?"

Brooke said, "Yeah."

Danny said, "Cool."

Brooke laid her head on his chest and they finished watching *Wall-E*, each wondering what it would be like to have intercourse with the other.

Kent was as nervous as he was excited about seeing Dawn again. He took a shower, did his hair, and then took the bottle containing five 100-milligram tablets of Viagra out of his medicine cabinet. He had already read the instructions multiple times and knew that one tablet was to be ingested approximately one hour before sexual interaction. He opened the bottle and took one of the tablets out, staring at it in his hand, wondering where he would conceal the tablet while on his date with Dawn, wondering how he would gauge her interest in engaging in any kind of sexual interaction. What if she was having her period? What if she just wasn't in the mood? Having to take the tablet an hour before sexual interaction seemed like it might present problems for Kent. The last thing he wanted was to take the tablet and not have sex, leaving him with what he assumed would be an insatiable erection for the rest of the night. Beyond that, he had a limited supply of the tablets, which were not cheap in Kent's mind, and he had no intention of wasting even one of them.

He left the tablet on his bathroom sink, put on his clothes, and then went to the kitchen and got a small piece of tin foil, which he wrapped the tablet in. He then put the foil-wrapped tablet in his wallet along with a condom from a pack of twelve he had purchased earlier that day at CVS. He knocked on his son's door before leaving for his date but got no answer. Kent cracked the door open to find Tim playing *World of Warcraft* with headphones on. Kent walked in and tapped his son on the shoulder, not thinking to read any of the scrolling green text in the guild chat window, which would have correctly revealed that his ex-wife was on the verge of getting remarried and would have incorrectly informed him that she was marrying a black man.

Tim took his headphones off and Kent said, "I'm leaving for my date. I left you some pizza money on the kitchen table if you want."

Tim said, "Okay, thanks."

Kent didn't know where he would be having sex with Dawn at the night's end, and he didn't really know how to broach the topic with his son. He said, "Um, I might be out pretty late tonight. Like, maybe the entire night."

Tim said, "It's cool. We're raiding all night."

Kent said, "Um, also, I might be coming back here early, but, um, with Dawn."

Tim said, "Okay."

Kent said, "Okay," happy to have avoided any perceptible awkwardness between him and his son. Then Kent left for his date.

Tim put his headphones back on and accepted a raid invitation he'd received from Mzo. Tim thought about his father moving on just as his mother had. He couldn't feel the emotions he knew were supposed to be there. He assumed this was because of the Anafranil. Tim had found some comfort in the fact that his father hadn't moved on like his mother had. He held no hope of his parents reuniting. He knew that was out of the question, especially based on the fact that his mother was on the verge of getting remarried, but he found his father's reluctance to replace his mother comforting. He had never told his father this, but he felt that this reluctance was something they shared. He knew that he should feel sad about that reluctance dissipating in his father, but instead he only felt hollow. It was a strange coincidence to Tim that the first Saturday his mother failed to call him from California was also the day his father was going to have sex with another woman. He wanted to feel something about all of this, but he found he couldn't even feel numb. There was simply nothing for him to feel at all. He put the absence of feeling out of his mind and continued his raid, sending e-mails to Brandy through her Freyja account during any break his guild would take and reminding himself that nothing mattered.

Kent took Dawn to a nice restaurant, as he had on many of their other dates, with the exception of one date on which they went bowling. The conversation was as engaging for each of them as it usually was, but an underlying nervousness on both of their parts heightened the experience for them. They were both acutely aware of the expectation of what the night's end would entail.

At the meal's end, Dawn said, "Should we go get a drink or something?"

Kent thought the introduction of alcohol would ease his nervousness. He said, "Yeah, sounds good."

They ended up making their way to Zoo Bar and listening to Fatbones Big Horn Band play as they drank. After the first drink, Dawn put her hand on Kent's leg and squeezed his knee. He returned the physical affection by placing his hand on the small of her back and moving his fingers in small circles. They had kissed each other and done so passionately, but Kent found these small massaging motions at Zoo Bar to be far more intimate than anything they had done previously.

After finishing their first drinks and ordering a second round, Dawn said, "I'm going to go to the ladies' room. I'll be right back," and then got up out of her chair. As she crossed Kent, she leaned down and kissed him, putting her fingers in his hair. After the kiss, she leaned her mouth close to his ear and said, "When I come back from the bathroom, I want you to tell me where we're going after our next drink." Then she headed for the restroom.

Kent was so nervous that he felt himself begin to sweat. He dabbed the back of his neck with a napkin and took a deep breath. He told himself that he was going to have sex with a woman who was very attractive and whom he liked a lot, and beyond these two things he had 100 milligrams of Viagra in his wallet, which would ensure an above-average sexual performance. He reminded himself that he had nothing to be nervous about.

The drinks arrived at their table while Dawn was still in the restroom. Kent assumed it would take twenty minutes to finish their drinks and then another twenty or thirty to drive to either his house or Dawn's. He had to decide, as soon as possible, when he would ingest the 100 milligrams of Viagra. Based on what Dawn whispered in his ear, Kent was almost positive that she wanted to have sex with him after their next drink. He took out his wallet, made sure no one was looking, unwrapped the tablet of Viagra, put it in his mouth, and swallowed it with a mouthful of the greyhound he had ordered, wondering if he would be able to feel the effects of the drug in any way other than it producing an erection.

Dawn eventually returned to the table, giving Kent a light squeeze on the shoulder as she did. They finished their drink with minimal conversation and then left Zoo Bar.

In Kent's car, Dawn said, "So, I don't want to be presumptuous or anything, but instead of dropping me off, would you maybe like to go back to your place or something?"

Kent would have preferred to go to Dawn's house, having had no time to put new sheets on his bed, but he said, "Yeah, we could do that."

Dawn reached over and squeezed his thigh nearer to his penis than to his knee and said, "Good."

After arriving at Kent's house, they made their way to his front porch, where they kissed each other urgently. Kent's ears and face began to feel flushed and hot. He assumed it was some side effect of the Viagra. He could also feel an erection beginning to form in his pants. It was harder than any erection he could remember having in his adult life. Dawn felt it poking her through Kent's pants. She said, "Oh, my. Looks like somebody's excited."

Kent said, "Well, you excite me."

They kissed for another minute or so as Dawn put her hand on Kent's erection. Kent was astounded at how hard it was. Dawn was as well. She said, "You are, like, rock hard."

Kent said, "Well, it's been a while since I've done . . . you know."

Dawn said, "It's okay."

Kent said, "My son might still be up. If he is, he'll probably be in his room playing video games, but, just to warn you, you might have to say hello or something."

Dawn said, "Okay," and Kent opened the door.

Tim was in his room. His raid had ended thirty minutes before, but he was still on his computer, logged into his Myspace account, chatting with Brandy. Kent saw that the light was on in Tim's room and motioned for Dawn to walk with him into his bedroom, avoiding the process of meeting Tim.

Once in Kent's bedroom, Dawn undressed him aggressively, kissing him and rubbing her hands over his body. Kent was built well. It seemed like he probably worked out with some regularity and didn't eat terribly. Once she had him down to his boxer shorts, she pushed him down on the bed and said, "Now it's my turn," and undressed herself in front of him. Kent knew that she had an attractive body, but it was made even more so as she stood in front of him in only her bra and panties. She removed her bra. Kent looked at her breasts. They were nicely shaped, with medium-sized brown nipples. They were much nicer than he remembered his ex-wife's to be. As he thought this, it occurred to him that Dawn's breasts were the first he had seen since his divorce, since his wife had stood in roughly that same spot in their bedroom with her breasts exposed. Kent knew that a thought of that nature would have deflated his erection had he not taken the 100-milligram tablet of Viagra. His erection was so stiff that each of his heartbeats made it throb a little bit. He was put at ease by the realization that nothing Dawn could say or do, nothing he could think about, nothing that could happen would make him lose his erection. He was going to perform well, which would almost ensure that Dawn would want to do this again.

Dawn moved onto the bed with him and they kissed for a few minutes, each of them moving their hands over the other's body, feeling skin touch skin. Kent's arms felt good to Dawn, as did his mouth and his body in general. She felt, for the first time in a long time, as though the man she was about to have sex with actually liked her. His touch was as at times gentle and at times aggressive. It conveyed a respect for her that was rarely present in her sexual partners, but it wasn't so timid as to lack the feeling of the expressly male carnal lust that Dawn required in order to be turned on. His hands were strong, and when Kent slid one of them under her panties to squeeze one of her buttocks, it caused her to exhale in a physical surrender to Kent—a feeling she wasn't positive she had ever known.

This was the first body Kent had felt close to his since his ex-wife's. It was impossible for him not to compare them, even though he hadn't had sex with his wife since their last awkward sexual encounter a few months after their official separation, almost a year before. He liked the way Dawn's body felt. She had taken care of herself. Although his ex-wife was physically attractive, and in what Kent had always considered to be good shape, Dawn's body was far more appealing to him. He could feel muscle under her skin. He could feel it tensing as she maneuvered her body in conjunction with his movements.

He slid her panties off, thought of how his wife's buttocks used to feel in his hands one last time, and then mentally forbade himself from thinking about his wife again that night. He slid off his boxer shorts and rolled underneath Dawn, forcing her to sit on top of him, straddling him. She could feel his erection between her buttocks. It was incredibly stiff, giving a resistance to her backward grinding motion that was notable to her.

Kent sat up a little, took one of Dawn's breasts in his hand, and licked at her nipple. He smelled her skin. He thought about how dissimilar from his ex-wife she smelled. His ex-wife, Lydia, was fond of using body lotions and soaps that smelled very floral. Kent had never had an opinion of her smell. It was neither attractive nor repellent to him. It was just how she smelled. Dawn, on the other hand, smelled like cinnamon, a scent that Kent found almost made him salivate. He became aware that he was, once again, thinking about his ex-wife as he felt Dawn's nipple become hard in his mouth. He breathed deeply, inhaling whatever the spiced scent was that she was wearing that night.

Dawn reached behind herself and took Kent's erect penis in her hand, stroking it. It was amazingly hard, harder than any erection she had felt in recent memory. This made her wet almost immediately. She took the hand Kent had on her buttock and moved it around to her vagina, guiding his fingers into it, showing him how aroused she was. Kent took this to mean that Dawn wanted him to give her some kind of clitoral stimulation before they began the act of intercourse.

He rolled her over on her back, spread her legs, and looked at her body as he knelt above her. She was an extremely attractive woman in Kent's mind, especially for one in what he guessed to be her late thirties or early forties. He kissed her neck and then moved his mouth lower on her body by increments, dragging his tongue over her nipples, down her stomach, and then to one of her hips and down to her inner thigh. He paused momentarily at her vagina, hoping that he would remember how to perform cunnilingus, hoping that the technique he had perfected with his ex-wife, a technique that was suited specifically to her sexual predilection, would be pleasurable to Dawn as well. And, again, Kent tried to banish the thought of his ex-wife as he spread Dawn's labia with his fingers and slowly slid his tongue over her clitoris.

Dawn's reaction to each shift of rhythm or direction with his tongue let Kent know that he was doing a decent job. After several minutes of Kent performing cunnilingus on her, Dawn reached down and pulled him toward her, saying, "Fuck me."

Kent was surprised to find that, not only did he still have an erection despite his penis having had no physical stimulation for the past several minutes, but the erection was also just as hard as it had been since it had first manifested itself. He moved over and got on his knees, reaching to the nightstand where he kept the pack of twelve condoms he purchased earlier that day. As he fumbled with the box, Dawn moved her head toward his penis and fellated him.

She ran a finger behind his testicles and applied a small amount of pressure to his perineum as she slid the entire length of his penis into her mouth and throat. She had mastered the ability to take the entire length of an average-sized penis into her mouth when she was in high school. It had served her well in life, and as Kent said, "Oh my god," in reaction to her performance, she correctly assumed that he was impressed with her skills.

She continued to fellate him in this manner for a minute or so until she became aware of the fact that he had opened the condom wrapper and was holding the condom, ready to place it on his penis. Kent had, in his marriage, been tasked with putting the condom on his own penis before every sexual encounter, without exception. So when Dawn took the condom from his hand and rolled it down the length of his penis herself, he was surprised and happy.

With the condom on, Kent rolled Dawn over on her back again, spread her legs, and very gently slid himself into her, looking into her eyes the entire time. Dawn was used to men having sex with her from behind or with her on top. Those seemed to be the only positions the men she had sex with employed. It was nice to look into Kent's eyes. Although she found it a strange thing to think about as she felt Kent's penis slide in and out of her, she couldn't help but feel good about being the first woman Kent was having sex with after his wife. She reached up and stroked his hair, bringing his face close to hers, and then kissed him gently to the rhythm of his thrusts.

Although his motion was slow at first, it was deep, and Dawn could feel him hitting her G-spot. The tenderness that had defined their initial moments of intercourse was quickly giving way to lust for Dawn. She reached behind Kent with both hands, grabbing his buttocks and pulling him into her, increasing his pace and thrust.

Kent was enjoying himself, but was finding it difficult to reach a level of sexual arousal that would even hint at a coming orgasm. He had heard that one of the potential drawbacks of taking Viagra was that an orgasm would be difficult to achieve. He didn't necessarily care if that was to be the outcome of the night as long as Dawn had one, but he felt that he should at least give it his best effort.

In the hour that followed, Dawn and Kent had sex in multiple positions, varying the speed, angle, and power of his thrusts. Dawn achieved three orgasms, the third coming simultaneously with Kent's first and only of the night, in the doggy-style position.

After ejaculating, Kent collapsed down next to Dawn. They were both exhausted. Kent was afraid that his penis might remain erect even after ejaculating, but it didn't. Dawn said, "Jesus fucking Christ. That was insane."

Kent said, "Yeah."

Dawn said, "Seriously. I don't think I've had sex like that since I was eighteen."

Kent said, "Yeah, I don't know if I have either." He thought about telling her that he had taken Viagra before their encounter, but then thought better of it. He did wonder what her reaction would be to future sexual encounters, however, if he chose not to employ Viagra. He looked at her lying in the spot where his ex-wife used to lay. He liked Dawn. He said, "So, I don't know if this is, like, a weird thing, or if you even want to do this, but if you want to stay here tonight, you can."

Dawn hadn't thought about that even being a possibility. Most of the men she was sexually active with in her adult life had been of the type who left her house or gave some reason that she had to leave theirs within fifteen minutes of having ejaculated. She liked Kent. She said, "Do you want me to stay? Don't feel like you have to say that because we just had sex or anything."

Kent said, "No, I'd really like you to stay, actually, if you want to."

Dawn said, "As long as it won't be weird for your son or anything tomorrow morning."

Kent said, "He'll be in his room playing video games. And, even if he's not, he should meet you. I mean, assuming you want to keep going out and everything."

Dawn said, "Well, after your performance tonight, I don't know if I can keep up with you."

Kent said, "I think you'll be okay," and then kissed her and felt his penis becoming erect again.

chapter twenty

For Allison Doss, the first day back at school after having a miscarriage wasn't as difficult as she thought it would be. None of
her peers or the faculty at Goodrich Junior High School knew
the truth about what had happened to her the week before. Her
mother and father decided it would be best if no one knew, and
she agreed with them. While she received sympathy from many
of her teachers and her fellow students, she found she was never
questioned about the event, never asked for any kind of explanation or elaboration. Even Brooke Benton didn't pry into the
details of the affair. She said only, "I'm glad to have you back.
We all missed you Friday night. And if you need anything, just
let me know."

After spending a little more than twenty-four hours in the
hospital and having to endure intravenous feeding, Allison was
glad to get back to her old routines of self-starvation and forced

vomiting. These were things that made her feel normal. It was during her lunch period, as she sat across from Brooke Benton chewing a piece of celery, that she received a notification on her phone alerting her that she had a new message from Brandon Lender on Facebook. The initial excitement she felt dissipated as she read his message and realized that he had no intention of seeing her again, but instead was merely making sure that he would not be implicated publicly in her failed pregnancy. His message read, "You didn't tell anybody that we fucked, right?"

She had come to feel some hatred for Brandon Lender, and this hatred was supported by many of the comments she was receiving in reaction to her posts on the various pro-anorexia websites of which she was a member—comments like, "You are beautiful & if he can't see that, he doesn't deserve you," and "You work so hard to look perfect, screw him," and "You proved you can get him, you don't need anything else," and "No guy is worth getting upset enough to eat over—remember that."

She didn't want to respond to him, but she couldn't help herself. She sought not only his approval but his continued affection. She needed him to see her as more than just one of many girls he had had sex with. She didn't need him to become emotionally involved with her, or to maintain a friendship with her, or even to have compassion for her. She just needed him to acknowledge her as the more beautiful version of the girl who used to be too fat to be sexually attractive. She just needed him to want to have sex with her more than once to prove that she wasn't just another meaningless conquest to him, that she was worthy of a repeat visit, that she was attractive enough to warrant having sex with again. She sent him a message that read, "I guess if you want to find out if I told anyone, we'll just have to hang out again and I can tell you in person." Brandon Lender replied to her message ten minutes later with one that read, "I'm not down with getting you preggers again, though. So we might have to fuck in the ass or something. Cool?"

This validation was all that Allison wanted. She wrote back, "Cool."

Tim Mooney and Brandy Beltmeyer held hands as they walked down the hall between classes. As Tanner Hodge passed them, he said, "I didn't know faggots could have girlfriends."

Brandy said, "What an asshole. Just ignore him."

Tim did even less than ignoring him. He found himself almost unaware of Tanner Hodge and Tanner Hodge's insult. He felt almost as if he were floating down the hallway, watching from a third person perspective similar to his point of view in *World of Warcraft*, looking down on himself from overhead as he walked through the environment. His motions were obligatory; he almost had no choice in what he did, no control. He walked through the hall. He held Brandy's hand. He carried his backpack. He made his way to American history. He thought about none of it as he kissed Brandy on the cheek and heard her say, "See you at lunch."

He almost enjoyed this feeling of extreme detachment from the world he lived in, but he found himself unable to enjoy anything. Even the happiness he usually felt in Brandy's company had slipped into something more like mild amusement, which was the strongest emotion he found himself capable of producing that Monday morning.

Kent Mooney spent his lunch hour at home installing Spector Pro on his son's computer. Once the program was installed, he selected certain settings that were designed to look specifically for account usernames and passwords. He linked the Spector Pro reporting function to his own computer and set the program to run invisibly whenever his son's computer was on.

He made himself a sandwich and turned on the television for

a few minutes but was too lost in his memories of sex with Dawn
Clint to watch. He thought specifically of the way her breasts
and thighs felt in his hands and of the way her vagina smelled
and tasted. That morning, he had received a text message from
Dawn Clint that read, "I can't wait to see you again, if you know
what I mean :)." After receiving the text, Kent thought briefly
about attempting a sexual encounter with Dawn without using
Viagra, but dismissed the possibility almost immediately.

After returning to work, he researched Viagra addiction on
the Internet and found that, although the drug was not found
to be responsible for physical addiction, it did sometimes trigger a strong psychological addiction in users who became fearful
that they would be unable to achieve a satisfactory level of sexual
performance without it. In most of these cases, the user merely
decided to use Viagra before every sexual encounter. Although
Kent wanted to know that he was still capable of performing sexually without the drug, he convinced himself that, at least for the
second sexual encounter with Dawn, he would use the drug. He
saw no harm in that.

On his way to the field house after school, Chris Truby crossed
paths with Hannah Clint. They hadn't communicated with each
other since Hannah spread the rumor that they had sexual intercourse. Hannah had no interest in being confronted by Chris,
being caught in her lie—especially not at school, where the truth
might be overheard by one of her peers. She made her best attempt
to avoid him, but he approached her and said, "Hey," and a conversation couldn't be helped. She was thankful they were alone.

She said, "Hey."

He said, "So how'd that video that I cut for you work out?"

She said, "We ended up sending it in—you know, like, using
it and everything. We're supposed to hear back this week, when
I'll be flying to L.A. for the next round of casting."

He said, "Wow. Cool."

She said, "Yeah." There was a pause as they stared at one another for a few seconds.

He said, "So, what's the deal?"

She said, "What do you mean?"

He said, "I mean, what's the deal?"

She said, "I don't know."

He said, "We haven't really talked since last week, and now, like, everyone in the school thinks we had sex. I don't get it."

She said, "Well, I'm pretty sure we had sex, and I might have told some of my friends about it. So I guess that's the deal."

He said, "We didn't really have sex, though."

She said, "Would you rather I tell everyone that you couldn't get it up?"

He said, "No, I guess I just don't know why you told anyone we had sex in the first place."

She said, "Because I thought you were my best shot at losing my V-card, but you seriously fucked that one up. So I just told everyone I lost it, and that's good enough. If they think I lost it, then I pretty much lost it, right?"

He said, "That's a pretty fucked-up way of looking at it, but whatever."

She said, "Whatever."

He said, "Well, so what's the deal?"

She said, "What do you mean?"

He said, "I mean, what's the fucking deal, like, with us?"

She said, "There is no deal with us. I'm pretty sure you're, like, a weird guy who has some serious sexual issues, and I'm not that into dealing with it."

He said, "So are we just supposed to not talk to each other anymore?"

She said, "We can talk if you want, but I don't see the point."

He said, "Whatever."

She said, "I know."

Chris continued walking down the hall toward the field house and did not turn to look back at Hannah as she walked down the hall in the opposite direction. He wondered if this would be a problem for the rest of his life, or if he would find a girl eventually who would indulge his sexual preferences, or if his preferences would change in time to be more normal. He hoped it was the latter. Hannah wondered if all guys were like Chris and would only be able to become sexually aroused through means that she found unappealing, or if Chris was an anomaly. She hoped it was the latter.

Dawn Clint received an e-mail alerting her that a new member had joined the private section of her daughter's website and wondered how long the website would remain viable. She assumed, but wouldn't consciously acknowledge, that the men who were subscribers were sexual deviants, quite possibly full-blown pedophiles, and presumed that their interest in her daughter would wane as she got older. She had gotten used to the extra money every month and was hopeful that her daughter would be selected as a member of the cast on the reality show they were waiting to hear back from. It would mean that perhaps her daughter would be able to generate a viable stream of income through her appearance on a legitimate television program.

Hannah had always told her mother that she wanted to be an actress, but Dawn knew that wasn't true. Dawn thought she wanted to be an actress, but she had realized at some point, while living in Los Angeles, that what she really wanted was to be a celebrity, to warrant attention from strangers, and to make a very good living doing what she felt was easy work. She knew her daughter felt the same way. She had no respect for the craft of acting, no interest in the art of it. She wanted to be on the covers of magazines and wanted to live in a mansion. That was all.

Dawn wondered what had changed—if it was generational.

Her mother, Nicole, *did* love acting, loved the craft, respected the art. For her mother, the minor amount of attention she had generated as a result of success in the field was secondary to the work itself. Dawn remembered having felt that way at some point as a little girl. She remembered watching the movies her mother was in, and listening to the stories her mother would tell her about working with amazing directors who were able to help guide her through emotional mazes in order to have her arrive at an amazing performance. Dawn had never experienced that, and after years of trying fruitlessly to navigate the seemingly impossible system of casting agents, talent agencies, commercial agents, fake producers and directors, and so on, somewhere along the way she had stopped caring about the quality of her work or the meaning behind the art. She had just wanted a job that would give her exposure and money. And she could see that her mother's interest in the art, which she had shared in the beginning, had just never existed in her daughter. For her daughter it had always been just about the fame, and Dawn saw no problem with that.

Just as she was about to log out of her e-mail account, a new message arrived in her in-box from the producers of the reality show *Undiscovered*. Dawn was nervous for her daughter. This e-mail contained news that could potentially change her life forever. Dawn opened the e-mail and read.

The e-mail was from a producer named Wendy Gruding. She explained that, although they had loved Hannah's initial application and subsequent video, they would be unable to invite her to Los Angeles for the formal casting interview. After doing some internal research, they had discovered Hannah's modeling website and come to the conclusion that it was material their parent company might deem unwholesome, due to the concerns of various advertisers that would likely be buyers of advertising time in the show once it aired. Wendy further explained that even taking the site down before the show aired wouldn't be enough to make their production company reconsider, because the images on the website could have been downloaded or copied to anyone's hard drive who had viewed the site, and once the show was on the air, they couldn't risk one of those images surfacing and causing potential damage to their parent company's reputation. Wendy thanked Dawn and Hannah for their time and patience during the selection process and wished them luck in the future with all of their endeavors.

Dawn archived the e-mail and logged out of her account. The sinking feeling in her stomach was one she hadn't felt since her youth, when she had been rejected for a television or movie role herself. She was unsure about how she should inform Hannah, and she felt as though it was partially her fault for maintaining her daughter's website. She convinced herself that she was not to blame, that this was the nature of the industry—no one was willing to take a chance on anything because of the potential loss of advertisers. In that moment it became clear to her why it was that no one cared about the craft anymore, why an entire generation of young actors, writers, and directors didn't care about the art they made. It was because the art was irrelevant. The only thing that mattered was how many cans of soda, how many bottles of laundry detergent could be sold. If the companies hiring the artists didn't care about the art, why should the artists?

It was this realization that ultimately changed Dawn's mind about the website. Dawn had found something in Kent that had substance and value. It was different and better than any relationship she had been in, even her relationship with Hannah's father in Los Angeles. It was real, and she wanted Hannah to have that one day, too. Dawn knew that her daughter wanted to pursue a career in entertainment, but she began to see that it had nothing to do with acting, it was about fame—it was the ideal of this new generation that wanted everything handed to it without carving out a place in the world through hard work and trial, without having to do anything other than exist. She wanted more for her daughter. She wanted her daughter to be a better person than that, to think in a different way from the rest of her generation. Dawn felt responsible, in some part, for this problem. She had been the one to encourage her daughter, even to create and maintain a website that she knew was of a questionable nature, in order to promote her daughter. In that moment, the website became a symbol to Dawn of everything she no longer wanted her daughter to be.

Dawn logged onto the hosting account for the website and took it down. She assumed her daughter would become aware of this transgression very quickly and decided that she would tell her the truth when asked. She would tell her daughter that the reality show had rejected her, and she would tell her daughter that her mother loved her and that she wanted better things for her in life than the things she herself ended up with.

chapter
twenty-one

Rachel Truby left work a few hours early on Friday, having already told her husband that she was spending the night and the following morning with her sister. She was, instead, spending the night and the following morning at a hotel with Secretluvur. As she drove, she realized that she'd forgotten to check the message from Secretluvur that contained the exact hotel where she was to meet him in a neighboring town. Rachel went home, packed a few things, and, for the first time since beginning her life of regular infidelity, logged into her account on AshleyMadison. com from the family desktop computer. She wrote down the name and address of the hotel on a Post-it note, put it in her pocket, and then went to shut her computer down. She noticed, however, that an update had been downloaded and was ready to be installed, which required a restart. She clicked the button authorizing the update to be installed and happily left her house, without realizing she had to click one more button in order for the computer to automatically restart itself after the installation was complete.

Don Truby came home from work that evening with the intention of scheduling another rendezvous with Angelique Ice, as he had done a few times before when his wife decided to spend the night at her sister's house. Don had meant to do this on his work computer, but now he noted that he was finally comfortable enough with the process to use the computer that he shared with his wife for this purpose.

He walked into their bedroom, sat down in the computer chair, ran his finger over the touchpad, and brought the screen out of its black energy-saving state to see his wife's Ashley Madison account become visible on the screen behind a pop-up window that asked if the user would like to automatically restart the computer upon installation of an update. It took Don Truby almost a minute to fully process exactly what it was that he was staring at. Initially he assumed it was a pop-up ad or some other result of adware, and he was a second away from closing the window when he realized that he was looking at an in-box that was full of messages from a user named Secretluvur. It took him a few moments of reading these messages before the possibility that this account belonged to his wife entered his mind, but eventually he understood exactly what he was looking at: a document of his wife's infidelity, with at least one man, that had been occurring for the better part of a month.

Don's initial emotional reaction was, he suspected, the common one: He was sad and outraged. He wanted to confront her, to demand some kind of explanation, possibly a divorce. He wanted to know why she would be more interested in having sex with a stranger she'd met online than she was in having sex with her own husband. All of these things formed Don's initial reaction.

His second reaction, however, was almost the opposite. As he sat in the chair, staring at a picture of Secretluvur and at the address of the hotel his wife was heading to—the hotel where she would have sex with this man—Don's original purpose for coming into the room came back to him. He logged off his wife's account and logged on to the Erotic Review on the computer he shared with his wife in order to communicate with Angelique Ice. The hypocrisy of his anger seemed absurd to him.

He realized in that moment that he had a decision to make. In the weeks since he had been cheating on Rachel with a prostitute, he was certainly happier, and it seemed to Don that his relationship with his wife had improved as a result of his happiness. With the new information that his wife's happiness had nothing to do with his own, but rather with her own experimentations in unfaithfulness, Don understood that they were more alike than he thought. He liked seeing his wife happy. He assumed she enjoyed seeing him happy. If their happiness could only come as a result of each of them having sex with other people, then Don decided he would have to deal with that. And, beyond their mutual happiness, Don never wanted to have to tell his wife the truth about his visits with Angelique Ice, which he thought would only be fair to divulge if he confronted her about her own secret life.

He logged back on to his wife's account and decided it would be best to install the update, as she had no doubt had planned to do. He saw no need to give her any reason to feel anxiety or suspect that he knew anything about her infidelity.

Don liked Angelique Ice, and although he knew he would purchase her services again in the future, he began to think about looking for something different that night. A new girl, a second girl, would signify to Don that, from that night forward, his sexuality would have nothing to do with his own wife. Despite this sentiment, Don found himself in the mood for a prostitute who looked more like Rachel than Angelique Ice did.

He entered his search criteria and found a prostitute named

Summer Sweet who looked enough like a younger version of Rachel that Don was persuaded to make an appointment with her for later that night after his son's football game. He hoped that having sex with her would remind him of having sex with his wife one last time, and then he would try never to think about his wife in a sexual capacity again. She would be the mother of his child, the warm body on the other side of the bed, and the person with whom he had occasional conversations about the minutiae of his life, and that is all she would be.

Kent Mooney received an e-mail notice at work from the Spector Pro software he installed on his son's computer that contained the username and password to his son's Battle.net account. This was what Tim used to log in to his *World of Warcraft* account. Kent decided he would eat lunch at home and log in to his son's account in order to experience firsthand exactly what it was that his son found so alluring about the game.

He made himself a sandwich and sat down at his son's computer, looking around his son's room as he waited for the machine to boot up. He realized he hadn't been very attentive to his son in the months since his ex-wife, Lydia, had moved to California. He had lost touch with his son, and he considered logging in to his son's *World of Warcraft* account as much an attempt to understand his son as it was an attempt to police his online activity. Some part of him thought that, if he could form a basic understanding of the things that were important in his son's life, then maybe they could repair their relationship on some small level, and maybe that repair would lead to Tim coming back to his former self just enough to give his father a glimmer of the way things used to be—just enough for Tim to want to play football again.

The computer finished booting up and Kent clicked on the *World of Warcraft* icon. Although he knew little about video games, he knew enough about computers in general to handle the process easily. He typed in the username and password supplied to him by the Spector Pro software and was taken to a screen that contained all of Tim's characters on the Shattered Hand server. Kent chose the character that was already selected, the last character Tim had played, his main character, Firehands, and entered the world. After a brief load screen, Kent was in control of Firehands, who stood in the center of a floating city called Dalaran. Other characters ran past him in all directions. It was a far more complex experience than Kent had expected. The city itself was too large and complicated for Kent to navigate properly. Beyond that, he didn't even know how to make the avatar move. He used the mouse to swivel the character's point of view but found that clicking on things only highlighted or targeted them.

After a few seconds of trying to discover how to move, Kent became aware of some green text scrolling up the left side of the screen. From a character named Selkis, Kent saw a message that read, "Yo nigger, your mom married to that homo in Cali yet? When's the wedding again?" From a character named Kenrogers, Kent saw a message that read, "Why would that homo buy the cow when he's getting the milk for free?" From a character named Mzo, Kent saw a message that read, "Is he a homo or a nigger? I thought he was a nigger?" From a character named Baratheon, Kent saw a message that read, "He's both."

Kent was stunned. The language used by the people his son played this game with was wildly offensive, but beyond that, they were clearly talking about his ex-wife, and beyond that, they seemed to know that she was getting married—information that Kent himself didn't have. All of which meant that Tim also had this information, and that he was more comfortable telling people he had never met than he was telling his own father.

Kent tried to respond but had too much difficulty writing a message in anything other than general chat. After reading a conversation among Tim's guildmates about how they all wanted to have various kinds of sex with his ex-wife before her wedding night, Kent shut the *World of Warcraft* program down and uninstalled it from his son's computer. He logged on to Blizzard Entertainment's customer-service website and canceled the account he had been paying for, enabling his son to play the game in exchange for fifteen dollars a month. The website offered the option of allowing his son's playing time to continue for the remainder of the current month, which was already paid for, but Kent declined, choosing instead to terminate the account immediately.

He didn't know what was more offensive, the fact that his son spent so much time in the virtual company of people who seemed to be racists and misogynists, or the fact that they knew more about his ex-wife's relationship status than he did. And then there was the information itself: Lydia was getting married. Kent had made some peace with the fact that his relationship with her was over. He had managed to find something in Dawn Clint that made it easier to move on. He had feelings for Dawn Clint, but the finality of Lydia marrying Greg Cherry was something he was unprepared for.

Although he was no longer hungry, he ate the sandwich he prepared for himself and returned to work. He planned to go to the eighth-grade Goodrich Junior High Olympians' final regular-season game after work and then return home to have a long conversation with his son.

Hannah Clint called her mother from the girls' dressing room in the gymnasium of Goodrich Junior High School an hour before the final game of the season. She said, "So . . . I'm pretty sure they said they were going to let us know by the end of this week, right? Well, it's, like, the end of the week, so what's the deal? Oh, also, the site's down."

Hannah's mother, who was driving to Goodrich Junior High School with her camera to document what might be the

Olympiannes' final performance of the year if the football team failed to claim a victory that night, said, "We need to talk about some things. I guess the best place to start is with the show. I got the e-mail. We didn't make it, baby."

Hannah said, "What? Why? I don't get it. I mean, I'm pretty sure I must have been one of the best ones. Did they not like the video or something? Should we have hired somebody instead of having Chris do it?"

She said, "They didn't like the website."

Hannah said, "Then screw them."

She said, "No, baby, I thought about it, and I think they're right. I took the site down."

Hannah said, "What?!? Why? What about my fans?"

She said, "Baby, if you want to act, you can act. We'll get you in as many theater programs as we can. But that website, and that show, that's not what you want to do."

Hannah, "Yes it is! It's all I want to do!"

Dawn said, "You know I've supported you in anything and everything, but you're better than that stupid show and you're way better than the website."

Hannah, "No I'm not! You have to put it back up!"

Dawn said, "I can't, baby."

And Hannah hung up on her mother.

Hannah was enraged. She felt no sorrow and no self-pity. She felt anger and rage toward her mother and toward the producers of the show. She was certain that, as soon as she turned eighteen, she would move to Los Angeles and never talk to her mother again, if that's what was necessary for her to achieve her goal of fame. As she slipped on her Olympiannes cheerleader skirt and made her way into the gymnasium to start stretching with the other girls, she thought about what she would do next, about how she would prove them wrong. She would start her own website. Chris probably knew how to make one, she reasoned, and on this website she could do whatever she wanted. She could interact with her fans directly. She could post any kind of video she wanted. She didn't need her mother, or a reality show, to make herself famous. She was determined to do it by herself and by any means necessary.

She envisioned herself sitting on a chair across from David Letterman as his featured guest. She heard herself telling him the story of how she was rejected from the first reality show she'd ever auditioned for. She heard his audience laughing in disbelief at the absurdity of the notion.

Patricia Beltmeyer glanced back and forth from an episode of *Are You Smarter Than a 5th Grader?* to the printout of every keystroke her daughter had made for the past week. She read every instant-message conversation she had, every e-mail she sent, and every paper she wrote for school. Nothing seemed out of the ordinary—until Patricia noticed a username and password that were unfamiliar to her: username Freyja, password luckycat2, only a slight variation on the password Brandy used on her other accounts: luckycat1. Her daughter had never used these during any of her weekly checks or her surprise checks.

Patricia's heart rate increased. She began to sweat. The realization that her daughter was engaging in online activity that she was not aware of was almost too much for her to handle. Her initial reaction was to disconnect her daughter's computer, give her an electronic typewriter for her schoolwork, and forbid her from any computer or cell-phone use until she was eighteen years old. She thought about logging in to the account immediately but couldn't tear herself from the keystroke document that she had in her hand. She continued reading and discovered multiple messages to and from another Myspace user named TimM.

Patricia read the messages, which detailed multiple visits to TimM's house, lunches eaten with TimM, holding hands with TimM, and TimM's continued promise to keep their relationship a secret from Patricia, who was conjuring images of TimM as a fifty-year-old pedophile luring her daughter to meet him in a seedy motel where he had no doubt defiled her. Patricia's worst nightmares were all written in the black-and-white text of a keystroke-log printout.

As she read on, she began to piece together that TimM was likely not the criminal adult that she had assumed he was, but rather one of Brandy's peers. The many references to events, people, and locations at Goodrich Junior High School, and to spending time with each other between classes, made it clear that TimM was a student, not an adult. This realization made Patricia feel only slightly better. She was still barely able to breathe as she thought about her daughter lying to her, sneaking to this boy's house when she was supposed to be visiting her friend Lauren, and maintaining a Myspace account she knew nothing about.

After reading the entire keystroke log, Patricia went to Brandy's room and logged into her Freyja account. She scoured the account's friend list, blogs, comments, and in-box for anything that might give her a clearer understanding of how exactly her daughter was using this account. Patricia never got the chance to see any of the overly sexual photos or read any of the blog entries about sexual activity that her daughter had posted before deleting them once she began her relationship with Tim. She saw only her daughter's Freyja account in its final form: a simple painted image of the goddess Freyja as a profile picture, no incriminating comments or messages from any other users, nothing but innocuous and innocent e-mails to and from TimM, which outlined the beginnings of an extremely normal and non-threatening teenage relationship. And, after seeing Tim's profile picture, Patricia accepted that he was one of her daughter's peers, not an adult sexual predator.

From everything the e-mails contained, Patricia concluded that this TimM was likely her daughter's boyfriend. Patricia found evidence that they had shared their first kiss but no sign that her daughter had engaged in any sexual behavior beyond kissing. Her daughter was merely growing up. Even in the face of this realization, Patricia was unwilling to accept the fact that her daughter was dating a boy behind her back.

It seemed from the pattern of communication that her daughter had been lying about going to Lauren's house every Friday night for the past several weeks and was, instead, spending her time at TimM's house. Patricia assumed that her daughter would attempt to initiate the same lie that night, and she devised a plan in which she would confront her daughter, catch her in her lie, and revoke all of her online privileges for at least one month. That would take care of deciding the consequences for her actions.

But the larger issue of what to do about her daughter's relationship with TimM was more difficult for Patricia to deal with. TimM seemed like a nice enough boy. Patricia knew that her daughter would have to start dating soon anyway, and she thought that a boy like TimM would probably be better than most, at least based on the exchanges he shared with her daughter on Myspace. She was tempted to let their relationship continue, after the grounding ended, of course. But something deep in Patricia's core, some need to control as many things as she could in her own life and in the life of her daughter, compelled her to end her daughter's relationship with TimM. Ending it would send the message to her daughter that she wasn't ready to date, and when she was, the first thing she should do would be to tell her mother.

So, while still logged in to her daughter's Freyja account, she assumed her daughter's identity and composed an e-mail to TimM that read, "Can't come over tonight and I don't think we should see each other or talk to each other anymore. Sorry. Bye." Patricia sent the message and thought about deleting the account, but instead opted to change the password to idontthinkso and log out.

chapter
twenty-two

Kent Mooney, Jim Vance, and Don Truby sat next to one another in the stands of the Goodrich Junior High School football
field, just as they had for every previous home game. Kent did
not mention his discovery that his ex-wife was getting remarried.
Don did not mention his discovery that his wife was cheating
on him with a man who went by the moniker Secretluvur and
whom she'd met on AshleyMadison.com. Jim Vance opened the
conversation by saying, "So, I'm getting a vasectomy tomorrow
morning."

Don said, "Good luck, man."

Kent said, "Yeah, good luck."

Don said, "Things going bad with Dawn or something? You
seem fucking depressed, man."

Kent said, "No, things are fine. Just wish Tim was playing in
this game. I thought he'd come around at some point during the

season, you know—snap out of whatever funk he was in—but this is it, the last game."

Jim said, "It's tough when they're this age. There's always next year."

They said nothing else as they watched the opening kickoff, which was returned by Tanner Hodge for twenty-six yards.

Every member of the Goodrich Junior High School Olympians eighth-grade football team understood the importance of a victory that night. Before the game, Coach Quinn had told them all that they should leave everything on the field. He highlighted the fact that some of them might not make the cut when they moved on to high school football, and so, without a victory, this would be the last organized football game that some of them would ever play. For that reason alone, he expected all of his players to give the greatest effort they had ever given in their lives for any single event. Danny Vance knew that he would play football again, no matter the outcome of the game, but he agreed with the basic premise that each player should play to the best of his capability to maximize the team's possibility of winning. It was with this attitude that he called the first play in the huddle: the Z cut left, a middle-distance passing play, with Chris Truby set up as the primary receiver.

The Olympians approached the line of scrimmage, got in their various stances, and waited for Danny Vance to initiate the play. Once initiated, the play was executed flawlessly. Each member of the offensive line found his block assignment and kept him from reaching the quarterback. The running backs effectively deceived the linebackers into thinking the play was an outside run. The receivers entangled the secondary, except for Chris Truby, who beat his defender off the line of scrimmage to such an extent that the defender twisted his ankle and fell down, leaving Chris wide open. Danny Vance threw a perfect pass to him, which was caught. Having no defender near him, Chris Truby turned up field and ran an additional sixty-four yards for a touchdown.

The play's result infused the Goodrich Junior High School Olympians with a level of confidence that made them each feel the game's outcome would be a predetermined victory for them. Danny Vance watched from the sidelines as the extra-point team took the field. Brooke Benton approached him and said, "That was awesome, babe. In my opinion, we should celebrate you guys winning tomorrow by"—and then she leaned in and whispered in his ear—"having sex." Danny attempted to maintain his focus on the game, on the task at hand, but found it difficult, as thoughts of sex with Brooke crept into his mind. She kissed him on the cheek and then returned to the far side of the sideline area, where the other Olympiannes, including Allison Doss, were in the process of cheering.

Brooke said, "I really think we're going to win this game. Seriously. Don't you?" Allison said, "Uh, yeah. Probably." Allison hadn't been thinking about the game's outcome at all. She instead was thinking about a series of text messages she had exchanged with Brandon Lender earlier that afternoon. Brandon had initiated the conversation by sending a text message to Allison that read, "So when can I fuck you in the ass?"

Allison had replied, "I don't know. When do you want to?"

Brandon wrote, "ASAP."

His enthusiasm made Allison happy. She wrote "I'm cheering tonight. After the game?"

Brandon wrote, "K. Meet me at my house after midnight."

Allison wrote, "You live like 2 miles away."

Brandon wrote, "Yeah, it's not too far to walk."

Allison wrote, "K."

Brandon wrote, "Make sure you shower good and get your ass really clean. If I can smell shit or anything, I'm out."

Allison wrote, "K."

Brandon wrote, "Just tap on my window when you get here and I'll open it for you. It's the one in front on the left of the front door."

Allison wrote, "K."

She had been thinking about her upcoming encounter with Brandon for most of the day. She hoped that she could clean her anus properly. The anxiety she felt about having anal sex for the first time had nothing to do with the pain she assumed would be associated with it, but instead was solely based on her fear of rejection by Brandon Lender for any reason. She hoped it would be over quickly and that he would hold her for just a few minutes before she would have to crawl back out of his window and walk home alone.

Allison tried to calm her anxiety by focusing her attention on the game. The Culler Cougars answered the Olympians' initial score with an eleven-play drive that resulted in a rushing touchdown. They followed the touchdown with an extra point and the game was tied seven to seven at the end of the first quarter.

Danny Vance found the second quarter more difficult than the first. He couldn't clear his mind of thoughts of sex with Brooke and as a result was unable to score again before the half. Over the course of two drives he completed only three passes out of seven attempts and the Olympian rushing game produced only one first down. The Culler Cougars, too, had difficulty scoring in the second half, with three offensive drives that combined for a single field goal resulting in a half time score of ten to seven in favor of the Cougars.

chapter twenty-three

Brandy Beltmeyer had begun to think that her mother was becoming suspicious of her increased time spent away from the house. She and Tim Mooney discussed it at lunch and decided that she would not visit him that Friday night for the first time in many weeks. Nor would she spend her time online talking to him. Instead, she would stay at home and watch television with her parents in an attempt to allay any suspicions about her activities outside the house.

Brandy had just finished eating dinner with her mother, father, and younger brother, when her mother said, "So, are you going over to Lauren's house tonight?"

Brandy couldn't identify her mother's tone. It wasn't suspicious, and it wasn't genuine. It was something in the middle. Brandy said, "No, I thought I'd just stay at home and hang out."

Patricia was surprised. She wondered if TimM had already

read the message she sent him posing as her daughter and decided to initiate some kind of fight that led to a breakup. She hoped this was the case. She said, "Oh, yeah, it'll be nice to have you home on a Friday night for once."

Brandy helped her mother clear the dishes and then went into the living room, where her father and little brother were already watching *Deal or No Deal*. Patricia was tempted to let the night continue without confronting her daughter. She was tempted to see what would happen in the coming days when Brandy found out that she would be unable to log in to her secret Myspace account because her mother had altered the password. She was tempted to do these things, but instead she came into the living room and said, "You know, since you're home, we could just do your Internet check right now instead of waiting until tomorrow."

Brandy said, "Okay."

They went into Brandy's room, and Patricia looked through all of her various online accounts just as she usually did. She found nothing abnormal, nothing that was cause for alarm. Brandy said, "Everything look okay?"

Patricia said, "Everything looks good on these accounts. But isn't there another account that we didn't check yet?"

Brandy said, "No, that's all of them."

Patricia said, "I think there's one more. Your Myspace account."

Brandy said, "No, we just did that one, remember? You said you thought that guy named GoofSlop had no business being my friend and we defriended him."

Patricia said, "Yeah, that's right. That's right. But, um, that's not the Myspace account I'm talking about."

Brandy could feel the cold sweat forming on the back of her neck. She had no idea how much her mother knew—if she knew anything at all or if this was some kind of psychological trick, an attempt to get her to divulge a secret, with her mother having only suspicion and no evidence of the secret's validity. She wondered if her mother had been monitoring everything she did on the Freyja account; if her mother had read the blogs she'd written when she first created the account; if her mother had seen the pictures she'd taken of herself in gothic makeup and lingerie. She concluded that if her mother had known about the blog posts and the images, she would have said something a long time ago. If her mother knew anything, it was a recent development, and the only information she could have possibly gleaned from the Freyja account was that she and Tim were a couple, which, she reasoned, wasn't that terrible.

Brandy said, "I only have one account, Mom. You just saw it."

Patricia said, "Oh. Because I was under the impression that you had another account, one that you can tell me about freely and maybe avoid some of the punishment that's coming your way, or you can keep playing dumb about it and get double the punishment. Your choice."

Brandy still was unable to detect any hint in her mother's accusation that enabled her to determine if this was all based on suspicion or if her mother had hard evidence against her. She chose to deny everything and hope that her mother had no evidence. She said, "Mom, I only have one Myspace account. I don't get what you're doing here."

Patricia said, "Then I guess you probably also have no idea who TimM is."

Brandy knew she'd been caught in her lie. She said, "Mom, I'm sorry. I just. I knew you'd never let me go out with him or see him or talk to him so I had to—"

Patricia said, "Lie to me at every turn? And engage in behavior that is absolutely unacceptable and more dangerous than you could possibly even imagine?"

Brandy said, "It's not dangerous, Mom. I like him and he likes me."

Patricia said, "Well, you can go on liking each other. But you can't do it using the service provider that your father pays for every month. I changed the password on your account, so don't even bother trying to log in. I have your cell phone downstairs, and I'm blocking your computer from the wireless router. And I know you probably think you can pick up the wireless signal from the neighbors, but you can't, because I blocked their router from your computer. And if you try to set up another network through their signal, your computer will send me an e-mail, so don't even try. I want you to stay up here and write me an apology—and it better be sincere. You are not to come out of your room for the rest of the night. Is that understood?"

Brandy was crying. She said, "Why are you like this? I wasn't doing anything wrong!"

Patricia said, "If that was the case, then you wouldn't be getting punished."

Patricia left her daughter's room listening to her cry.

Tim Mooney was looking forward to a night of doing nothing but playing *World of Warcraft*. He had been meaning to raise his reputation with the Oracles for some time, and viewed a Friday night with no other obligations as the perfect time to run a few daily quests with various factions that he had neglected.

His father usually left him money for pizza or fast food, but that wasn't the case tonight. Tim looked in the usual places that his father normally left money, a note about food, or the food itself, and found nothing. He assumed it was just forgetfulness on his father's part and made himself a sandwich, which he took into his room and set on his desk as he started up his computer. At the start-up screen, he noticed that the *World of Warcraft* shortcut icon was gone. He opened his hard drive folder, then opened the programs folder to look for *World of Warcraft*, and found nothing. He did an exhaustive search of every folder on his computer's hard drive in an effort to find *World of Warcraft* but found nothing. Not wanting to reinstall the entire game, and not knowing exactly what was going on, Tim searched for possible explanations online and still found nothing explaining any spontaneous uninstalls of *World of Warcraft*. He reasoned that there must be something wrong with his computer and ran a full scan for viruses, spyware, adware, and so on. The scan returned nothing abnormal. He resigned himself to a fate that he was not looking forward to: reinstalling the entire game, a process he knew would take at least an hour.

He put the first of four disks needed to install the original game in his disk drive and began the reinstallation, eating his sandwich as he waited. Nothing seemed to be out of the ordinary as he ejected the fourth and final disc, having completed the original game's installation. He accepted the end-user license agreement and began downloading the first of several patches that were necessary to play the game, the last of which indicated that it would take twenty-five minutes to download. Tim left his computer and went to the living room, where he spent twenty-five minutes watching an episode of *Wife Swap* that didn't interest him. He then returned to his bedroom to find that the patch had finished downloading. He applied the patch and was finally ready to play *World of Warcraft* again.

Tim Mooney entered his username and password, an action that had become a physical reflex for him when he was prompted by the site's log-in screen, and received a message that read, "This account needs to be converted to a Battle.net account. Please [click here] or go to: [http://us.battle.net/account/creation/landing.xml] to begin conversion." Tim retyped his username and password, assuming he'd made an error the first time and again received the same message. He had converted his account to a Battle.net account on the first day. It was mandatory to do so in order to play. He was unsure if this had something to do with the game being uninstalled from his computer, so he contacted the Blizzard support center via chat and, after some time spent waiting, finally received a response.

After a minute or so of chatting, the customer-support representative for Blizzard informed Tim that his account had been canceled earlier that day, and that a special request had been made to cancel the account as soon as possible, not even allowing for play to continue through the end of the month. When Tim asked who was responsible for this error, he was told that the account holder, Kent Mooney, had canceled the account.

Tim ended the call and stared blankly at the inoperable log-in screen. His father had canceled his *World of Warcraft* account. He should be furious, but found it impossible to generate anger. He just stared at the log-in screen, feeling detached from it all, having no control of any of it. He watched the "Pale Blue Dot" video on YouTube and found no comfort in it. Where before it had made him feel as though the insignificance shared by all humanity gave greater importance to each individual's experiences, he now found that that same insight made him feel that nothing mattered. There was nothing anyone could do that would mean anything. The whole of life, of existence itself, was pointless. He went back into the living room and watched an episode of *16 and Pregnant*, waiting for his father to return home so he could ask him why he had canceled his *World of Warcraft* account.

chapter
twenty-four

The second half began with a forty-six-yard kickoff return by the Culler Cougars and a subsequent touchdown and extra point after a drive of three rushing plays, making the score seventeen-seven in their favor. Coach Quinn could feel the head-coaching job slipping away from him. On the sideline he said, "We have to win this game. We have no other option. They have a good defense and a good offense, so we're just going to have to be better. Hit your blocks and let's make some plays out there."

Danny Vance led the Olympians on a thirteen-play scoring drive of his own, culminating in a screen pass to Tanner Hodge for the touchdown and bringing the score to seventeen to fourteen. His thoughts of having sex with Brooke Benton had subsided to some degree, and he found it much easier to concentrate on the task at hand. The next kickoff was dropped by the Cougars' returner and recovered by the Olympians on the thirty-five-yard line. Coach Quinn said, "That's a gift from God, boys. Let's not waste it."

Danny Vance led the Olympians to another touchdown after eight plays, this scoring drive culminating in a pass over the middle to Chris Truby, making the score twenty-one to seventeen in favor of the Olympians. The score remained the same for the remainder of the third quarter and well into the fourth.

With three minutes left on the clock, the Olympians were forced to punt. Jeremy Kelms, assuming that he might have been one of the players Coach Quinn was referring to in his pregame speech, exerted himself to his fullest capacity as he kicked a thirty-eight-yard punt that put the Cougars on their own fourteen-yard line.

Coach Quinn gathered the defense before they took the field and said, "This is it. The game—hell, the entire season—is' riding on your shoulders right now. You stop them, we win, we go to the playoffs. You don't, we don't. So·don't let me down." He sent them onto the field and thought to himself how absurd it was that his professional future depended on the performance of a group of eleven thirteen-year-old children. He had no control in the matter.

After two successful three-play drives for first downs, the Culler Cougars found themselves on the fifty-yard line with one minute and twelve seconds left of play. Three rushing plays later, they were faced with fourth down and eight yards to go, with forty-eight seconds of play left in the game. Culler's coach knew that a punt was pointless. He used the last of his time-outs and brought his offense to the sideline. He gave his players a speech very similar to Coach Quinn's pregame speech, citing the fact that many of his players would not play in high school and this might very well be their last chance to do something meaningful on an organized level. He explained what they already knew: that without at least a first down, the game and their season would be over. He insisted that their best plan of attack was a run directly up the middle. It would be unexpected, as they had eight yards to gain for a first down. It was likely that the other team would spread the defense somewhat, in order to protect against a pass, and as long as the offensive line hit their blocks, the play should be successful.

The play was run just as Culler's coach had instructed, and the Olympians' defense was spread out just as he predicted. His offensive line hit their blocks just as they were asked to do, and the Culler Cougars' fullback had an open hole straight up the middle, directly to Bill Francis, the middle linebacker. For Bill, the play happened in slow motion, each second storing itself in his memory forever. He would remember the images, smells, tastes, and sounds of the next five seconds for the rest of his life.

The Cougars' fullback ran through the hole in the line and made no effort to sidestep, or spin, or in any way avoid Bill Francis. He lowered his head, tucked the football under his arm, and ran as hard as he could directly toward Bill Francis, who leaned back on his heels out of fear for the impact he could see coming. The Cougars' fullback planted his helmet squarely in the chest of Bill Francis, who made an awkward attempt to tackle him but failed. Instead, Bill Francis found himself lying on his back, wheezing from having the wind knocked out of him, as he watched the Cougars' fullback run unobstructed fifty yards down field and score a touchdown.

In the stands, Don Truby said, "Tim would have stopped him."

Kent Mooney said, "I know. I know."

The Cougars scored their extra point, bringing the score to twenty-four to twenty-one in their favor. The Olympians kicked off to Tanner Hodge, who returned the ball to the thirty-four-yard line with twenty-six seconds left in the game. Danny Vance gathered himself and led the Olympians back on the field for their final offensive attempt. He knew they likely had enough time for three plays, which had to result in a touchdown. A field goal would result in a tie, which would put their overall record at six wins, two losses, and one tie. This was an identical record to the Pound Squires, who had a higher points-per-game average than the Olympians, a factor that would determine which team would receive a playoff berth.

The first play of the drive was a thirteen-yard pass completion to Chris Truby for a first down, leaving twenty seconds on the clock. The second play was a pitch to Tanner Hodge, resulting in a seventeen-yard gain, leaving twelve seconds on the clock. The third play was another pitch to Tanner Hodge, resulting in a gain of twelve yards and leaving five seconds on the clock. Coach Quinn called his final time-out of the game and brought his team to the sideline. His team needed twenty-four yards for a touchdown, and they had one play left. He had become used to the idea that the outcome of this game—and, consequently, his career—was out of his control. He looked to Danny Vance and said, "Danny, this is your moment. You've grown a lot this season, and I think you know better than anyone on this field what play is going to get us in that end zone. I believe in each and every one of you guys, and your season comes down to the next five seconds. Okay, now, Olympians on three. One, two, three—Olympians!"

Danny jogged back onto the field and into the huddle. He saw Brooke on the sidelines cheering, her position slightly exposing her buttocks. He thought briefly about winning the game and then celebrating by having sex with his cheerleader girlfriend. He felt no more ready, psychologically or emotionally, to have sex than he had at the beginning of the season, but the idea of sex as a trophy for his victory was alluring. He assumed the Cougars would be playing a deep-pass prevention defense, so he called an X flat left, a pass play designed to be thrown to a receiver approximately eight to ten yards from the line of scrimmage in order to gain a first down.

Chris Truby said, "But we need to score a fucking touchdown here, man."

Danny said, "We need to get twenty-four yards down the field to do that. If they're going to give us the first ten, I say we take it. I'll put the pass right in your numbers, Chris. No one will be near you. Catch it and run your ass off."

Chris said, "Thanks, Coach."

They broke from the huddle and approached the line of scrimmage. Danny initiated the play, and everything unfolded before him just as he had assumed it would. The Cougars were backed up to protect against the deep pass, allowing Chris to slip into the flat with no one covering him. Danny threw him the perfect pass he had promised, and Chris caught it. Chris turned to run upfield and saw that he had to beat only two defenders; the rest had been so spread out that they had no chance of getting to him before he reached the end zone. He employed a spin move to avoid the first defender, and as he approached the second defender, he attempted a head fake. But he was unsuccessful in duping the free safety, and he was tackled on the eight-yard line with no time left on the clock.

Danny Vance looked at Brooke Benton on the sideline. She was frowning in a display of sympathy for Danny. He stayed on the field longer than necessary, staring at the scoreboard, slowly accepting the fact that his season was over and his freshman year in high school would be more difficult than he expected or wanted in terms of winning the starting quarterback position on the junior varsity team.

He thought about all the decisions that led to that moment—decisions made by both him and Coach Quinn. He wondered whether, if he had not gone against Coach Quinn's early desire to run the ball so much, it would have made a difference. He came to no conclusion. Once all the other players had left the field, Coach Quinn said, "Danny, come on," and Danny joined the rest of his team as they made their way into the field house.

Coach Quinn had no interest in coaching eighth-grade football at Goodrich Junior High School for another year, but that was beyond his control. As his team gathered around him in the field house, he said, "Guys, you played hard. That's all I asked of you, and you gave me that. Sometimes in life things just don't work out the way they're supposed to, and you have to learn from that, pick yourself up, and give it another shot. Those of you who go on to play high school football: Remember tonight and become stronger from it. Those of you who just played your last organized football game: You should remember this night, too. Remember that, for one night, you put it all on the line and gave your best effort for something. That's an important thing, an important moment in your life, and even though we didn't get the win tonight, you guys should all be proud of a great season and a great last game. Olympians on three."

They all put their hands together in the middle of the field house and the words rang hollow to Danny Vance as Coach Quinn said, "One, two, three—Olympians!" He hung his shoulder pads in his locker next to his helmet, knowing that he would not wear them again that year. His next set of shoulder pads and his next helmet would be issued to him by the North East High School equipment manager. It was over.

On the drive back home, Jim Vance told his son many of the same things Coach Quinn had told him in the field house: to be proud of his effort, to realize that something was to be learned from the experience, and to know that he had played well. Danny wondered if he could have played better, if he could have led a scoring drive in the second quarter had he not been preoccupied with thinking about Brooke and having sex with her. He reasoned that he might have been able to win the game. Jim said, "You know, if anyone is to blame, it's that Bill Francis kid. Jesus, what kind of tackle was that supposed to be? He was sitting back on his heels, not moving into the tackle at all. It looked like he was scared out of his mind. You can't beat yourself up."

Danny said, "I know," and thought about Brooke.

•   •   •

Chris rode home with his father, who attempted to convince him that he'd done everything correctly. There just wasn't enough time to win the game. Chris said, "Dad, it's cool. It's not that big a deal. Seriously." Chris didn't care about the game. His thoughts had already refocused on how he could take advantage of the belief, now held by his entire class, that he was no longer a virgin. He wondered if it would make it easier for him to find a girl willing to engage in some of the stranger sexual acts he found himself interested in. If not at Goodrich, Chris thought, certainly once he got to high school he would be able to find at least one girl who had similar sexual tastes, and who had seen enough Internet pornography to know how to indulge them with some proficiency. Football was the last thing on his mind.

His phone vibrated and he saw that Hannah Clint had sent him a text message. He was surprised to be hearing from her at all. The message read, "Hey, know anything about websites? I'll make it worth your while. We can do whatever you want."

Across town, Chris's mother, Rachel Truby, found herself licking Secretluvur's anus as she stroked his penis. She had never been commanded to do anything similar by any of her sexual partners, and she found it enjoyable. She knew that her son's final game of the regular season was happening simultaneously, but she found it difficult to care. She had no regrets about missing the game in order to meet up with Secretluvur, and she wondered briefly if this made her a bad mother.

As Secretluvur ejaculated all over her face and hand, she thought less about her son and about her husband. They were becoming increasingly ghostlike to her. In the bathroom of the hotel room, Rachel cleaned Secretluvur's semen from her hand and face. She knew she didn't want a divorce. It would be far more trouble than it would be worth. Chris would be eighteen soon enough. She assumed he would go to college. She hoped it would be out of state. In the past month or so it seemed that Don's attempts to have sex with her had diminished. Rachel knew he was a decent husband and pleasant enough to be around. As long as their relationship could exist without a sexual component, Rachel could see herself staying married to Don for the rest of her life. She would even have sex with him a few times a year. That seemed a small price to pay to avoid the turmoil of a divorce, of moving to another house, of trying to find another man. Rachel knew that logically she didn't need a man in her life in the capacity of a husband, but she had become used to it, and she had to admit that she would feel like something of a failure if she were to get a divorce.

She turned off the light in the bathroom and went back to Secretluvur, who was sleeping in the bed. She ran her fingers though the coarse hair on his chest, and for the first time she wondered why her husband's attempts to have sex with her had subsided. She wondered if he had simply given up, or if perhaps he had found a sexual release outside of their marriage, as she had. She reasoned that the latter was far more likely, and she found that she didn't care. She knew that she would never ask him if this was the case, and as long as he was good about being secretive, she couldn't fault him for doing the same thing she was. This was the last thought that went through Rachel Truby's mind as she fell asleep on Secretluvur's chest with the faint smell of his semen and anus still in her nose.

chapter twenty-five

Kent Mooney was angry with his son, and he used the time it took him to drive home from the football game to think about the game, and about his son knowing that his ex-wife was getting remarried, and about his son telling the people he played *World of Warcraft* with about it, but not telling him. That anger soon grew into rage. His son, Tim, would have made that tackle. He had no doubt about that. And somehow, if Tim had just been there to make that tackle, everything else could have been forgiven. But Tim wasn't there to make that tackle.

He walked into his house to find Tim sitting on the couch watching *America's Best Dance Crew*. Kent said, "So, your team lost tonight because the kid they replaced you with got run over on basically the last play of the game."

Tim said, "That's too bad. Do you know what happened to my *Warcraft* account?"

Kent said, "Yeah. I, uh—I canceled it."

Tim said, "Why?"

Kent said, "Because I wanted to. I pay for it and I can cancel it whenever the fuck I want to, Tim."

Tim could see that his father was beyond angry. Tim wanted to find anger in himself, but he couldn't. In the same unfeeling tone he'd become accustomed to using over the past month, he said, "I still don't understand why you would do that, though."

Kent said, "You don't have to understand. I guess it's kind of like how I don't understand why you wouldn't tell me that your mom is getting remarried."

Tim tried to deduce how his father could have known this. He said, "I thought Dr. Fong couldn't tell you things like that."

Kent said, "So you told all of your little video-game pals and you told your fucking psychiatrist?"

Still not raising his voice above a normal speaking tone, still unable to feel fear in the face of his father's rage, or anger in response to his father's actions, Tim said, "How did you know about my guild knowing?"

Kent said, "I logged on to your account, Tim. Nice group of people you play that game with. They had some real nice things to say about how they wanted to have sex with your mother and about black people."

Tim said, "You don't know them. They're not really like that. It's just jokes."

Kent said, "Well, it's jokes you're not going to be hearing for the foreseeable future."

Tim said, "It doesn't make sense not to let me play."

Kent said, "Tim, you didn't tell me about your mom getting remarried. Why?"

Tim said, "I don't know. I guess I just didn't want to talk about it. She didn't even want me to know about it, either, if it makes you feel any better. I found out about it through her Facebook page by accident."

Kent said, "I don't give a fuck how you found out about it. You should have told me. We're all we've got, Tim. Your mom is gone. It's just you and me, and that's the way it's going to be, probably forever."

Tim said, "Okay, but how does taking away *Warcraft* change that?"

Kent said, "Fuck that stupid game, Tim. It's a waste of time. You should be playing football like you used to. I don't know what happened this year, but you belong on the football field. And next year you're trying out for the team."

Tim said, "I don't even like football anymore, Dad."

Kent said, "Yes, you do."

Tim said, "No, I don't. I like *Warcraft*."

Kent said, "It's just a game, Tim."

Tim said, "So is football, Dad."

Kent said, "Well, football is the game you're playing next year."

Kent left the conversation and headed into his bedroom, too angry to deal with his son anymore. He turned on the television in his bedroom and watched an episode of *So You Think You Can Dance* as he thought about his son and about Dawn Clint. He had a date with her the following night and had been looking forward to it for most of the week. He assumed the date would end with what would be their second sexual encounter. The memories of how her body felt against his, and how her breasts felt in his hands and mouth, were fading, becoming less accessible to Kent. He was excited to refresh them.

Tim went to his bedroom as well. He tried to conjure sorrow, self-pity, anger, rage, fear, and any other emotion he thought might be appropriate, but he found himself unable to feel anything except complete detachment from the event. He logged onto his Facebook account and looked through his mother's pictures. There were a few of her and Greg Cherry together, but the photo album containing the images of their engagement was still private. Tim again tried to force himself to feel anything, to have some emotional reaction to the reality that his family had disintegrated, never to be repaired. And again he was unable.

He logged onto his Myspace account and saw that he had a message in his in-box from Brandy Beltmeyer's Freyja account. He found this strange, based on their conversation at school, in which they'd decided to postpone any communication until the following week. He opened the message and read it. The tone of Brandy's message was different; the writing style was different. At first it didn't even seem like she'd written the message, but he eventually decided that its unfamiliar style and tone was due to the nature of its content. It was clear that she was breaking up with him. No explanation was given, and Tim found that none was necessary. After reading the message, he logged out of his Myspace account and watched "The Pale Blue Dot" multiple times, thinking about how meaningless everything was.

Anything any person would ever do would be erased at some point. There was no point to life, to having goals, to having a family. And, since Tim found himself without a family, he began to embrace the notion that he was the perfect example of the meaninglessness that defined existence. His mother had a new life that he wasn't a part of, and that was the way she preferred things. His father wanted him to be the child he used to be, but he knew he could never be that child again. The girl he thought he loved had decided to end that experience, for reasons unknown to Tim. And, beyond all that, the one thing he had been able to find comfort in for the past year or so, *World of Warcraft*, had now been excised from his life against his will. He tried to imagine what possible future his life held but found himself again unable to conjure even the most rudimentary image of being at college or in an office or in a home with a family of his own. He couldn't imagine anything beyond that night. He had no control over anything that was happening to him, and even if he had, it wouldn't have mattered.

Tim sat at his computer, watching various clips of cosmologists and philosophers discussing the insignificance of humanity for several hours after he heard his father turn off the television in his room. He brushed his teeth, and, with no anger or fear, and no need to prove anything to his father or to lash out against him, Tim quietly went to the kitchen, took a steak knife from the silverware drawer, and made his way to the bathroom. He ran a hot bath, got in, thought one last time about the fact that nothing would ever matter, and used the steak knife to sever his femoral arteries. The warm water made the experience almost pleasant to Tim. He closed his eyes and wondered what his mother's new neighborhood looked like, the one where she would live with Greg Cherry.

Awakened and annoyed by the sound of running water in the bathroom, Kent Mooney said, "Tim!" After receiving no response, he angrily got out of bed and made his way to the bathroom, where he discovered Tim, unconscious, naked and floating in a bathtub full of his own blood.

Frantic, Kent dragged his son out of the bathtub and dialed 911. Once it was determined that his son was still breathing, Kent was instructed to tie towels around his son's thighs at the location of the serrations and wait for the paramedics, who were already en route. Once they arrived and assessed the situation, they informed Kent that he was very lucky to have found Tim so soon after the initial injuries were sustained. They maintained that if another thirty minutes had passed, Tim would most likely have bled to death. It was the first time Kent had cried since he and his wife separated.

chapter
twenty-six

Tracey Vance and her husband Jim put on their shoes Saturday afternoon, and she took her car keys from the kitchen table. She looked at Danny and said, "We should be back in a few hours. You and Brooke can get a movie on demand if you want, and there's money to order food if you want, too. Be good."

Danny said, "Okay."

Jim said, "I know you're disappointed about the game, but trust me, everything is going to be okay. You're in the eighth grade. You still have your whole life ahead of you, and this game really didn't matter."

Danny said, "I know," even though he didn't believe it.

Tracey said, "Come on, we don't want to be late." She was looking forward to having sex with her husband without a condom, and she felt, in some small way, as though she had achieved a certain feminine victory on that day. It was similar to what she felt the day she'd gotten her diamond ring from Jim. She was happier than she had been in a long time.

Jim looked at his son, who still looked forlorn, and as he walked out the door he said, "Look on the bright side—at least you're not getting a laser beam in your balls." Which made Danny smile.

Brooke Benton arrived at Danny's house a few minutes after his parents left to get Jim's vasectomy. Brooke said, "I'm sorry, babe. I know that game was important to you, but you played really well, and, in my opinion, you still have, like, the best shot at being the starting JV quarterback next year."

Danny said, "Yeah, who knows? It's all out of my hands at this point. Nothing I can do about it except try out next year and see what happens, I guess."

Brooke said, "Yeah, I guess so. So what are we going to do?"

Danny said, "My mom said we could get a movie or something and she left money for food if you want to order something."

Brooke said, "Oh, yeah, we could do that. Or, I was thinking . . . how long are your parents gone for?"

Danny said, "A few hours."

Brooke said, "Well, what if we . . . you know . . ."

Danny said, "You want to have sex still?"

Brooke said, "Yeah. In my opinion, we totally should. It's not like we're not going to be safe or anything. You still have those condoms your dad gave you, right?"

Danny said, "Yeah, but I just—I still don't know if we're ready for this, you know?"

Brooke said, "Well, I'm ready for it, and I think we should do it just once, and then we don't have to again if you don't want to."

Danny looked at Brooke. He remembered the second quarter of the football game, when he was unable to score. He placed some blame on her for that, and some part of him did feel that having sex with her forcefully would yield a certain amount of vindication. Beyond that, he felt that, if he got it out of the way, that would be one less thing he would have to worry about as he approached high school. He said, "Okay."

They went into Danny's bedroom. Danny got a condom from the box his father had given him and set it on the bed next to them. They took off their clothes and Brooke reached down, stroking his penis, which became erect almost instantaneously. She said, "Okay, put it on." Danny rolled the condom down the length of his penis. Brooke said, "Okay, I'm ready."

Danny slid his penis inside her. She experienced pain and said, "Ouch, slow down a little." Danny did not comply. As his father was undergoing a vasectomy, Danny Vance broke through Brooke Benton's hymen and continued to thrust his penis into her vagina with as much force as he could generate until he ejaculated. When he slid his penis out of her he saw blood, and when he looked in her eyes he saw tears.

THE NOVELS OF CHAD KULTGEN

MEN, WOMEN & CHILDREN
A Novel

ISBN 978-0-06-165731-3 (paperback)

"*Men, Women & Children* explores all of the things that most Americans don't talk about, and in the course of showing what happens when we don't communicate with each other it deftly exposes how we can be both tender and frightening, moving and bizarre, in one of the most beautiful ways I've seen outside of real life." —Stoya

THE LIE
A Novel

ISBN 978-0-06-165730-6 (paperback)

From a writer whose unsettling, brutally honest, and undeniably riotous take on male inner life has rocked readers everywhere comes a dry and cynical tale of three college students who deserve each other.

THE AVERAGE AMERICAN MALE
A Novel

ISBN 978-0-06-123167-4 (paperback)

"It's so primal, so dangerous, it might be the most ingenious book I've ever read."
—Josh Kilmer-Purcell,
New York Times bestselling author of
I Am Not Myself These Days

Visit www.AuthorTracker.com
for exclusive information on your favorite HarperCollins authors.

Available wherever books are sold, or call 1-800-331-3761 to order.